SQUIRE'S HAZARD

BOOKS BY CAROLYN HUGHES

THE MEONBRIDGE CHRONICLES

Fortune's Wheel

A Woman's Lot

De Bohun's Destiny

Children's Fate

Squire's Hazard

THE FIFTH MEONBRIDGE CHRONICLE

Squire's Hazard

CAROLYN HUGHES

Riverdown

Published in 2022 by Riverdown Books

Riverdown Books
Southampton, SO32 3QG, United Kingdom
www.riverdownbooks.co.uk

ISBN 978-1-9160598-8-7 (paperback)
ISBN 978-1-9160598-9-4 (eBook)

British Library Cataloguing in Publication Data
A CIP catalogue record for this book is available from the British
Library

Cover design by Avalon Graphics www.avalongraphics.org

CAST OF CHARACTERS

IN MEONBRIDGE, HAMPSHIRE

DICKON DE BOHUN, Lord of Meonbridge in waiting, squire in training in Steyning
MARGARET, LADY DE BOHUN, his grandmother, currently "Lord" of Meonbridge
Piers Arundale, Dickon's squire and friend
ELIZABETH (LIBBY) FLETCHER, Margaret's companion

Alice atte Wode, villein, Lady Margaret's close friend of 30 years
John atte Wode, Alice's son and Meonbridge's bailiff
Agnes Sawyer, Alice's daughter, mother of Dickon de Bohun
Jack, Agnes's husband, a carpenter
James Paynter, journeyman to Jack
Eleanor Nash, formerly Titherige, a freewoman

MARGERY TYLER, Libby's aunt, servant to the Browghtons
Gabriel Browghton, freeman farmer
Philippa, his wife
Piers Cokewell, a labourer
Jan and Ellen, Mistress Browghton's dairymaids
The Browghton children's nursemaid

Sir Giles Fitzpeyne, knight of Shropshire, once comrade-in-arms of
Margaret's late husband, Sir Richard de Bohun
Lady Gwynedd, his wife
Angharad, their elder daughter

IN STEYNING, SUSSEX

EARL RAOUL DE FOUGÈRE, liege lord of Margaret's late husband,
Sir Richard, and Sir Giles Fitzpeyne
Jeanne, his wife
Sir Eustace Beneyt, knight in service to the earl
EDWIN DE COURTENAY, squire in training, grandson of
Hildegard, Lady de Courtenay
Alan de Clyffe and Nicholas Fenecote, squires in training

IN HASLEMERE, SURREY

HILDEGARD, LADY DE COURTENAY, once mother-in-law to the
de Bohuns' son, Sir Philip
Hugh de Courtenay, knight, her husband

PROLOGUE

E dwin clapped a hand across his mouth, stifling a snigger. Nick and Alan, crouching beside him just behind the stables entrance, sniggered too. Their hiding place was out of sight of Sir Eustace Beneyt and his squire, but they had a good view of the unfolding skirmish.

Edwin held his breath, and he could sense his friends' excitement too at what might happen next.

And, when it did, it was exactly what he had hoped for.

With a resounding slap, the knight struck the squire's ear with an open-handed blow. The clout was hard and heavy, and the boy cried out. Tears burst from his astonished eyes. He bit down upon his lip, drawing blood. Pressing his hand to his assaulted ear, he looked up at Sir Eustace's furious face, red and purple now, his bushy eyebrows merging.

Edwin nudged the others and snorted softly, and they snorted back but did not speak.

Sir Eustace had a reputation for ferocity on the battlefield, but here at Steyning he was known to be a man of modest temper, who

1

rarely raised a hand against his squire. He would shout at him, yes, and damn him for his failings, but, as far as Edwin could remember, he had never struck him before.

But never before had the knight's beloved mare, Morel, been harmed whilst in the squire's supposed care.

Edwin punched the air, delighted with the way the prank had worked. It was the best so far, though the other tricks they had played upon Dickon de Bohun had been good too. Like when Alan stole one of Sir Eustace's armoured gauntlets, and the matter of the missing piece of Morel's bridle.

Both times, Sir Eustace had been so furious Edwin expected him to punish de Bohun severely. But his chastisements then were still not physical, which was frustrating. It was then Edwin decided to make Sir Eustace absolutely mad with anger at his squire, and he had known exactly what would do it.

And he was right. Of course, it was a shame poor Morel had to suffer too, but it was worth it for the sight of de Bohun's humiliation.

It had been a clever plan.

Alan had called Dickon away when he was part way through preparing Morel for Sir Eustace to go out hunting. 'Dick,' he had said, coming over, 'can you help me? I've got a problem with some harness.'

Dickon had hesitated. He was already behind with saddling Morel. But he followed Alan down the stable to a stall right at the far end. Of course, Alan had no real problem, but had tangled up the straps on purpose.

Anyway, whilst they were away from Morel's stall, Edwin had crept in and hidden one small but especially spiny chestnut between the folds of the thick blanket Dickon had just thrown over the mare's back. Naturally she whinnied when he placed it there, but he managed to soothe her and she was calm enough when Dickon returned, out of breath and agitated, now even more behindhand with his work.

Edwin had by then vanished, hunkering down in a nearby stall, where the others joined him. It was dark inside the stables and easy enough to keep out of sight.

Horses were often nervous in the moments before they took the saddle, and Dickon, who was, even Edwin would admit, good with horses, murmured to her as he lifted the fine leather saddle and lowered it with care over the blanket. Morel whinnied shrilly as soon as she felt it touch her, arching her back, and kicking out. Yet Dickon was now in such a hurry, he just continued buckling the girth and fixing the bridle, by turns whispering into Morel's ear and stroking her on the muzzle.

When Sir Eustace came to mount her, he was puzzled by her skittishness. 'What's amiss with her?' he said, as she pranced and whickered out on the bailey.

Dickon shuffled his feet. 'Naught I know of, sir,' though his face betrayed unease. Nonetheless, he brought the mounting block and, as Sir Eustace stepped up onto it, Edwin and his chums each held their breath.

The knight put his foot into the stirrup and, bouncing, swung his leg up and over the restless horse's back. He lowered himself into the saddle and Morel screamed and bucked. Then, snorting, she took off across the bailey, her rider clinging to the pommel on the saddle, until at length she reared in fury and threw him off, to land with a heavy thud upon the dusty ground.

The conspirators had scuttled to the stable door to watch the ensuing spectacle. It took the knight a while to recover both himself and his mare and walk her back to the stables. As he approached, they retreated once more into the gloom.

'De Bohun,' Sir Eustace yelled, and Dickon, white and shaking, had run forward.

'Take off the saddle,' roared the knight and, with trembling fingers, Dickon had unbuckled the girth and lifted off the saddle, and the blanket. 'Shake it,' snarled Sir Eustace, and Dickon opened the blanket out and flapped it. And out dropped the sweet chestnut husk, falling to the ground.

The knight lunged forward and, snatching up the spiteful object, advanced upon Dickon, his face purple. 'Your hand,' he commanded and, when Dickon held it out, Sir Eustace pressed the chestnut into it. Then, wrapping his big fist over Dickon's, he squeezed. Dickon had yelped like a whipped puppy, as the chestnut's spines bit into his palm.

Then came the first blow to Dickon's ear, then a second and a third. 'You heedless dolt,' Sir Eustace cried. 'I'm done with all your carelessness. No longer will I have you as my squire. I shall tell the earl you are dismissed from my service.'

He turned back to the mare and rubbed his face against the side of hers, running his hand over her muzzle and cooing. Then he stood up straight and yelled 'Alan', and Edwin slapped his friend upon the back as he slunk out of the stables.

Eustace's eyebrows knit. 'Were you hiding?'

'Of course not, sir, just tidying.'

The knight grunted. 'Right, I shall tell Lord Raoul you are my squire now.' He gestured to Morel with his head. 'Take good care of her. I shall give hunting a miss today.'

When Alan led Morel back into the stable, Edwin slapped him again upon the shoulder. 'Excellent. Puts de Bohun right back down where he belongs. And gives you a new knight to serve.'

Alan's previous knight left Steyning two weeks ago, and he had not yet been allocated another. He smirked. 'Couldn't have worked out better.'

Edwin peeped once more out of the stables to gloat upon the sight of Dickon's face, red and snot-covered, distraught with grief and shame. Then, remembering his own knight had also ordered up his rouncey, he hurried back inside.

Raoul de Fougère paced up and down the hall a little, then returned to face the knight. He shook his head. 'I am disappointed, Eustace. I had high hopes of young de Bohun, that he might prove the best of squires.'

'He's been excellent with the horses,' said the knight, 'and is coming on well with all the skills of battle. But, for months now, he's been careless, losing things and causing me great inconvenience. I must say, I've been surprised. It's not what we have squires for, my lord, to cause us nuisance, but to avoid it.' He raised his ample eyebrows. 'But this last incident was no mere nuisance. I can't have my beloved Morel put in danger—'

'Hardly "danger", Eustace,' interrupted the earl. 'One small chestnut? Painful, I am sure, but not life-threatening...'

4

'Maybe, but why? That's what I don't understand.'

'Did one of the other squires play a prank on him, perhaps?'

'I have wondered that. Not that I've questioned them. But, prank or no, Dickon's particular neglect was in not noticing the mare's distress when he put on the saddle. I can't tolerate such lack of attention. What else might he fail to notice? In more urgent circumstances?'

Raoul nodded. 'I do understand your concern. But you are happy with Alan de Clyffe?'

Eustace grimaced. 'A supercilious little knave, but yes, he'll do.'

'Very well, I shall take young de Bohun under my own wing. See if I can train the inattention out of him.'

———

COURTENAY CASTLE, SURREY
CHRISTMAS 1363

Lady Hildegard de Courtenay was old, her back a little bowed, but her mind was sharp enough, and her temper was as prickly as a teasel. She was anticipating her forthcoming visitor with anything but pleasure, for, the first time she met him, this time last year, she found her grandson Edwin quite unpleasant.

In truth, she scarcely knew the boy. His father, Benedict, her second eldest son, lived in France, and Edwin had been born and brought up in Burgundy, in the chateau of his mother's parents.

Last year, he had come to England to pursue his knightly training at Steyning Castle. It was in Steyning that Benedict himself had done his training and, some years ago, Lord Raoul had suggested he might wish his own sons to gain their knighthoods here in England, rather than in France.

Benedict was not sure he did, and Anne-Marie and her haughty parents were vehemently against it. This was what Hildegard's husband, Hugh, who maintained an occasional exchange of letters with their son, had told her. Yet an offer from a man of Raoul de Fougère's standing could not be wholly spurned. Moreover, Benedict was keen to keep on good terms with the earl for any future advantage it might bring him. Thus he recommended to his wife that they send *one* son to England. Anne-Marie was adamant that the two older boys would remain in France. However, both she and her parents had apparently seemed delighted at the prospect of foisting Edwin onto the earl.

"Foist" was the term Hugh chose to use. When, in the autumn of last year, he advised her that their hitherto unknown grandson was coming to England, she questioned why *he* had been chosen rather than his brothers. Hugh frowned. 'I understand that young Edwin appears somewhat "difficult", whatever that might mean. Of course, we have never met him and cannot verify the truth of it until we do. But I regret to say, my dear, that the boy is, shall we say, unloved.'

She sighed on learning that, for the next few years, Edwin would have to consider Courtenay Castle as his home, and return here for the Christmas holidays. This was an arrangement that, for any of their other grandchildren, she and Hugh might have viewed with pleasure. But Edwin was "difficult".

When Benedict had first brought his son to England, he simply left the boy at Steyning Castle, and returned to France. Even in Hildegard's largely pitiless view of parenting, that did seem most unkind. At twelve, he was not exactly a child, but even so... She had wondered what black mood he might adopt when he first came to stay with his English grandparents.

Three months later, when Edwin arrived for Christmas, her fears were fully realised.

Not that she had spent much time with him that year, for by chance an ague kept her confined to bed for several days. Though, from their initial meeting, she was grateful to be discharged from her grandmotherly duties.

She remembered that first meeting with great clarity.

Edwin was tall even then, and upright, with a mane of light-brown curly hair. But he was not handsome. Benedict was fine-featured, so perhaps the boy took his visage from his mother? She had never seen her.

His lack of good looks was aggravated by the scowl that rested upon his mouth and in his eyes and did not fade for their entire interview; a conversation in which she asked questions, and he mostly failed to answer.

Obviously, his grasp of the English language had then been somewhat limited. She did feel a certain sympathy for the boy, abandoned in a country where he struggled to understand or be understood. Nonetheless, despite his surliness and lack of English, she managed to establish that he seemed content enough at Steyning Castle. It was a great honour for a boy to be selected to join the earl's entourage of young squires, for de Fougère's reputation for turning out fine knights was formidable. She wondered how such a surly boy was faring, both with the other squires and with Lord Raoul himself, but could get nothing from him to enlighten her. Neither could she discover anything about his life in Burgundy. He simply did not want to talk.

When she was forced to take to her bed, she was relieved to leave him in Hugh's entire care.

Though even she appreciated it must have been a lonely Christmas for the boy. For, that year, none of her other grandchildren came to visit, their parents pleading other arrangements for the entire festive season. When the time came for him to return to Steyning, he seemed keen to go.

Another year had now passed since she last saw young Edwin. Might his mood have lightened somewhat? Would his training have helped to loosen his tongue a little? Might his English have improved? Made him more willing to engage? In truth, she was not hopeful.

She tottered up and down her chamber, her cane tap-tapping on the wooden floor, as she awaited his arrival. When at last there came a knock upon her chamber door, she cried "Wait" and lurched over to her grand armchair, where she sat straight-backed, her hand atop her cane.

'Enter,' she called, and a servant ushered the boy inside.

She beckoned Edwin forward. He seemed even taller and more stiff-backed. But was that a glimmer of a smile upon his lips? She arched an eyebrow and held out her hand. 'Come, give your grandmother a kiss.'

Edwin did not particularly want to kiss his grandmother's dry and wrinkly skin, but he came forward nonetheless and, leaning over, dropped the briefest of pecks upon her hand.

'*Grandmère*,' he said, stepping back, 'you look well.' He did not mean it. She was ancient, much older and more wrinkled than his French grandmother.

'As well as can be expected,' she said. She placed her free hand upon her lap and he noticed how gnarled and bony it was. 'But tell me, child, how are you enjoying life at Steyning Castle?'

He bristled at the "child". 'Well enough,' he said, wondering how much to tell her, and what she might want to hear. He did not know her well.

When he last saw her, a year ago, he was so angry at being torn from his home in Burgundy and dumped alone in England, he could not bring himself even to be polite. Moreover, speaking English then was hard and he could barely be bothered to make the effort.

But, this year, his English was much better and life in Steyning Castle was proving so much more agreeable, he decided he could be affable towards this weird old woman. At least she was showing some interest in him: his French *grandmère* would not even have bothered to ask after his welfare.

'Go on,' she said, her voice impatient. 'Tell me how you spend your time.' She gestured to a low stool, which he took, albeit he was affronted to be crouching at her feet. Yet, despite her great age, he sensed this grandmother was someone to whom it might advantage him to show esteem.

However, when he told her about the training, she leaned back against her cushion and her eyelids drooped. He stopped talking and her eyelids flicked open.

He smirked. 'Perhaps you do not find my life at Steyning of much interest?'

She waved her hand. 'It is clear you are enjoying yourself. But what of the other squires? The earl chooses only the best, you know. Have you made some suitable friends?'

'My best friends are Alan de Clyffe—he is heir to some important family in the north of England, and Nicholas Fenecote, whose *papa* is also an earl.'

Her thin lips stretched into a generous smile. 'Excellent choices. It is always wise to forge allegiances with the scions of the most reputable and honourable families.' Her cane tapped. 'And what do you and your friends do for amusement?'

He hesitated. What might someone so ancient consider amusing? Would she disapprove of teasing? He was not sure. Yet his father had told him she herself was not above a little acerbic wit. 'My mother may be old,' he had said, 'but her tongue can be as sharp as a serpent's if she takes against someone.' He had winked.

Edwin moved his stool a little closer to her. 'Well, there is a boy—another squire—who is such a churl that Alan, Nick and me cannot help but tease him.' She arched an eyebrow. 'Oh, it is just small stuff, *Grandmère*, nothing that gets us into any trouble.'

At first, she laughed, but then her forehead creased. Was she about to reprimand him? She tapped her cane again, so sharply it made him jump. 'I suppose teasing others *is* what boys of your age do. But what has this boy done to deserve your loathing?'

'He is so timid—is that the right word, *Grandmère*? Not like the rest of us at all.'

'Is this boy not from a noble family?'

'He is a de Bohun—'

Her eyes grew wide. 'A scion of the Earl of Hereford? Where is his family seat?'

'Hampshire, I think.'

'Ah, not a Hereford, then... A minor branch of the family...' Her brow then wrinkled. 'Hampshire, you say? And what is the boy's first name?'

'Richard, I suppose, though we call him Dickon—'

At that she glowered. 'Dickon?'

'And Lord Raoul really likes him—' He could not help but sneer.

Her eyes were glittering now. 'Dickon de Bohun? Pah! The little bastard always was going to return to Steyning, after a spell with Giles Fitzpeyne.'

'You know of him, *Grandmère*?' Edwin was surprised, and amused by her sudden venom.

She tossed her head. 'Indeed I do.'

By the time he had left his grandmother's chamber, he felt

vindicated in teasing Dickon de Bohun. He had known it all along, that de Bohun was not quite what he appeared to be. And he would have no hesitation whatsoever in telling Nick and Alan who he really was.

'For you can be sure,' *Grandmère* had said, 'that no one in Steyning other than the earl, and perhaps Countess Jeanne, will know the truth about young de Bohun's birth.'

Hildegard's conversation with her grandson stirred up all the old rancour she harboured against the Meonbridge de Bohuns. It was intolerable that the *bastard* boy was now training alongside her own grandson, apparently under the favoured patronage of Raoul de Fougère.

She thought back to those few months when the boy had been at Courtenay Castle, after Hugh had—misguidedly, in her opinion— agreed to admit him as a page-in-training, despite the ignominy the de Bohuns had wrought upon them.

Margaret de Bohun had almost *begged* them to take the boy. Indeed, she had thrown herself upon their mercy. Hugh was excessively soft-hearted. And look what it all led to.

Despite the passing of the years, it still rankled that Sir Richard de Bohun had drawn her family into his mendacious plot to elevate the boy to the position of his rightful heir, when he was in fact the result of some sordid liaison between Sir Richard's son, Philip, and a village wench. The de Bohuns, Richard and Margaret, claimed they knew nothing of the child until a year after he was born. Whether they did or not, she had no way of proving. But it turned out the boy was born nine months or thereabouts after Philip was married to her own darling Isabella, and the de Bohuns used that fact to claim that *Isabella* was his mother.

Poor Isabella had died in the Mortality, taking her *unborn* child with her. Soon after her death, Philip was murdered and his sister, Johanna, decided to become a nun. "Sister Dolorosa", she called herself. What a ridiculous name! Thus, the de Bohuns were left without an heir until the wench turned up again in Meonbridge, bringing her bastard offspring with her.

Inevitably, the de Bohuns were pleased enough to find they had a grandchild after all, legitimate or not, but it was not until seven years later that the matter of the child's legitimacy came to a head.

Obviously, she understood why Sir Richard made his mendacious claim, but that did not assuage her indignation that her daughter—and her own august family—had been *used*.

For, when Richard claimed Dickon as his heir, things were looking awkward for him. A distant and unscrupulous, indeed malevolent, cousin—Morys Boune—was claiming his right to the de Bohun estates, in the apparent absence of a de Bohun heir. It was then that Richard lied, declaring the bastard boy was his *legitimate* grandson, and that Isabella had "died in the birthing of him".

How incensed Hildegard had been that her dead daughter was implicated in such gross deception—as she had put it then, and still felt now. The elevation of a half-peasant brat to the status of heir to the vast de Bohun estates was an intolerable insult to her daughter's memory.

It was true that, with the passing of the years, she had somewhat forgotten her resentment. But now, with Edwin's news, the old bitterness resurfaced. It was interesting that Edwin had somehow discerned the boy's inferiority, whilst not knowing the reason for it.

She did not wish serious harm upon young de Bohun, but did rather relish hearing news of his humiliation. She doubted he would ever admit his ignominy to his grandmother, but how satisfactory it would be for Margaret too to suffer a little of the same? Hildegard smirked to herself and tapped her cane. It would be a small but fitting recompense for the humiliation she herself had once suffered at the hands of the de Bohuns.

1

MEONBRIDGE, HAMPSHIRE
CHRISTMAS 1363

The waters of the river glinted in the winter sun, as it dipped towards the tops of distant trees. Dickon's heart beat faster at the sight of it, for he and his small retinue had at last reached the final mile of their long ride to Meonbridge from Steyning. He'd never have thought he would care for it quite so much, the Meon, the river of his childhood.

He called out to Piers Arundale and, when his grandmother's squire turned his head in answer, he pointed. 'Home,' he cried, and Piers trotted over.

'You're glad to be back, my lord?' Piers's eyes were quizzical.

'I've missed the place.' He'd not tell Piers the true reason for his yearning to be home. If asked, simple pleasure in being amongst family and friends again would be enough. Indeed, now he was here, he wondered if he could somehow arrange it so he stayed for good. Though of course his grandmother wouldn't let him.

He'd been relieved when Piers arrived at Steyning Castle with two de Bohun men-at-arms to accompany him on the journey back to

Meonbridge for the Christmas festivities. Yet the prospect of the two-day ride, in the chill December weather, was still daunting.

He'd done this journey many times before. When he was small, he'd ridden pillion behind his uncle, John. But, for the last two years, he'd travelled the long distance on his own horse, albeit still with the small retinue to protect him. He had to keep his wits about him, for the roads and tracks were treacherous at the best of times, even more so at this time of year. Though the courser Piers brought for him, his favourite, Bayard, was a fine, sure-footed horse. Indeed, Bayard lived up to his reputation so well, he could let his mind wander to the events of the past few months.

He'd been at Steyning now for a year and a half. When he went there the first time, years ago when he was much younger, he wasn't at all happy. At home in Meonbridge, he'd always felt confident and strong. But Steyning Castle was big and frightening, and all the other boys seemed arrogant and proud. He was glad when Sir Giles Fitzpeyne had suggested he went to Shropshire instead, to continue his page training. Sir Giles had only two pages, and they lived as part of the family. But, by the time he was twelve, Dickon was ready for a more martial atmosphere, and content, if not eager, to return to Steyning.

At first, it was all he'd hoped. He soon made friends with two fellow squires in training, Alan de Clyffe and Nicholas Fenecote, both of whom were from noble families, and displayed it in their bold and mannerly demeanour.

He'd been nervous about exposing his own background. His grandmother had made it clear that there was no need to speak of it: no one at Steyning except Lord Raoul knew the truth about his birth. And the confidence he'd gained at Fitzpeyne Castle was enough to make him feel their equal, and for Alan and Nicholas to accept him.

But when Edwin de Courtenay arrived in Steyning a few months later, the mood entirely changed.

First, Edwin lured his friends away. Then, after a while, the "gang of three", as he thought of them, began to taunt him, always at Edwin's instigation, making him look stupid, calling him "churl" and "dullard", though never within earshot of their knights or the earl, or even any of the castle servants.

Dickon didn't understand what made Edwin take against him. It seemed clear he considered him inferior. But why? Surely he didn't know his secret? How could he? So, was his true background showing after all?

He found it hard to assert himself more strongly, but pretended to ignore their taunts, determined to put on a brave face, not let the others see how alone and scared he felt.

What they did at first was not much more than teasing. Like the time Dickon came to dress Sir Eustace for a tournament and one of his gauntlets was missing, and he couldn't explain its loss, though he was certain Edwin or one of the others had taken it. He had to endure a lashing from the knight's blasphemous tongue, before running to the earl's armourer to beg for a substitution. How vexed Sir Eustace had been when the replacement didn't match his other gauntlet, though he'd joined the tourney, nonetheless.

But, next day, when all the other squires had time off their normal duties, to play a game of camp-ball, Sir Eustace had made him search for the missing gauntlet. All day he looked for the wretched thing, searching in all the places it might have been. By late afternoon, he reported to Sir Eustace that the gauntlet was nowhere to be found. But, a short while later, it appeared as if by magic in Sir Eustace's armoury chamber.

The knight came looking for him, demanding his presence in the chamber. He pointed. 'What is that then, boy?' he said, his scruffy eyebrows arched.

And there it was, the missing gauntlet, sitting with its fellow.

His face had grown hot. Certain though he was that Edwin de Courtenay was responsible for the mysterious reappearance, he'd not say so. He just had to accept that his knight considered him inept.

There were other instances too of objects going missing, sometimes making it impossible for Sir Eustace to ride out that day. Each time, the knight had been so furious, Dickon imagined he'd be beaten at the very least. But, fierce as Sir Eustace often was, he usually held back from a physical reprimand. Yet Dickon would have preferred a beating, rather than have his knight so disappointed and frustrated with him.

But the prank that resulted in poor Morel's anguish was quite a different matter, for him and for Sir Eustace.

Dickon bit down hard upon his lip to stop tears welling at the memory, of the horse's suffering, the knight's fury and the stinging blows that followed. But worst of all was being dismissed from Sir Eustace's service. How mortified he was to be cast aside. Sad too, for he liked Sir Eustace and knew the knight was fond of him.

What's more, Lord Raoul deciding Dickon would join his personal entourage of squires made it all much worse. The "gang" surely resented what seemed like his advancement. And, unless he told the earl what was going on, no amount of bravado on his part would stop Edwin continuing to make his life a misery.

Yet, how could he tell the earl? He'd ask him to prove that the mislayings and the incident with Morel resulted from others' pranks, rather than his own carelessness. Then ask him to prove it was Edwin who was behind them. How could he possibly do that?

Of course, he knew it *was* Edwin and the others, from hints they dropped within his hearing and winks that passed between them whilst in his company. But those things weren't any sort of proof.

Besides, blabbing about a fellow squire just wasn't done; it was dishonourable. He couldn't—wouldn't—do it.

As they crossed the bridge, Dickon clicked his tongue and Bayard spurred his pace. Piers did the same and together they broke into a canter, leaving the men-at-arms to follow on. The road that led through the village up towards the manor house was muddy from the autumn rains, but not yet a slough. That would come, when the road ran almost as slickly as the Meon, the usual dirt and rubble churned up by deluges of rain and snow into a murky torrent tumbling with rocks and debris liable to hobble the unwary rider's horse or even break its leg. But, for now, they could ride apace even as the road inclined uphill towards the knoll from which the great house overlooked the village.

Someone must have sent word up to the house, for his grandmother was awaiting him.

'My darling boy,' she cried, as Piers shoved open the heavy bailey door and ushered Dickon into the great hall. A welcome mantle of muggy warmth at once enfolded him. He threw off his damp and chilly cloak and eased off his soggy gloves, letting them all fall onto the floor, as his grandmother came forward, her arms outstretched. 'How glad I am to see you.'

He was glad to let himself be embraced. 'And I you, Grandmama,' he said, and meant it, more so this time than he'd ever done before.

She took his arm and drew him over to the fire, blazing in the wide stone hearth and sending its smoky billows skywards up the towering chimney. He slumped down onto a nearby bench, all of a sudden exhausted and looking forward to his bed.

But Grandmama was eager for conversation. 'How was your journey? Not too onerous? Or cold?'

'Bayard made it easier. But the cold...' He grimaced and, despite the fire's heat, his whole body gave a shudder. Yet he managed a rueful grin. 'It's a pity Christmas is in December. Riding from Steyning to Meonbridge in midsummer would be almost a pleasure. Perhaps I'll ask his lordship if he can change our annual holiday to June?'

His grandmother threw back her head and laughed. 'What a wonderful idea. But even as powerful a man as Raoul de Fougère cannot alter the Church's calendar.'

He shivered again, then couldn't stop, and Grandmama called to a servant to bring a fur-lined wrap. Moments later, a snug fox fur was enveloping his shoulders, and he held out his icy hands towards the fire and kneaded at his fingers.

Piers came over, bearing a cup of steaming spiced ale. 'Here, my lord, this'll warm you up.'

'I'm not sure I can hold it,' said Dickon, grimacing again. 'Best put it on the table.' Leaning forward, he wrapped his hands around the cup and waited for his tingling fingers to thaw out.

'Do tell me your news,' said his grandmother, after they'd shared a little supper in the privacy of her chamber. They were sitting before the fire until it was time to retire to bed. 'Last Christmas, you were so full of excitement about your new life at Steyning. Has this year been even better?'

Dickon bent down, pretending to fiddle with the buckle on his shoe. He was sure his face must betray the anxiety that had built up during the long ride home. He'd tried to work out what he was going to tell his grandmother about his squiring life. As he rode, he practised what to say, about the training and about his move to the earl's personal retinue, though not why it had happened. But now he was confronted with the need to *say* it, he feared he might without intention betray the truth.

'Actually, Grandmama, I'm very tired,' he said at last, glad, as he sat up again, that the light in the room was dim enough to conceal his face. 'Do you mind if I tell you all about it in the morning?'

It wasn't that he'd never lied to her before: he'd become quite practised at it as a boy. But those lies had been trifling matters, not a bald concealment of something so humiliating as being dismissed from Sir Eustace's service.

'Oh, my dear boy,' she cried, 'of course. How unthinking of me to keep you from your bed, when you must be so weary from your journey.' She leaned across and patted him on the arm, her smile tender. 'In the morning, then.'

In his own chamber, Dickon was alone a while, though Piers would soon come to share it with him, as he'd done for many years when he was younger. He rolled out the truckle from beneath his fine oak bed in readiness for Piers, then threw himself down upon his own mattress. He felt bad about putting off his grandmother, when she was so eager to hear his news. Maybe, by the morning, he'd feel both stronger and more certain about how to paint his life at Steyning in the most favourable light.

Dickon was used to rising before dawn, along with all the other Steyning Castle servants, of both gentle birth and lowly. His early morning tasks were rigorous. Even in the coldest, wettest weather, the horses had to be groomed and fed, their stalls cleaned out and hay replenished. He loved horses, but that particular aspect of the squire's life was not his favourite.

Home in Meonbridge, he took advantage of being freed from such obligations and lay in his bed a full hour longer than Piers, who, as a squire in this household, did have those duties to perform. He'd leapt from his low bed as soon as the Matins bell sounded from Saint Peter's and, having rolled the truckle back into place, stood at Dickon's side.

'You coming to help muck out Bayard?' Piers whispered in his ear.

'Tomorrow,' Dickon murmured, drawing the edge of his blanket up over his chin. 'I'll be up by the time you're back.'

Though, moments after Piers had left, Dickon realised going with him would have given him a bit more time before having to face his grandmother. Whereas, by the time Piers returned from tending to the horses in his care, he'd already have had to present himself before her and tell her what she was so keen to hear.

Light was seeping through and around the shutter at the chamber's tiny window as he tumbled off the bed. He splashed his face with the icy water in the bowl, and pulled on his hose and tunic. When he was dressed, he took a deep breath and walked as confidently as he could manage along the passage to his grandmother's chamber. He tapped upon the door and waited to be summoned.

His eyes widened when he found Libby Fletcher standing beside the open door, her head at a slight angle. 'My lord,' she said, then giggled. He couldn't help but grin.

Yet why should he be surprised to see her? She'd been his grandmother's companion ever since her own mother, Matilda, was banished.

He wondered—if briefly—at the momentary tremor in his chest. He'd not seen Libby for twelve months, and she looked somehow different now. A year older, obviously, and maybe a fraction taller, but also... He couldn't stop his eyes from straying downwards, but flicked them away, as a flush rose to his neck.

Hoping she hadn't noticed his wandering eyes, he peered around her into the chamber. 'Is my grandmother awaiting me?'

Libby nodded, and held the door open a little wider. 'Thanks,' he muttered, then pushed past her, keeping his warming face averted.

'Ah, Dickon,' said his grandmother. 'Splendid. You can leave us, Libby, for an hour or two.'

'Yes, milady,' he heard Libby mumble, as she closed the door behind her.

His grandmother was sitting at the table, sipping from a cup of what he supposed was small ale, and nibbling at some soft wheaten bread. She got up and stepped over to the two chairs standing before the hearth. 'Let us sit down by the fire.' She beamed. 'I am most eager for your news.'

As he sat, his heart was thumping. 'It's become much harder this year...' he began. 'The castle's so big, and the earl has so many knights, and stables so full of horses for us squires to tend.'

'I visited Steyning Castle some years ago,' she said. 'I recall how very grand it was. It makes our manor house here in Meonbridge seem scarcely any greater than a cottage.' She laughed.

He joined in. 'It makes even Sir Giles's castle seem small.'

'But you enjoy working with the horses?' She gave a slight tilt of her head. 'You learned quickly at Fitzpeyne Castle, I recall.'

'Oh yes, it's still the best part. I never thought I'd love horses quite so much.' He hesitated. 'They seem to like me too.'

'How many animals are you responsible for?'

'Well, my knight, Sir Eustace—' he said, then stumbled. He pretended to clear his throat. 'Oh, how stupid of me... Sir Eustace was my knight but, just a few days ago, the earl decided to appoint me to his personal retinue.' He squirmed in his chair.

'How thrilling! An advancement, eh?'

'Well, yes.' He swallowed. 'I liked Sir Eustace a lot, but it's an honour to serve his lordship. Anyway, he has lots of horses, and each of us looks after two or three. Obviously, the grooms do a lot of the heavy work, but the earl insists us squires do our fair share, so we understand all the tasks required.' He wrinkled his nose. 'I don't much like mucking out the stables on a freezing winter's morning. But I love grooming the horses and getting them ready for the day.' Or at least he *did*.

'Ha, yes. Working outdoors in this weather can be testing. I noticed the other day how white and waxy our squires' fingers were when they came back to the hall for breakfast. Their lips were blue and their poor teeth clacking. I insisted they eat a bowlful of hot pottage before they went outside again.'

'The earl does the same. If it were up to our training masters, I'm sure coarse bread and plain water would suffice. Which, in the summer months, is fine. But, on winter mornings, his lordship always orders up a great cauldron of steaming pottage for us all.'

'Quite right too. And what else do you enjoy? Riding, I imagine?'

He nodded eagerly. He'd not ridden as a child—not like the sons of gentry—but he'd learned fast under Sir Giles's instruction. When the time came for him to return to Steyning to become a squire, not only did he ride well, but he could handle weapons too and knew the basics of courtesy and service.

'The earl considers riding practice more important than weapons training. "If you can't ride as if you and the horse are one," he says, "you'll never learn to fight on horseback." Every day we practise in the yard, then go for a canter across the downs.' He knew his eyes were shining. That was always the best part of his day.

'Yet I suppose you do also practise the martial skills?'

'With swords and little lances, though it's mostly still like playing. But, when we return in January, for those of us who are fourteen, it'll become more serious. Real weapons.' Yet, despite his excitement at the thought of wielding a proper sword, he was still fearful of how Edwin might act if he were to meet him face-to-face.

'I remember how much your father enjoyed his years at Steyning. You sound just like him—riding and fighting were his favourite occupations too.'

'Was there anything he didn't like?'

'Oh, yes. What he did *not* enjoy was serving at table—'

He giggled. 'Me too! I'm always afraid I'm going to drop the platter on the floor. It'd be so embarrassing.'

'I recall Philip saying much the same, but it never happened, you know. It is important that you learn all aspects of etiquette and courtesy, even if they are not the most exciting parts of your training. Moreover, it is an honour to serve your lord at table. If you are invited to be cup bearer to the earl, you will know that he favours you most highly.'

'I'd much rather pour wine into his cup than serve him from a platter of sloppy brewet.'

'You will learn, my darling boy, and I am delighted that the earl has taken you into his own service. You must be showing great promise.'

He twisted away again. He regretted his grandmother's misinterpretation of what had happened, but he couldn't tell her the truth. At least, not yet.

But she noticed his discomfort. 'Is something amiss, my boy? You seem somehow not yourself.'

'No, Grandmama, I'm fine. A little tired maybe.' How he wished he could stop his cheeks from flushing.

'A boy of your age should not be tired,' she said, her eyes wide, 'but be full of boundless energy and vigour.'

'Maybe it was the ride. It's difficult this time of year.'

'Indeed. But you have plenty of time now to regain your usual energy, and catch up with your friends and family in Meonbridge. Your mother, I know, as well as your maternal grandmother, are both most eager for you to visit them.'

'And I will, Grandmama, I promise, but not right now. I'm going to the stables to see Bayard.'

Glad to escape his grandmother's probing, if just for now, Dickon ran out through the hall door and across the bailey towards the fine new stables that had been built earlier in the year.

A groom met him at the door. 'Mornin', milord, you looking for Bayard?'

At Dickon's nod, the lad led him past the long line of stalls to the far end, where Bayard's head was jutting out from his stall, looking his way, as if he was waiting for him.

'You wan' 'im saddled, milord?' said the groom, as Bayard whinnied.

'No thanks. I've done enough riding for a few days. I've just come to see him.'

Left alone with the horse, he pushed open the stall door and stepped inside. Bayard backed away a little, snickering softly, and Dickon held his hand out flat for him to snuffle. Going closer, he stroked the horse's muzzle, murmuring all the while. He laid his face against the warm dark hair on Bayard's neck, and closed his eyes.

Tears oozed from beneath his eyelids. It wasn't only the journey that had exhausted him. He'd been shocked by the increasing violence of Edwin's bullying, ending with the dreadful incident with poor Morel. How good it'd be just to stay here and ride Bayard every day. He could practise his combat skills with Piers, and learn more about his estates, in preparation for the day when—

Jerking his head back from the comfort of Bayard's quivering neck, he spun around and thumped his fist against the sturdy timber of the stall. His knuckles swiftly stung with pain, and the blow's thud made Bayard start back and whinny. At once regretting his outburst, he turned and soothed the horse's muzzle once again.

Dickon hadn't moved from Bayard's side when he heard Piers calling out his name. He sighed. Much as he liked Piers, he was fearful the squire might, like his grandmother, ask him questions he didn't want to answer. But he could hardly pretend not to be in the stall, when the groom knew well where he was. Giving Bayard a final pat, he stepped out into the aisle and called to Piers.

'You planning a ride?' said Piers.

He shook his head. 'Tomorrow, maybe. I'm still too stiff from the journey.'

'Me too. It's keeping alert that's so hard in winter: your back and shoulders tense, your eyes peeled for hazards underfoot.'

He agreed, though, in fact, this time he'd let Bayard take most of the strain.

'Though I must say,' Piers went on, 'I thought you seemed more distracted yesterday than alert...' He raked his fingers through his hair. 'Is something wrong?'

Dickon was affronted for a moment. Yet Piers only ever had his best interests at heart. He stared down at his feet and lifted a shoulder in a fleeting shrug.

'So, *is* anything wrong, Dick?'

He shook his head, and Piers frowned. 'I'm sorry,' he said, 'but it doesn't look that way to me. Since you've been back, you've seemed far away. Her ladyship's noticed too. She asked me to find out.'

Dickon flinched, and Piers must have read it as alarm. He put up his hands. 'Don't fret, I'll not tell her anything you don't want me to. But I'll need to tell her something to stop her worrying.'

He quelled a groan. Of course, Piers knew what training to be a squire was like. Years ago, when he was helping him prepare for going away to Courtenay Castle to start his page training, Piers had told him tales of his own life as a young squire. He'd made it sound fun and exciting, but Dickon suspected he understood well enough how it really was.

If he was going to tell anyone what was happening in Steyning, it would be Piers. He longed to share the burden of it but hesitated, nonetheless.

Piers drew him away, down the aisle to an empty stall, and they flopped down onto the freshly strewn hay. 'So, what is it?' he said. 'Are you mooning over a girl?'

Dickon snorted. 'Hardly. There aren't any girls at Steyning Castle.'

'That can't be quite true. There must be at least one or two serving girls.'

'Well, yes, but I never talk to them. Anyway, I wouldn't...' He looked away a moment and cleared his throat. 'The other squires talk about them sometimes, but not in a chivalrous way. You know, it's all about their—' His neck felt hot. 'And what it might be like to squeeze them—' His ears were surely flaming. 'Did you ever talk about girls like that?'

'I suppose so, though I'd never have laid hand on a servant when I was in training, for fear of being caught.'

'What about since then?'

'Well, yes, but only if they're willing. And there aren't many of those in Meonbridge.' He grinned.

Dickon didn't speak again for several moments, thinking this talk of girls might divert Piers for a while. 'Libby Fletcher's pretty, isn't she?' he said at length.

Piers smirked. 'Growing up now too...'

'I'd noticed.' He flushed again. 'You know we were playmates for years?'

'Since you were five or so, you told me.'

'I grew very fond of her. And I think maybe I still am.'

'That's understandable...' Piers cleared his throat. 'But, if you're thinking your fondness could become something more...?' Dickon's eyes widened, and Piers shook his head. 'She's your grandmother's servant, Dick. You mustn't take advantage...'

What Piers said was true. He shouldn't be thinking of Libby that way. Next time he saw her, he'd make it clear they couldn't continue to be friends.

'Anyway,' Piers went on, 'somehow I don't think that's what's troubling you.'

Dickon pouted and plucked at the hay, like he used to pick at his straw pallet when he was a boy. Damn Piers! He always somehow *knew*... He stayed silent a little longer, but sharing it would surely be better than keeping it bottled up inside. 'If I tell you, you mustn't tell my grandmother.'

He then described all that had happened to him since Edwin de Courtenay came to Steyning, the teasing, then the bullying, and the final incident with Morel.

As he came to the end of his sorry tale, Piers was scowling. 'Why haven't you told the earl?'

He winced. 'I'm not likely to do that, am I? It'd make me look even more a fool. A blab.'

'What are you going to do?'

He looked away. 'I can handle it.'

'Can you? It seems to be troubling you a great deal...'

'I'm just trying to work out what to do. How to get back at him. I'll think of something.' He stared at Piers, whose brow was furrowed, evidently unconvinced by his bravado.

As, in truth, was he.

2

***

L ibby had hoped she might be allowed to stay and listen to Dickon's tales of life in Steyning, but of course her ladyship dismissed her, wanting to be alone with her grandson.

'You can have an hour or two to yourself,' she said, and waved her away. Libby didn't want time to herself. She wanted to sit in her ladyship's chamber and gaze upon the vision of manhood Dickon had become.

Naturally he'd grown taller, as had she. But how handsome he was now: his black hair so glossy and his blue eyes sharp and steely. And his chin was definitely stronger. From what she'd heard, he looked just like his father, Philip.

She'd seen him for only moments, as she stood at the chamber door, then ushered him inside But she could tell he was surprised too by how much *she'd* grown since he last saw her, for, as he cast his eyes over her, they sparkled, and his smile was warm. Her heart had flipped. But he'd then stared beyond her, asking for his grandmother and, when she stepped aside to let him enter, he just pushed past her, without another glance.

By the time she returned to her ladyship's chamber, he'd gone.

She'd come back from the kitchen with a plate of sweetmeats, and placed them on the table. 'Cook asked if you'd care to taste these, milady. It's a new recipe he's trying, for the Christmas feast. He said he'd value your opinion.'

Lady Margaret gazed at the plate of almond delicacies. 'How delightful.' She picked one up between two fingers and popped it into her mouth. She savoured it a little. 'Delicious. Why don't you try one, Libby dear?'

Libby was glad to taste one of the little morsels and agreed it was delectable. Her ladyship took a second one, then a third, declaring all most appetising, and bid Libby pass on her approval to Cook.

She nodded but, as her ladyship seemed so merry, she thought she might risk asking about Dickon. 'And is his lordship content at Steyning Castle?' It seemed silly calling her childhood friend "his lordship", but she didn't want to seem disrespectful.

Lady Margaret's eyes lit up. 'Oh yes, very happy. It is clear he has inherited his skill with horses from his father, despite the lowly nature of his early upbringing, and his late start in knightly pursuits.'

'I suppose he doesn't miss Meonbridge at all?'

'Oh, I am not at all sure that is true. He seems content enough to be back here for a while, although of course, one day, albeit many years ahead, when he is lord, he will make Meonbridge his home.'

That "when he is lord" lay heavily upon Libby's heart. Was that why he'd brushed past her earlier? He no longer thought of her as his friend, but just another servant?

During dinner, Dickon did glance Libby's way from time to time, causing flutterings in her belly and confusion in her mind. She hoped to have a chance to speak to him afterwards but, as soon as Lady Margaret declared the meal finished, he left the hall with Piers Arundale. So she helped the other servants clear away, as she usually did. Then she went upstairs to sit with her ladyship a while, as usual in the hour following dinner, when she'd do some sewing whilst her ladyship slipped into a doze.

It was so much better in the summer, when after dinner they might go outside, to walk or work together in the garden. Libby didn't care all that much for gardening but, years ago, her ladyship had insisted on teaching her how to sow and plant and nurture vegetables and herbs, so that, when she married, she'd know how to manage her own potager. She'd knuckled down and learned and had come to realise that working out of doors was much more pleasurable than being cooped up inside the house.

But it was too cold and wet today for being out of doors, and anyway there was no gardening to be done. One benefit of her ladyship's chamber was the comforting warmth of the fire. In winter, the great hall downstairs was freezing, for the fire, large as it was, left most of the huge high room unheated. At dinner, she and the other servants, sitting furthest from the flames, shivered through every meal. To spend any time downstairs in winter, you had to wrap up warm and keep on the move.

When her sewing hour was done, and Lady Margaret had awoken and bid her take a message, Libby wrapped her thickest woollen cloak about her and went down to the hall. But at the bottom of the stairs, as she was about to run across towards the kitchens, she saw Dickon and Piers were indoors again, standing by the hearth, their backs towards the fire.

She hesitated, one foot on the bottom step. Could she approach him, or had the time for any intimacy between them already passed? Anyway, she'd instructions from her ladyship, and had no choice but to cross the hall.

As she came closer, Dickon looked up. She couldn't read his face. Was he pleased to see her, or maybe it mattered little to him? But he spoke her name, and moved away from Piers. Coming up to her, he smiled. 'Libby? How are you?'

She bobbed a curtsey, despite still feeling silly. 'Well enough, my lord.'

'We didn't have a chance earlier to talk. Can you sit a moment?'

'Her ladyship's expecting me back.'

'A few minutes then.' He pointed to one of the stone seats built into the long walls of the hall. Each seat was underneath one of the tall narrow windows, which had glass panes at the top but were merely shuttered at the bottom. Wind whistled between the wooden slats, sending shivers down her back. But she didn't mind the chill for the chance of a few words with Dickon, and pulled the hood of her cloak up a little more around her neck.

For several moments they were silent. She wanted to jump in but thought it best to wait for him to speak. It hadn't been like this last year. Now it felt more awkward. Not only did he seem much older, but he was also moving ever closer to becoming lord of Meonbridge, whereas she was just a servant. She supposed they could no longer be the friends that they once were.

But Dickon took her hand. 'Do you ever think about the way it used to be, when we were children?'

She was surprised. Had he after all been thinking the same as her? 'When you first came up here, supposedly to play with me?'

'We saw each other every week for years.'

'We used to have such fun together, especially when we were older...'

'And didn't we get into scrapes?' He squeezed her hand, and he talked about the day when the wicked Bounes got a so-called friar to try to kidnap him. Libby's bravery had saved him, when she hobbled the man by thwacking at his legs with a stout branch.

'Piers was brave as well,' she said and he agreed. Piers had chased off the "friar" by charging at him with his sword.

He went quiet again. 'But those times have gone, Libby. My life has changed, for the better, of course, though sometimes it doesn't always seem so.' His eyes suddenly looked sad. 'Soon enough I'll inherit my grandfather's domains, with all the duties that entails....' He let go her hand.

Libby couldn't think what to say. His eyes now seemed to suggest maybe he wasn't quite as contented as her ladyship implied.

'But surely that's years away?' she said. 'You don't have to worry about all that yet.'

'Oh, but I *do*, Libby.'

She started in surprise. His words were spoken with a sudden sharpness, when moments ago his mood had been relaxed, as he reminisced about their past. She didn't know what more to say.

For a few moments, it seemed he didn't either, but at length he gave her a wan smile. 'What I meant to say, Libby, was that we'll no longer be able to spend much time together, if any.'

A tightness gripped her chest. Surely he didn't mean it? They could always find a little time... She wanted to say so, but how could she gainsay him?

'Anyway, I must go,' he said, jumping up from the seat. 'Things to do...' He raked his fingers through his hair.

She wondered what it was he had to do, as rain was once more lashing at the window glass above her head. But it wasn't for her to ask. She got up as well. No suitable leave-taking came to mind, so she just bobbed a curtsey and hurried off towards the kitchens.

Later, when she was on her own, Libby thought over her brief conversation with Dickon, still confused.

At first it seemed he wanted to relive his happy memories of their years as children. He'd taken her hand, and even squeezed it. Only moments later, he changed, as if he'd forgotten what close companions they once had been.

She'd known him a long time, and for a year or so they'd been almost constantly together. The last year before he went away to be a page, he'd spent more time with her here than with his Sawyer family.

She didn't know it at the time but, when she was a little older, she learned from her mother the true reason Dickon came to the manor house. It must have seemed—to those who even thought of it—an odd thing for her ladyship to do, to invite the son of the village carpenter to play with her companion's daughter. But it was a ruse on Lady Margaret's part to enable her to see more of her grandson. Though, at that time, no one in Meonbridge knew he was her grandson apart from the de Bohuns and the Sawyers.

When he first came, Dickon didn't seem to like Libby much. But eventually they became good friends. He found out she was just as eager as he was for a lark or two. They often escaped her mother's— and her ladyship's—attention, and ran into the woods or down to the river. It had surely been most improper behaviour for a girl, but her mother never tried to stop her, indeed she seemed almost to encourage her waywardness.

She never wanted their friendship to end. But end it did, a few months after that day she'd helped to save him from that horrible friar. They were seven or thereabouts by then, and that was when Dickon went away from Meonbridge to start his new life as Sir Richard's heir.

She'd seen much less of him since. For the first few years, he came home twice a year, though later only at Christmas. Yet, during those few precious weeks, he still spent a day or two with her, doing things they'd done when they were children.

But, this year, he seemed different. He'd smiled at her and briefly held her hand. Yet, only a moment later he'd said he could no longer spend any time with her. She couldn't believe her ears.

And, if he truly meant what he had said, she wasn't sure she could bear it.

3

'You can leave us, Libby,' Margaret said, as the girl laid the tray of sweetmeats on the table. 'We shall serve ourselves.'

Libby pouted, but nonetheless she dropped a curtsey and left the chamber.

'That girl is just like her mother. Hates to miss out on any gossip.' Margaret laughed lightly, and Eleanor and Alice joined in.

'Oh, I don't think she's quite as fond of gossip as Matilda,' said Alice, her eyes alight. 'Nor so wily?'

Alice's son, John, had once courted Matilda Tyler, although Matilda's father, Robert, then Meonbridge's bailiff, had deemed John an unsuitable match for his daughter. How amusing it was that John eventually became the bailiff, quite trouncing Robert's lowly opinion of him. Yet how differently life might have been for poor Matilda if Robert had not been so disdainful.

'You are right, Alice dear. Libby is a good girl.' Margaret refilled the three cups with more spiced wine and brought them over to the table. Alice pushed aside the mass of greenery piled up on the table's surface, to make space for the cups. 'Thank you,' said Margaret and sat down.

'Speaking of Matilda,' said Eleanor, taking one of the cups and folding her hands around it, 'I saw someone yesterday whom I have not seen for, well, at least a couple of years. Her sister, Margery Tyler.'

Eleanor had been close to Matilda when they were young. In fact, they were the best of friends. Which Margaret always considered strange, for they were very different characters, Matilda dashing and flighty, Eleanor far more modest and restrained.

'Oh yes,' said Alice, 'I too saw her the other day.'

'Margery?' Margaret frowned. 'I cannot think when the last time was that I saw her. Where is she now?'

'Where's she been ever since her father died,' said Alice. 'As a servant with the Browghtons.'

'The Browghtons?'

'Their property is that sprawling farmstead four miles or so along the road to Middle Brooking. They came to Meonbridge two years before the Mortality, I think it was.'

'I do not think I have ever seen them,' said Eleanor, 'yet they have lived here all this time—'

'Aha!' cried Margaret, as recognition dawned. 'I recall them now. Foreigners. From Devon, was it, or Somerset? Anyway, not Hampshire. I believe it was Mistress Browghton who inherited the property...' Eleanor and Alice both shrugged. 'I do remember Robert saying they were queer folk, who intended to keep themselves apart from village life.' She took a sip of her wine. 'They have never come to our Christmas feast, nor to any village celebration that I recall.'

Alice nodded. 'I remember Stephen, when he was reeve, taking the trouble to walk down there, to welcome them to Meonbridge. Almost rude, he said they were. No interest in the village. Which is perhaps why we never see Mistress Browghton here. Nor her children, though I believe her husband deals with tradesmen and other farmers in the village. Otherwise, they seem to keep almost entirely to themselves.'

'Do they not even come to church?' said Eleanor.

'I understand they have a private chapel. Maybe they have their own cleric too?' Alice was tying together stems of pine and ivy. 'Anyway, neither the family nor their servants ever attend Saint Peter's.'

Eleanor winced as she picked up a bunch of holly, pricking a finger on the spiky leaves. 'And that is where poor Margery has been living all these years? It is bad enough she had no choice but to become a servant, but in such an isolated place as that...'

'Not at all what she might have expected from her life.' Margaret's hands were still for a moment.

'No indeed,' continued Alice. 'She was no beauty, Margery, unlike her sister. But, as the bailiff's elder daughter, she'd have expected to make a decent match and become a goodwife and a mother.'

Margaret noticed a rueful grin pass between Eleanor and Alice. 'Am I missing some playful banter?'

Alice pulled a face. 'There's nothing amusing in Margery's situation but, years ago, Eleanor and I used to jest maybe she'd make a suitable match for my John.'

'Surely not?' said Margaret. 'A handsome and important man like our bailiff deserves a much comelier wife than what I recall of Margery Tyler.'

'Indeed,' said Eleanor. 'That is what Alice and I concluded. In truth, it was not just her glum looks that made her unsuitable for John, but her gloomy temper too. But I would not have wished for her to become a servant, especially in such a place.'

'Is she their housekeeper perhaps?' said Margaret.

Alice shook her head. 'A lowly maid, so I believe.'

Margaret pondered a moment. 'Yet, if the family do not come to Meonbridge, it seems their servants do?'

Eleanor was struggling to tie a couple of bushy stems of ivy around the holly to make into a swag. She set it aside a moment and looked up. 'I have seen Margery only the once, and she seemed to be on some errand for her mistress. Mistress Browghton refuses to engage with tradespeople herself, or so I understand.'

'Did you speak to Margery?'

'I did not know quite what to say. But, if I see her again, I will make it my business to speak. If only to find out how she is.'

'How did she look?'

'She always looked somewhat older than her years, but the other day I thought she looked truly *old*. Thin, in body and in face, and her back was almost bowed.'

Alice agreed. 'It's a sad end for a young woman who might have hoped for so much more.'

. . .

The gloomy conversation about poor Margery Tyler had cast a brief pall over what was supposed to be a merry afternoon, weaving Christmas swags and garlands to decorate the hall. Margaret refilled the wine cups and pressed more of Cook's delicious sweetmeats on her companions. They spoke of more cheerful topics for a while and gradually their spirits lifted.

At which point Alice asked about their grandson.

'Have you not seen him?' Margaret said, surprised. 'How remiss of him not to have visited you already.'

'Yet I suppose he's only been home a day?'

'Indeed. And the journey was exhausting.'

Alice nodded understanding. 'But Agnes is most anxious to see her son. Geoffrey and the girls are eager too to see their brother...'

'I will insist he visit the Sawyers soon, and you too, Alice dear.' A pang of guilt reminded her that, however strongly she might feel that Dickon was a de Bohun now rather than a Sawyer, it would be unkind not to urge him to spend time with the family who had brought him up.

'And how is Dickon enjoying his knightly training?' asked Eleanor.

'Oh, very much.' Margaret repeated what he had told her about the horses and his promotion to Lord Raoul's personal entourage of squires. She knew her eyes were shining as she spoke of him. It was easy to make his life at Steyning appear a great success, as indeed he had done himself.

Yet she felt sure something was not quite right at Steyning, although what it might be she could not imagine, and she doubted Dickon would tell her. But she would not mention such concerns to Eleanor, and especially not to Alice. She did not want to worry her, nor betray Dickon if he had some difficulty he was trying to resolve. Though she had asked Piers Arundale to try to find out what was wrong.

She also would not mention the spark she was sure she saw between Dickon and young Libby. It had occurred to her that Dickon might do something foolish, as young men often did. Though he was only fourteen, and she did not think that even Philip bedded girls

35

quite so young... But perhaps the answer was to marry Libby off. She always had intended to find the girl a decent match, but now wondered if she should do it sooner than she'd planned. She must give some consideration to the matter—but in private.

However, she could speak of her other plans and, finishing the last drops of her wine, she beamed. 'I do have some wonderful news concerning Dickon.'

Alice put down her swag of pine and ivy. 'What news?'

'I am sure you both remember Sir Giles Fitzpeyne? Richard's old comrade-in-arms, who gave us such support when those dreadful Bounes came to steal Meonbridge from us.'

'It was to Fitzpeyne Castle that Dickon went after all the upset with the Bounes,' said Alice.

'Indeed. Dickon so enjoyed his time up there. Well, three days ago I received a letter from Sir Giles, suggesting that his daughter Angharad might make a suitable match for Dickon.'

'What does Dickon think of the idea?' asked Eleanor.

'I have not yet told him of it, but I think he will be pleased. He grew quite fond of little Angharad.'

'You must be delighted to ally the de Bohuns and the Fitzpeynes, after all that Sir Richard and Sir Giles had been to each other,' said Alice.

'I am.' Margaret felt cheerful at the prospect. 'Of course, Angharad is yet a child—only six—so the marriage would be years away. But a betrothal in a year or so will affiliate our houses and put the plan in place. One of the steps our young lord needs to take to establish himself as a member of society.'

4

Dickon wished his grandmother hadn't felt she needed to prompt him to visit his mother and the rest of his Sawyer family. He did intend to see them, and, after all, he'd only been home two days.

Nonetheless, the following morning, he put on a thick cloak and sturdy boots to walk down to the village.

He decided to call in at Grandma Alice's, as her house was on the way. His uncles, John, the Meonbridge bailiff, and his younger brother Matthew, were both already out about their work, but his maternal grandmother was pottering in the house.

With her reminder yesterday, Grandmama had hinted that his mother and Grandma Alice were offended he'd not already been to see them. But when Grandma opened the door to him, the broad smile on her face showed she was anything but upset with him.

'My dear boy,' she cried, and stepped back to let him in. 'Am I allowed to hug you?'

'Of course you are, Grandma,' he said, sheepish but understanding it was what grandmothers liked to do. He let her embrace him, and folded his arms around her too.

'Are you on your way to see your mother?' she asked.

'I wondered if you wanted to come down with me?'

'I'd like that.' She reached out for her cloak, but he stayed her hand. 'There's no hurry, if you're busy.'

'You're sure you don't mind waiting?'

He shook his head. 'I'll watch you. Are you making pottage?'

'As I always do of a morning. Either making or replenishing it.' She beamed.

'Can I help?' He could just imagine the hoots of derision from Edwin and the others at the very idea of helping to make pottage. He was sure neither Edwin or Alan ever helped their grandmothers in the kitchen. But he supposed neither of them had a grandmother quite like Grandma Alice, who actually prepared meals for her family.

She handed him an onion and a knife. 'Do you know how to do it?'

He chuckled, then sliced the vegetable in half and peeled off the skin.

When the chopped up vegetables had softened in the great black cauldron, Grandma Alice poured in water from a jug and stirred. 'I'll let it bubble a little while, then we can go.'

At length she buckled on her boots and wrapped her winter cloak about her shoulders. 'This was your Grandpa Stephen's. Good and thick. I always wear it in the winter. It's a good shield against the wind and a reminder of your grandpa's loving arms.' Dickon blushed.

They stepped out onto the road that led down to the village. Already it was worse than when he'd ridden up it three days ago, with the central channel a near torrent now after all the rain. If he'd been alone he would have run, skipping over the surging water and the stones and debris caught up in the flood. But his grandmother's steps were slow and cautious, and he offered her his arm.

'Thank you, dear,' she said. 'What a kind boy you are.'

It was his youngest sister, Elizabeth, known as Lizbet, who answered their knock at the door. She squealed and, running back inside, cried out 'Dickon's come!'

'Let's go in,' said Grandma Alice, 'and close the door against the weather.'

They were taking off their damp and chilly cloaks when his mother came forward and held out her hands to him.

He took them. 'Ma,' he said. 'You look well.' He meant it: her eyes were bright, and her mouth was curving upwards.

She stepped back a little to gaze at him. 'My, how you've grown.' She giggled. 'All mothers say that. But you have—again. You are so like your father now.'

She held out her arms again. 'Am I allowed?'

He snorted. 'Grandma said that too.' He stepped into her arms. She held him for several moments and he didn't resist, happy to be amongst those who loved him rather than those who wished him harm.

They all took stools around the hearth and chatted for a while, with Dickon retelling the same not-quite-true story of his life in Steyning that he'd told Grandmama Margaret.

But, at a lull in the conversation, his sisters, Lizbet and little Alice, who'd been hovering at his side, jiggling from foot to foot, tugged at his sleeve and demanded he play with them.

His ma shooed them away. 'Dickon's no interest in poppets, no more than Geoffrey does.'

But he put his hand upon hers. 'No, Ma, really, I love poppets.' He winked at her, then followed the girls over to the bed and let them show him their cloth family.

After a while, sensing he was being watched, he looked across at his mother, and saw her gazing at him, her head tipped to one side, a smile upon her lips. She was so much happier than she used to be. It was two years ago last summer that Jack, and Dickon's brothers, Stephen and Geoffrey, all got the plague. And Stephen died. Ma went almost mad with grief. Then, for a long while after that dreadful time, she barely spoke, and Jack did almost everything, with the help of Grandma Alice.

But, twelve months ago, the black cloud lifted. Ma's heartache seemed to ease at last and she had more energy and cheer than he'd ever known. How glad he'd been to see it then, and how much gladder he was now to see her bustling around, preparing a dinner he'd agreed to share, her melancholy and her anguish seemingly melted away.

'Where's Geoffrey?' he said at last, leaving his sisters to their poppets.

'He works full time now with his pa.'

Noticing the "his", he was wistful. Jack was the only father he'd ever known, but his mother was now careful to refer to *Philip* as his father. Had Grandmama perhaps insisted that she did, to reinforce his de Bohun bonds?

'Will they all come back for dinner?'

'Oh yes. Geoffrey's looking forward to seeing you, and so is Jack.'

'And what of Christopher?'

'He left us earlier this year, once his apprenticeship was done. Went to be a journeyman in Winchester. But James Paynter's still with us, though I daresay he'll move on before too long, to set up his own shop.'

He nodded. If life had turned out differently, that would have been his lot too: working for Jack, or gone to be an apprentice to another craftsman. He wondered often if he'd have liked that life more or less than he liked the one he had. 'Can I go down to the workshop?'

'They'll be back soon.'

'Yes, but I'd like to see it, see what they're making.'

'If you pop over now, you can tell them I'm expecting them at the *Sext* bell, as usual.'

The workshop was a few short steps away, sheltered by an enclosed passageway Jack had built to keep the house and workshop warm and dry.

As he approached, the sweet earthy scent of sawn timber and shavings wafted through the door. The smell of it took him back to his childhood; to the few days he had spent in Jack's workshop, not wanting to be there at all but out playing in the woods and meadows. He grinned to himself: what a difficult boy he'd been. He'd led his parents a merry dance. Did he somehow *know* he wasn't destined for a carpenter's life? Yet how could he have done? But he did now regret causing Jack such trouble, when he was the best of fathers.

He rapped upon the doorpost to announce his presence, then stepped inside. The room was full of activity. Closest to him, James, the journeyman who'd been with Jack since before Dickon first left for his page training, was bent over a long plank of cut timber, planing it smooth. His face was red and slick with sweat, and locks of his thick fair hair were escaping from his close-fitting coif. Dickon's brother, Geoffrey, was sweeping the chips and curls of wood piling up on the floor around James's bench. At the far end of the workshop, Jack was leaning forwards, sawing planed lengths into shorter pieces with shaped ends.

No one saw him standing in the doorway, so Dickon called out and waved his arm to attract attention. At that moment, Jack stood up, as a cut length fell to the floor, and a broad smile creased his face as he put down his saw and strode across to Dickon.

'How glad I am to see you, son,' he said then winced. 'Sorry... *My lord.*'

Dickon grimaced. 'No, Pa, "son" was right. I can't have you of all people calling me "my lord".' He stepped forward, holding out his arms, and Jack, seeming nervous, accepted his embrace, folding his own arms around Dickon's back. A ripple of joy fizzed along his spine at the comfort of his father's clasp.

'It's good to see you,' Jack repeated, as he stepped away again. 'Have you seen your mother?'

'Yes, I've come from the house. She says to come for dinner at the *Sext* bell.' Dickon gestured around the workshop. 'You look busy.'

'Very. I need to take on another journeyman, and an apprentice or two.'

'Ma says Christopher has gone.'

'To be a journeyman. Earlier this year.'

'He didn't say he was leaving when I last saw him.'

'Nay, a chance came up in Winchester, and I encouraged him to take it.' He rubbed his cheeks. 'But I haven't had time to find another.'

Jack called to James and Geoffrey to stop what they were doing and come and meet their guest. Dickon bit his lip. He didn't want to be thought of as a "guest". As if he was a stranger here, and not part of this family. But he swallowed down his disappointment.

'Your brother and sisters have missed you.'

'I've missed them too.'

'Though I daresay you've made lots of friends?'

'I have, but family's still family.'

He heard a delicate cough behind him and, turning, saw Geoffrey was standing stiff and awkward behind a bench.

'Good to see you, brother,' said Dickon. 'Ma says you're working full time now? Do you like it?'

Jack chortled. 'He's very good. Isn't he, James?'

41

The tall frame of James Paynter loomed beside him. 'Geoffrey's got the makings of a fine joiner,' he said, raising his fingers to his forehead. 'Welcome home, milord.'

Dickon shook his head. 'No need for "milord", James.' He grinned. 'We're all family.'

James flushed then returned the grin.

But Geoffrey still held back a little, shuffling his shoes amidst the shavings. Jack nudged him with his elbow and Geoffrey mumbled 'Milord', so Dickon had to repeat his assertion about not wanting to be addressed differently from the way he'd always been. 'I'm still your brother, Geoffrey.' He wrapped his arm about his shoulder. 'And I'm going to spend a bit more time with you whenever I'm back in Meonbridge.' He turned to his pa. 'What are you making?'

'You really want to know?'

'Why not? I'm interested.' As he said it, he wondered if he truly was but, despite his more-or-less contentment with being a de Bohun, he felt he'd never *not* also be a Sawyer. It was one of the things he'd decided on his long ride home, that he would make more time for *this* family, the one that had nurtured him. Even if—or perhaps because— he hadn't much honoured them for it in the past.

5

MEONBRIDGE

APRIL 1364

Margery stood at the door of Martin Webber's cloth mill, her arms clasped around the bolt of bright blue woollen fabric her mistress had demanded she collect. The linen-wrapped bundle was so cumbersome and heavy, she wondered if she could get it all the way back to the Browghtons' farmstead without it slipping to the ground.

She grunted. It was typical of Philippa Browghton to give no thought to the practicalities of carrying the fabric. She wished now she had thought of it herself, although she had not imagined the "length of fine wool" ordered especially from Master Webber would be quite so hefty. But, if she took it slowly and stopped every so often for a rest...

She stepped across the threshold, and turned onto the narrow path that led back up to Meonbridge's main thoroughfare. She waited, as a young woman was walking down the path towards the mill, pulling a small, wheeled barrow behind her. As the girl came closer, Margery gasped. She looked exactly like her sister Matilda, with her pretty face and thick dark hair. Was this Matilda's daughter, Elizabeth? She was a babe the last, and only, time she saw her.

When the girl was a few steps distant, Margery hailed her. 'You seem to have a similar errand to my own,' she said. 'Though you are better equipped for carrying your purchase home.' She pointed to the barrow.

The girl looked startled, then noticed Margery's bundle. 'Yes, her ladyship's ordered two bolts of cloth for new spring gowns, and said I should bring the barrow to fetch them home.'

So, it *was* her niece, and she was still serving Lady Margaret de Bohun.

'You must be Elizabeth. I am Margery Tyler, your mother's sister.'

The girl's mouth fell open. 'Ma's sister? I knew I had an aunt... But how odd we've never met before. I thought you must no longer live in Meonbridge, as her ladyship's never spoken of you.'

'She wouldn't have.' Margery was aware her tone was sour. 'I live a distance down the road to Middle Brooking. I rarely come to Meonbridge, just to run the occasional errand for my mis—'. She stopped. Need she explain the depth of her disgrace, if the girl did not already know?

But then, why not? She might as well admit the truth, or a version of it, anyway. For the child was herself a servant, and must surely know her mother was banished by her ladyship, sent miles from Meonbridge, to another county, to be a maid to some decrepit knight.

'The occasional errand for my mistress,' she continued. 'She does not care to visit Meonbridge herself. She sends her orders courtesy of her husband then gets her servants to collect them. Thinks herself too grand for shopping.' She sneered.

'You're a servant too?' Elizabeth said. 'I didn't know.'

'I had no choice, after Father died. Your mother was taken in by Lady de Bohun, but there was no place for me. Our family was unjustly stripped of all our wealth and standing, so I lost my home and livelihood...' She hesitated again. Did Elizabeth even know what had happened to her grandfather?

But the girl did not query what she had said, so she carried on. 'I took a position with the Browghtons, newly come to Meonbridge. They were prosperous, with a large household, and it seemed a fitting enough situation...' She could not help another sneer twisting her mouth, but she would say no more. No need to explain how *unfitting* the situation had turned out to be. 'How do you like working for Lady de Bohun, Elizabeth?'

'It's Libby, actually,' the girl said, flushing. 'Ma always called me Libby.'

Margery rolled her eyes. Matilda gave the girl a graceful name then chose to demean it. How like her. 'Very well, *Libby*,' she said, more tersely than was necessary.

'Anyway, I don't mind it,' said her niece, not noticing. 'The work's not hard and her ladyship's quite kind.' She indicated the barrow. 'I could help you if you like.'

Margery hefted her bundle and repositioned it in her arms. 'It would be too far out of your way. Your mistress will be expecting you.'

'Oh, she'll probably not notice if I'm not back for a while.'

Margery glowered. Not *notice*? Philippa Browghton was heedful of every move her servants made: none of them could leave the farm without her permission, nor for any reason she deemed unwarranted. Maybe Lady de Bohun *was* kinder. It would scarcely take much effort to be more so than Mistress Browghton.

'A little of the way, perhaps,' she said. 'We can talk some more.'

'I'll just pick up her ladyship's order.' Libby darted into the mill, leaving her barrow at the door.

Margery walked the last two miles to Browghtons farmstead on her own, with her bundle slung across her back. She had taken off her shawl and Libby helped her to retie it with the bolt of fabric held inside, like some women carried babies. She should have thought of it herself.

But she had enjoyed, or almost so, talking to her niece, despite her lingering resentment against Matilda. It seemed the girl was happy to have met her too.

How strange that, in all the fourteen years of her niece's life, she had not seen or spoken to her. Yet, whilst it would be strange for most people, it was not so for her. The Browghtons' farm was a fair walk out of Meonbridge and, because her mistress shunned the company of anyone outside her household, she spent all her days in the house or garden, and expected her women servants to do the same. Margery worked long hours and had no friends, and visited Meonbridge for no other reason than rare errands for her mistress. Her visits had been so infrequent, it was scarcely surprising she had never run into the girl.

Before they parted, Elizabeth asked if they might meet again, and Margery had agreed, although how she might arrange it she had no idea. What plea might she make to Mistress Browghton?

Though, what did it really matter if she never saw her niece again? The girl seemed content enough with her life. What else might she have to say to her that she had not said already? She could tell her nothing about Matilda, far away in Dorset, and she scarcely wanted to regale the girl with tales of her own miserable life at the Browghtons'.

Matilda, she suspected, had told her daughter little or nothing of the Tylers' change of fortune. She would not have wished to expose the family's humiliation to anyone who did not already know it.

Yet, hours later, when Margery was lying awake in the dark, in the upstairs chamber she shared with the other maids, she mused that maybe, after all, her niece *should* know the truth.

When she was a girl, Margery had much disliked her younger sister. Matilda was pretty and vivacious, and their father indulged her in her love of finery. Until, of course, she was seduced by Philip de Bohun, and she found herself with child. Then their father went quite mad, not only arranging for Matilda's child to be aborted but forcing her then to marry his henchman, Gilbert Fletcher. Then, a few months later, so it was said, Father, in league with Matilda's husband, arranged Sir Philip's murder.

At the time, Margery was not sorry for her sister. For she herself was plain—no man even wanted to seduce her and how deeply that aggrieved her. Then, after the turmoil of the seduction, the abortion, the murder and, the last cruel turn, her father's self-inflicted death, the Tyler family was entirely disgraced.

Their father's presumed guilt as a murderer left Margery and her sister with nothing, the family's property forfeit to the king. Gilbert too had died and Matilda, pregnant again with Elizabeth, drew Lady de Bohun's sympathy, and she took her in as her companion.

Elizabeth thought her ladyship was "kind". But Margery received no compassion. She had no choice but to find herself a job.

Thus, penniless and tainted through no fault of her own, Margery no longer had any chance of finding a husband. A servant's job was all she could do to stay alive.

How much she had resented that her sister seemed to have fallen on her feet, whilst she, the elder daughter of a once high-ranking villein, was forced into a life of servitude. She and Matilda scarcely spoke to each other after that. When, five years ago, the de Bohuns claimed Matilda betrayed them by plotting with the Bounes to kidnap Dickon, and banished her from Meonbridge, Margery had been rather pleased to see her sister get her come-uppance.

She had not thought about Matilda or her family for years. It was only seeing Elizabeth that brought it back to her. The unhappy memories roiled round and round inside her head, keeping her awake. By the time her eyes were closing in blessed sleep, she had decided *not* to see her niece again.

If the girl was ignorant of all the misery she was heir to, perhaps it was best that she remained so.

6

'You might be surprised, milady, who I met there,' Libby had said, in answer to Lady Margaret's enquiry about her visit to Master Webber's.

But her ladyship was not surprised. 'Oh dear, I should have told you months ago that Margery had been seen in Meonbridge. I imagined she had left Meonbridge altogether. Yet, Mistress atte Wode mentioned before Christmas that she had seen her, and Mistress Nash saw her too. I am so sorry, Libby, for not telling you. With all the excitement of the festivities, it quite slipped my mind.'

Libby had felt a little aggrieved her ladyship had not told her about her aunt. It was strange that she had simply forgotten, especially when she seemed so sad about Margery being "brought low", as she put it.

'Poor Margery,' Lady Margaret continued. 'She did deserve much better. After all the expectations she must have harboured, of a suitable marriage and a prosperous life. None of it her doing, either, but entirely brought upon her by her father...' She'd paused, as if she was remembering. 'Robert Tyler—your grandfather, Libby—was once such a fine man... I have never understood what went so wrong... But it was cruel that Margery should have had to become a lowly servant because of his misdeeds...'

She'd wondered why her ladyship couldn't have found Margery a job as she had her mother, though didn't say it.

'How did she look?' said Lady Margaret.

'She's very different from my mama. Not a bit pretty, with a narrow face and sort of pinched-in cheeks...' She bit her lip as she realised how unkind that description sounded.

But her ladyship nodded. 'She was always very plain, in stark contrast to your mother. In her humour, too, she was quite different. How did she seem to you?'

'Cheerful enough, I think, milady. But we only talked a little while, and she didn't tell me much about her work, apart from the fact she was a servant, a dairymaid I think she said.'

'Not at all what she would have expected, poor Margery,' Lady Margaret said again. 'Nonetheless, I hope she is content enough.'

Libby ran out through the manor house gate and down the road towards the mill. She hadn't visited her friend Maud for months. It was well before Christmas that they'd last spoken.

As she ran along the narrow track that led down to the mill cottage, Libby remembered her Aunt Margery saying she wasn't allowed out for any purpose other than running errands for her mistress. Which was really mean. Whereas Lady Margaret was perfectly happy for her to visit Maud. She did seem very kind compared to the horrid Mistress Browghton.

A little out of breath, Libby knocked upon the cottage door. She knew it was Maud coming to answer, from the slight scuffing sound as she dragged her twisted leg across the floor. It took a long time for her leg to mend after she broke it years ago, but mend it did, albeit not quite straight. But the cheerful, energetic Maud she'd known before the accident never did return. She rarely went outside, staying indoors with her ma, doing what she could to help around the house and mind the little ones. Her mood was mostly solemn too, though she did seem to enjoy her chats with Libby, even laughing a bit more than she used to.

Libby had been dying to tell her about Dickon.

Not that Maud was much interested in boys. When she confided her own secrets to Libby, they were never about boys. Mostly, Libby presumed, because Maud thought they wouldn't be much interested in her. Yet, despite her wonky leg, Maud was just as pretty as she'd always been, and it was obvious she'd make a good wife and mother, with all her years of looking after the cottage and the babies.

But she'd not yet mentioned Dickon when the cottage door flew open and Mistress Miller burst through, a basket on each arm. She'd been down to the village for supplies. Maud got up at once. 'Shall I help you, Ma?'

Mistress Miller shook her head. 'No, sweeting, you sit with Libby, as she's come to see you.' She looked sidelong at Libby. 'Why don't you go out into the garden? It's chilly still, but it's a lovely afternoon.'

Libby slipped off her stool. Even if it was cold, it would be easier out there to tell Maud about Dickon. She didn't want Mistress Miller to overhear her. 'We could walk down to your orchard, Maudie.'

Maud looked up. 'You sure you don't mind, Ma?'

''Course not, sweeting. It'll do you good, a breath of fresh air.' She caught Libby's eye again. 'But wrap up warm.'

Outside, Libby set off through the potager down towards the orchard, which lay beyond the gate at the far end of the garden. There was a bench under the fruit trees where they might sit. Eager to get there, so she could tell Maud what was on her mind, she almost broke into a run. But she soon realised Maud wasn't close behind her. She was several yards back up the garden, tottering a little on the uneven ground. 'Are you all right?' she called.

'It's this tufty grass,' said Maud. 'I still wobble if I step on a lumpy bit.'

'I'm sorry, I should've waited.'

Maud caught her up. She was breathing hard.

'D'you still want to go down to the orchard?' said Libby.

'Oh, yes. The blossom might be coming out on some of the trees. It is so pretty.'

The pear tree under which they sat was covered with white flowers, and its branches hung low around them. They pulled the frothy sprigs towards their noses and sniffed in the sweet, fruity scent.

Libby took Maud's hand. 'If I tell you something, will you promise not to tell anyone else?'

Maud's eyes widened. 'Have you got a secret?'

Libby giggled. 'Promise?' Maud nodded.

'It's about Dickon—' she began.

Maud interrupted. 'Libby, you can't call him "Dickon" any more...'

She pouted. 'He doesn't mind. I've always called him Dickon and, till he's lord, he won't expect me not to.' She said it with confidence. Though maybe he *did* mind now and that was why he had been strange with her? 'Anyway, I wanted to tell you what happened when he came home for Christmas. Did you see him at the feast?' Maud shrugged. 'What did you think?'

'I didn't think anything.'

'Not even how handsome he's become?'

'Well, yes, of course, he's handsome. But what of it? It's not for me to admire him.'

'Oh, Maudie, you're so prissy!' Though she did feel a prickle of unease. 'Anyway, why not?'

'You know why not. Anyway, does he admire you?'

Libby hesitated. She was certain she'd seen something in his eyes when he caught sight of her, standing at the door of her ladyship's chamber. They *had* sparkled, hadn't they? Then, later, when he spoke to her in the hall, he'd taken her hand in his, and held it. 'I'm sure he does.'

Maud shrugged. 'As long as you're not thinking something more can come of it.'

Libby flushed. 'Whatever do you mean?'

'Oh, Libby, stop it! You *know* what.'

When Libby was home again, she thought about what Maud had said. How shocked she'd seemed. She suspected she'd never had feelings for a boy.

Yet she'd not told Maud the whole truth about Dickon. She'd made out he had eyes for her, as much as she had for him. When, really, he had dismissed her, hadn't he, or did she just imagine it?

7

COURTENAY CASTLE
APRIL 1364

When Hildegard told Edwin the truth about Dickon de Bohun's birth, that day over the Christmas holiday that they had spent together, she had been rather delighted at his reaction. It was clear he already loathed the boy, as if he had instinctively recognised his lack of breeding. But, when he discovered the boy's mother was indeed a peasant girl, he was undeniably elated.

'I knew it,' he crowed, and punched the air. 'I always thought there was something not quite right about him.'

She had nodded coolly, gratified.

It was pitiful of course that a person of her age and standing might gain pleasure from the humiliation of a child, but it felt like some small grain of recompense for the ignominy the de Bohuns had caused *her*, as well as for the effrontery of them implicating her darling Isabella in their duplicity. Not that she had told Edwin about his aunt.

She had however discovered that the boy knew little about his English family.

She realised that Benedict had rarely, if ever, discussed his siblings with his son. It seemed he had not even mentioned his youngest sister, and certainly not said how she had died. But why would he? He scarcely knew Isabella, who was thirteen years his junior. Although she died the same year that this son, Edwin, had been born, Benedict was living in France, as he had done ever since he was dubbed a knight. After that, he had come only once to England, to leave this boy in Steyning. On that occasion he visited his parents for a short while before going home, clearly out of duty rather than affection. If he had ever commented to her on his lost sister then or at any other time, Hildegard did not recall it.

Edwin, she must presume, knew nothing of Isabella, nor of his other de Courtenay aunts and uncles.

'But I should like to learn more about my de Courtenay family, *Grandmère*,' he had said to her. 'The only heritage I know of is Burgundian.'

She had agreed. Though she knew all the spouses of her other children, she had never met Benedict's wife, Anne-Marie. She suspected their lack of acquaintance was no loss. When Benedict married the woman, Hildegard and Hugh were not invited to the wedding. It was the plague year, so journeying to France would anyway have been difficult, if not impossible. Nonetheless, she might have expected the woman would wish to meet her in-laws in the years that followed.

Apparently not.

No matter. This grandson was now in England, wanting to know more about his English family. It was vexing that Benedict had not bothered to tell him anything, but she was glad to do so. She would resist turning the boy against the French side of his heritage, but surely she should take the opportunity to encourage him to defend the name he bore, de Courtenay?

She had started by outlining the lineage of her husband, Hugh, and showed Edwin the chart that Hugh had had drawn up, illustrating the family's ancestry and adding the many children that she had borne him. For a boy of fourteen, Edwin seemed surprisingly fascinated by his heritage and spent hours poring over the chart, asking questions about this and that branch of the de Courtenays.

So engrossed did he become that she ran out of time to tell him the story she had been planning to impart: about his Aunt Isabella. It rankled for a long while that she had not told Edwin about how Sir Richard insulted her daughter's memory. During the long dark days of winter, she had spent many days in her chamber, tap-tapping up and down, vacillating back and forth over whether to write to her grandson, to tell him the full, appalling tale.

Yet, now spring had arrived, her dour mood had lightened a little. Perhaps it was best after all that she had not told him. Hugh had long since set aside his disquiet about it all, and would be furious if he discovered she was stirring it all up again and passing it on to Edwin. Not that that would stop her. Nonetheless, bitter as her resentment was, it should perhaps be hers to endure alone. Edwin's initial antipathy to Dickon, for his apparent lack of breeding, was already burning more fiercely with what she had told him about Dickon's birth.

In truth, she need tell him nothing more.

STEYNING CASTLE
APRIL 1364

The pranks Edwin and his chums had played upon de Bohun had, up till now, been secret, witnessed only by the three of them. He did not mind that at first. All he wanted was to make de Bohun cringe, to make him feel a fool.

But when, at Christmas, he had learned from his *grandmère* what he had suspected all along, that Dickon was not of wholly gentle birth, he wanted more. Outraged that such a half-peasant oaf should be training alongside him and his other elite friends, his desire to humiliate him became even greater.

So much so that he now craved a much more public shaming.

He had been gleeful when he returned to Steyning in January, eager to tell Nick and Alan what he had learned. They were sprawled together in an empty stable stall, as they often did, catching up with each other's news. Not that the others had anything of much interest to tell. Their Christmases had been full of family and friends, day after day of feasting, games and entertainments. The sort of festivities

Edwin's family would have had in France. But Christmas at Courtenay Castle had been intolerably dull. He now knew he had many cousins, but they had visited briefly with their parents and did not stay. Most days he had spent almost entirely alone.

The best day had been one spent with his *grandmère*, when she told him the thrilling truth about de Bohun.

'You know what a churl we think de Bohun is,' he said to his friends, when he had had enough of hearing about the merriment in Castle Clyffe and Fenecote Hall.

Alan scoffed. 'I wonder he's got the impudence to come back here.'

'I agree,' said Edwin. 'Guess what I have found out about him.'

'What?' said Alan and Nick as one.

Edwin smirked. 'I now know for sure he isn't what he claims to be.'

'What do you mean?' said Nick.

'What I thought, he's not one of us at all. Not born of a noble family. Or rather only half of him is...' He guffawed.

'What's the other half? A pig?' Alan pulled on his nose. 'Oink, oink!'

Edwin hooted. 'Almost! His mother was a *peasant*. Probably a whore...'

'So he's a—'

'A bastard, yes. What a hoot is that?'

Yet Nick gave a slight shake of his head. 'He's done well, then, for Lord Raoul to let him come here.'

'I suppose you might be right,' mumbled Alan.

Edwin sat forward, irritated his news seemed to have fallen rather flat. 'So you don't think he still needs keeping down where he belongs?' His words came out slightly strangled.

The other two were quiet for a few moments then Alan sat up too. 'Well, it's still fun seeing him made to look a fool... You got something more in mind?'

At the time, he had not thought up any new plan. Then, training and hectic activity took over the squires' lives and he had little time to himself. But, whenever he did have the chance, he went to the stables, to sink back into the hay and think.

For de Bohun to be truly humiliated—as *he* still wanted, even if the others no longer seemed quite so keen—it would have to happen in front of the earl, indeed in front of the entire company. And what more public place was there than when he was serving at the earl's high table?

He had observed that, after a slightly shaky start, de Bohun had learned quickly. Edwin himself served only at the table of his own knight, his lady and his immediate followers, but he remembered well enough his own anxiety when he first started, a few weeks before they left Steyning for the Christmas holiday.

"Ere you go,' the server in the kitchen had said, handing him a platter of meat and sauce. ''Old it steady now, lad.' He had winked. But, as he lifted it to his shoulder, the platter seemed impossibly unwieldy to be borne all the way into the dining hall. It wobbled as he walked, even though he tried to keep it steady with his hand. He was terrified the sauce might slop over the side, and hugely relieved when he arrived at his knight's table and put the platter down for the diners to serve themselves.

At high table, though, the squires served the first portions directly to the earl and countess and their most honoured guests, before leaving the platter on the table. He had observed how awkward it was for the server to come up behind the diner and lean between him and his neighbour, especially as they were sitting on high-backed chairs.

Next time he was able to hunker down in private with Nick and Alan, he told them of his idea.

'What I've been thinking is...' He paused. 'How about when he's waiting at table? You know, some sort of "mishap"?'

'"Mishap"?' Alan's eyes were alight.

'The idea came to me when I remembered my first time carrying a platter. It contained a brewet of meat and almond sauce, and I was worried the sauce might slop. But that brewet had been well made, with sufficient sauce but not too much. Whereas if I could persuade one of the kitchen servers—for a fee, of course—to add a little extra sauce to the platter Dickon was about to take...?'

Alan's forehead creased. 'But how can you be sure it would be *that* platter he took? And what are the chances of him actually spilling it? He's become quite good at serving.'

Edwin grimaced. He could see the plot had flaws. 'But, if it worked, how thrilling it would be to see de Bohun tip the platter and the sauce dribble off the side, to land who knows where?' He guffawed and Alan joined in, though Nick just frowned.

Edwin flumped back onto the hay. He was glad Alan still seemed to be on side, though it was disappointing about Nick. But, as far as *he* was concerned, de Bohun did not merit his place amongst the chosen here at Steyning, and he could not stomach the injustice of it. He had to find a way to make this new plot work.

8

I t was the part of his duties that Dickon liked the least. When he'd been squire to Sir Eustace, waiting on only him and his small retinue of followers, he'd not minded it too much. For all he had to do was carry the platters of food into the hall and place them on the tables.

However, as a member of the earl's personal entourage, it was a different matter.

For serving the earl and countess and their important guests meant not only bearing in the great platters of food, but serving portions to each person. What's more, at the high table, they were all in full view of everyone else dining in the hall. It was terrifying. How glad he was he didn't have to do it every day: at least the earl's squires took turns.

Though he still didn't much enjoy doing it. It did feel somehow demeaning, despite Piers assuring him it was an honour to serve your knight, especially when he was as important a man as Lord Raoul.

He'd taken his turn several times and was now reasonably adept, having learned to balance the platter on one arm whilst spooning up a portion of food and placing it on each individual trencher, not letting any of it spill or drip.

Yet, despite his growing skill, how Dickon wished it had not been his turn today of all days.

It was an important occasion. Guest of honour was the countess's mother, a French lady of supreme dignity and grandeur, the widow of an English duke. It was her birthday, and Countess Jeanne had taken particular care with the menu, ensuring every dish was one of her mother's favourites.

As he made his way towards the kitchen, his stomach flipped. He hoped he'd be given an easy dish to serve. He passed through the screen wall separating the great hall from the passage that led out to the kitchen. A table was set up behind the screen, which shielded the diners from draughts and noise. Beside it stood the seneschal, supposedly inspecting each dish brought from the kitchen before it was carried into the hall. But, red-faced and unusually tense, he was barely glancing at the dishes before he waved them on.

'Quickly, quickly,' hissed the seneschal to the platter-bearers, his customary formality and stiffness slipping. The servers screwed up their faces, as they hefted their platters and hurried out into the hall.

Seeing the seneschal so unlike himself, Dickon presumed the serving of this special dinner must have somehow become delayed. The seneschal was clearly most displeased: it was his responsibility to marshal the dishes and the servers and ensure an efficient routine that worked every time. Dickon's mouth felt suddenly dry. No dallying would be permitted once he'd got his platter.

At the entrance to the kitchen, he saw the dishes lined up on a table, attended as usual by a kitchen boy, whose job it was to hand them to the servers. Dickon stepped up and reached forward for the nearest plate. It was a dish of small pies, filled with chicken he presumed, for tiny pastry hens decorated the crisp, golden lids. Simple to serve. His fingers were already gripping the edge of the platter when the kitchen boy whipped around.

'Not *that* one,' he cried and, lunging forward, slapped Dickon's hand away. 'This is yours.' He pointed to another platter, which contained what Dickon recognised as a Sarcenes brewet, a spicy meat stew, its sauce coloured red with root of alkanet. The pieces of meat were almost awash with the garish sauce.

'Why that one?' Dickon said. 'This one's next.' He pointed to the pies.

But the boy shook his head. 'Got swapped by mistake. This one's for you, young master.' He took hold of the dish of brewet. It rocked slightly and sauce sloshed a little from side to side.

Dickon gulped. 'But there's too much sauce.'

'Nay,' said the boy. 'His lordship likes lots o' gravy.' He thrust the platter into Dickon's hands.

His stomach lurched. This was what he'd feared. Yet he *was* good at serving; surely he could keep the platter steady. He hesitated a moment more, but the kitchen boy was already handing the pies to another server, and the seneschal was glaring at him.

'Hurry along, de Bohun,' he called. 'His lordship and his lady are a-waiting.'

Dickon pressed his lips together. Should he point out the excess of sauce? As he reached the seneschal, he leaned forward to show him the dish. But the old man waved his hand. 'No time for that today. Just go.'

What choice did he have?

He held the wide platter out in front of him, resolved to keep it level, and advanced towards the high table. He served the earl and countess first, holding the platter more or less steady on his left arm whilst spooning a small portion of the brewet and a little sauce onto each of their bread trenchers. But when he came to serve the duchess, she turned her head to see what was on the platter, and her cry of delight—'Brewet Sarcenes!'—took him by surprise. His arm wobbled and the platter tipped. The meat and sauce slithered sideways and, slipping off the plate, dropped onto the duchess's breast.

The old lady screamed, and Dickon gazed in horror. Red drops speckled the pristine whiteness of her wimple, and a crimson stain was seeping across the bodice of her grey silk gown. The countess dabbed with a napkin at her mother's breast, then raised astonished eyes to Dickon.

He flinched and stepped back, holding fast to the wretched platter, as Lord Raoul sprang to his feet. He took a single stride towards him and hissed in his ear. 'Return that to the kitchen, de Bohun, then leave. Go to your quarters and stay there till I send for you.'

Dickon turned and stumbled back the way he'd come, holding his head high but fighting to keep the tears from bursting forth.

Dickon cringed, fixing his gaze upon a nail embedded in the timber floor. The earl was pacing up and down his private chamber, gesticulating and shaking his head. His chastising words had stung even more sharply than if he'd yelled at him and lashed out with his hands. For they'd been spoken quietly, and were heavy with disappointment.

'I do not comprehend what has happened to you in recent months, Dickon,' he continued, coming to stand before him and lifting his dipped chin with his fingers. 'When you first came here, it was clear that Sir Giles had trained you well. You rode as if you had done so all your life, and your attention to your stable duties was faultless.'

Dickon gave a single nod, afraid to speak in case his emotions caused the hovering tears to overflow.

'So, what has changed? How have you become so careless? Eustace has told me of several instances of you apparently losing items of equipment, in one case causing him to miss a tourney. That was inexcusable enough. Far worse was the appalling incident with his horse. Sir Eustace doubted you placed the offending chestnut there deliberately, but was aggrieved that you did not recognise the mare's evident distress and act at once upon it.'

It was true. Morel had whinnied loudly when he put on her saddle. She'd arched her back. Yet he'd put it down to her high spirits, when he should have looked for the source of her unrest. But then he was also in a hurry, knowing Sir Eustace wanted her at once to go out hunting. He'd been delayed by Alan supposedly needing his help, and it was only afterwards he understood the whole thing was yet another of Edwin's pranks. He cursed himself for not realising it sooner, and for letting his haste undermine his concentration.

'What on earth was the problem earlier at dinner?' continued Lord Raoul. 'I assume it was an accident but, Dickon, for such a mishap to happen with *such* a guest, and on such a day.' He let out a deep sigh.

'Besides, I do not expect mishaps of any kind from squires in my personal entourage.'

Dickon swallowed. Still he couldn't speak. Though he wasn't sure the earl expected him to answer.

His lordship stepped away a moment and made a circuit of the chamber. When he returned, his eyebrows were arched. 'Well, do you have nothing to say? No explanation for your carelessness and inattention?'

He gulped again. What could he say? What he *wanted* to say, of course, was that none of it was his fault. Apart from the incident with Morel, when he could have saved her anguish if he'd not been in such haste, everything was surely down to Edwin de Courtenay and his gang. But he'd not say that to the earl. Edwin would know that. It was a code of honour. You simply didn't blab.

He lowered his eyes again. 'I don't know, my lord...'

'"Don't know"? Well, you have to know, de Bohun, if you wish to continue in my service. You have to take a good long look at yourself, and mend your ways.'

'Yes, my lord,' he muttered, wanting this torture to end so he could run outside and allow the brimming tears to flood. He half turned, as if to leave, but the earl's hand landed upon his shoulder with a thump.

'I have not yet said that you can go.' He grunted. 'Look at me, Dickon.'

He looked up at the earl once more: his lordship's eyes looked more sad than angry. 'You must know, lad, that I want your career here at Steyning to succeed. I think it could, although not without a great deal more effort on your part.' He sighed again. 'Nonetheless, I cannot allow this carelessness—if that indeed is what it is—to go unpunished.'

Dickon's tongue filled his mouth. Was he to be flogged? Dismissed from the earl's entourage and given over to one of the lesser knights? Even dismissed from Steyning altogether? He thought of his grandmother, how dreadfully disappointed in him she'd be.

'My decision,' continued the earl, 'is that you are banned from serving at my table for a month. Moreover, during those weeks, you will undertake daily practice of the art of table service under the close tutelage of the seneschal.' He squeezed Dickon's shoulder. 'Otherwise, lad, you may continue in your duties, and your training.'

Dickon's legs were wobbly. Being banned from serving the earl at table was a terrible dishonour, but at least he'd not been dismissed from Steyning. Nor sent home to Meonbridge in disgrace... He was so grateful and relieved, he wanted to cry out but, instead, he bowed his head and whispered, 'Thank you, my lord. I will try hard not to let you down again.'

Lord Raoul nodded, and patted Dickon on the shoulder once again. 'Go.'

As Dickon hurried from the earl's chamber and skittered down the narrow winding staircase to the great hall, he was trying to hold back the tears, but several times was forced to swipe his sleeve across his face. He ran out of the hall door onto the vast bailey, and down towards the stables, which, at this time in the afternoon, would be mostly empty of horses and of men. Sliding inside the stables entrance, he crept down the aisle, wanting an empty stall to sit in for a while. He heard the soft snickering of a horse, but most stalls were unoccupied, and he chose one with a good pile of dry unused hay. Throwing himself down onto the mound, he let out a long, shuddering breath of relief. The tears had already subsided and, as he lay back in the sweet-smelling hay, just one or two last drops trickled down his cheeks.

A few moments later, he heard someone entering the stables. Wasn't it too early for everyone to be returning? But someone was walking down the aisle, opening the empty stable doors. Dickon held his breath. He hoped it wasn't Edwin. As he thought it, the face of Nick Fenecote appeared at the entrance to the stall.

'Hello, Dick. Can I join you?'

He breathed out. He'd always liked Nick more than Alan de Clyffe, who seemed much more like Edwin. When Edwin cajoled them both away, it was the loss of Nick's friendship he'd regretted more.

'Why aren't you with the others?'

'I was, but I wanted to come and find you, so I made a lame excuse.' He snorted. 'The Master was too busy chiding one of the others about some offence to bother arguing with me.'

Dickon grinned. 'What do you want?'

'To say I was sorry about what happened...' He paused. 'You do know Edwin arranged it, don't you?'

He gave a light shrug. 'I didn't know, but I suspected. Anyway, why are you sorry?'

'I think he's gone too far.' Nick looked down at his feet. 'Teasing's one thing, but what happened with Morel, and today, is quite another.'

'Do you know why he's doing it, Nick?'

'He says you don't deserve to be here, training alongside the rest of us.'

Dickon swallowed. 'Don't *deserve* it?'

'Because you're only half a de Bohun, he says. Because your mother wasn't of gentle birth.'

'How does he know that?'

'He told Alan and me about it when we came back after Christmas, so maybe he learned it from someone at Courtenay Castle?'

'But he's been bullying me for a lot longer than just since Christmas.'

'He used to say he suspected your heritage wasn't, you know, pure.'

'And you believed him?'

Nick flushed. 'I wasn't sure.' He plucked at the hay on the stable floor. 'I'm sorry now I let him take me in. Because if it's true, Dick, I admire you for what you've achieved here at Steyning.' He looked up. 'Is it?'

Dickon nodded. 'But don't tell anyone else, Nick, please. The earl knows and the countess, but no one else as far as I'm aware. Except for Edwin.'

'And Alan.' He chewed on a quill of hay. 'I'll tell no one, Dick, I promise. If Edwin wants to play any more pranks on you, I'm having nothing more to do with it.'

Dickon stayed in the stall a while longer after Nick had gone. He was pleased he'd sought him out. Perhaps they could become friends again?

But he was glad too that he now understood about Edwin. He'd somehow learned the truth about his birth and, arrogant pig that he was, he couldn't tolerate someone like himself—someone so "undeserving"—being in his company or that of his highborn friends.

Nick agreed it was likely no one else in Steyning knew about his birth. But was that true?

He recalled Ma saying, years ago, when he first went to Courtenay Castle for his page training, he must tell no one his mother was the carpenter's wife. He was then only a child, and didn't understand why he had to keep her a secret. As he got older, his grandmother told him more about his birth, and about his grandfather's insistence that Dickon was his true heir. Grandpapa lost his life because of it, and Dickon almost lost his too, but Grandmama continued to advise him not to tell anyone the truth.

'Naturally, the earl and countess know,' she'd said, 'but there is no necessity for any others at Steyning to be privy to our family's private affairs.'

He wondered why Edwin hadn't just told everyone. But maybe even a de Courtenay was wary of what might happen if the earl found out he was spreading rumours. Gossip of any kind, as well as blabbing, was roundly condemned. Presumably even Edwin wouldn't risk losing the earl's regard?

Weeks passed and Dickon's life progressed with no more trouble. Perhaps Edwin's desire for pranking had waned, though it seemed more likely he was lying low for a while. Dickon didn't imagine for one moment Edwin's gleeful venom had vanished.

In January, those squires who were at least fourteen had begun training with real weapons: steel swords; heavy lances twice their own height; and unwieldy maces and pollaxes.

Dickon had been excited by the prospect of handling a proper sword, if nervous of his ability to do so. Until now, weapons training had been more like play. They used to fight on piggyback, and learning to thrust and parry whilst balancing upon a fellow's back was good practice for fighting atop a horse. But the swords and shields they used then were hardly any better than those given as toys to children.

Even now, the swords weren't really dangerous, with their blunted edges and shielded tips. The important difference was the weight: the steel sword was so heavy his arms ached mightily at the end of every training day. But it was good to feel he was on the way at last to becoming a true knight, a noble fighter, as his father and grandfather had been. Eager to justify his grandfather entrusting him with the de Bohun heritage, he determined to work hard and concentrate, and ensure he made no more errors.

In some ways, it was easy enough to concentrate on the sword training, when he was always working with one of the weapons masters, or hand-to-hand with one other squire—so far, never Edwin.

But learning to tilt a lance was quite another matter.

How he'd enjoyed the lance training when he was a page. For him and Sir Giles's other page, it was like a game. They took it in turns to climb onto a wheeled wooden horse, a little wooden lance clutched beneath one arm. Then one of Sir Giles's squires would loop the harness around his shoulders and run towards the quintain, pulling the "horse" behind him, whilst the page aimed at the target with his lance. It had been fun, and how they laughed when they failed often even to touch the mark.

Both boys grew steadily in skill, at length striking the target every time, and with greater force. When Dickon first came to Steyning, the young squires were still practising lance tilting the same way, from a wooden horse. He was proud of the skill he'd gained already, and proved one of the most accurate at hitting even the smallest targets.

Now, though, it was a game no longer: it was much harder, and it *was* dangerous.

Despite his late start at riding, Dickon had taken to it and, these days, he felt as comfortable sitting upon a horse as any of the others. Which was just as well, because lance training now had to be done from astride a saddle.

The quintain still comprised a pole and crossbar, with the target at one end and a heavy sandbag hung from the other, so it was harder to make the crossbar move and spin. But, now they were on horseback, the skill to be perfected was not so much wielding the lance as controlling your horse as it charged towards the target. Yet, now that the lances were longer and heavier, balancing such an unwieldy thing beneath one arm, whilst trying to govern your galloping mount with the other, was exhausting.

'We're building up your muscles here,' the master yelled from the edge of the training ground, 'as well as teaching you control of yourself and of your steed. This is what all those years of riding practice were for.' He thwacked his whip against the ground, as Dickon sped past on a rouncey. 'Remember what you've been told: you'll never be able to fight on horseback unless you and the beast move as one.'

Tiring as this training was, Dickon was pleased with his own progress. He wasn't the only one: most of the others were improving day by day. Except for Edwin de Courtenay. Which was odd. For Edwin was an excellent horseman, yet somehow he found it difficult to coordinate his handling of both horse and lance.

Not that Dickon felt sorry for him. He was glad Edwin was getting a taste of humiliation. But, one afternoon, Edwin missed the target so often, when everyone else was hitting it spot on, that Dickon saw one or two of the other squires were making fun of him. He went to join them.

'Strange, isn't it, when he's so good on horseback?'

'It's like he's got the palsy,' said one of the others, and everyone laughed again. But then somebody pushed past him, and Dickon saw Alan de Clyffe striding across the training ground towards Edwin. He said something to him, and they both looked back towards where Dickon and the other squires were huddled. Edwin scowled before he and Alan walked off in the direction of the stables.

Dickon grimaced at the others. Presumably Alan had told Edwin what he and the others had been saying, and Edwin would likely have taken it badly. They all shrugged and, gathering up their weapons and equipment, strolled back towards the castle.

Later that afternoon, Edwin waylaid Dickon in the stables. He blocked his path, standing legs apart, his arms folded across his chest.

'What do you want, Edwin?' Dickon said, though he was sure he knew the answer.

Edwin sneered. 'It's time you were taught a lesson.'

'What do you have in mind?' Dickon's heart turned over. If it was knives, he reckoned he'd not stand much of a chance. Of course, he carried a knife—everybody did—but fighting with one wasn't something he'd ever done.

'Wrestling?'

'Fine.' His momentary terror faded.

Wrestling held few fears for him. As a boy in Meonbridge, he'd invariably won any fights. At Fitzpeyne Castle, he and the other page used to wrestle often, albeit it was only play, and they became skilful at it, Dickon especially. But, here at Steyning, they did little unarmed fighting, either for recreation or to supplement their martial skills. They were training here to fight as knights, so that meant on horseback and with weapons.

As Dickon walked back to the castle, after they'd agreed the when and where, he was smirking to himself. Edwin might be good at wrestling too, he didn't know, but at least he felt he had a chance of besting him.

It was early the following evening, after supper, that Dickon left the hall and made his way towards a clearing in a small patch of woodland beyond the castle's orchards. Despite his earlier mood of confidence, he'd eaten little. Anyway, wrestling on a full stomach probably wasn't a good idea.

Did anyone other than he and Edwin know about the challenge? He'd seen Edwin in the hall at supper and they'd exchanged curt nods, but none of the other squires, not even Alan, showed any sign of being party to Edwin's plan. But, when he reached the clearing, he saw that Alan, though not Nick, was there with Edwin, and a small band of squires and servants was gathering to watch.

Dickon wished now he'd asked someone to second him. Not that he'd know whom to ask, though Nick might have agreed. Looking around the onlookers, he feared they would likely be taking Edwin's part. He worried too that if, by chance, the fight was going his way, Alan might step in to help Edwin. He didn't trust him to keep out of it. But it was too late for misgivings now.

Standing at the edge of the clearing, on the opposite side to Edwin, and some distance from the band of witnesses, he stripped off his belt and tunic and laid them carefully on the ground. Edwin then strode forward, his chest thrust out, to the grassy centre of the clearing. One or two of the onlookers cheered.

Dickon stepped forward too. Each of them took up a stance, legs tensed, arms out.

Then Edwin lunged, grasping Dickon's wrist with one hand and his elbow with the other. He leered as he thrust a knee forward, clearly intending to unbalance Dickon. But Dickon flicked his free hand up and drove it hard against Edwin's inner arm, making him let go. Unbalanced then himself, Edwin staggered, giving Dickon time to grab one of his flailing hands. Squeezing it hard, he flipped it up and twisted it at the wrist, causing Edwin to cry out, then grabbed the rest of Edwin's arm with his other hand. Quickly putting out a leg in front of Edwin's and pushing hard against his arm, he threw Edwin over and he fell back onto the ground.

A collective groan rose from the group of bystanders, but Edwin recovered fast and, leaping up, he glowered at Dickon. 'Right, de Bohun,' he hissed, 'now you're really for it.' He lunged again.

At first it felt an even match in terms of strength and skill. Dickon would trounce Edwin, then Edwin would do the same to him. But, as each of them tumbled onto the grass time and time again, Dickon realised that Edwin's energy was waning: his grip was becoming weaker, and he was finding it harder to throw him over. Yet there was still power left in his own hands. When Edwin lurched towards him yet again, but with little vigour, Dickon threw up his hands to fend him off and caught him hard upon the nose. He heard a slight crunch, and Edwin screamed, stepped back and flung his hands up to his face, where blood was already flowing freely.

All those who, moments earlier, had been cheering Edwin on, now fell into silence.

Dickon, aghast at what he'd done, turned, intending to collect his things and leave. But, just beyond the clearing, thrashing through the trees towards them, came shouting men and barking dogs. He hurried to where his belt and tunic lay, but the men had already arrived before he had time even to pick them up.

'Stay where you are, all of you,' yelled one of the men. It was a training master, accompanied by some servants, all of whom were wielding sticks.

How had the master found out about the fight? Perhaps one of the onlookers had slipped away? Dickon looked around: all were standing stock still, their eyes wide. He couldn't tell if anyone was missing. Edwin was snivelling, his fine tunic now clamped to his nose, blood staining its yellow fustian bright red.

Ordering a servant to stand with Dickon, the master strode over to Edwin. 'What's been going on?' he said. 'How came you by that bloody nose?'

'It's not bloody,' Edwin cried, 'it's broken!' He lifted a hand and pointed a finger at Dickon. '*He* did it. He started it.'

Dickon grimaced. Of course, he would say that. Edwin de Courtenay had no aversion to blabbing.

The master came back to Dickon. 'Why, de Bohun?' He lowered his eyes, and the master clicked his tongue. 'I do insist upon an explanation for this unseemly brawl.'

Dickon still didn't answer. He *should* counter Edwin's lie by saying it was he who'd challenged him to the match, in the expectation, presumably, that he'd win. But he'd not do that. Even if he couldn't now avoid the worst of punishments, he was damned if he was going to act with dishonour.

9

MEONBRIDGE
APRIL 1364

It was such a beautiful morning, Margaret could not resist putting on her hessian apron and heavy gloves and going down to her rose garden. The snowdrops were long gone but violets and primroses should still be abundant, carpeting the ground beneath the still bare-stemmed roses. The blue irises she loved so much would also be pushing through and might even be in bloom.

She decided not to ask Libby to go with her, and none of the gardeners would be in that particular part of the garden. She would have it to herself, and could relish the gentle warmth of the early sun upon her back, breathe in the earth's scent as she drew her little mattock through it, and marvel at the hum of insects as they began their daily toil from plant to plant.

Collecting her tools and wheelbarrow from the little wooden shed just inside the entrance to the gardens from the bailey, she trudged happily along the paths that criss-crossed the grand potager and herbier to the flowery gardens beyond. The gardeners had made a good start on tilling the soil in readiness for the cabbages and colewort, turnips, beets and fennel. The onions they had sown last month were already nudging through.

Margaret was wistful about the potager: she so enjoyed the occupation of growing vegetables. She remembered times past when growing food rather than flowers had been a necessity. She was still a small child when famine struck every community in the land, and her mother taught her that there was no shame in a lady, however gentle, ensuring her manor's gardens were productive, even if it meant dirtying her own hands. Few of her mamma's acquaintances shared her view, but Margaret grew up finding pleasure in working out of doors, setting an example of diligence to her servants and her tenants.

When she married Richard, he had been surprised to find he had such an industrious wife but if, initially, he thought her outdoor toiling somehow unbecoming, he soon learned that Margaret would not be gainsaid when it came to managing the manor grounds. Thus she had continued ever since.

However, although she was not yet old, her body was less forgiving than it once was. She had found that beginning early in the day, and preferring days when the sun's warmth eased her aching bones, she could manage almost a whole morning's labour before fatigue drove her back indoors.

Naturally, it was vexing to be so constrained, but what choice did she have? Yet she would not forego the pleasures of her labour until she was absolutely forced to do so.

Although, last winter, she did decide to give up working in the potager. She would leave that to the gardeners, and focus her own efforts on the flower gardens.

Today she was going to work in one of her favourite parts, her "inner sanctum": a circular tunnel trellis, profuse in summer with a heady mix of honeysuckle and roses, with a little enclosed herbier half way round with a fountain and a seat. Two months ago, she had taken one of the gardeners away from his labours on the potager to help her prune the roses. Despite the chilly air, she had been determined to do some of the work, but she had so many roses now, and the plants were so exuberant, she could not do it all by herself. Between them, they had done a good job, for leaf buds were now bursting everywhere, and the flowers would soon follow.

But the task today was one she could do alone: tying in the fast-growing shoots of honeysuckle. There were a huge number, but she would do some today and more another time.

Starting inside the tunnel, she secured a dozen shoots to the willow trellis. But several whippy shoots were growing on the outside and out of reach, and she walked round onto the burgeoning bed. She edged carefully between the thorny rose stems and the sturdy leaves of sprouting irises and mats of pale yellow primroses, but she soon wished she had left the errant honeysuckle to its own devices. For her skirts kept snagging on the spiky thorns and it was tricky to avoid crushing the iris tubers underfoot, as she tried to disentangle the fabric.

Before long, her back was aching so much with the effort of it that, in vexation, she decided to retreat. But she turned too quickly, and her foot caught in the tough stems of some roses. She heard a crack and such a dreadful pain shot through her leg she almost swooned. The dizziness was swiftly followed by a gripping sensation in her chest, and suddenly she could not catch her breath. Alarmed and in agony, she tried to cry out for help but her voice was too weak to carry. Moments later, she was toppling forward, into the trellis and the vicious roses, her foot still trapped and her leg on fire. Powerless to prevent the fall, she landed heavily and, moments later, darkness closed her eyes.

When Margaret's eyes opened once again, Libby was peering down into her face.

'Milady?' said the girl, her mouth twisted in concern.

Margaret found she was lying on a stretcher on the lawn next to the fountain, though it was still. How she would have welcomed its soothing whisper, its cool spray upon her skin. 'Libby, dear...' she started, then cried out, as she tried to lift her head, and hot pain seared through her leg. She recalled what happened earlier. 'I caught my foot... and fell...'

'Yes, milady. Your leg's broken, Simon says. You must've twisted it when you fell...'

Margaret groaned, as she shifted, and pain sliced through her once again.

Then the surgeon was at her side. 'Please lay quiet, my lady. I must

73

try and set the break. You know well enough what that entails...' She nodded. 'Can I give you a little dwale, to help with the pain?'

Her mind was foggy, yet she understood what Simon said. Dwale was poison but it would dull her senses sufficient for him to wrench and twist her leg back into shape. 'Do what you must,' she whispered.

How much time had passed she did not know, but when she gained her senses once again, she was in her chamber, in her bed, her comforting pillow beneath her reeling head, her coverlet tucked up beneath her chin.

'Your ladyship?' whispered Libby, leaning forward.

Margaret forced her eyes open, to see the girl's stricken face searching hers. 'Libby, dear,' she croaked. 'I am alive?'

'Of course, milady. Simon's the best of surgeons. You've said so yourself.'

Margaret would have smiled agreement, but her face would not oblige. She gave a single nod, and closed her eyes again.

It was Alice's dear face that greeted her when she next awoke.

'Margaret?' she said. 'At last. How glad I am to see your open eyes.'

'How long, Alice?'

'Two days. You needed rest.' Alice touched her arm. 'And you'll need much more. Much, much more.'

Margaret tried to lift her head, but it was as heavy as a cannonball. She slumped back onto the pillow. 'Am I not mended?' she asked.

'Simon has set your leg. It was a nasty break. Your arm too was hurt but not so badly.' She looked into her eyes. 'No more gardening for you this summer.'

Margaret sighed. Perhaps she would never work again in her beloved garden? Grief-stricken at the prospect, her breathing faltered. Invisible fingers then seemed to clutch at her chest for a few moments before releasing her. She let out a small cry.

Alice gasped. 'Is something amiss, my lady? Are you in pain?'

Margaret recalled then the same gripping sensation just before she collapsed amongst the roses. How frightened she had been by it. But, when she awoke later from her swoon, the pain in her leg was so appalling it must have driven the fear, and the memory of it, away. It was only now that she remembered, now it had come again. She gave Alice a thin smile. 'My leg is very sore.'

Alice patted her arm. 'For a moment, you seemed to be struggling for breath,' she said, her eyes wide with concern.

But Margaret shook her head. 'It was just the pain.' She laid a finger upon Alice's hand. 'I shall sleep now, Alice dear. As you said, more rest is needed.'

She closed her eyes, willing her incipient tears to keep at bay.

A week later, Margaret was feeling so much better that she refused to lie in bed all day. Nonetheless, she was obliged to accept sitting in a chair.

'It'll be weeks, my lady, maybe months,' the surgeon said, 'before the leg has healed.'

'Like poor little Maud Miller?'

'Indeed. Though her break was awkward, whereas the setting of your leg went well.' He rubbed his neck. 'Nonetheless, your ladyship, you have to give it time. You must let your servants and Mistress atte Wode take care of you.'

Margaret pouted, but Simon shook his head. 'I'm sorry, my lady. You really must put no weight on the leg for at least another week or two. Then maybe try a few gentle steps around your chamber, with the help of crutches.'

Alice, sitting in the other chair, leaned forward. 'If you want to garden again, my lady, you simply have to let it mend.'

Margaret grunted. She was angry with herself for being careless, for overtiring herself, for not being more vigilant about where she put her feet. Perhaps solitary gardening was no longer a suitable occupation? She waved her hand. 'Very well, I hear you both. But how can I rest when I have this and all our other demesnes to run?'

'You will have to let your bailiffs and your steward manage your estates, and your servants run this house,' said Alice. 'They can come to ask for your advice but, for now, *you* must do nothing more than rest.' She glanced up at Simon, who nodded.

After Simon left, Alice asked Libby to fetch her ladyship some wine and sweetmeats. She sat down again at Margaret's side. 'I know you will find it hard, but you have no choice.'

For the first time, a few tears gathered in her eyes. 'I feel so helpless. Like an infant.'

Alice touched her hand. 'It's vexing, when you are by nature so energetic. But time will pass.'

'Not fast enough, I am sure of it. But what of you, Alice? Simon said I was to let you take care of me. But you have your own household to run.'

'My sons are quite capable of fending for themselves, and Agnes will help.'

'It is good of you all, Alice.'

'Nonsense. I can scarcely abandon you.'

Margaret sighed. She was a terrible, ungrateful patient. Resting was just not in her nature. She wanted to be outside and working, especially as the weather was so delightfully warm. For three weeks now, Alice had come soon after breakfast every day and watched her hawk-like for any unsuitable activity.

Margaret had to admire her friend's resolve. 'You know how much I appreciate your company, Alice dear, but is it necessary for you to be quite so *vigilant?*'

Alice pressed her lips together. 'I believe it is. I know you well. You're like a filly yearning to slip the reins.'

Margaret threw back her head and laughed. 'Some filly! More like an old nag.'

'I'm glad to see you merry again at least.'

It was true that she had regained a little of her sense of humour. Because, for the last two days, she had been hobbling around her chamber, with a crutch under one arm and Alice supporting her on the other side. It was not much but it was a start. But Simon had warned her that she should not attempt to rush her recovery.

'I'm sorry, my lady,' he had said, 'but I'm afraid it'll be a good while yet before you'll be able to stroll outdoors.'

Yet how she longed to feel the sun upon her head again, and the soft summer breeze wafting against her face.

However, the shuffling around the chamber was going well and, after another week, she was certain her leg was much stronger. 'I am looking forward to my descent into the hall,' she said to Alice, tilting her head.

'Has Simon said you can?'

'Well, no, but I am sure I can manage it, if you help me.'

Alice's forehead wrinkled. 'I understand how eager you are to escape your chamber, but do you think it's wise?'

Undoubtedly it was not wise, but Margaret thought she might go mad with all this waiting and inactivity. 'If we take it slowly...' She raised an eyebrow.

Poor Alice. It was clear she did not agree with Margaret's plan, but she could scarcely refuse to help her. Margaret knew it was unkind to press her into doing something she disapproved of, but she was going to try it, nonetheless.

In the middle of the afternoon next day, Libby came to tell her that all the trappings of the midday meal had been cleared away, and the hall was relatively quiet.

'Then why not pay a visit to little Maud?' Margaret said to her.

'It's not my usual day, milady.'

'No matter.' Margaret glanced at Alice. 'Why not surprise her?'

Libby's eyes lit up. 'If you're sure, milady?'

When the girl had gone, Margaret took up her crutch and turned to Alice. 'Right. The stairs.'

'I really don't think this is a good idea.'

'I want at least to try it, Alice. I cannot stay cooped up in this room much longer.' Her heart was beating a little faster, as the prospect of her freedom beckoned.

This must be how a liberated prisoner must feel, after weeks or months spent chained up in a dungeon. Although it was also not much different from the release she herself had felt after the weeks of lying-in, confined to her chamber, following the birthing of her babies.

. . .

She did not openly admit it, but climbing down the narrow staircase to the hall had been much more testing than she had anticipated. By the time she reached the bottom, her breath was short with the effort of it, her neck was slick with perspiration, and her heart was pounding not from excitement but unease. She held out her arm to Alice for support, and tottered over to a bench seat underneath a window.

'Let us sit here a while,' she said, taking in deep breaths. 'Then perhaps we can take a turn about the hall.'

Alice shook her head. 'You're pushing yourself too hard. I know how impatient you are to return to your active life, but overdoing it won't speed your recovery. Indeed, it might slow it down.'

Margaret pouted. 'But it is so frustrating, Alice, not to be able to work as I am accustomed to.'

'But the house is running smoothly enough, and John tells me the work outdoors is proceeding as it should.'

Margaret pressed her lips together. 'It is not that I do not trust them all to do what is required. But rather that I like to lead by example.'

'Like a commander leading his troops onto the battlefield?'

'A little like that, yes.'

Shortly, her breathing settled back to normal and, leaning on her crutch, she pushed herself to her feet. 'A circuit of the hall, I think.' Alice held out her hand, but Margaret did not take it. 'Let me try it on my own.'

Yet, moments later, she was groaning and slumped onto another bench. 'Oh, Alice, I do think I have overdone it. My poor leg is throbbing. Perhaps the descent overburdened it? To think I must soon ascend the stairs again. I might as well be climbing one of the high peaks in my Cheshire home.'

'Peaks?' Alice's eyes were wide. 'I have never seen one. Are they higher than Riverdown?'

'Oh, yes. Twice as much, or more. Much different too, with steep tracks, loose gravel underfoot and bare jutting rocks on every side.'

'And have you climbed them?'

Margaret let out a sigh. Her leg was hurting badly now, and she was afraid she might have damaged Simon's skilful repair. The pain reminded her of the walk she once took with her brothers up the slopes of Shutlingsloe. She had been fifteen, and it was just a few months before she married Richard. Her brothers had teased her for thinking she could climb the hill as easily as they and, affronted, she had determined to prove them wrong. But she turned her ankle on a treacherous patch of scree early in the walk and had to be carried home. Naturally, she had been mortified, but now she remembered too how very painful her foot had been, and how long it took to mend.

She related this to Alice. 'I had then not even broken my ankle. Yet now I am trying to force my battered leg to function when it is not ready.' She turned her eyes to Alice. 'I am a foolish old woman!'

'Neither old nor foolish. Just a woman with a busy life, who wishes to resume it. But, yes, I'm afraid you must be patient.' She stood up. 'And now I think it's time you returned to your chamber, and stayed there a good while longer.'

Margaret pushed out her lips, a gesture she remembered employing as a child. Yet, this time, she had no good reason for defiance. 'I accept your counsel, dear friend. Perhaps I do simply have to rest.'

By the time they had struggled up the stairs again, she wanted nothing other than her bed. She let Alice help her change into her night chemise before sinking gratefully onto the mattress, and laying her head upon the pillow.

'Do go home, Alice,' she said, 'and please tell Libby I will keep to my bed for the remainder of the day.' She pouted once again. 'Would you please also tell Simon that I wish him to come and inspect my leg, to be sure I have not undone his labours.'

'It's likely just the strain of going down and up the stairs. But, yes, I'll tell him. When I come tomorrow morning, I trust you will feel rested.'

The next morning, Margaret was still in bed when Alice came. Libby had brought her up some soft wheaten bread and small ale for breakfast, but she hated trying to eat in bed, and had given up after a single sip and bite. Hearing the knock upon her chamber door, she bid Libby answer it, and was delighted when Alice's cheerful face greeted her.

'Rested, I hope?' said Alice.

Margaret could not agree. 'The throbbing in my leg would not let up, and I tossed and turned the whole night long.'

Alice frowned. 'What did Simon say?'

'That the leg is fine, but I have overtaxed it.'

'His remedy?'

'Confinement to my chamber.' She smacked her hand down upon the bed. 'Oh, Alice, what a fool I was!'

She sent Libby off with messages for Cook and the laundress, and let Alice help her to get dressed. Though that task was getting easier, now that her arm at least was almost mended. They sat together in her comfortable cushioned chairs, moved to stand by the window instead of before the hearth. The window was not large but afforded a grand view of the broad countryside around Meonbridge, with its fields and meadows, orchards and woodlands, the sparkling river in the valley and the heights of Riverdown. She was wistful, wanting to be out there, but was grateful for the casement that let in the delicious warm spring breeze.

Alice opened her scrip and, pulling out a sealed letter, she handed it to Margaret. 'John gave me this last night. He brought it back with him from the priory after his visit to Sister Rosa, his first since February. I believe it is a personal letter from your daughter.'

Margaret's chest tightened as she took the parchment. 'Ah, he told her of my accident?'

Alice nodded, and Margaret's stomach fluttered. Her daughter was still "Johanna" in her heart, even though she entered the priory, as "Sister Rosa", twelve years ago. Yet "Johanna" had rarely been a happy girl, whereas "Rosa" was a woman who had found fulfilment and Margaret was delighted. But, Rosa's fulfilment did embrace a slight sternness in her outlook, and Margaret knew her daughter would be vexed with her for continuing to garden at an age when, Rosa doubtless assumed, her health was failing. Not that Margaret thought herself at all unhealthy, just a little weary in her limbs and back. Although Rosa had already suggested she let others do the toiling, Margaret was by no means yet willing to give her garden up.

She hesitated to break the letter's seal. She suspected her daughter's words would involve chastisement for refusing to heed her advice, and would probably accuse her—in the kindest possible, Sisterly, manner—of being irresponsible.

'She will be cross with me, you know.'

'I fear she will, for John told me of her vexation when he relayed the news.' Her voice softened. 'You can't blame her for being concerned about you.'

'No, I do not blame her at all. I do wish, nonetheless, she did not think of me as *old*.' She chuckled softly. 'It is amusing that some of the priory's most active sisters—the almoner, say, and the cellarer—are ten years my senior, yet she does not seem to think that they need to rest.'

She tucked the unopened letter down by her side. 'I will read it later. Now I would rather talk to you.'

'John will return to the priory in three weeks for another consultation with Sister Rosa about the priory's demesne, so if you wish to send her a reply he will take it for you.'

Margaret inclined her head. 'It is time I think for John to come and consult with me. My accident has not affected either my tongue or my brain, so if I cannot be outside, at least we can discuss the needs of our demesne and any problems with the tenants.'

'I know he wants to come but is anxious not to intrude till you are well enough.'

'I most assuredly *am* well enough for a consultation with my bailiff. So, yes please, Alice, ask him to come here to my chamber tomorrow morning.'

The light cascading through the open window was bright as well as warm, and Alice suggested they take advantage of it to undertake some sewing. Margaret gave her friend a little pout. Embroidery was not her favourite occupation, but at least it kept her fingers busy, and she agreed. Alice was of course an expert needlewoman, and would stitch whenever she had a moment spare.

It was pleasant enough, however, stitching quietly together, exchanging an occasional word but with no need for constant chatter.

Suddenly Alice put down her sewing and gave a little laugh. 'I don't know what made me think of her, but Matilda Fletcher has just popped into my head.' Margaret grunted. 'A particular memory I have of her, throwing her embroidery aside in sheer frustration.'

Margaret laughed too. 'Oh, yes, poor Matilda. She was never good at needle craft.'

'I often wondered why. She had aspirations to be a lady, so embroidery was a skill she might have sought to cultivate. Yet she never did it well. Her stitches were always too tight or too loose.' Alice tied off some threads in her piece. 'Is Libby any better?'

'She is. I do not set her to embroidery, not wanting to give her ideas above her station.' She raised an eyebrow. 'But she does plain sewing, and does it excellently well.'

'Is she as ambitious as her mother?'

'She might be, but I shall heartily discourage it, and soon.'

Alice's eyes widened. 'Where do her ambitions lie?'

'With our grandson, I suspect.' Alice gasped, and Margaret lay her embroidery down upon her lap. 'Perhaps it was inevitable. They were childhood friends for many years, and each grew fond of the other. I imagined that, when Dickon went away, he would lose interest in her and, when he came home to Meonbridge for the holidays, he would no longer wish to see her.'

'But of course, he does see her, often, here in your chamber.'

'Indeed. Then, at Christmas, it was evident that both had changed—grown up, you understand—and each noticed the difference in the other. I saw it in their eyes.'

'But they can have no future together, not now. He must surely have a bride of gentle birth?'

'Which is why I have agreed to Giles Fitzpeyne's proposal that Dickon marries his elder daughter Angharad.'

'Oh yes, you mentioned it some months ago.'

Margaret put down the cushion she was embroidering. 'Angharad is still a child, but I know Dickon became fond of her when he was at Fitzpeyne Castle. It would be a good match...' She paused. 'Despite Giles's wife, Lady Gwynedd, being a Boune.' She arched an eyebrow. 'But Giles tells me she has thrown off entirely her association with her family and never sees her only living brother, Gunnar.'

'Didn't she have sisters too?'

'Several. Gwynedd's mother, Alwyn, remarried after Morys died, and arranged marriages for all her daughters outside the county, so they could all throw off the Boune name.'

'It's understandable Gwynedd too wants no more to do with them.'

'Indeed. Yet, although she doesn't speak to Gunnar, evidently Giles, out of some sense of familial duty, goes twice a year to Hereford to check he is still alive. For the man is a recluse, with neither wife nor children, and few servants. One day, Giles says, he expects to find him dead.'

'At least that will be the end of that hateful line.' Alice's mouth twisted a moment but then she smiled. 'Anyway, more happily, when are you thinking Dickon and Angharad might marry?'

'Oh, the marriage will not take place for many years, not until Dickon has won his knighthood. But I think perhaps we might organise a betrothal in the spring of *next* year, when little Angharad will be eight?'

'I imagine Libby will be sad at the prospect of his betrothal. But it has to be.'

'It does.'

'But you have a plan for her as well?'

'When I sent Matilda away,' said Margaret, 'I promised to care for Libby and find her a decent husband as soon as she was old enough. She will be fifteen in December, and I propose to have her married off by then. I think it best if she leaves Meonbridge or marries well before Dickon is betrothed.'

'Do you have a suitor in mind for her as well?'

She shook her head. 'I need to find one. A respectable villein, I am thinking, not too old. A man who is looking for a young, industrious wife. Libby does have something of her mother's wilfulness, but she is also a brave, helpful girl. Do you recall how, years ago, she stopped that evil Boune lackey snatching Dickon away?'

'I do. She was exceptionally bold and fearless.'

'Moreover, she *is* hard-working. I have taught her well, and she will make some man an efficient wife.'

'I'll ask John if he knows of any such men.'

Just then Margaret heard a creak, like the opening of her chamber door. 'Libby?' she called and looked around. But no one entered the room.

'It must have been the breeze,' said Alice, and Margaret nodded.

10

MEONBRIDGE
MAY 1364

S he knew it would happen one day, but now Libby was terrified it might happen soon and she'd not have the chance to tell Dickon how she felt about him.

When she returned to Lady Margaret's chamber, the door had been ajar. Her hand was poised to push it open when she heard her ladyship speak her name. She stayed outside, her ear against the opening. She was soon trembling at what she heard. If her ladyship had her way, she'd be married off before Dickon even came back to Meonbridge for Christmas. She spun around and ran back downstairs, into the hall, out onto the bailey and on down towards the gardens. Lady Margaret would wonder where she'd gone, but she didn't care. She had to be alone, to think about what to do.

Yet what could she do? If her ladyship found her a husband, she'd have no choice but to marry him. It seemed Lady Margaret did at least want a suitable match for her, not just some rich old man. But suitable or not, she didn't want any *other* man. She wanted Dickon!

. . .

She'd been thinking of visiting Maud again, even though she'd seen her only days ago. But Maud hadn't been in the least sympathetic about Dickon, and Libby wasn't in the mood for idle chatter. Yet she did want to talk to someone about her new predicament.

Her aunt, perhaps? It was a long walk to the Browghtons' farmstead, there and back again, and she'd be away much longer than if she called on Maud. But Aunt Margery was family and would surely agree her ladyship's plans for her were unfair?

At the risk of vexing Lady Margaret by returning later than usual, Libby at length decided to make the journey to the farm. Last time, she'd walked only half way down the Middle Brooking road so, not knowing quite how far the farmstead was, she ran some of the way.

Today was warmer than it had been and, by the time she reached the farm, her kirtle was sticking to her back and she could hardly breathe. She stood a while by the entrance to the broad yard, recovering. As she took in the sight of the huge farmhouse and all the buildings round it, she quailed. How would she even find her aunt?

Dogs barked, and her throat went dry as she remembered Aunt Margery saying her mistress didn't much like people. If the woman rushed out of the house to scold her or chase her off, or even set the dogs on her, what would she say or do?

Maybe coming here had been a bad idea after all?

She dithered a while longer. Perhaps she should go home again? But then a woman lurched from one of the outbuildings, carrying a pail of something—milk perhaps?—and Libby could scarce believe her luck when she saw that it was Margery.

Despite her unease, she ran forward, calling her aunt's name. The woman stopped and looked towards her, squinting, and Libby was certain she saw her scowl. Anyway, she banged the pail down onto the ground, slopping a little of the milk, and strode across towards her.

Her face was dark. 'What are you doing here, girl?' she said, her voice a hiss. 'You shouldn't be here. I told you Mistress Browghton doesn't welcome strangers.'

Libby fiddled with her hair. 'I just wanted to see you, Aunt. To ask you something.'

'But why on earth did you imagine coming here was the right thing to do?'

'I didn't know how else to see you.'

Margery grunted but didn't answer.

Libby jiggled from foot to foot. 'Can't we talk a little while?'

Margery tutted. 'Wait here,' she said then hurried back to the pail of milk and, hefting it, went into another building, close to the farmhouse. Moments later, she ran back to Libby and, gripping her elbow, pulled her over to a barn, where bales of last year's hay were still piled up in one corner. 'I've only a few moments, girl, before I will be missed. So, say what you want to and be quick.'

Her aunt's urgent tone flustered Libby. She'd so much to say, she couldn't say it all in moments. Not knowing what order to say things in, she blurted out what first urged her to come.

'Lady Margaret's getting rid of me! She's going to marry me off. And soon...'

'How soon?'

Tears were pricking at her eyes. 'Much earlier than I thought. I've always known she'd get me a husband when I was old enough. She promised Ma.' She sniffed. 'But I thought she meant when I was eighteen, not now...'

Aunt Margery scowled. 'That is typical of the de Bohuns. Pushing people around to suit themselves. It is what her *lady*ship did to your mother. Took her in out of seeming kindness, then banished her on some false pretext.'

'What d'you mean?'

Margery frowned. 'You must know about the plot to kidnap Dickon and seize Meonbridge?'

'I helped save him from his kidnapper—'

'Really?' said Margery, in a dismissive tone. Libby was momentarily aggrieved her aunt didn't seem to know about her bravery. 'Anyway,' continued Margery, 'Lady de Bohun claimed my sister was involved in the plot—'

Libby gasped. 'Involved?'

'You didn't know? It was why she sent Matilda away from Meonbridge.'

'I didn't realise.'

'Anyway, I never believed it of my sister.' She looked away.

'You don't think she would?'

'She was flighty and self-willed, but why would she get involved with such rogues?'

Libby wasn't sure what "flighty" or "self-willed" meant. Even though she'd known her mother was unhappy, she never discussed it with her. She could recall the day when those horrible men came to attack Meonbridge and kidnap Dickon, though she was injured when she tried to stop the man running off with him, and her memory of what happened afterwards was hazy. But she'd never thought her mother was involved in the attack. How could she have been? Hadn't she run forward too to stop the man escaping, and been assaulted by his henchmen?

She'd never really understood why her mother had gone away, leaving her behind. Nobody had explained it to her, either then or since.

'But why would Lady Margaret send her away if she didn't deserve it?' she said at last.

'Who knows how the gentry think? Maybe she believed Matilda was to blame? But you see what I mean, girl? People like the de Bohuns can do whatever they like with their servants, whether or not it is just or fair.'

'And now she's going to do the same with me,' said Libby. 'She wants to get me away from Dickon.' A sudden heat spread across her throat: where had *that* come from? She'd not thought it before. But it was surely possible Lady Margaret did somehow know how she felt about Dickon, and wanted her married soon to prevent anything happening between them.

Her aunt's eyes widened. 'Dickon de Bohun?'

She nodded. 'But I don't want to marry anyone else. I want to be with Dickon.'

'How would that be possible?' Aunt Margery was frowning.

'I love him, Aunt, and he loves me too,' she cried. 'We're meant to be together, I know we are.'

'But he could never marry a girl like you.' Her voice softened. 'Anyway, what makes you think he cares for you?'

She described his shining eyes and the warmth of his smile, and his approaching her and taking her hand, though she didn't mention his later coolness.

'Hand holding and smiles aren't much, are they?'

'Oh, but it's not just that.' Her heart was thudding with frustration. 'We grew up together. By the time he left Meonbridge, we were *really* close.'

'Yet he's been away for years. He will have grown up, changed. He's not your childhood sweetheart any more—'

Libby threw up her arms. 'But it's not like that,' she cried. 'I'm certain he loves me as much as I love him. And it's not just a childish thing, but proper, grown-up love.' The tears were brimming now.

Her aunt shook her head. 'If you want my advice, girl, Lady de Bohun's offer would be the best for you—'

'No! She's trying to keep us apart, denying me the chance to talk to Dickon properly.' Her neck flushed again: what evidence did she have for such a claim against her ladyship? Yet, shouldn't Dickon have a say in who to marry? 'Anyway, it can't be just his grandmother's decision, can't it?'

'It doesn't work that way with the gentry, girl, you must know that. Remember what happened to Dickon's mother? Philip was destined to be lord of Meonbridge, whilst Agnes was one of his tenants. Even though she was carrying his child, he was already betrothed to some fine lady. I daresay Agnes imagined she loved him but, even if he did love her, there was no question of them marrying.'

Libby pouted. 'But her baby's grown up to be lord of Meonbridge.'

'That is scarcely the point, girl, is it? Agnes could never marry Philip, just as *you* can never marry Dickon. He's a de Bohun and you can be sure his grandmother will find him a bride of gentle birth.'

She wished now she hadn't come. 'I thought you'd understand.'

'I do. More than you do, it appears. Accept the husband Lady de Bohun finds for you. If he's a well-off villein and even a half decent man, you'll be content enough.'

'But I want Dickon,' wailed Libby, 'and he wants me. We're meant to be together.'

Aunt Margery flapped her hand at her. 'Will you stop making such a racket.' Her lip curled. 'I daresay you can resist Lady de Bohun's attempts to marry you off till he returns to Meonbridge. Then you can tell him how you feel. I doubt it will make a difference but you can try.'

Libby nodded, her heart lightening a little.

But her aunt's brow was furrowed. 'But beware, girl,' she said. 'If that boy is anything like his father, he will take full and foul advantage of your declaration. Then, having had his way with you, he'll walk away.'

Libby didn't believe he would do either.

Her aunt's eyes were glittering. 'I daresay you'll take no notice, but my advice to you remains the same: forget Dickon de Bohun.'

11

STEYNING CASTLE
MAY 1364

'My dear, whatever is troubling you?' said Lady Jeanne, removing her light cloak after her stroll around the gardens to inspect the progress of the spring tidying and give the gardeners their instructions for early plantings.

Raoul was pacing their private chamber, as he was given to doing when he was vexed or had some problem to resolve.

Shortly he came to a standstill beside her. 'It is young de Bohun,' he said. 'I do not know what has happened to him.'

'What *has* happened?'

He stroked his beard. 'It is hard to know. When he first came here, he was so full of enthusiasm, and it was clear Giles Fitzpeyne had trained him well. For a boy of such an essentially lowly upbringing, he had already mastered horsemanship to a remarkable degree, and even his fighting skills were admirable.'

'But now?'

'For several months, he was the best of students, eager to learn, and quick to progress. But, then, he seemed to lose his concentration. He kept losing things, making mistakes. The sort of mistakes he'd not made before. Then, last autumn, there was the incident with Eustace's mare, Morel, do you remember?'

The countess nodded. 'That poor horse. Sir Eustace refused to keep young Dickon in his service after that, I recall. Yet you found it hard to believe Dickon had harmed the horse deliberately?'

'Eustace did not think so, either. It was so unlike him. He had proved himself most adept with horses. No, it seemed more like carelessness. Distraction... I really do not know what. But, it has continued, mostly in small ways. Then there was the incident in the dining hall the other week.'

'Yes, that was most unfortunate. In truth, my heart went out to the boy. Although I do wish it had not been my dearest mama, of all people, whose dignity and finest silk gown bore the brunt of it.' She took her husband's arm. 'Come, Raoul, let us sit a while. This constant pacing will wear you out, as well as put holes in your shoes.' She drew him over to the table, where stood an untouched flagon of wine. She poured some into a large mazer and put it into Raoul's hands, as he pulled out a stool and sat.

'The final straw,' he continued, 'was yesterday, when Dickon apparently assaulted Edwin de Courtenay over some disagreement at the quintain, and was so violent he broke his nose.'

She sat beside him. 'Goodness, that sounds much unlike the boy I understood him to be. Did you find out why he did it?'

'He refused to say. I threatened to dismiss him altogether, but I cannot bring myself to do that, Jeanne. Instead, I have banned him from training, with indoor duties, for a month, and confined him to a solitary cell. It is a punishment of sorts, but how can I change him back into the careful, diligent and thoughtful squire he used to be?'

'Have you considered the reasons for these changes in the boy?'

'As I said, I had thought them inattention, lack of concentration.' He turned to his wife. 'You think there might be something more?'

'Those are not reasons, but effects. Why would Dickon stop being a diligent boy and become a careless one? He has much at stake, has he not? The trust his grandfather placed in him? His father's reputation on the battlefield? Surely he would not risk dishonouring those fine men by allowing his diligence to lapse and jeopardise his knighthood? There must be something more.'

Raoul nodded. Following yesterday's fight, he had been pondering upon the nature of the relationship between Dickon and Edwin. It was clear they were not friends. Yet they shared a familial connection, with Dickon's father, Philip, being once married to Isabella, Edwin's aunt. Richard de Bohun implicated Isabella in his deception over Dickon's legitimacy, in an attempt to repulse Morys Boune's claim to the inheritance of the de Bohun domains.

He drained his cup of wine and poured another.

Jeanne was gazing at him. 'You are deep in thought, my love?'

He took her hand, and told her what he had just been thinking. 'But do you remember also,' he continued, 'that, after Richard's death, Margaret persuaded Sir Hugh de Courtenay to accept Dickon as a page? Hugh agreed, even though Hildegard took the greatest umbrage at Richard involving Isabella in his falsehood.'

'I remember you telling me how affronted she was by Richard claiming Isabella was Dickon's mother. Poor Hildegard, she can get very worked up. But it was understandable enough, especially as Isabella had died, along with her unborn child, years before Richard made his claim.'

'Indeed, yet how much could Edwin know of it all? He was still a child at the time, and living in France. It is possible his father told his family little, if anything, of events back here in England.'

'Perhaps, then, Edwin has learned of it recently?' said Jeanne. 'Are you thinking, perhaps, that he is somehow aggrieved about the past and Dickon's connection with it?'

Raoul squeezed her hand. 'It has only just begun to dawn on me that it could be the case.'

'Yet how does that explain the change in Dickon's behaviour?'

He raised an eyebrow. 'It might, if Dickon's so-called "accidents" have in fact been somehow engineered by young de Courtenay as a form of retribution. I do not know why I had not thought of it before, because I do recall such incidents occurring when I was a squire, between boys who, for one reason or another, loathed each other.'

'Can you find out if your suspicion is well-founded?'

'I could talk to Sir Eustace again, and the training masters. See if they have noticed anything untoward between the boys prior to yesterday. In truth, my love, I should look into it. For, the more I think of it, the more I do wonder if young Dickon is the butt of bullying. I imagine he is well able to stand up for himself. The fight yesterday showed that to be true. Nonetheless, I cannot permit intimidation. If that is what is happening, I want to root it out, and punish the perpetrators, whether that is Edwin de Courtenay or another.'

'Only "want"? You are king in your own castle, my love. Whatever you want, you can surely do?'

He laughed. 'Yes, of course I can, but I believe we have a well-run and contented community here, Jeanne, and I do not want to threaten that harmony by stirring up a hornet's nest.'

She smiled. 'I understand. But if Dickon is being ill-treated, you must discover it. If those boys are at loggerheads, and bullying is going on, the harmony of Steyning will be undermined.'

12

STEYNING CASTLE

MAY 1364

Dickon had never slept alone in all his life: as a boy he lay alongside his Sawyer brothers on the cottage floor, then later he shared his chamber in the manor house with Piers. As a page and as a squire, he bedded down alongside his fellows in the great hall – in winter, close-packed for warmth.

He was terrified at the prospect of spending a month of nights in a solitary cell.

His first night, one of the earl's older squires, Ivo, mumbled good night, took away the candle and locked the door. Dickon lay down on the pallet, painfully thin against the hard cold floor and, pulling his hood up over his head and wrapping his blanket tight about his body, he couldn't help but quake. He was sure he'd not be able to sleep. He was used to the faint light of the hall fire's dying embers, or streaks of moonlight piercing the shutters. But the cell was so dark he couldn't even see his fingers held close up to his face. He was used too to the sounds of scampering feet, as a mouse or rat ran across the great hall's rush-strewn floor, in search of fallen morsels, but this chamber seemed entirely *full* of creatures, scurrying back and forth.

However, he wasn't really fearful of the creatures. What frightened him was being all alone.

His cell was a small chamber in the cellar, set aside for miscreants. He shared the space with casks of wine, barrels of ale, and sacks of grain and other produce. He was sure the rodents weren't just scuttling but gnawing too, probably at the baskets full of vegetables and fruit.

He did, in fact, sleep well. Managing to ignore the scuttling and gnawing, he found he enjoyed the relative silence, his ears no longer obliged to hear the mumblings and mutterings, snores and farts of other sleepers. He must have fallen asleep quickly and slept soundly all night long. When Ivo unlocked the door and took him up into the brightness of the new summer's day, he was pleased but not desperate, as he thought he'd be. And, the following night, his fear did not return.

The other part of his punishment hit him much harder. Not that he had to spend his days entirely on menial tasks, but that the earl had forbidden him from taking part in any of the training. He wasn't even allowed to tend the horses. After a month of missing it all, he worried that he might have fallen behind the others. He'd have to work all the harder to catch up.

Yet at least Lord Raoul hadn't sent him away. For that, he was very grateful.

When the period of his punishment ended, Dickon was nervous, wondering how the other squires would treat him now. The morning of his last day, he asked Ivo if he thought the others would consider him no longer one of them.

'Nay, lad,' Ivo said, 'you aren't the first young squire to spend a spell down here. I reckon your fellows 'll consider it a badge of honour. They did in my day.' The man was far beyond the age when normally a squire became a knight, and Dickon wondered, but wouldn't ask, if Lord Raoul had denied him advancement for some misdemeanour. Anyway, he hoped Ivo was right about the other squires.

When he re-joined his fellows on the training field, only de Courtenay failed to shake his hand or pat him on the back. Edwin stood alone in the middle of the jousting field, inspecting one of the quintains, pointedly ignoring Dickon's return.

Alan wasn't effusive in his welcome but did step forward with the others. Nick, however, beamed as he offered his hand to Dickon. 'Glad to see you back, Dick,' he said.

Dickon gestured towards Edwin, and Alan smirked. 'He'll not be welcoming your return. He'll not forgive you for the broken nose.'

'He shouldn't have challenged me—' Dickon started, but Alan held up his hands.

'I'm not taking sides,' he said, his eyes wide.

Dickon was surprised at Alan's amiability: had he fallen out with Edwin since he'd been in solitary confinement?

A month later, life seemed once more like it had been when he'd first come to Steyning. Dickon fulfilled all his tasks and training without mishap, and Alan and Nick were both as friendly to him as they used to be before Edwin came. It was clear that they were no longer Edwin's exclusive friends—the "gang of three" no more. Edwin himself maintained his distance, and Dickon noticed the training masters seemed to be keeping the two of them apart, for they were never pitted against each other in one-to-one encounters.

He was glad: he'd no wish to get into any more fights.

Best of all, he was sure Lord Raoul had set aside his fury with him. He could once more serve at table, and he was especially careful about everything he did. It did seem, too, that Edwin had given up his bullying, for now at least. Had the outcome of the fight discouraged him? Even if it had, Dickon doubted Edwin's restraint would last.

Dickon was alarmed when Lord Raoul sent a message demanding he attend him in his private chamber. The tone of the message, delivered curtly by the squire Ivo, suggested the earl might be annoyed with him yet again. When he knocked on the chamber door, and Lord Raoul barked 'Enter' in what sounded like an angry voice, Dickon swallowed hard to dislodge the lump rising in his throat. He pushed the door open and slunk inside.

But, when he raised his eyes, he saw the earl was smiling. 'Ah, Dickon, my boy, come in.'

Dickon breathed out: he wasn't vexed with him after all. 'You wanted to see me, my lord?'

'Nothing to worry about, I am sure, but I have received a letter from your aunt, Sister Rosa—'

'Sister Rosa?' Dickon's mouth fell open. 'Why?'

'Ha! Do not distress yourself, lad. However, there seems to be a problem back in Meonbridge, and your aunt clearly felt that I—and you—should know of it.' He gestured Dickon to the table. 'Come, sit down.'

The letter was lying in front of him. Dickon glanced at it as he took a stool. He spotted the word "Margaret". 'Is there something the matter with my grandmother?'

Lord Raoul stroked his beard. 'Yes, there is, but I repeat, you need not be alarmed. Read the letter and you will see.'

Dickon bit his lip. Although he recognised "Margaret", he doubted he could read the entire letter. He picked it up. But, however hard he stared at it, he knew he'd not be able to make out all the words. He put it down again. He was certain his face had reddened.

'That was quick,' said Lord Raoul, beaming, but Dickon shook his head.

'No, sir, I haven't read it. I don't think I can.' He bit his lip again and lowered his eyes. How he wished he'd been more diligent in his reading lessons. He'd been trying to learn to read since before he first left Meonbridge, seven years ago. Throughout his time with Sir Giles, and ever since he'd been here, tutors had worked hard to help him. But somehow he always found it too difficult, and not nearly as much fun as learning horsemanship and fighting. Thus he'd reached the age of almost fifteen still mostly unable to decipher a simple letter.

'Ah. Reading not your strong suit, lad?'

He looked up. The earl's eyes were twinkling. 'No, sir,' he mumbled.

'Well, I think you are going to have to rectify that failing. Learning to ride and handle weapons are of course essential for a knight. But reading and writing are useful too, particularly when you have estates to manage, as you will have when, at length, you return to Meonbridge to take up your responsibilities.' Dickon nodded, feeling sheepish. 'I had not realised this deficit in your accomplishments.' The earl seemed to be trying to frown, yet his eyes were still alight. 'So, extra literacy lessons for you, I think?'

Dickon groaned inside, but the earl was right. Both his grandmother and his aunt could read and write, and used their skills daily in running their households and domains. Even the only father he'd ever known, Jack Sawyer, could do both, and he was just a carpenter. And his uncle, John, the bailiff, he was certain he could too. If he was honest with himself, he was ashamed to have failed in this part of his training. 'Thank you, my lord, I promise to pay better attention in the future.'

'Good man. Now, this letter. It is important that you know its contents.' He picked up the paper and began to read out loud.

Despite the earl's insistence that he need not worry, Dickon was at once dismayed by what he heard. For his grandmother had had an accident in the garden, several weeks ago, and was not mending as quickly as both she, and his aunt, had hoped. Lady Margaret was still mostly confined to her chamber, which made managing the de Bohun estates most difficult.

'I wonder how badly hurt she is,' said Dickon, his voice catching.

Lord Raoul knit his brow. 'Sister Rosa does not say precisely, but I think we must presume Lady Margaret has broken a limb, for your aunt refers to the need both for her bones to mend and for her to regain her strength.'

Dickon was troubled. His grandmother had always seemed so strong and hearty, he couldn't imagine her ailing and confined. 'What shall I do?' he said, lifting wide eyes to the earl.

Lord Raoul patted his shoulder. 'I have already decided that you should go home to Meonbridge for a while. There, you can set your mind at rest about your grandmother's state of health, and give her a few weeks of your time to help with the estates. I know you have a fine bailiff in Meonbridge and a most capable steward managing your wider domains. Nonetheless, the summer period is the busiest of the year, and Lady Margaret will undoubtedly be concerned that she cannot oversee the day-to-day running of affairs to which she is accustomed. I am sure she will welcome your presence at her side. I believe that is what your aunt thinks too, for why else would she have written?'

Worried as he was, Dickon was torn by this decision of the earl's.

Naturally, he wanted to go to help his grandmother, but at the same time he didn't want to leave his training. Now it was ramping up into more serious practice, he didn't want to miss out on anything. Especially as the trouble with Edwin seemed to have died down for the time being.

'It's a pity to have to go away just now——'

'But if your aunt has thought it necessary to write,' said Lord Raoul, his eyebrows lifting, 'she must be concerned about her mother.'

Dickon reddened, alarmed the earl might consider him unfeeling. But the earl seemed not to have noticed, for he stood up, and Dickon scrambled to his feet. The decision had been made.

Yet Lord Raoul took both his shoulders in his hands and smiled down at him. 'I know it is a nuisance, lad, but you owe it to your grandmother, and to the memory of your grandfather, to go home and take charge for a while. None of the other squires here have your responsibilities. You are young, but you have a sensible head upon these shoulders.' He gripped them as he said it. 'I am certain that your grandmother will benefit greatly from your help. Shall we say three months? We will review it when we know how Lady Margaret is faring.'

When Dickon left the earl's chamber once again, his heart and mind were a jumble of conflicts. Troubled as he was about missing so many weeks of training, he was excited too by the prospect of spending the summer months in Meonbridge. His time would not be idle, but he would perhaps have the chance of riding out on Bayard with Piers Arundale, and perhaps going down to the river for a swim?

And of course, he'd be seeing Libby Fletcher.

13

I n hot summers, the buttery was stifling and airless. Even in cooler weather, the room was still oppressive. Gloomy, too, for it had the tiniest of windows.

Whatever the weather, it was a room where Margery did not like to linger.

She had come to fetch a basket for the cheeses she, Jan and Ellen had been making this afternoon. As usual, she left the buttery's door ajar, to give a little extra light as well as let in some of the breeze wafting along the cross passage from the open door that gave out onto the yard.

She was crouching on her haunches, to reach the lower shelves, when the shaft of light went dim. She heard a rustle behind her, then the room darkened further as the door was pushed fully shut. Her stomach lurched as the familiar stink of sheep and sweat assailed her nose. She stood up, and at once she felt his hands grip her waist.

'Sir,' she murmured, 'the mistress is expecting me back in the dairy.'

'No, Margery,' he said, his voice low, 'she is not.' He dug his fingers

100

into her sides, making her wince. 'My wife has gone upstairs to tend the children, and the witless maids are scrubbing down the dairy. You'll not be missed a while.'

Margery swallowed. He always seemed to know. As if he had been watching her. Yet how could he? He had been out in the fields all morning, shearing the yearlings with his shepherd. It was her bad luck that he must have seen her slip from the dairy as he came back into the yard.

She tried to turn, but he held her fast.

'No, Margery, as you are.' He breathed onto her neck. When working in the dairy, she plaited her hair and wound it around her head, covering it with a linen cap. It was cool and practical, but left the skin of her neck exposed to the touch of others, whether she wanted it or not. She did not want it now, but made no attempt to stop him brushing his rough lips across the nape, then up towards her ears.

He had done this so many times, he knew well enough how, despite her wishes, her body would respond. She felt betrayed by the uninvited sensation low down in her belly, knowing that what it promised would not be fulfilled. It never was. The hunger gnawing in her at this moment would soon turn to disgust, of him and of herself.

Of course, Gabriel Browghton cared nothing for her. He never had. Even when she first came here, scarcely much more than a girl, he took her often, not from his desire for her but because he could. She had wondered if he also assaulted the household's then only other woman servant, the children's nursemaid, but suspected his opportunities for catching her alone were few.

At that time, women came in daily from Middle Brooking to help with the dairying and calves, and Margery imagined they too were difficult to catch. But, a couple of years ago, Jan and Ellen arrived to work with her in the expanding dairy, girls who would, like her, live in. Before long, he was paying more attention to them than to her, presumably because they were young and pretty, whereas Margery was well over thirty, and always had been plain.

Yet he waylaid her still from time to time.

Shifting his hands from her waist up to her breasts, he crushed them hard in his great fists, squeezing until she whimpered. He seemed to relish her discomfort. He kissed her neck and ears again, swinging her from pain to something like desire and back again.

It always ended the same way. Her skirts pulled up, a calloused hand between her legs, then... She clenched her teeth hard together and waited for it to be over.

Gabriel was never gentle. But this time he seemed to have some anger to resolve. Perhaps the dairymaids had vexed him? Maybe one or other of them had turned him down? As he bored into her, time and time again, she wanted to cry out, but kept her mouth tight shut. She simply had to endure.

When he was done, he stood a while behind her, his hands heavy upon her shoulders, breathing fast. Gradually the panting eased, and she heard the rustle as he adjusted his braies and surcoat. Then, without a word, he opened the buttery door, letting in once more the beam of light, and slipped silently away.

She smoothed down her skirt and turned towards the light. But she stumbled, as a stab of pain shot through her, and she thrust out a hand to steady herself against a shelf full of terracotta ware. She groaned: he had damaged her again. She could feel the stickiness between her legs and the familiar metallic smell was faint but undeniable. Pushing away from the shelf, she stepped to the open door and peered outside. No one was about. The mistress was presumably still upstairs, and Jan and Ellen in the dairy. If she could walk, this was her chance to clean herself, to conceal what had just happened.

Turning around again, she picked up a small pail, and took a clean folded rag from the pile used for wiping out utensils in the dairy. It was scarcely any distance to the pond but, in her present state, it would seem an expedition. Yet she had no choice. There was nowhere private in the house where she could take a pail of water and lift her skirts. But, with a little water from the pond, she could find a few moments' quiet in the nearby byre, for the cows now spent all day in the fields. She had done so many times before.

But she had to hurry, for her mistress might soon return downstairs.

Wincing at her discomfort, she forced herself to move, walking as quickly as she could out of the house and across the yard towards the pond. She was fortunate that the only other person in the yard had no interest in her movements, so she reached the pond unchallenged. She bent to half-fill her pail with the murky water. Checking once again no one was about to see her, she hurried to the byre and, slipping inside, entered one of the stalls.

It did not take long. She cleaned herself, then rinsed out the cloth, turning the water in the pail a muddy red. She had to go back to the dairy but, hearing men's voices just outside the byre, she froze, not wanting to be seen. As the voices faded, she tipped the water into the already rancid hay, and hid the cloth and pail beneath it. No one would come to clear the cows' old bedding for weeks yet.

Peering from the byre, she saw the men had now reached the dairy. Even from a distance, she could see they were the two farm labourers from Middle Brooking, two idiots Gabriel Browghton employed to do menial tasks around the place. The girls seemed to have finished in the dairy, for they were outside now, chatting and giggling with the men, as they so often did. She grunted. They had best be careful for, if the mistress caught them acting the strumpet, as she would think it, they would be in trouble. Though Margery hardly cared. The girls were an irritation although, as dairymaids, they were efficient enough, which was perhaps why the mistress kept them on, despite their brazen behaviour.

She felt a little better now, and the discomfort had eased sufficiently for her to cross the yard back towards the house. Hoping the labourers would ignore her, she kept her head down as she tried to hurry past. Yet it was difficult to step around them, and one of them, Pers Cokewell, spun around and grabbed her arm.

'Well, well, if it ain't Mistress Tyler?' He sneered. 'Wind changed when you were a lass, eh?'

He always said much the same thing. He had been saying it ever since he came here. She had never asked him how he knew she was a Tyler but, from what he said, he seemed aware of her family's fall from grace.

'Aw, Pers,' said Ellen, 'don't be mean. Marg can't 'elp her gloomy face.' She giggled, and Jan joined in.

Margery gritted her teeth. She wanted to slap the girl for her insolence, but ignoring her was better for her temper. She threw off

Pers's hand. 'You'd do well to keep your comments to yourself,' she hissed and strode away, leaving sneers and giggles in her wake.

Lying on her pallet in the dark, Margery could not find a comfortable position. The pallet was thin and the plank floor hard, and her body still ached from her encounter with her master. Jan and Ellen had long since dropped off to sleep, after whispering and sniggering together, although Margery had not heard what it was about, and did not wish to know.

Warm as it was in the upstairs chamber, she wrapped her blanket around her, craving comfort.

Comfort! How long ago was it she had received any of that? Her father had never seemed to like her, always favouring her sister. Even her mother, Anne, had shown her little love, no matter how hard she tried to please. Her mother had been ill at ease with her position as the bailiff's wife; never quite adapting from the deprivation of her lowly cottar life to the one of comfort and even luxury her husband was intent upon providing. She continued to labour in the house and garden, despite having servants to do it for her. Margery sought to win her mother's affection by doing as she did. But she failed. Anne doted on her sons, and admired Matilda's beauty.

But, for Margery, she seemed to have no feelings.

When Anne died in the first outbreak of the plague, alongside her two precious boys, Margery felt scarcely any grief.

How humiliating it was that the sole source of "comfort" she had ever received was Gabriel Browghton.

When she first came here, she had thought she should resist him, yet fear that he might dismiss her if she did not submit stayed her hand. Wretched and degrading as it was, what she had at the Browghtons was not just a job, but her only home.

In the beginning, she was also terrified she might get with child, and that *Mistress* Browghton would throw her out. But, in all the long years of Gabriel's unwelcome attentions, her belly had never swelled. It was both a relief and a regret. She had kept her home and job, but denied her only likely source of love, a child.

She assumed the reason for her barrenness was the nature of her and Gabriel's union. Everyone knew that, for a woman to conceive, she must enjoy the act of love. Yet she never had enjoyed it. Unlike her sister, who evidently exulted in her romp with Philip de Bohun. Bile rose in Margery's throat whenever she thought of Matilda's manifest joy, and its outcome. Not that *that* child survived, of course.

How often she had told herself she was not obliged to endure her master's violent misuse, nor yet the contempt of everyone else here. She should leave, find herself another position, with kinder people. But what if no one else would employ her? The prospect frightened her: she would be not only jobless but homeless too, a vagabond, a beggar.

Yet might such an outcome be better than being so abused? From time to time, she thought it might.

14

Libby found herself a little breathless at Piers Arundale's announcement. Knocking on her ladyship's chamber door, he stepped inside. 'Your grandson has arrived, my lady. Shall he come up to see you?'

Lady Margaret's eyes lit up, and she stood up from her chair. 'How I wish I could go downstairs to greet him, but I am still not quite ready to risk those stairs again.'

'Simon says it won't be too long now, milady,' said Libby. She was sure her own eyes too were bright with anticipation.

'Nonetheless, it is most frustrating, being so confined.' Her ladyship took up her stick and, straightening her back, stepped over to the small coffer where she kept her mirror. She picked it up and held it up to her face. 'How do I look? Not too old?'

Anxious as she still was about Lady Margaret's plans for her, Libby was saddened nonetheless by her ladyship's present mood. She'd never troubled herself overmuch with her appearance: she was always well groomed, but never too particular about what she wore or the arrangement of her hair. She'd been grumbling for a while about her fading eyesight and aching limbs, but put both down simply to the passing of the years. Nonetheless, Libby was certain her ladyship didn't think of herself as truly "old".

Yet, despite her excitement at Dickon's return, Lady Margaret seemed to think his decision to come back—as well as Sister Rosa's to write to the earl telling him of her accident—suggested both her daughter and her grandson considered her incapable of governing Meonbridge alone. Libby had heard her saying as much to Mistress atte Wode.

'You look the same as ever, milady.'

'Thank you, child.' She pinched her lips between her teeth to make them a little redder. 'Now run down to the hall, and ask my grandson to attend me.'

Libby bobbed a curtsey and hurried from the room. She could hardly wait to see Dickon again. It had been half a year since he was last here, and she had so much to say to him. She'd put behind her the unsettling conversation she'd had with her aunt, and her advice to forget all about him. Her ladyship seemed to have made no progress with her plans for marrying her off. Her accident had, Libby thought, diverted her from everything but mending her broken leg. So, not only did she still have a chance to tell Dickon how she felt but, with him home for several weeks, she also had the time in which to do it.

She clattered down the narrow stairs and, stopping on the bottom step, plucked the arras aside and peered across the hall.

He was taking off his cloak, and chatting merrily to a few of the servants who'd come forward to greet him. She lingered a moment, to watch him. Wasn't he even more handsome than before? What would he say to her? Nothing now perhaps, but hopefully later.

Hurrying forward, she dropped a curtsey. Then, looking up into his face, she gave him her brightest smile. 'Welcome home, my lord,' she said, and his eyes seemed to light up.

'Thank you, Libby. How's my grandmother?'

'She's asking for you.'

'Now?'

'She's eager to speak with you again, my lord.' As am I, she'd have liked to add.

Dickon turned to Piers. 'You can deal with everything, can't you? The horses, baggage and so on.'

Piers nodded, and ran out through the door and back onto the bailey.

Dickon started towards the stairs. 'How is my grandmother really, Libby? My aunt's letter to Lord Raoul was worrying.'

'She's well in many ways,' said Libby, 'but her leg still pains her, and she's frustrated by her confinement to her chamber.'

'I can imagine how vexing it must be to be prevented from doing as you wish. Grandmama is usually so full of energy.'

At the door of the chamber, she knocked and awaited Lady Margaret's call of "Enter" before going in. 'His lordship's here, milady,' she said, and he brushed past her and almost ran towards his grandmother. He kissed her on the cheek, and she embraced him.

She looked back at Libby, who was hovering at the door. 'Thank you, Libby dear. I shall send for you later.'

Libby winced. Dismissed again. Well, of course she would be; her ladyship was hardly going to let her listen in to her private conversation with her grandson.

But Dickon turned his face towards her too and smiled, and her stomach did a flip.

Having nothing particular to do, she took the chance for a stroll in the garden. She'd go to her ladyship's secret arbour. It wasn't truly "secret", but it was supposed to be Lady Margaret's private sitting place. But, since her accident, nobody had sat there except for Libby—taking advantage of her mistress's confinement—and even she hadn't been there for a while.

She sneaked unseen into the tunnel pergola, overflowing with the flowers she knew were honeysuckle and roses. But, the moment she saw them, even she could see the flowers were all out of control, with thorny branches and whippy stems shooting in all directions, in some places hindering her passage through the tunnel. It was where Lady Margaret had had her accident, and these very flowers were the ones she'd been trying to bring under control.

Her ladyship would be sad to know her precious roses were

growing so wild. She ought to tell her, so a gardener could come. Yet, Lady Margaret would then know she'd been here.

She shrugged: she'd decide about it later. Now all she wanted was to sit a while and think.

Pushing her way through the spiky thicket, she came to the arch that led into the arbour, with its lawn and fountain, and the turf seat overwhelmed by yet more roses. They too were growing wildly, but it was lovely to have some of the blossoms hanging low, their delicious perfume wafting about her face.

It was such a romantic spot, a place where lovers might sit together, hidden from others' prying eyes. She and Dickon never came here when they were children. They'd usually escaped the gardens altogether, to the orchard or, even better, to the meadows, the river or the woods beyond.

How relieved she was that he'd come back to Meonbridge—for three whole months, her ladyship had said. She admired him for giving up his exciting life in Steyning to come and help his grandmother.

She was longing to talk to him. She practised in her head what she might say. But she urged herself to be patient, to let him get used to being in her company. Then, when they were easy with each other once again, she'd tell him how she felt about him and how much she hoped he'd say the same of her.

However, in the week or two that followed, Libby was disappointed that Dickon seemed preoccupied almost entirely with his grandmother and the manor estates. He hardly even spoke to her.

Of course, she saw him almost every day, when he came to talk to Lady Margaret. She wasn't always sent away. She suspected her ladyship might prefer her not to be there, but Dickon sometimes suggested she stay, to sit by the window, sewing or practising her letters. Grateful for his seeming thoughtfulness, she sat quietly, her back to the low-voiced conversation, but glancing sideways from time to time. Occasionally she caught him looking her way, and they exchanged a smile.

His conversations with his grandmother were usually about the estates, about her plans and expectations, and what could and couldn't be done over the summer.

A few days after his arrival, he'd told her that John atte Wode, the bailiff, had suggested they make a tour of all Meonbridge's acreages and farmsteads to check on the progress of the crops and animals, and the plans for harvest.

'That is an admirable idea,' her ladyship had said. 'Your uncle is the best bailiff we have ever had, clear-headed and forward thinking. He will be an excellent adviser.' She stretched out a hand to pat his arm. 'Enjoy your tour.'

'I will. Learning about Meonbridge and its domains is going to be much more agreeable than I'd expected.'

Lady Margaret had thrown back her head and laughed. 'How glad I am to hear you say it.'

When Dickon wasn't with her ladyship or the bailiff, he was invariably in Piers's company, galloping across the fields and hills, or practising with weapons on the bailey, she supposed.

But even though Dickon scarcely ever spoke to her, he didn't entirely ignore her. Once or twice, when she came into the chamber, bringing refreshments for them both, he got up to clear a space for her on the table. As he did so, his arm brushed lightly against hers, and she was sure he meant to do it.

She hugged herself inside. Was he trying to show her he *did* want her around? Yet there never seemed to be an opportunity for them to be alone.

A few days later, Lady Margaret raised with Dickon the subject of her flower gardens.

'It has been weeks since my accident. I was trying to tie up the honeysuckle in the arbour, and intended to do the same with all the roses. I realised only this morning that I have forgotten all about it.' Her face looked stricken.

Libby bit her lip. Should she say?

'Do you want me to have a look, Grandmama?' said Dickon. 'See what needs doing?'

'I could show you,' Libby said. 'I know where it was her ladyship fell...'

Lady Margaret turned. 'Oh, yes, you found me. I have wondered how you knew where to look?'

'You'd said to me that morning, milady, that's where you were going.'

'Ah, did I? How wise of me.' Her eyes twinkled. 'Else I might be lying there still.'

'So, shall I show you where?' Libby said to Dickon.

Her ladyship gave a little laugh. 'I am sure Dickon can find it for himself, Libby dear. The flower gardens are not so very large.'

'But it might be easier if Libby showed me, Grandmama.'

'We could run down there after dinner.' Libby's heart pounded at the prospect.

Her ladyship's brow crinkled, but Dickon nodded. 'The sooner we get a gardener to tackle it, the better, Grandmama.'

Libby felt like a child again, running across the bailey and down towards the gardens with Dickon at her side. As she led Dickon through the great potager, her heart was racing, and not because she was hurrying.

'It's strange,' he said, stopping and gazing at the neat rows of onions and cabbages in the potager's long beds. 'I've hardly ever been in these gardens. I wonder why?'

'Because the orchard was always much more fun. We could steal apples or some cherries.' She pointed to some tall spiky leaves. 'We'd hardly want to eat an onion.' She put her fingers to her throat and pretended to gag.

He sniggered. 'Yeah, maybe that was it.'

He opened the gate that marked the entrance to the herbier and flower gardens. It pierced the fence put there to keep out the sheep and goats that sometimes grazed the orchard. He didn't shut the gate behind him, and she tutted.

'You mustn't leave it open, Dickon, else the animals might get in and munch her ladyship's precious flowers.'

'But there aren't any animals around.' He smirked.

'Not right now, but there often are. It's best not to risk it.'

His eyes crinkled as he agreed, and how she longed to grab his hand. But she steeled herself against it. Despite their childhood friendship, he *was* the lord of Meonbridge, strange as that did seem. Even if he felt the same for her as she did for him, she still had to take it slowly.

They soon came to the opening to the arbour.

'It was here,' she said, pointing to the patch of broken honeysuckle stems and roses where her ladyship had lain, unable to move, until she'd found her. Many of the broken stems were dead now and blackened, though others had recovered from being crushed and seemed more rampant than ever.

He waved his hand at the overflowing pergola. 'I suppose it's not meant to look like that?'

She shook her head. 'By now, her ladyship would've trimmed back all those long wavy shoots and tied them to the framework. I've watched her do it. But she prefers working by herself, especially in the early morning. That day, she went without me.'

'But you went to look for her?'

'She'd been away much longer than I expected. I don't know what made me think it, but I felt I needed to make sure she was all right.'

How horrified she'd been to find her mistress lying upon the ground, amidst the tangle of wiry tendrils and thorny shoots, her leg twisted underneath her. She must have been there quite a while. Libby remembered crying out as she ran forward, fearful her ladyship might be dead. But Lady Margaret raised her head.

'Libby?' she said, her voice quavery. 'Is that you?'

She knelt down at her side. 'Oh, my lady, are you hurt?'

Her ladyship nodded feebly. 'My leg, I think it is broken...' She moved slightly and at once cried out. 'Oh, my goodness, how it hurts.'

Libby jumped up again. 'I must get help, milady.' Yet she was afraid to leave her alone.

But Lady Margaret groaned. 'You must. And do please hurry.'

She ran faster than she ever had before, back towards the house. By chance, she saw Piers Arundale as she reached the bailey, and called out to him. 'Her ladyship's h-hurt,' she cried. 'P-please, Piers, get a litter and fetch Simon Hogge.'

'Where is she?' Piers called back, hurrying towards her.

'In the f-flower gardens... By the t-tunnel...' She stopped running as he approached, and bent over, trying to catch her breath. 'But I must go back to her. Can you arrange it?'

He nodded. 'We'll be there soon.'

She could trust him to act quickly, and hurried back to the arbour.

'They weren't all that long,' she said to Dickon, 'but, by the time they came, her ladyship was struggling to stay awake.' She looked up at him, and her eyes filled with tears. 'I was so afraid.'

'Goodness, Libby, I'd no idea it was so awful. Thank God you went to find her. Else she might not have...' He grimaced. 'You seem to make a habit of saving us de Bohuns.'

She blushed, proud he thought of it like that.

'The first time at the river, with the false friar,' he continued. 'Then, when Thorkell Boune was carrying me off.'

'He did still run away with you.'

'But you were brave, Libby. Grandmama told me how you charged at him.'

It was because I loved you even then, she thought. And I still do. How she longed to say the words out loud, but it was too soon.

Dickon stepped into the tunnel, pulling at the tangled vegetation with his bare hands. She followed. 'If you continue along here,' she said, 'you come to her ladyship's secret arbour.'

'Secret?'

'Only because it's her private sitting place.'

'I wonder if she and my grandfather used to come here, for—' He reddened, and she giggled.

'Let's go and see,' he said, walking on.

He let out a whistle when they reached the arbour. 'All these years, I've not known this was here.' The fountain was still, but he dabbled his fingers in its pool. The water was rather green. 'Lord Raoul's got a garden much like this at Steyning, or rather the countess has. Not that she works in the garden, like my grandmother.' He chuckled. 'She just tells the gardeners what to do.'

'Lady Margaret does love her gardening.' She dipped her fingers too. 'She'll be so upset if she can't go back to it.'

He looked up, his eyes wide. 'But surely she'll get better?'

'I suppose so. But maybe she should be more careful. Not come here on her own?'

'She'll hate not being able to do just as she wishes.'

'Maybe I should always come with her?' She'd not thought of that before. Perhaps making herself indispensable might delay the day when her ladyship sent her away?

He brightened. 'I'd like to think she always had some company.'

'She'd hate to know we're talking about her as if she's an old lady.'

'We'll not tell her, eh?'

She nodded, but was gazing at the arbour seat. The afternoon air was hot and the bower delightfully shady. It would be lovely to sit there with him, beneath the perfumed flowery arch. She was on the point of suggesting it, when a spray of cold water struck her cheek. She gasped and spun around.

'I thought you were looking hot.' Dickon had a wide grin on his lips.

She laughed. 'I was thinking we might sit in the shade a while—'

His fingers flicked more drops from the fountain's pool towards her. It wasn't especially cold, but the water tingled on her skin. He guffawed, and she leaned forward and, plunging her own fingers into the murky liquid, scooped some up and flung it across at him. There was rather more than she expected and greenish water dribbled down his cheeks.

'Hey,' he cried, and lunged towards her. But she was quick and dodged his outstretched hands, scooting around the fountain to the other side. He chased her, dipping and flicking water as he went, till she turned suddenly and they collided, and his flailing arms encircled her, as if to stop her toppling over.

All at once their faces were so close she could feel the moisture on his skin, and the warm breath from his lips. She giggled. 'Well...' she started, but couldn't think what else to say.

His cheeks were flushed, but he didn't pull away, and neither did she. After all, having his arms about her was exactly what she wanted.

After a few moments, he giggled. 'Sorry.'

'There's no need for sorry,' she said, wanting to say more. 'Shall we sit?'

Unfolding his arms, he took her hand and drew her to the arbour seat. Her face felt warm, and her heart was thudding once again. She was alone with him at last, and so very close. She put a hand down on the seat beside her and, as she'd hoped, he laid his lightly on top.

'I suppose we shouldn't really be alone together,' he said.

'We've been so often enough before.'

He sighed. 'I know, but it's different now. We're not children any more...'

All at once her stomach churned. What did he mean by saying that? He was holding her hand, yet did he think he shouldn't be? Her heart's pounding seemed to have reached her ears. Surely she should tell him how she felt? Wasn't this the chance she'd been waiting for? If she didn't do it now, she might not get another.

'I feel differently about you now,' she said, her voice a whisper. Her gaze was fixed upon her skirt.

'How?'

She hesitated. 'When we were little, we grew very fond of each other, don't you think?'

'Like brother and sister...'

'Maybe more than that?' She felt him shrug. 'We were so close... It seemed like we were always *meant* to be together...' She stopped, as he lifted his hand off hers.

After a few moments he stood up. 'I think we'd better report back to my grandmother,' he said softly.

She didn't look up, not wanting to see his face, certain she might cry. She'd said too much, and now everything was spoiled. 'Yes, I suppose we had,' she mumbled, and stood up too, smoothing down her kirtle, even though it wasn't crumpled. 'She'll be wondering where we are.'

As they walked back to the house, he kept a foot or so away from her. She longed to reach out for his hand but perhaps the time for holding hands had already passed.

15

W hen Dickon and Libby returned from inspecting the damage in her flower garden, they both seemed a little quiet. As they entered her chamber, Margaret greeted them warmly, despite her anxiety at what Dickon might be about to tell her.

'What have you discovered?' she said, gesturing them to come forward.

Both wore long, melancholy faces. Their shoulders sagged. Had they had some sort of argument? A lovers' tiff, perhaps?

She caught her breath at that unbidden thought. Had she been naïve?

When Dickon said he would inspect her garden, and Libby suggested showing him where to see the damage, she had said that he could go alone. All she was thinking was that Dickon was perfectly capable of finding the place himself. But he had agreed with Libby it would be quicker if she showed him, and she had not demurred.

'Grandmama?' Dickon was standing by her chair.

Shaken from her thoughts, she looked up at him. 'Yes?'

'Shall I tell you what we found?'

She pointed to the other chair. 'Is it all a dreadful tangle?'

'Everything's so overgrown.' He sat down. 'The sooner a gardener tackles it, the better.'

She let out a sigh. 'Very well. Though you must make sure it is Will Greenfinger who attends to it. He is the only one I trust to make a fair job of it without my supervision.'

'I'll speak to him,' said Dickon. 'The work needs to be done soon, Grandmama, so I'm afraid you can't oversee it.' He got up. 'But how is your leg? Have you tried to go downstairs? It can't be much longer before it's mended, and you can be your old self again?'

She laughed at that. 'Not so much of the "old".'

Dickon reddened. 'I didn't mean that sort of old.'

'I know, dear boy. I am teasing you.' She leaned forward to pat his arm. 'Thank you for your encouragement. I do feel that, before too long, I shall be able to walk again.'

'I'll talk to the gardener tomorrow. But may I go now?'

She agreed, and he hurried from the chamber. He barely glanced at Libby, who had said nothing at all since they had arrived.

'Are you feeling unwell, my dear?' said Margaret.

The girl looked up. Her face was glum. 'I'm fine, thank you, milady.' She seemed to give herself a little shake. 'Is there something you'd like me to do?'

She sent Libby off with several messages, and settled back into her chair, to think more about what might have passed between her grandson and her maid.

The next afternoon, Alice paid Margaret a visit. Margaret held her friend in great affection but, in the early days of her recovery, Alice had taken Simon Hogge's instructions overmuch to heart. Day after day, she had watched her like a hawk, determined she would do nothing to jeopardise her recuperation.

If truth be told, she was grateful that Alice visited a little less often now.

At length, of course, she had frustrated Alice's vigilance by insisting on the attempt to go downstairs. Alice had been much against it, and was proved right. Margaret cringed at the memory of it:

the exercise was a disaster and had given her confidence a considerable knock.

But, now, when she and Alice were settled down with some refreshments, she dismissed Libby, then related what Dickon had told her about her flower garden. 'It is so frustrating not to see it for myself. Even more so not to be able to do the work.'

'I do recall,' said Alice, 'how exasperated I was all those months when I was ill. Unable to do my usual chores, when so much needed to be done.' She took a sip of wine. 'But you have no choice but to wait until your leg is strong enough.'

'Dickon said he thought I should soon attempt the stairs...' Margaret arched an eyebrow.

'Didn't you tell him you already have?'

'No.' She turned her wine cup in her hands. 'I know now it was too soon, as you tried earnestly to tell me, Alice dear, and I think my grandson might be vexed if he knew I ignored both Simon's advice and yours. Therefore, I have not mentioned it.'

'Your secret is safe with me.'

Margaret could not suppress a deep sigh. 'What a foolish old woman I am.'

Alice shook her head. 'You shouldn't be so hard upon yourself. Your frustration was understandable. You must be sure that, when you do next attempt it, your leg is ready.'

Margaret took a long draught of her wine. 'Yet I do have to recover soon, so Dickon can return to Steyning.'

'I thought it was agreed he'd stay in Meonbridge till Michaelmas?'

'It is. But I do think, Alice, that he should not stay so long. I worry that he is missing important schooling.' She put down her cup and clasped her hands together in her lap. 'There is too another matter...'

'What is that?'

'I scarce know if I should even mention it, but I am concerned, and would welcome airing my anxieties with you.'

'You know I never repeat anything you tell me,' said Alice, and Margaret nodded.

'It is in relation to what I told you earlier, about Dickon going to inspect my flower garden, and report back on the state of the plants. You will remember that, when I had my accident, I was working on

118

the honeysuckle, tying in the fast-growing shoots. There were a vast number, and I had done very few of them before I caught my foot in that errant rose and fell.'

'So, the shoots you hadn't done are now rampaging everywhere?'

'Exactly. I suspected as much, and Dickon confirmed it.' She took another sip of her wine. 'But that is not the source of my anxiety.'

'Oh?'

'Dickon did not inspect the flower garden alone. Libby went with him.'

'It's nice for them to spend a little time together, whilst they are still young.'

'Yet I am not sure it is, Alice. Not any more.'

'What do you mean?'

Putting her wine cup down, she smoothed the fabric of her skirt then clasped her hands together in her lap. 'We spoke of it a few weeks ago. I mentioned that I thought Libby had hopes of Dickon, despite the impossibility of such an outcome.'

'Indeed. Which was why you'd agreed to Dickon marrying Sir Giles's daughter, and are hoping to find Libby a suitable husband before too long.'

'I had planned to arrange a marriage for her before Dickon returned here for Christmas but, because of Rosa's interference...' Alice's lips parted, and Margaret smiled thinly. 'Oh, well enough meant, I know, but Dickon is now home again, with every opportunity for spending time with Libby.'

'Can you not prevent it?'

She sighed deeply. 'My efforts to do so have been feeble. When I told Dickon how concerned I was about the flower garden, he offered to go down to look at it. Libby was here with us, and at once suggested she might show him where it was. I did not think he needed her to show him and said so, but he demurred, and it seemed overbearing to insist. So, I allowed them both to go.'

'"Allowed"?'

'Well, yes. To be honest, Alice, they both seemed gleeful at the prospect, and it was only after they had run off together that I grasped what I had just witnessed. There was a spark between the two of them that was not simply friendship—not the amity of children—but something more.'

'Ah. Your earlier suspicions were confirmed?'

'Indeed. I knew for certain then that, ever since last Christmas, Libby had been flirting with our grandson, the way girls of her age do when they are thrown together with a good-looking boy. I was not sure if he was responding to her longing gazes and advances, but I now think he was. It was as if they were noticing each other, the changes wrought recently in their young bodies...'

'They are both very handsome. And certainly the right age for *noticing*...' There was a glint in Alice's eyes.

'However, when they returned from their little outing to the gardens, they were no longer gleeful but morose and distant from each other. It popped into my head quite unbidden that they had had a lovers' tiff. *That* was what I thought, Alice. Lovers!'

She stood up and took up the flagon of wine. Offering it first to Alice, who declined, she poured herself some more.

Sitting down again, she took several large sips from her cup. 'It was then, Alice, that I understood that letting them go off together on their own was a mistake. I had been naïve...' She looked at Alice. 'Letting them be alone together, out of sight of other people, might suggest that I approve of their relationship.'

'When you don't.'

'Not when it is evidently much more than mere friendship. How can I? Dickon is going to marry Angharad. I will soon arrange a suitable match for Libby. They can never be together, not in that way.'

'So, letting them be alone together now is... risky?'

'I believe it is.' She unclasped her hands. 'Indeed, Alice, I have wondered if Libby somehow engineered the outing to the garden, so she could be alone with him.'

'That sounds like something Matilda might have done, but is Libby devious like her mother?'

'I do not think so. Certainly I did not consider it at the time. It is only now that I am wondering...'

Alice leaned forward. 'Have you told Dickon of your concerns? Or of your plans for his betrothal?'

'Neither. I suppose I should. Tell him that, if he is imagining that Libby might be a potential bride, it simply is not possible.'

'Or at least just tell him of Sir Giles's proposal? So that he understands what the future holds for him.' Alice took a sweetmeat and bit into it. 'And what it doesn't.'

16

MEONBRIDGE

JUNE 1364

Dickon was astonished at the scale of the Meonbridge domains. When he was a boy, he'd thought himself the expert on the fields and woods of Meonbridge, but he now realised he'd hardly known them at all.

He was enjoying walking them all with his Uncle John. They'd gone out together almost every day since he'd been back, and John explained which fields and pastures were part of the de Bohun demesne, which were farmed by tenants, and which owned by freemen with no obligations to her ladyship. As their visits took them further afield, they went on horseback, and took the opportunity for a trot along shady woodland tracks or an exhilarating canter across the downs.

John was more than twice Dickon's age. When he was younger, he'd always seemed a cheerful sort of fellow but, these days, he was serious and rather earnest.

Grandmama considered him the best of bailiffs. Maybe John's work was the cause of his stern demeanour? Even Dickon could see his tasks were considerable and onerous. Nonetheless, he wondered why his uncle wasn't married. He was tall and strong—indeed, he had the bearing of a knight—and his face was handsome if often glum. Dickon grinned to himself: was John's face dour because he hadn't found a wife, or was the dourness the reason he didn't have one?

But his uncle's eyes lit up when he talked about the arrangement and extent of the de Bohun lands, about the tenants and the other farmers, and about the cycle of works and events that took place every year. 'Her ladyship has bid me tell you all I can whilst you're back in Meonbridge.' He grinned. 'There's a lot to know.'

Most boys in the village grew up spending at least some time working in the fields alongside their fathers—their mothers too—and always helped bring in the hay and the grain harvest. But, as the sons of a carpenter, Dickon and his brothers rarely did that kind of work: if they did any, it was in their father's workshop. Though, now he thought about it, *he'd* spent much of his childhood running wild in the woods and by the river, rather than in the workshop.

When he began spending time up at the manor house, for a reason he didn't then understand, play was again the main occupation of his days. After he left Meonbridge to start his knightly training, his brothers were apprenticed to their father, but he'd grown up knowing almost nothing about the work of carpenters or farmers or any of the other folk in Meonbridge.

'There's a lot more than I'd imagined,' he said to John, pulling a wry grin. 'Thank you for taking the time to tell me.' He wiped his sleeve across his face. 'God's bones, it's hot.' The sun was right overhead, blazing bright in a cloudless sky.

John glanced up, shielding his eyes from the glare. 'Dinnertime? Let's find a shady spot to eat.' Pointing ahead to a nearby patch of woodland, he clicked his tongue and his horse ambled towards it. Dickon followed. They dismounted in a dappled grassy clearing and, setting the animals loose to graze, sat down on the mossy trunk of a long-ago fallen tree.

His uncle took a linen-wrapped bundle from his saddlebag. 'Ma's made us both some dinner. Meat pies, and bread and cheese.' He held up a flask. 'As well as some of her best ale.' He shared out the food and they ate in silence for a while.

'Her ladyship's asked Adam Wragge to come back to Meonbridge soon,' said John, flicking his beard free of a few crumbs from his pie,

'so he can tell you about your other estates, in Dorset and in Sussex.'
He grinned again. 'As I said, there's a lot to know.'

Dickon rolled his eyes. 'I'm not sure I can take it all in.'

'You will, milord, in time. Her ladyship's idea is that you use some
of the next few weeks to get a broad understanding. The details can
come later.'

Dickon bit his lip. 'Please just call me Dickon, John. "Milord"
doesn't seem right. Especially when we're alone.'

What a peculiar situation he was in. He might be heir to the de
Bohun estates, but the atte Wodes were still his family, albeit they were
villeins. After all, he was half a villein too. Jack Sawyer might not be his
real father, but he was the only one he'd known, and he'd brought him
up the same as his two other sons—well, almost.

On the long ride back from Steyning, he'd given much thought to
how he should behave towards his villein family—the atte Wodes and
the Sawyers—both now and in the future, when he took over from his
grandmother responsibility for the estates. Wouldn't it be wrong, as
well as awkward, to act in any way superior? He certainly didn't want
them to "milord" him. Indeed, did he want anyone in Meonbridge to
do so? It was troubling, not knowing the proper way to act.

Yet didn't his grandmother provide a good example for him to
follow?

As far as he could tell, she had an easy relationship with her
tenants. She'd told him long ago how she and Grandma Alice had been
friends, ever since their two daughters—Johanna and his mother,
Agnes—had been little girls. He'd seen how freely she talked with all
the villagers. Yet it seemed they—or most of them, at any rate—still
held her in respect. He didn't remember his grandfather, Sir Richard,
all that well, but thought he'd held himself much more aloof, perhaps
believing himself grander than everyone else in Meonbridge.

But *he* wasn't going to be like that.

Grandmama was close to trying the stairs again. He'd been
encouraging her for days, ever since, with a sheepish grin, she told him
she'd tried a while ago, before her leg was ready, and it had all gone
wrong. He'd pretended to be cross with her. Yet it had clearly shaken

her confidence, which was so unlike her, and it troubled him: she needed to return to her usual way of life, her gardening, her command of the manor's affairs, her conversations with her tenants. He was pleased that she was, at last, bolstering herself for the great descent, as she called it.

Already, her mood was lighter. 'It is wonderful to see you throwing yourself with such energy into learning about your estates,' she said to him. 'I am so proud of you.'

'I'm enjoying it, Grandmama. John's opening my eyes to how much I don't know.'

'As I knew he would.'

'And I'm enjoying being talked to as if I'm an adult.'

'But, my dear boy, you *are* an adult.'

'I'm only just fifteen. But, with John, I feel I'm having a grown-up conversation, discussing the estate's undertakings and affairs.' He sucked in his lips. 'But I told him I don't want him calling me "milord". It seems wrong, when he's my uncle...'

'You are in a difficult position. Perhaps, with your family, you should be more informal.'

'I *must* be, Grandmama. I can't bear for them to think I imagine myself grander than them.'

'I understand. I am sure you will work out what is best to do.' She leaned forward and touched his arm. 'You can talk to me, you know, about anything that is troubling you.'

He stared down at the floor. How he wished he could tell her more. She was wise, and kind, and could surely give him good advice about his problems back in Steyning. But he couldn't stomach telling her about the bullying, or what Edwin knew about his birth.

No, this was something he had to deal with by himself. If he could act the adult here, couldn't he do the same in Steyning?

Yet, in order to tackle it, he wanted to know the truth about his past. Edwin had learned that Dickon's mother was a Meonbridge tenant, which, in his eyes, made Dickon unworthy of training to be a knight. But was that all Edwin knew about him, or was there more? How vexing it would be if he knew more than he did himself.

Neither his mother nor father, nor either of his grandmothers, had ever told him the whole story. How was it his father and mother, a de

Bohun and an atte Wode, had him? What happened to Agnes, and how did she come to marry Jack? What happened when his grandfather made him his heir?

He'd lots of questions, and he needed answers. But who would tell him? He didn't like to ask his grandmothers, or his parents. But maybe his uncle would be willing?

Late in the afternoon, after a quiet day indoors talking to his grandmother, Dickon went down to the stables and asked the groom to saddle Bayard. He needed to escape the house a while and a good gallop would help him think.

All day, Libby had been in and out of his grandmother's chamber. She'd not lingered, for he and Grandmama were talking about deeds and contracts, and he doubted Libby was much interested in listening in. But, several times, she'd come over to the table where they were sitting with documents strewn around them, to replenish their refreshments, and bring answers to sundry messages she'd carried for his grandmother.

On reflection, it had been unkind to reject Libby when they were together in the garden, and he regretted spoiling their happy mood. Yet, if he'd thought then it was his duty to curb their fun, *now* he wasn't sure he wanted to. For every time Libby's body brushed close to his, his groin tensed, and he had to stop his fingers reaching out to touch her.

It was clear enough she felt the same.

When he was some miles from Meonbridge, bringing Bayard to a halt, he dismounted, close to a great oak tree standing in the middle of lush meadowland that ran alongside the river. He let Bayard graze the flower-filled meadow grass whilst he sat beneath the tree and, leaning against the ancient trunk, rubbed his shoulder blades against the sharp grooves of the bark.

He conjured a vision of Libby as she was the other day, prancing around the fountain, her dark hair flying, her lips parted in merry laughter. His groin tensed once more, as he imagined what it might feel like to stroke her skin, to cup her breasts.

He thought again about the way the other squires at Steyning talked about the castle maids. Obviously, it could all have just been swagger, but he recalled his envy at the thought they'd touched a girl when he hadn't.

But perhaps he could touch Libby? She was flirting with him, wasn't she? Offering herself to him?

Moments later, he was grinding his shoulder blades once more, hard against the bark. What was he thinking? Libby wasn't like those Steyning maids. He couldn't treat her as if she was one of them, even if she *was* flirting.

Leaping up, he strode across to Bayard. He took the reins and rested his face against the warm quiver of the horse's neck. Bayard whickered and twisted his head around for the muzzle rub he knew would come.

Dickon sighed. Everything seemed to be pushing him towards what he—and Libby too—desired. But his head was telling him that his desires—or hers—were not what was important. He needed to talk to someone about it. But who? Piers, perhaps? Yet he knew well enough what he'd say. And it wasn't something he could talk to John about.

No, this was something else he'd have to work out for himself.

He remounted Bayard and trotted across the meadow and on towards much higher ground. Climbing the hill, he urged Bayard into a canter and then a gallop and, with the wind rushing past his ears, and his hair streaming out behind, he let his uncertainties and worries blow away.

Despite his anxieties, and his coolness with Libby the other day, their friendship soon enough recovered, though they'd not been on their own again.

But, one afternoon just after dinner, when he came up to his grandmother's chamber to discuss something with her before he went out again with John, he found her sleeping. Libby was sitting sewing on the window seat. He sat down beside her.

'Has Grandmama been sleeping long?' he said in a whisper.

'She often snoozes for an hour or so after dinner.'

'Maybe I'll not wait, then. I'm meeting my uncle shortly.'

She nodded, but he didn't get up to go. 'Libby, I hope we can stay friends?' She tilted her head but didn't answer. 'When I said things were different now,' he went on, 'it's true, but...' He wasn't sure what exactly he was trying to say. 'But perhaps not in the way you thought I meant?'

'So, what did you mean?'

'You were right when you said we'd been close for years.'

Libby put down her sewing. 'Dickon, are you saying you'd like us to meet alone again?'

He stared down at the space between his feet. She certainly was willing. Was it wrong for him to want it too? He thought yet again of the lewd conversations at Steyning with the other squires. He really *didn't* think of Libby that way.

Yet here she was, her lovely body warm and close, the feathery ends of her unbound hair skimming the gap between her little breasts. His heart was pounding just below his ear, and he clasped his hands together and jammed them between his thighs.

But at length he looked up: her head was tilted again, her lips parted.

He ignored the tremor in his stomach. 'That would be fun.'

17

STEYNING CASTLE

JULY 1364

E dwin's writing skills were not quite as proficient as his reading. Letter writing was a chore he scarcely had the patience for: trimming the quill; being careful to take up just the right amount of ink to make marks on the paper yet not cause a flood; thinking up what in the world to say...

His grandmother had written to him weeks ago, and he had intended to respond, but somehow could never summon the enthusiasm to make the effort.

He had been pleased to receive her letter. When he returned to Steyning after Christmas, he was already excited by what he had learned of Dickon de Bohun's birth.

He had always known that de Bohun was inferior, but his conversation with his grandmother confirmed it. How gleeful he had been. He felt entirely justified in continuing to keep de Bohun in his rightful place.

What *Grandmère* imparted in her letter, telling him about the unjust involvement of his Aunt Isabella in a ruse to make de Bohun appear what he was not, strengthened his belief that he did not deserve his place at Steyning. He determined at that moment to do all in his power to ensure that, somehow, de Bohun was humiliated and sent away.

Yet had that already happened, without his intervention?

De Bohun's departure from Steyning a few weeks ago was one of two things that had happened that he wanted to tell his grandmother, and which he thought she would like to know. Even though writing it was going to be a chore, he might quite enjoy describing the events.

He smoothed out a sheet of paper and, taking up one of the quills he had sharpened in preparation, he dipped it in the ink. But how much should he tell her? How should he start?

"*Right worshipful and well-beloved Grandmère Hildegard,*" he wrote then paused, his quill poised above the page. What next? He would thank her for her letter and tell her he was well. He dipped his quill again and continued writing.

Now for the interesting part: his news. But what should he say first? Perhaps the duchess's birthday dinner?

He smirked to himself: how very well that prank had worked, much better than he had dared to hope. Of course, he had not planned for the victim to be that particular guest. It could have been the countess or even the earl, but de Bohun managed to serve both of them without mishap.

But he would not tell his grandmother that he had arranged what happened next.

"*I think, Grandmère,*" he wrote, "*you might be amused to hear what happened to Dickon de Bohun when he was serving at high table. It was a special dinner, held in honour of the countess's mother. It was when Dickon was serving the noble duchess herself that the platter he was holding tipped and the meat and sauce slid sideways, down onto the duchess's chest. It caused an uproar, as you can imagine.*" He giggled to himself thinking about it again.

The kitchen boy he had paid to do it had done his job well. What luck that the duchess had cried out in delight at what was on the platter and made de Bohun jump. *Parfait!*

Perfect, too, because the earl and countess were enraged as well as embarrassed. Best of all, the *whole company* saw it happen. De Bohun could not have been more humiliated.

He told his grandmother about de Bohun's punishment for the

130

"mishap" and paused again. He lay down the quill. What now? He was sure she would be interested to learn of the much harsher punishment de Bohun received after the fight. Though, naturally, he would not say what happened at the quintain, nor who actually proposed the bout.

He would not admit it to anyone else, but the challenge had been a mistake. Yet it had never occurred to him that he might lose. He would never forgive de Bohun for breaking his nose, and for making him look weak. Who fetched the master he did not know, but he had been relieved when he arrived. He was exhausted, his bloodied nose was agony, and he saw at once that he could land de Bohun in trouble yet again.

When the master demanded to know what was going on, he took his chance, making a show of whimpering and staunching the blood flowing from his nose. And when he accused de Bohun of starting the fight, he just stared at his feet, saying nothing. *Quel crétin!*

He sniggered to himself as he continued writing.

"Lord Raoul was so angry with him for starting a fight with me, and for damaging my nose, he punished him with a whole month of solitary confinement and no training. Hourra!"

In his excitement, he flicked the pen, and a drop of ink flew off and landed silently on the paper, close to the top. The dark bead trembled a little but did not burst. Annoyed his hitherto pristine page was sullied—and right by his grandmother's name—he grabbed a rag and dipped a corner into the bead, hoping to suck up the spilled ink. The droplet dwindled a little but, in his impatience, he withdrew the rag too quickly, and the ink seeped into the "ard" of "Hildegard". He groaned: he could not bear to screw this page into a ball and have to write everything he had written all over again. It would have to do: he would apologise for it at the end of the letter.

It was disappointing that, given how angry he was, the earl had still not dismissed de Bohun. The solitary cell must have been horrible, and being banned from training for a month would have set de Bohun's progress back against the rest of them. All that was good. But why did the earl think de Bohun *still* deserved to stay at Steyning, when he had broken one of his cardinal rules? It was exasperating.

"However, Grandmère," he continued, *"I wonder now if de Bohun's punishment has been taken further. For he has left Steyning, and returned to*

Meonbridge, supposedly because Lady de Bohun has had an accident. But perhaps that is not true? I wonder if Lord Raoul has lost patience with him after all?"

He said it, although he did not believe it. But no announcement had been made about when or whether de Bohun would return. He wondered if one of the other squires knew more.

Only Nick Fenecote had an answer. Edwin did not talk to him much these days, since he had transferred his loyalties to de Bohun.

Nick snorted at his question. 'Why would you care about that, de Courtenay?'

He ignored the comment. 'Has he gone for good?'

'You'd like that, wouldn't you? You've been trying to get rid of him for months.'

Edwin did not deny it. 'Well, has he?'

'Sorry to disappoint you. He'll be back by Michaelmas.'

Yes, that *was* disappointing. But three months was long enough for him to come up with an idea to ensure that, by the time he did come back, Dickon de Bohun would be an outcast to all the other squires.

Except perhaps for Nicholas Fenecote.

Edwin was surprised at how quickly he received another letter back from *Grandmère* Hildegard. His heart sank a moment, as he supposed he would have to go to all the trouble of writing to her yet again within a week or two.

But, when he read the letter, apart from her saying she had enjoyed reading all about Dickon's "little misadventure", he saw she was responding largely to a brief comment he had made about the hunting expeditions he and his fellow squires would soon take part in.

It was not the first time they had been out hunting. But the master told them that, this time, the stakes would be much higher: they were expected to play a greater part. And, this time, they were to hunt for boars.

He had been greatly excited at the prospect. But his grandmother's letter sounded a note of caution.

"I wish to ensure, Edwin, that you understand the perils," she wrote. *"Long before I met him, when he was perhaps not much older than you, your*

grandfather Hugh came close to dying, after an incident in which he was gored by the antlers of a stag. Of course, he did survive, but I understand that he teetered betwixt life and death for many days..."

Edwin was impressed, and made a mental note to talk to his grandfather about it all next time he was at Courtenay Castle.

"Hunting boars," she continued, *"is <u>many</u> times more perilous, for boars are brutes. They will run at you like thunder and stick you with their vicious tusks."*

How could *Grandmère* Hildegard possibly know that? Women did not hunt, except perhaps with falcons. He snorted. Who knew what the old dragon might have got up to in her youth?

But she then referred to another hunting episode, when *Dickon's* grandfather, Sir Richard, actually died.

"At first, it looked to be an accident, but later it appeared that Richard was murdered by those execrable Bounes..."

This startling information gave him an idea. He did not yet know how he might do it but he decided that, whilst Dickon was away, he would learn the rules of hunting so well that he would be able to contrive an "accident" of some kind.

18

For days, Libby had heard Dickon encouraging her ladyship to try the stairs again. Simon Hogge now agreed she should, declaring her leg was much improved. Lady Margaret had been nervous but, one morning, when Libby came to help her dress, her eyes were wide. 'Right, Libby,' she said, 'today is the day.'

She swung her legs off the bed and planted her feet upon the floor. 'When I am dressed, you will please send for Simon, and ask my grandson also to attend me. I am determined to visit the rest of my house again.'

An hour later, Dickon and the surgeon—one above her, one below—helped her to descend each narrow step with care. Libby followed on behind.

Lady Margaret was joyful when she reached the bottom. 'Oh, my dear boy,' she cried, squeezing Dickon's shoulder. 'Freedom at last.'

'Does the leg feel stronger, milady?' Simon said, his face still creased with anxiety.

'Remarkably so. Not that I shall be running around the grounds this afternoon.' She laughed lightly.

'Indeed not, milady. Small steps still, I think.'

Libby was relieved to see her mistress merry once again. Though, in a sudden panic, she wondered if it might mean Dickon would now go back to Steyning much sooner than he'd planned.

As if she was thinking the same thing, Lady Margaret turned to Dickon. 'Perhaps you do not after all need to stay in Meonbridge till Michaelmas?'

He scoffed. 'This is your *first* day downstairs, Grandmama. You still have to recover your full strength.' He took her arm. 'Shall we walk a little?'

'You are right. But might we go outside? I am sure I can manage the bailey steps.'

Dickon looked across at Simon, who nodded. 'It's a fine day, milady. A little sunshine will be beneficial.'

Libby went outside with them. The air was warm, but a light breeze plucked at her ladyship's gauzy veil. 'How wonderful it is to feel the elements once more upon my face,' Lady Margaret said, her eyes alight. 'Thank you, dear boy, for persuading me to make this little outing. I had become quite fearful that I might never see the outside of my house again.'

'*You* fearful, Grandmama? Never. Your leg just needed to be ready. And now it seems it is.'

She beamed. 'I think we should take a stroll around the bailey. Slowly, of course. Can you spare the time, or shall Libby go with me?'

Dickon looked at Libby. 'I do have time, but Libby can walk with us.'

Her heart leapt at his invitation. Though she was sure she saw a cloud flicker across Lady Margaret's face. And it wasn't long before her ladyship decided she was a little chilly after all and sent her indoors to fetch a shawl. Libby thought it likely the shawl was a ruse, though she'd no choice but to go.

When she returned, Dickon and his grandmother were nowhere to be seen. Surely they hadn't already gone as far as the garden? She stood at the top of the steps, scouring the bailey for sight of them, when one of the young grooms came up, on his way indoors.

'If you're looking for 'er ladyship,' he said, ''er and 'is lordship's down with the 'orses.'

Libby ran off towards the stables. As she approached, she slowed her pace. If the shawl had been a ploy, she might catch what they were saying. She waited a few moments just outside the stables entrance, her ear against the doorpost. She could hear them murmuring, about something she was sure she wasn't supposed to hear.

She listened for a short while longer then stepped inside. As she handed her the shawl, Lady Margaret abruptly stopped what she was saying and patted a horse's muzzle. Libby was pretty sure the horse was Dickon's favourite, Bayard.

'Thank you, dear,' her ladyship said to her, as she threw the shawl around her shoulders, then turned back to Bayard. 'We are talking horses, so perhaps you would like to go to help prepare for dinner?'

Of course she didn't want to, but she curtseyed and walked back to the house. As she helped spread the cloths upon the trestles, and set out the bread trenchers and the drinking cups, she considered the brief but troubling snatches of conversation she'd just overheard.

It seemed Dickon was quite happy about marrying this Angharad, who Libby thought must be the daughter of Sir Giles Fitzpeyne. After the attack on Meonbridge, Dickon had gone to Fitzpeyne Castle to finish his page training, and stayed there for three years before he moved to Steyning. She supposed he must have got to know the girl quite well.

Yet Angharad was still a child—only seven, did she hear her ladyship say? It would be years—at least five?—before they married.

What might Dickon think of that, not bedding her till he was twenty? Yet maybe he'd already bedded girls in Steyning? A mazer slipped from her grasp and clattered to the table. She swallowed, and a flush of heat rose to her throat. Might she be already sharing him? She'd not even considered that till now. Though, if Steyning Castle was anything like here, there'd not be many serving girls, but there might be a nearby village, where squires could go if they were looking for a swive...

Her flush spread across her neck, making her uncomfortable and hot. She thought again about that day in the arbour, when for a few moments they'd played together much like children—or maybe more like lovers? All at once they'd been in each other's arms. And he'd not pulled away. He'd wanted to hold her. Yet, when she spoke to him later of what she felt, he'd dismissed it.

How confused she was about it all.

His wedding plans hardly mattered, they were so far ahead. There was surely time enough for her to make him see that *she* was his intended, and not Angharad. But, her confidence lasted mere moments. Perhaps she didn't have very long at all: for, even if it might be years before Dickon's marriage, it might be only *months* before her own.

For a week or so ago Lady Margaret had hinted once again that it was time to find her a husband. 'I will start looking as soon as I am on my feet again,' she'd said. 'Which will, I am sure, be before too long.'

Libby had been thrown into a panic. 'A husband, my lady? But I'm too young.'

'Oh, I do not think so, dear. I promised your mother that I would find you a good man to wed when you were of a fitting age. You will be fifteen in December, will you not?'

'Yes, but—'

Her ladyship held up her hand. 'No "buts", I think. You do not want forever to remain a servant.'

Of course she didn't. But neither did she want to be married off. Aunt Margery had been right. Lady Margaret did push everyone around—Dickon as well as her. Her time for convincing Dickon might after all be short. He mustn't go back to Steyning till she'd got his promise.

Yet what could she say or do to make him understand? He'd so obviously noticed she was almost a woman, and his behaviour at the fountain surely proved his feelings for her? And, the other day, when she'd wondered out loud if they might meet alone together again, he *had* said yes.

Her excitement mounted at the prospect of lying in Dickon's arms. Yet, moments later, a different emotion gripped her: mightn't he think her a strumpet if she offered herself to him? Shouldn't it be he who made the first move? But, if he didn't, what other option did she have?

19

After dinner one hot July afternoon, Dickon left the manor house and sauntered down the road into the village, to Jack's workshop. It had always been his intention to spend a bit more of this time in Meonbridge with his Sawyer family. He'd wanted to show them they were still his family, and that wouldn't change, even when the day arrived that he became the lord of Meonbridge.

He'd go to see his mother later but first he wanted to see more of the carpenters' work in action. With John's help, he was beginning to understand something about farming, but he wanted to know about everything that went on in his domains.

Jack was hearty in his greeting, clasping him by the shoulder. 'What are you doing with your time back here in Meonbridge?'

'John's trying to teach me all I need to know about the estates and how they work. I'm learning things I never knew about farming.' He beamed. 'But I want to understand everything that goes on in Meonbridge, including in this workshop.'

James looked up. 'Is that necessary?' He reddened. 'Sorry, that were impertinent.'

Dickon held up his hands. 'No, no. I just want to. My grandmother's made it her business over the years to do so, and I plan to follow her example.'

'You couldn't do better,' said Jack. 'Her ladyship's been a good lord of Meonbridge, when Sir Richard was away on the king's business, and since his death. She's been much missed.'

'Well, I'm glad to say she's recovering. She's tramping the grounds and gardens again, though still under orders from me and Simon Hogge to take things slowly yet a while.'

'So, you'll be returning to Steyning soon?'

'Not yet. I'm enjoying myself here too much. The earl gave me till Michaelmas, and that suits me well enough.'

Nonetheless, he did miss his life in Steyning, or the good parts of it anyway. Since Edwin's rancour seemed to have cooled, the daily round of activities and training had become enjoyable again. He'd regretted having to leave it all behind. Though it was true too he felt more at ease here in Meonbridge. For here, despite his wish not to appear "superior", he did feel more in command of both himself and life around him. Because, he supposed, in Meonbridge he *was* in charge, whilst, in Steyning, the other more naturally "knightly" squires somehow still made him aware of his lowly standing.

James offered to show him the timber yard, and Dickon was glad of the chance to talk. James was almost as old as John but, once he'd got over his awkwardness over what to call Dickon, they fell into an easy way of conversation.

Like John, James enjoyed talking about his work, and explaining aspects of it Dickon didn't immediately understand. But it wasn't long before the heat of the afternoon drove them to seek shelter from the sun and they slipped into the cool of the shed where trees hauled back from the forest were cut up. They sat down side-by-side on one of the benches used to balance the long tree boles being sawn into manageable lengths.

'Are you planning to stay with Jack?' said Dickon, thinking of what his pa had said about needing more hands.

It was hard to be sure, with James's face already pink and shiny

139

from the sun, but his cheeks seemed to redden further. 'To be honest, no, I'm not. But I ain't told Jack yet.' He looked embarrassed, as if he already wished he'd not mentioned it after all. 'Not that I'm going soon. I'd not let Jack down. He's been the best of masters.'

'But it's time for you to move?'

'Jack would not deny me the opportunity. He knows I'm ready to set up on my own.'

Dickon recalled his mother mentioning James might leave before too long. 'I daresay he won't be surprised, if the time has come for it. So, you'd move away from Meonbridge?'

'If I stayed, I'd be competing with Jack for work, and that wouldn't be good for either of us. I'm planning to get married, and set up a home and business somewhere else. But not all that far away, I hope.'

'Who's the lucky maid? Do I know her?'

'Ha, no, there's no one yet. But it's high time I wed, started a family.'

'Perhaps you should help Jack find another journeyman? A couple of apprentices too?'

'That's a good idea. It'd ease my guilt, as well as speed things up, as Jack's so busy. But you'd be surprised how hard it is to find skilled men.' He rubbed his close-trimmed beard. 'Jack's got contacts, but we're so busy all the time.'

Dickon nodded. He wished he could help, but what did he know about apprentices and journeymen?

On the final day of Dickon's tour of the Meonbridge domains with John, they were going to ride to its furthest point, a small enclave of land occupied by a single tenant farmer, an old man who was the fifth generation of his family to farm the holding.

'But he'll be the last,' said John. 'For his two sons, his only children, both died in accidents, and neither of them were married. With no grandchildren to carry on, and no other relatives we know of, when the old man dies, we'll have to find a new tenant for the holding.'

'Will that be difficult?'

'Not necessarily. But, as you'll see, it's an out of the way place. It might be better to sell it to a freeman who wants to make more of the surrounding pastureland. A sheep farmer.'

Dickon nodded. So many decisions to be made. The estate certainly didn't run itself.

When they'd inspected the old man's holding and held an awkward conversation with him about the future, they rode away and up onto the downs. Once more John had brought food prepared by Grandma Alice and, finding shelter under a spreading tree, they sat down onto the grass beneath.

When he'd finished eating, John folded his hood into a pillow and, putting it behind his head, leaned back against the tree. He closed his eyes. Dickon chewed his lip. He didn't want to disturb his uncle's rest, but now was the perfect time for him to answer all his questions.

He coughed, and John lifted an eyelid. 'Sorry, just fancied a doze.'

'No, *I'm* sorry, because I hate to stop you, but I've been wondering if you'd...' He looked away a moment. 'If you'd tell me more about my past.'

'Your past?' John sat forward. 'What do you want to know?'

'Everything. There's a lot I don't know about, and I don't want to ask my parents or my grandmother—either of them—in case it might be painful to recall.'

John frowned, though not unkindly. 'What are you thinking of?'

'How was it my father and mother had me?' He blushed. 'I mean, how did your sister and Sir Philip—?'

John held up his hand. 'I understand.'

'Then what happened to my mother, and how come she married Jack? And how did my father die? And what happened when my grandfather made me his heir?' He pressed his lips together. 'All these are things I don't know about, or not enough. My memory's hazy and I do think I should understand my background, now I'm almost a man.'

John sat up straight. 'I agree, you should. I'm happy to tell you what I know.'

'Can we stay here a while and talk?'

'I can spare a little time. But what's made you think about this now?'

Dickon looked away a moment. He'd no intention of telling John about Edwin and the bullying. But he did have to give some reason why he wanted to know more about his family.

'When I was little,' he began, 'Pa was working all the time, and Ma was always melancholy. They never told me how they met, or about my real father, and I never asked them. I'd no reason to think I *wasn't* Jack's son. When I went up to the manor house to play with Libby, nobody told me why I was there. I remember thinking how stupid it was, me going to play with a girl, but I was only five or six, so I suppose I didn't trouble myself all that much about it.'

'I always wondered whether Jack or Agnes ever talked to you about those things.'

'Hardly anything. Yet, when my grandmother told me I was Sir Philip's son, I was only a bit surprised. I suppose because some of my friends kept saying Jack couldn't be my pa because my hair was black and his was fair.'

John chuckled. 'I remember you saying that. But Jack and me used to wonder if you did somehow know all along you were a de Bohun?'

'I dunno,' said Dickon. 'I did feel sort of different, but I hadn't worked out what the difference was. Anyway, Grandmama didn't tell me anything much about my father. She said she'd tell me one day how he died, but she never has.' He stared at the ground between his feet a moment, then looked up. 'I've lived all these years not knowing the truth about my heritage and, now I'm going to be lord of Meonbridge, I think I should.'

'Very well. Where shall I begin?'

'At the beginning?' said Dickon.

John pressed his lips together. 'Which won't, I'm afraid, show your father, Philip, in a good light. For he seduced my sister, and got her with child.'

Dickon swallowed: in a way, it was like him and Libby, except his father *had* taken advantage of the girl he coveted. 'If he seduced her, didn't he care for her at all?'

'Oh, I think he did. Yet he knew he couldn't marry her. He was already betrothed, and was married not long after. My sister was so distraught when he abandoned her, she ran away from Meonbridge. We didn't see her again for a whole year, when she returned with Jack, and you, a babe.'

'What did my father think of me?'

'He never knew you. He was killed a few months before Agnes came back.'

'Killed? In an accident?'

John's face went dark. 'I'm sorry to tell you he was murdered.'

Dickon gulped. Why didn't he already know that? 'Who did it?'

He grimaced. 'It was my predecessor as bailiff, Robert Tyler, or rather he put his henchman up to it.'

'But why would the bailiff want my father killed?'

'To be honest, Dickon, I don't know. In those months, Robert seemed to be losing his wits. I do know he resented Sir Richard making Philip steward, giving him authority he believed would undermine his own. Moreover, Philip had ideas on how to rebuild the estate after the devastations of the plague that Robert didn't agree with.'

'But that isn't enough to want him dead.'

'I agree. But Robert had become brainsick and, soon after Philip's death, he died himself, falling from Saint Peter's tower.' He hesitated. 'Many folk thought he meant to fall... But we never learned the true motive for Philip's murder, for the henchman who was arrested for it revealed nothing more before he was hanged.'

This was difficult to hear: his father, hailed as a great knight at just eighteen, and destined to be one of the king's favourites—or so his grandmother had once proudly said—had been cut down by a madman, out of some sort of resentment. What an ignoble end!

'And what of my mother? Didn't you go looking for her?'

'We couldn't. Plague came to Meonbridge only days after she left, and Sir Richard forbade anyone to leave the village. After the plague passed on, I did spend time searching, with Philip's help—'

'So, he *did* care for her?'

'I believe so, yes. He *said* he thought of her as a sister, because as a child she spent a lot of time up at the manor house as companion to his real sister, Johanna, and he played with her too occasionally. That was the reason he gave for wanting to look for her. Despite my probing, he never admitted he'd got my sister with child, nor that he loved her in *that* way.' His forehead wrinkled. 'In what way he *did* care for her, I was never sure. Agnes did claim later that he truly loved her,

143

and regretted his behaviour towards her. Anyway, not long afterwards, he was killed. I'd become reeve and there was so much work to do to put the estate and the village back together, I had to stop my searching for a while.'

John was silent for a moment then looked up at the sky. 'It's time we went back to the manor house. But I can carry on talking as we ride.' He packed the leavings of their dinner into his satchel.

Dickon jumped up too. 'I'm sorry to—'

John held up his hand. 'No, no, it's not a problem. But I have something I must do this afternoon.' He strode over to his horse and took up the reins. 'A bailiff's work is never done.' His eyes crinkled and Dickon laughed.

They mounted and John led the way back at walking pace towards the village.

'Anyway, to continue,' he said, 'I'd had to stop looking for Agnes but, a couple of months later, she and Jack turned up with you, the little boy Jack had agreed to raise as his own. It was a time of great rejoicing.'

Dickon steered his horse close to John's, so it was easier for them to talk. 'Were my grandfather and Grandmama pleased too?'

'Very much so, because Philip's wife, poor Isabella, had died in the plague—and, as you know, your aunt, Johanna—'

'Sister Rosa...'

He nodded. 'She'd decided to enter the priory, and Sir Richard and Lady Margaret assumed they'd never have a grandchild. So, when you appeared, they were delighted. But it was agreed your position as their grandson and heir would remain a secret within the family. No one in Meonbridge knew the truth of it at first, beyond the de Bohuns, the atte Wodes and the Sawyers.'

'When was it made known?'

'Sir Richard was forced to announce it when, in all honesty, I don't think he'd thought about the consequences.'

'Was that when those men came to attack Meonbridge?'

John scowled. 'The Bounes: your grandfather's cousin, Morys, and his sons. They'd somehow heard of Philip's death and came to discover if he'd left an heir. If he hadn't, Morys would inherit Sir Richard's estates. So, his lordship claimed you were his heir. And, to reinforce the claim, he lied, saying Philip's wife, Isabella, was your mother, thus making you legitimately born.'

'I hardly remember anything about it, except there was a great fuss.'

'Indeed there was. For what Sir Richard said was, of course, a lie. I can't tell you everything now—it's a long and complicated story.' He raked his fingers through his hair. 'But Isabella's family, and especially her mother, Lady Hildegard, were furious that she'd been implicated in the lie. Anyway, the Bounes brought their case to court, claiming you were in fact my sister's son, and therefore *ill*egitimate—'

'How did they find out?'

He shrugged. 'As I say, it's complicated… However, with the help of Lord Raoul, the Bounes lost their claim, and you were acknowledged as the de Bohun heir. But it was then the Bounes murdered Sir Richard, then tried to kidnap you and attacked Meonbridge, when you were badly hurt. Do you remember any of that?'

He did, though the details were still hazy. 'I suppose I was still only seven, so perhaps it's not surprising I don't remember it all that clearly.'

They were at the edge of the village now.

'Right,' said John, leaning back in the saddle so his horse came to a halt. 'I'm afraid I'll have to leave you for now. Business to attend to. I'll tell you more another time.'

Dickon rode slowly back to the stables. What a story John had told him. Why had no one told him before that his father had been murdered? Perhaps Grandmama had intended to tell him once, yet it would hardly be a memory she'd be eager to relive. He understood that. He wondered if Libby knew about it all. For Robert Tyler, the man who'd killed his father, was *her* grandfather. Did she know he was a murderer, or had that been kept from her as well as from him?

Could he ask her what she knew? Yet it was a difficult subject to raise. If she didn't know, she surely would be horrified. He didn't want to be the bearer of such knowledge.

But now he was even more confused about his feelings for her.

The other day he'd said it would be fun for them to meet again— and he'd meant it at the time. Every time he saw her, he couldn't stop an image of how she'd look without her kirtle worming itself into his

145

head. And sometimes his cock responded too in a way he wished it wouldn't.

Ever since he'd said it, she'd been pressing him to suggest a time. Not that she said as much. But, whenever their paths crossed, in his grandmother's chamber, or at dinner, or sometimes just passing in the hall, she'd tilt her head at him and smile, or lower her eyes and simper.

Yet he never should have said it, however much he wanted to hold her in his arms and stroke her skin. Piers was right: swiving Libby would be wrong. Dangerous. After all, when his father seduced his mother, she got with child and ran away from Meonbridge when he couldn't marry her. How could he risk that happening to Libby?

So, he'd been resisting her flirtations simply on the grounds of what was right. By not speaking to her unless they were in the company of others, he'd thus far avoided making any arrangement.

But didn't he now have *another* reason for not allowing their friendship to become something more? Now he knew how his father died, and that it was at *her* grandfather's behest, surely he couldn't carry on their friendship as if he didn't know.

For the best part of each day, when he was busy with John or Piers, he could push the anxiety and confusion from his mind. But when he was alone, the turmoil returned. The reasons why he should avoid any further relationship with Libby roiled in his head, convincing him to keep away from her. Yet then he'd see her, albeit at a distance, and his desire diminished his resolve.

When the turmoil got too much, he ran off to the stables and slipped into Bayard's stall. He'd like to share his worries, but couldn't bring himself to talk to Piers, knowing what he'd say. But here he could lean his face against the horse's neck and whisper them. And, in the calm he found in Bayard's company, he made a decision. He didn't need advice about what to do: he knew the answer well enough. In the weeks remaining of his time here in Meonbridge, he had to ensure that he and Libby were never alone again.

Two weeks passed, and he'd managed to stick to his resolve. But, one afternoon, shortly after dinner, he had some time to spare before his usual practice bout with Piers and ran up to his grandmother's chamber, thinking to ask her if she'd like to walk with him in the gardens.

It had been a careless move, for he'd forgotten she nearly always fell asleep for an hour or so after dinner. He was still standing by his grandmother's chair, gazing down into her peaceful face, when he heard a noise and, out of the corner of his eye, saw Libby scuttle to the chamber door and put her back against it. She was smirking.

'Libby...' he said, his heart hammering in his chest. 'I must go.'

She tilted her head. 'Not without keeping the promise you made.'

'I made no promise.' Hadn't it just been a throwaway remark?

'Oh, I think you did.' The tip of her tongue grazed her bottom lip, and his groin shuddered.

He couldn't think how or what to answer and, in the silence, she answered for him. 'As it's so very hot, I thought you might like to go down to the river. You always did enjoy a swim when we were children, and I don't think you've done that since you've been back.'

Both were true. He loved swimming in the river, and he'd not thought of going down there in all the weeks he'd been back home. Of course, there'd been many other things to do but also, these days, when he wanted exercise, his first thought was always Bayard. But how much he'd enjoy immersing himself in the Meon's cooling waters. He couldn't help but sigh at the thought of it.

He was relieved she'd not suggested finding an empty chamber or seeking out an isolated barn. The river was a public place, where anyone might come. Even the particular spot they used to favour, where a bend in the river created a deep pool, was surely open enough there'd be no opportunity for any intimacy.

He agreed to meet Libby by the river the following afternoon. She'd told him it was her afternoon for visiting her friend.

'Maudie won't mind if I miss a week with her. We don't always have much to talk about. But her ladyship won't expect me back till later.'

She was already sitting on the riverbank when he arrived, her feet dangling in the water. She was by "their" pool, where the tips of the willows' long slender branches skimmed the river's gentle current. He removed his shoes and tunic and sat down by her side. He dipped his toes into the water too.

'Chilly,' he said.

'That's why I can't bear the idea of swimming in it.'

'I thought you couldn't swim?'

'Well, no, I can't. Though I suppose I could just bob about.' She giggled.

His back was already clammy from the heat, and his shirt was sticking to it. He longed to take it off and slip into the water. At length, he grasped the bottom of it and pulled it up and over his head. He sat a while longer, enjoying the warmth of the sun on his bare shoulders, imagining how wonderfully the water would cool his skin.

A moment later, he flicked his eyes at Libby and, grinning, toppled forwards into the pool. He gasped as the cold water folded over him, then he rotated in a somersault. He laughed as his head bobbed above the surface. 'You should try it, Libby,' he cried.

Unusually, she hesitated, but at length she smiled and shook her head. He wasn't sure if it was fear that was still stopping her, or shyness. 'Very well. I'm going for a swim.' Giving her another grin, he struck off downstream.

A short while later, when he was treading water, hoping to see the otter he'd spotted running in the undergrowth flop into the river from the bank, he heard a splash behind him. As he spun around, expecting the otter, he saw Libby was in the water after all, submerged up to her ears. Her long dark hair fanned out around her head, and she was bobbing gently up and down. He swam back towards her and, as he came close, he saw her shoulders glistening as they broke the surface. He assumed she'd have kept on her chemise, but it was obvious she was naked.

She wasn't looking his way, so, not wanting to alarm her, he called out before he came too close. 'You decided to come in after all.'

She spun around to look at him. 'It's so hot today. The water's lovely, isn't it?' She spread out her arms and twirled, giggling, teasing him with her eyes.

The thought of her naked body beneath the water was arousing. He couldn't see it clearly but, if he got a little closer, he might be able to touch it. What would she say? Wasn't it what she wanted him to do?

Why else had she taken off her kirtle and chemise? He approached her, getting close enough to run his fingers through her fanning hair. His cock nudged against his braies.

She laughed, spun around again to face him. Her eyes were alight, her cheeks glowing. She held out a hand to him and he took it. When he drew her closer, she didn't resist.

He could no longer help himself, and it seemed neither could she. When he laid his hand upon her shoulder, she lifted it slightly then tipped her head to rub her chin against his fingers. She parted her lips. When he shifted his hand from her shoulder to her waist, she moaned softly and clasped her hands around his neck, pulling him closer still.

When their faces were so close they were almost touching, she kissed him. Then, bouncing slightly, she brought up her legs and wrapped them around his waist.

20

How humiliated she was when Piers Arundale appeared suddenly at the river and caught them together in the water. His face flushed red, and he stumbled to a halt yards from the riverbank. How shaken he must have been by what he saw. He turned his head aside, staring towards some trees on the other side of the meadow. And he didn't mention what he'd seen, but just told Dickon he was needed. Then he spun around and hurried away.

She and Dickon were still clasped in each other's arms.

He sniggered. 'Oh dear, I think poor Piers was shocked.'

'D'you think he'll tell her ladyship?'

'Doubt it. Though he might want to talk to *me*, if you know what I mean.'

'But he's no right—'

He put a finger to her lips. 'No "right", maybe, but Piers always has my best interests at heart.'

What did he mean by that?

A chill skimmed her shoulders, and she unwrapped her legs and lowered her feet onto the riverbed. 'Shall we get out?' she whispered.

'I suppose I'd better go soon, anyway.'

'D'you think it's true, about you being needed? Maybe her ladyship sent Piers to find you?'

He shook his head. 'More likely he came looking for me himself.'

She unfolded her arms from Dickon's neck. 'You think he already knows? About us?'

He shrugged then took her hand, and they waded to the bank. Dickon stepped up onto the grass, his braies clinging to his body, water flowing down his legs. He held out both his hands to her. She hesitated, not wanting to leave the water. They'd been having such fun together, but the spell was broken. Piers's intrusion had prevented what she was sure was just about to happen. Was that chance now lost? After all the effort of getting Dickon to come here... A lump filled her throat.

At length, she let him help her climb out. Shivering, and feeling all at once exposed, she pulled her hands free from his and folded her arms across her breast and belly.

Dickon squeezed the water from the legs of his braies, and rubbed briskly at his wet body with his shirt. He was gazing at her as he did it, a playful smile upon his lips, but somehow she couldn't return it. She bent down to pick up her chemise and, turning away from him, patted the rumpled fabric over her skin. But it wasn't drying quickly enough and, opening the chemise out, she dragged it over her head and tugged it down her damp body to cover herself up.

When they were both dressed, Dickon reached for her hand again and drew her down onto the grass. He put his arm around her waist and pulled her close. 'That was fun,' he said.

She leaned her head against his shoulder. 'Can we do it again, d'you think?'

'Maybe.'

They sat a few moments longer, arms about each other, the warmth and closeness of Dickon's body easing the embarrassment of Piers's untimely interruption. At length, they untwined and, getting to their feet, ran back to the manor house wall.

Dickon gently pushed her through the little gate. 'Go to the flower garden,' he said, 'and stay there a while. Maybe pick a posy? I'll go and find out if I'm really needed.' He rolled his eyes, and she giggled. But then he took her hand again and lightly squeezed it.

As Libby busied herself later with her customary tasks, the bliss of the afternoon's events hummed in her head. She wanted to hug herself with joy: what she'd so much longed for had happened. Of course, there'd been no chance to declare her feelings to him, but Dickon had said there'd be another time. Hadn't he? How she hoped it would be soon.

But she didn't see him again that day. It seemed he had been needed after all, though for what she never did find out. Then her ladyship took her supper in her chamber, as she'd done ever since her accident, and, as usual, she asked Libby to eat with her.

Dickon must have eaten downstairs with all the others in the household. Raucous laughter drifted upstairs from the hall, and Libby felt a little peevish, hating to be excluded. 'I wonder what's so funny?' She heard the tartness in her voice.

As further bursts of merriment rose to their ears, her ladyship huffed. 'You can be sure that, without my presence these past weeks, the conversation will have become entirely unfit for delicate ears.' She laughed a little. 'I think it is time I took all my meals downstairs again. There is no reason any longer to keep myself apart. Tomorrow, Libby, we shall make the effort.'

Hours later, as she lay on the low truckle cot beside her ladyship's vast wooden bed, Libby was finding it hard to fall asleep. Lady Margaret was snoring lightly, as she always did, but that wasn't what was keeping her awake. For, alone at last, and cloaked by the darkness of the room, she could think again about what had happened at the river, remembering the tingling on her skin when Dickon touched her, and the stirring deep inside. She let her fingers touch where he had stroked, and quivered.

She wrapped her arms around herself. It was working out as she'd hoped it might. He *did* feel the same as she did. He'd proved that by his actions. He *wanted* her, just as much as she did him.

21

MEONBRIDGE

JULY 1364

For almost fifteen years Gabriel Browghton had been assaulting her. Margery was grateful when Jan and Ellen had come. She had not expected it, but it was not long before she realised she was being spared at least some of his unwanted attentions. He did not avoid her altogether, but it was clear he preferred the younger women. Of course he did. Yet, more recently, she was sure at least one of them was not always letting him have his way. She always knew when he had been fobbed off, for he then came to her, and his mood was ugly. She wished she knew too how to defy him, but he was so practised at catching her unawares she had become unable to resist.

He was angry when he found her earlier in the byre. She had gone there for a few moments' rest between working in the dairy and going to do the afternoon milking. How he knew she was in there, she did not know. She never knew. She often felt he must be watching her, yet that made no sense.

She had been lolling amongst the few remaining bales of last year's hay, easing her sore back and massaging her aching legs, when she heard someone come into the byre. She tensed, hoping it was not the

153

mistress about to catch her shirking. But when Gabriel stepped forward, his mouth twisted in an unpleasant sneer, she almost wished it had been his wife. He had swived her only days ago, and she had not yet recovered.

Not that it lasted long. It rarely did. But twice in one week was really too much to bear.

The first cow milked, Margery hefted the full pail in one hand, and the empty one and three-legged milking stool in the other. She hobbled over to the next cow, the stool's legs, as always, getting snarled up in her skirts. She cursed under her breath.

As she reached the animal, she changed her mind: she would take the full pail back to the dairy now and make three more trips to milk this one, Belle and Flora. It meant more walking back and forth, and would take longer. But carrying two heavy, slopping vessels at once was just too difficult, and she was sick of complying with Philippa Browghton's arbitrary demands, on top of being forced to submit to those of her husband.

Margery Tyler should not be carrying out this drudgery at all!

It was not what her father had planned for her, nor what she had imagined for herself. By now, she should be the mistress of a household, perhaps much like this one. She should be *commanding* dairymaids, not making her hands red raw, and her back bent and frail, doing all the work herself.

She grabbed the handle of the pail again and stomped off towards the field gate and the dairy.

Back in the meadow, she determinedly cast her angry thoughts aside. Calm was crucial for the cow to submit to her kneading fingers. Besides, the act of milking was a balm to her own troubled spirit, and she did not want to sully these few moments' peace.

She maintained her composure long enough to carry the next full pail to the dairy, and to fill the third pail with Flora's creamy milk.

But, as she stumbled back to the dairy yet again, the thump of the pail's hard edge against her shin, and the slop of milk soaking her skirts, goaded her resentful thoughts once more. If it had not been for her sister's wild romp with Philip de Bohun, *none* of what followed would have happened. All of it was the result of Matilda's reckless act.

Yet it was not her sister that she blamed.

Philip cozened Matilda into his bed. Then, having got her with child, he abandoned her. And his mother then took control—

Was that really true? That *was* what Father told her, was it not? She shook her head, to cast the memories away again, for she was back at the dairy door. She leaned her shoulder against it to push it open. In her weariness, she let the heavy pail slip to the floor, and the milk swirled and slopped over the rim.

'Damn!' she muttered and looked up at Ellen. 'Can you mop this up, whilst I go to milk the last one?'

'You want *me* to clean up after you?' said Ellen, tossing her head.

Margery stared at the milky puddle a moment, seeping into the cracks in the earthen floor, then snorted. 'Oh, what do I care?' Picking up the final empty pail, she stumbled back out into the yard.

In the meadow, she once more bid her rancorous thoughts be still as she put her stool down by her favourite, Belle, and stroked her belly. 'Your turn now,' she murmured. 'You ready for me?'

Belle lowed softly and, lifting her head from the grass she had been cropping, turned towards her. Not much made Margery smile these days, if it ever had, but the sight of Belle's brown eyes gazing at her did, and the touch of her velvety muzzle. She raised a hand and laid it gently on the wet, downy snout. Bending forward, she wiped and massaged Belle's udder before reaching for the pail and placing it underneath.

'Let's go, Belle, shall we?' she murmured, and began pulling on the teats. Belle gave a single low then dipped her head.

The rasp of her cropping teeth mingled with the swoosh of her milk gushing into the pail, and the faint hum of the flies pestering her tail. The soft sounds eased Margery's unsettled mind. She rested her forehead against Belle's twitching flank. How much happier she would be to spend all her days with Belle than have to consort with people.

Soon enough the milk stopped spurting, and the vessel was full. She exhaled and, heaving herself upright from the stool, eased her back. 'Well done, lady.' She patted the cow's rump. Then, lifting the pail and picking up the stool, she turned to go. 'Tomorrow,' she whispered, and Belle raised her head a moment before returning to her grazing.

As she set down the pail to open the meadow's gate, Margery groaned. Across the yard towards the dairy, Pers Cokewell and his mate were there again, chatting to Jan and Ellen. She would not have thought the girls had finished their work, but it was not her job to chivvy them.

She had no choice but to pass them all, standing right outside the dairy door. She presumed Pers would, as always, favour her with one of his crass remarks. He was an idiot, of course, but that did not stop her feeling aggrieved.

She lurched across the yard, the pail thumping against her leg. As she approached, Pers snorted. 'My, you do look 'ot, Missus Tyler. Sweaty... Red... It don't 'elp none to improve yer—'

She banged the pail down, deliberately catching the toe of his thin shoe.

He yelped. 'Hey! Watch out.'

'No, *you* watch out,' she snarled. 'Else one day you'll find your insults reaping a whirlwind of their own.'

He scratched at his matted hair. 'What d'ya mean by that, yer old besom?'

"Old besom"? How dare he! But she would not rise to that taunt now. In truth, she had no idea what she meant, but her patience was wearing thin. If only she could find a way to silence Pers's slurs.

How long had she been lying on this lumpy pallet, staring wide-eyed into the chamber's gloom? All night, it seemed. Jan and Ellen were still snoring. But the turmoil in her head endured.

It was hopeless to continue struggling.

She did not often leave the sleeping chamber at night, in case she disturbed the Browghtons or their children. Occasionally, during hours of wakefulness, she heard someone else moving about downstairs, and wondered if it was the mistress who was restless, or the master. She had arisen herself a few times, unable to bear the discomfort and frustration any longer, trusting to experience to move towards the stairs, without tripping over the other maids. But, tonight, light from a full moon was piercing the window shutters, relieving the blackness just a little.

Stilling her mind a moment, she listened. All seemed quiet in the house, and at length, she eased herself up from her pallet, felt for her shawl and tiptoed across the room. It was fortunate the house was sturdily built, for none of the floorboards in the chamber creaked. Yet a number of the treads on the steep stairway did, and she took each one carefully until she reached the bottom.

Right next to the stairway's last step was the door into the buttery and, opening it quietly, she slipped inside. Her heart quickened. She abhorred this airless room. But Gabriel would scarcely come looking for her at this hour of the night.

Wrapping her shawl around her shoulders, she pushed the door closed and shuffled over to where a low wooden chest that held table linens stood against the wall. She sat down. Sitting in the gloom was not much better than lying in it, but at least the girls' snuffles would not distract her.

The churning in her head continued, the constantly repeating themes: the injustices of her life, and who was to blame for them. What had befallen her was not her fault. She was a victim of others' misdemeanours and betrayals: Matilda's seduction by Philip de Bohun, her pregnancy, the ending of it, their father's madness, Philip's murder, the family's plunge into dishonour and the loss of everything they had.

And weren't the *de Bohuns* at the root of it all?

First, Philip violated Matilda. Then, when she got with child, his mother had stepped in to conceal the inconvenience— That *was* what Father told her.

He had so revered the de Bohuns, Sir Richard and Lady Margaret, and especially their son.

She remembered Philip as a boy. They were the same age. As a young child he had been unruly. When he was five or so, Lady de Bohun was finding him so difficult to control, she asked Father—at that time the manor clerk, and one of the few men in Meonbridge who could read and write—to take her son in hand whilst Sir Richard was away, fighting the king's wars. In the two years before Philip left Meonbridge to begin his knightly training, he and her father became very close. It was Father's great affection for him that made what happened later so confounding.

For then, when, in the months following the plague, Sir Richard appointed Philip as steward, enabling him to make decisions over Father's head, Father obviously resented it.

Not that he ever said so directly.

But she had seen it, in his narrowed eyes and angry demeanour. Poor Father. After all the efforts he had made to elevate himself from his lowly start in life, and give his family such a prominent position in Meonbridge.

Yet what happened next was far, far worse, for it tipped him over from an angry man into a mad one.

Perhaps she should not have told him of Matilda's pregnancy? Though surely he would have learned of it eventually? But she was shocked by his solution to the problem: Alys Ward was sent for, to get rid of the child, and Father told her, but not her sister, what was happening only moments before the wretched woman arrived. She remembered what he said to her quite clearly.

'Sir Philip is a married man and Lady Isabella is already with child herself. The family can't have a scandal such as this becoming common knowledge. Or have a bastard child born at the same time as the true de Bohun heir. It can't be tolerated.' He glowered then, taking a kerchief from the sleeve of his gown, wiped away the beads of perspiration gathering on his face. 'Anyway,' he said, not looking her in the eye, 'Lady de Bohun has demanded it.'

Margery gasped: *Matilda* was to suffer for Philip's sins? Surely that was unspeakable? Was there not some alternative solution? 'Perhaps Matilda could go away,' she said. 'Have the child in secret.'

He seemed to consider the idea a moment. 'Where would she go?' But then he looked away again. 'No, no, I must do her ladyship's bidding.'

Yet was it not astonishing that her father would make his favourite daughter suffer so? Why had he agreed to it? To save Matilda's reputation? Or was he thinking of his own? Or had Lady de Bohun forced his hand, threatening his position in the household and the Tyler family's standing?

Her father did not elaborate, as Alys knocked at the door, and events then took their course.

It had been about that time, or maybe a little earlier, that Margery had noticed that her father was not only angry but disturbed, seeing iniquity and fornication everywhere in Meonbridge. He ranted daily about the upsurge of immorality amongst the tenants.

It was not just his ranting. At times, he seemed almost to have lost his wits, and reports of his eccentric and tempestuous behaviour had come often to her ears.

Now, she rocked back and forth upon her uncomfortable perch, her eyes closed. When she opened them again, she could see across the room. The slivers of light filtering through the tiny shutter's slats were sun rather than moon. No more chance for sleep, then: she would have to be about the first tasks of her day before too long. She must return soon to the sleeping chamber, so Jan and Ellen had no cause for asking questions.

But she had a few moments yet.

She thought again about what her father said of Lady de Bohun's part in the ridding of Matilda's child. Was she the only one who knew of it? Or did Matilda know it too? Margery had supposed Father intended to tell her sister that it was at her *ladyship's* insistence her child was to be expelled. But, as far as she knew, he never did, for Matilda never mentioned it.

When did she have that conversation with her sister? Shortly after their father vanished... October of that year? She had been alone in her father's house, bewildered by his disappearance from Meonbridge without a word of explanation. Matilda's visit was a surprise, for she had seen little of her sister since she had, unwillingly, been married, three months earlier. Matilda's belly was surprisingly rounded, and she was a little breathless as she came into the hall.

Margery bid her sit. 'You look exhausted, sister.'

'It's this one.' Matilda placed a hand on either side of the bulge and pressed rather vehemently. 'Trying to kick its way out.' She scowled.

Margery had been most puzzled by the pregnancy. After all, she had been there when Alys Ward had come with the draught that initiated Matilda's suffering and, supposedly, the expulsion of her shame. That was in early March.

'When's the child due?' she said, in the manner of simple enquiry, although she could not suppress a frown.

'December or thereabouts.'

She narrowed her eyes. 'December? Yet you married only in July.'

Matilda did not respond at once. 'What are you saying, Margery?' she said at last.

'I suppose I was wondering if Alys's draught did not work after all, and a de Bohun child is still growing in your belly?'

'Ha! How delighted I'd be if that were true.' Matilda scowled again. 'But it isn't. That child was indeed lost. Then my vile husband took the betrothal Father offered him as permission to stake his immediate claim on me. He swived me a mere week after the abortion. *One week*, Margery. Can you believe it?'

'Oh, Matilda, how appalling.' Despite her dislike of her sister, Margery's dismay was truly meant. As she understood it, consummation of a marriage before the ceremony was commonplace, but to insist upon it, in Matilda's delicate state, was surely the action of a brute.

'Yes, Margery, he raped me.' Her sister's eyes were wide.

'Did Father not know he was such a man?'

'Perhaps, in his madness, he no longer cared? I'd soon enough be wed and off his hands.'

'You believe Father is mad?'

'Don't you?'

Of course, she did. She told Matilda about his ravings, and her sister rolled her eyes. 'I've heard that too. All of a sudden, our father is preaching the terrors of the fiery furnace.'

'You shouldn't jest about such matters.'

Matilda pouted. 'I'm not. It's assuredly what drove him to punish me—'

'The ridding of the child, you mean?'

'Punishment for *my* so-called debauchery. For bringing shame upon him, and risking *his* respectability in Meonbridge, and most especially in the eyes of the de Bohuns.' She grimaced. 'He robbed me of a child born out of love. Marrying me off was penance too, for I'm sure he knew my husband's vile nature well enough.'

'How extraordinary he would so ill-use his own daughter.'

Her smile was thin-lipped. 'I'd fallen so very far, from the summit of his love to the deepest pit of his revulsion.' She pressed on her belly once again. 'I imagine the same applied to Philip—'

'What do you mean?'

'The boy he loved so well, who had gained such glory on the battlefield, also fell from perfect grace to the foulness of a common fornicator. In Father's eyes, he too had to be chastised.'

'You mean *Father* was involved in Philip's murder?' Margery had been aghast.

'You must realise that's why he's disappeared?'

Astonishing as it later seemed, at that moment she truly had not suspected their father of implication in Philip's murder. Yet, when Father vanished, most people in Meonbridge undoubtedly already assumed as much.

Everyone except for her.

'You think this desire to chastise Philip made Father have him killed?' she said.

'That and his resentment of Philip's new authority,' said Matilda, 'and his dread of losing his own.'

'All of it drove him mad?'

'The Devil found chinks in Father's armour of morality and power, and goaded him into actions the man we once knew never would have taken.'

In all that conversation Matilda had made no mention of Lady de Bohun, and Margery did not enlighten her with what their father claimed. In Matilda's eyes, *he* was entirely to blame for everything that happened.

But Margery knew differently.

It was true that her father was unsettled by Philip's advancement and his trespass onto his own authority. He was disturbed too by what he saw as an upsurge of depravity amongst the tenants. But, when he discovered the wickedness of the two people he had loved the most, sheer grief overwhelmed him.

Then, when Lady de Bohun, a woman he held in high admiration and respect, demanded that he sacrifice Matilda for the sake of the honour of *her* family, he struggled to reconcile her ultimatum with what his heart told him was right. A struggle that plunged the grief he was already suffering into madness.

That surely had to be the answer?

The *de Bohuns* were to blame for her father's insanity and for everything that followed. Philip struck the first blow, and his mother struck the second.

And, from what her niece had told her back in May, it seemed that Philip's bastard son would be cozening her into his bed just as Philip had Matilda. If he did, the whole cycle of misery and devastation might be about to begin again.

22

He couldn't keep avoiding being alone with Piers. After the incident at the river, Dickon knew full well Piers would be itching to talk to him about it, but he'd only do so in private. He knew too what Piers would say: he was playing a dangerous game.

But he couldn't elude Piers's company for long, when up till now he'd spent at least some of every day either riding with him or practising sword skills on the bailey. Even if Piers said nothing, his grandmother would surely notice and ask if anything was amiss.

After a third day of excuses, he agreed when Piers suggested they take the horses for a canter, and they rode up onto a quiet part of Riverdown and flew across the wide open hills, until the horses needed rest. They stopped close by a copse of trees and dismounted, letting their mounts crop the flower-filled grass, whilst they flopped down in the shade. The tree's canopy was a welcome respite from the sun's heat, and Piers had brought a flask of small ale for them to share.

He offered it to Dickon first. He took a swig and handed it back. His heart was thudding, knowing Piers had brought him up here for a reason.

Yet Piers stayed silent, and Dickon lay back with his arms folded behind his head. It wasn't comfortable, for the ground was already parched, and the grass was prickly against the thin fabric of his shirt. He closed his eyes and waited for Piers to speak.

But Piers was fidgety, fingering a lump of chalk he'd picked up from the ground. Was Grandmama suspicious of his relationship with Libby? *Had* she put Piers up to talking to him about it? Yet he was as sure as he could be she didn't know he'd been alone with Libby at the river. He was certain Piers wouldn't have told her what he'd seen.

At length he opened his eyes and sat up. 'I know you want to say something, Piers, so why don't you spit it out?'

Piers reddened. 'Because it's not my place to say it.' He chewed his lip. 'Yet I want to safeguard you from dishonour.'

Dickon frowned. 'You don't approve of my behaviour—'

He held up his hands. 'It's not for me to approve or disapprove. I just feel I should warn you against indiscretion, for the consequences that might follow.'

'What consequences?'

'Oh, Dick, I don't need to spell them out. You know well enough what it might lead to. And what I know of you makes me believe you wouldn't want that.'

Dickon plucked at the grass between his feet. 'Perhaps it's already too late—'

Piers snorted. 'Don't you know?'

Dickon looked away. It was humiliating, Piers questioning him like this, even if he was doing it for the best of reasons. He didn't have to stay and listen. He tugged at the grass more fiercely. Should he just get up and leave? But at length he nodded. 'It isn't too late.'

'Good.' Piers turned to face him. 'Dick, I know you're fond of Libby...'

'She's very pretty...'

'Yes, but that's not what I mean. You care for her like... like a friend, or perhaps more like a brother? You care what happens to her.'

What happened at the river was hardly the action of a brother. Yet, if he was honest with himself, neither was it the action of a swain, or not an honourable one. He was no different from those squires at Steyning who talked of the serving girls with such contempt.

He thought back to what John had told him about the way his father felt about his mother: he admitted only to caring for her as a sister. Knowing he was going to marry another woman, he seduced Agnes nonetheless, leaving her dishonoured, and so ashamed she ran away. As John had said, she'd been fortunate, to find an employer who took her in, and supported her despite her condition. Doubly fortunate to meet Jack, a man who cared enough for her to raise another man's child as his own.

'It might've turned out much different,' John had said. 'My sister might've died alone, and so might you, or she might've been assaulted, or found only a life of degradation.'

If he and Libby continued on their present path, might that not also be the outcome for her?

'You think I should give her up?' he said at last.

Piers rubbed at his neck. 'I've seen the look in Libby's eyes, Dick. She has hopes you know can never be fulfilled. It's unkind and deceitful to let her imagine she might ever be your wife.'

'You think she does imagine that?'

'I don't pretend to understand the minds of maids, but I suspect she *hopes* for it, even if in her heart she knows it can never be.'

'She's said more than once we're meant to be together—'

'That's it, then. I can't believe she doesn't know it's not possible, but maybe she's hoping somehow to persuade you?' He reddened. 'Aagh, I've just had a thought. Might she be *trying* to get with child? To force your hand?'

Dickon groaned. 'You could be right. I do feel she's been seducing *me*. You know, leading me on. And, because she's so pretty, it's hard not to let myself be tempted.' He stared down at the ground. 'Pitiful, eh? Blaming her.'

'It is certainly most ungallant.' Dickon looked up again and nodded. 'Yet you couldn't marry her, Dick, even if she did get with child. Her ladyship wouldn't permit it. Perhaps Libby doesn't realise that?'

Of course, Piers had hit upon the truth. Libby had been very provocative, teasing him with her eyes and lips, pressing him to meet. *She'd* suggested the river. And he'd agreed, naïvely imagining it safe. But perhaps she'd planned all along to follow him into the water, naked? He did think that might be the way of things. He'd fallen for it because of his own lust, not thinking of the consequences, as Piers would have it.

But, if he got her with child, her chances of winning a decent man would be undone. It could ruin her, and her future happiness. If the worst happened and she chose to do as his mother did, she might have no future at all.

'I've been an idiot,' he said. 'I think you're right, even though it's hateful to speak ill of her. I must stop it at once. Make it clear we can't "be together".'

'Do it soon, Dick. She won't thank you for it now but, in time, she'll understand.'

They rode back to the manor more or less in silence. Dickon kept turning over in his head how foolish and dishonourable he'd been. He should have better recognised Libby's true intentions. Hadn't he led *her* on, allowing her to imagine that what she wanted was not impossible? He must bear some of—or even all—the blame for what had happened. But, at least, Piers's intervention that afternoon, which had seemed untimely and frustrating, had saved them.

Yet, what he feared most now was telling Libby their intimacy could go no further. She'd be quite justified in declaring him false-hearted, but he'd try to explain he was now thinking of her and her future. He doubted she'd accept his explanation. But, maybe, in time, she'd realise it was for the best.

Now, instead of trying to avoid Piers, Dickon was constantly on the alert for Libby. He spent less time with his grandmother simply to avoid crossing paths with her companion. Whenever she did enter the chamber, he couldn't look her in the eye.

Perhaps he should return to Steyning earlier than planned? Despite the problems with Edwin, he did miss the rough and tumble of life there, and he worried about the training he wasn't doing. Also Grandmama was much recovered, and he was sure she could manage without him now.

But he couldn't go away without speaking to Libby. He *had* to face her.

He wasn't looking forward to it at all. But, once he'd told her they

166

could never be together, perhaps he should leave Meonbridge straightaway? Wouldn't that be for the best?

The thought of seeing Edwin de Courtenay again was the part of going back to Steyning that Dickon was least looking forward to. Edwin's anger had calmed down in the weeks before Dickon left to come back here. But he had no way of knowing now if Edwin was eagerly awaiting his return so he could ramp up his bullying once more.

Thinking about Edwin reminded him of what John had told him, about the de Bohuns' connection to Edwin's family, the de Courtenays. When John first told him about Philip's wife, Isabella, he'd not said she was a de Courtenay. It was only in a later conversation he'd mentioned it.

'A *de Courtenay?*' cried Dickon. So, was Edwin from the same family?

'Yes. The daughter of Sir Hugh and Lady Hildegard, from Surrey, where you went first for your page training. You were there only a few months before you moved to Steyning. You weren't very happy there, and you were quite young.'

'Perhaps you're right. Anyway, did my father and Isabella marry after I was born?'

'No, soon after you were conceived.' He frowned. 'Philip was already betrothed to her and they married a few months later. Which is when my sister ran away from Meonbridge.'

Dickon felt faintly nauseous. John's story shed a poor light on his father's honour. Not only had he betrayed Agnes, but his behaviour towards his wife was shameful. He wondered if Edwin somehow knew this story too? Might it explain why he felt so aggrieved against him?

Even if it did, he was no nearer knowing how to deal with Edwin's bullying.

23

Margaret had been delighted at Dickon's cheerful acceptance of the prospect of marrying Angharad Fitzpeyne. Not that she had imagined he would not be pleased. She was certain that he had grown fond of the girl when he was living at Fitzpeyne Castle as a page, albeit she was still very little when he returned to Steyning. But he had often spoken of her, and her younger sister Nesta, with affection. By the time Dickon left Fitzpeyne Castle, Giles also had two male heirs. But it was clear that Dickon liked Angharad best of all the Fitzpeyne children.

When, during their walk together a few weeks ago, she told him of Giles's proposal and her agreement to it, she was so glad when his face lit up.

'I'm sure Angharad will make me a fine wife,' he had said. 'Though of course she's still quite little.' He chuckled.

'Indeed, it is many years before you would marry. Six, perhaps?'

He had nodded but then Libby arrived with the shawl she had sent her for, interrupting the conversation. She had sent Libby away again, but Bayard suddenly let out a shrill whinny, alarming Dickon, and further discussion of betrothal plans was forgotten.

But Dickon continued the conversation himself again a week or so later. They were sitting in her chamber, each occupied with their own thoughts. 'Seven years seems a long time to wait,' he said, without preamble.

Her forehead creased. 'Wait for what?'

'My wedding?'

'Ha!' She laughed. 'I realise it seems a long time in a young person's life. But Angharad is still a child and needs to grow into a woman. Whilst you must complete your training and win your knighthood.'

He pouted. 'But in six years I'll be three years older than my father was when he was knighted.'

She could not resist a beam of pride. 'But that was because he excelled himself at Crécy.' She pursed her lips. 'Yet, I will admit, Dickon, that I did not want him to fight for the king at all.'

'He was very brave.' His eyes shone, as they so often did when he spoke of his father.

'He was scarcely more than a boy. Not so much older than you. But your grandfather was a doughty knight and expected his son to be the same, whether I agreed or no. Naturally, your father too was eager for the fray. Nothing I said could dissuade them both from riding alongside Lord Raoul.'

'And my father was knighted by King Edward himself.'

'He was, because of his prowess on the battlefield. As the mother of such a knight, how could I be anything but proud?'

Dickon then looked glum. 'I'd like you to be proud of me too, Grandmama.'

Margaret laid a hand on her grandson's arm. Given all that happened afterwards, part of her regretted her maternal pride in Philip or, rather, she regretted *his* pride in his own prowess and adulation. It had not served him well. She squeezed Dickon's arm. 'My dear boy, I am very proud of you, just as you are. You do not need to go to war. Indeed, I am thankful there is no prospect of it now, since the king renounced his claim to France.'

Dickon half smiled at her but disappointment seemed to cloud his face. She was sorry if he was frustrated that his life showed no possibility of being as exciting as his father's. But much more was she relieved that, for a few years yet at least, he would be spared the perils of the king's military excesses.

'I imagine,' she continued, 'that you will follow the customary path, and be knighted when you are twenty-one or so. I would expect it to be then that you will marry. Angharad will be fourteen, a good age for a bride of gentle birth. By then, too, the difference in your ages will not seem so great.'

'It's still a very long time away,' he said.

'Yet you have much to do in the intervening years, and to achieve, becoming a knight being the most important.'

He agreed but again seemed distracted by his thoughts. She wondered once more what they were, just the customary ponderings of a fifteen-year-old boy, or something more difficult and worrying? But she would not ask. If he wanted her to know, she had to trust that he would tell her in due course.

A few days later, Dickon came to her with a request. She was strolling in the flower garden when he hurried through the gate towards her. Libby, some distance away, was gathering a posy. Margaret saw him gaze in Libby's direction and hesitate a moment, before he turned and came up to her. He seemed a little breathless.

'Would you mind, Grandmama, if I returned to Steyning earlier than we'd planned?'

She was surprised. 'I thought you were much enjoying your time here?'

'Oh, I am. But I'm missing the life at Steyning too, and I'm worried about the training.'

'I agree with you, dear boy. I am, after all, more or less recovered and, as much as I enjoy your company, I too believe you should return to your training.'

'Should I just go, do you think, or do I need to warn Lord Raoul of my return?'

'Oh, the second. It would be most discourteous to turn up without asking if he agrees to you changing the original arrangement.' She shook her head. 'You must write to him.'

He grimaced then reddened. 'Yes, I suppose I must.'

She suppressed a chuckle. So, had he *still* not mastered his letters? But she did not enquire. Writing was a skill he had to grasp. A letter to Lord Raoul would be excellent practice.

He was on the point of leaving when he saw Libby coming towards them with a sheaf of flowers in her arms. 'I'm glad Libby's keeping you company when you come outside, Grandmama.'

'But it is not necessary. I do not need a nursemaid.' She appreciated his concern, but how humiliating it was to have her grandson speak as if she was an old woman.

He sniggered. 'Libby's not your "nursemaid", Grandmama, but your companion.'

She puckered her lips. 'That is as it may be, but it will not be the case for much longer.'

'What do you mean?' His eyes widened.

His evident alarm reminded her, too late, that she had intended not to tell him of her plans for Libby. Yet, perhaps after all she should? For, when he next returned to Meonbridge, at Christmas, the girl might be gone. She was not so unkind as to send her away without giving them both the opportunity to say goodbye. 'When I took Libby on as my companion in her mother's place, I promised I would give her a home until she was old enough to marry. I would find Libby a suitable husband and ensure that her future was secure.'

'"Suitable husband"?' Dickon's voice was thick. 'But she's still only fourteen, Grandmama. Isn't that too young?'

'I do not believe so. After all, Angharad will be that age when you marry her. Moreover, Libby is quite ready. She will make a man a good wife. She is intelligent and resourceful, and I have trained her well in all the housewifely arts.'

Dickon visibly gulped. She regretted his seeming distress at her news. Even if she had not planned to say it, she did now think it was right to do so. Keeping him in the dark about her intentions would have been heartless.

'And have you found her such a husband?' he said quietly.

'Not yet. I have asked the bailiff if he knows of any likely suitors, and dear Alice is always a useful source of information—'

He gazed again across the flowerbeds towards Libby, who had

paused in her progress to pick a few more flowers. 'I must go,' he said. 'I'm glad you told me, Grandmama.'

That probably was not true. Yet perhaps he did understand it was something he had to know.

Just as it would have been unkind not to tell Dickon about her plans for Libby, it would also be uncharitable not to ensure that Libby knew of *his* plans too.

Of course, Dickon *should* tell her himself, and perhaps he would. Yet she was confident that they had not seen or spoken to other for some weeks. Unless they had been meeting in secret, which she doubted, as she was also certain they had had a falling out. Dickon was avoiding Libby, she was certain. If he was proposing to leave Meonbridge without seeing Libby again, whilst knowing that by the time he returned she might be gone, well, she could not allow the poor girl to be kept so in the dark.

But she would not say it yet.

24

MEONBRIDGE

JULY 1364

Now he was thinking of returning to Steyning sooner than originally planned, Dickon realised with a stab of guilt that he'd not spent as much time with his mother as he should have done—as he'd promised his pa he would. Pa had reminded him often enough, but somehow he always ran out of time or had somewhere else to be. He'd visited her only once in all the weeks he'd been here.

What kind of a son was he, when she'd endured so much for him?

He'd make a point of going to see her more often whilst he was still here. Go there instead of seeing his pa and brother. Maybe even instead of spending an afternoon with Piers.

It was a fine oak door he knocked upon that afternoon. It was new. He smiled to himself: Pa was an expert in his craft, and anyone who stood before his house could see the superiority of his work.

Despite the evident thickness of the door, he heard the sound of childish squeals behind it. He'd warned his mother to expect his visit this afternoon, and she must have told his sisters he was coming. A lump came to his throat, regretting his neglect of them, as well as of their mother. The girls hadn't been at home the last time he came, so he'd not seen them since last Christmas.

It was little Alice who heaved open the door, her chubby face alight with giggles as she peeked out at him through the gap. Lizzie then ran forwards and stood just behind her bigger sister, her thumb tucked into her mouth.

'Hello, little ones,' he said, beaming. 'Are you going to let me come in?'

His mother called out, 'Don't make your brother stand on the doorstep.' She hurried forward to swing the door fully open and gestured to him to enter. 'They're such sillies. They've been so excited about you coming, and now they're too shy to greet you.'

He stepped inside. 'If I'd come more often, I might not seem such a stranger. I'm sorry.'

She shook her head. 'I know you're busy.'

'Not so busy I couldn't—'

She held up her hand. 'Let's sit outside, as the weather is so pleasant.'

Little Alice led the way, skipping along the cross passage to the door that gave out onto the garden. As he followed on behind, he realised Ma didn't even try to call him "milord". To her he was just "Dickon", and his sisters' "brother". How very glad of it he was.

The arbour and turf seat Pa had built years ago still stood part way down the path that continued on towards Ma's potager. A blanket was spread out upon the little grassy area before the arbour and the two girls raced towards it and threw themselves down.

Ma gestured to him to sit beside her, but he flopped down onto the blanket beside his sisters, intending to play with them a little whilst he and Ma were talking.

He'd told her all about his life at Steyning the last time he visited. Now he thought he'd ask her about herself.

Her eyes lit up. 'You might be pleased to hear I'm weaving again.'

'I didn't know you had a loom.'

'My pa bought me one when I was a girl, to encourage me to take up a craft. Did you know your grandma Alice had been a weaver?' He shook his head. 'Anyway, I enjoyed it for a while. But, after what happened, you know, with your father, well, I gave it up.'

Dickon looked away, sure his face had reddened. Ma assumed he knew what had happened with his true father, even though neither she nor Jack had ever told him the full story. He'd not say her brother John had now told him everything. 'You never took it up again?'

'I had you, and married Jack, then we came to Meonbridge, and Jack took on the carpenter's shop. It was difficult to start with, not finding quite enough work nor earning enough money. He needed an apprentice but couldn't afford one. He suggested I help him out, making small items of furniture, chests and boxes. Later on, I learned to use the lathe to make turned bowls and cups.' Her eyes brightened. 'I enjoyed that too, and it worked well for a year or two. But Jack decided he didn't want to make furniture any more, only doors, windows and roof beams.'

'Pa told me how he decided to move into what he called building manufacture.'

'Indeed. He wanted to build houses and repair barns, not bother with the "small stuff", as he called it. And for that he needed skilled journeymen and apprentices. There was no longer any place in his business for me.' She let out a deeper sigh.

'You were sad to give it up?'

'I was.' She looked away. 'But I had three boys to care for, and all this.' She gestured towards the potager, now much larger than he remembered it being years ago. 'Your pa thought it was enough. For a long while so it proved to be.'

She gazed across the garden. Her eyes seemed to be glistening. Was she perhaps thinking of all those years of melancholy, when she struggled to care for either the garden or her children?

But she was composed when she turned back to him. 'You went to begin your knightly training, and the two girls came along, and then...' Her face clouded over briefly. 'Oh, Dickon, so much has happened in these past years.'

'Stephen?' he said simply.

She sighed. 'And, in my grief...' Turning her face towards a yellow rose dangling close by her ear, she pulled it to her nose and sniffed its perfume. She said no more, but put both hands in her lap and gazed at them a while. Then at last she looked up. 'But, at length, the melancholy passed.'

He nodded and, getting up from the blanket, went to sit beside her. 'You were telling me about your loom, Ma. I'd like to hear more about it.'

'Oh, yes, so we were. I'm sorry for allowing my memories to intrude.'

'When did you start weaving again?'

She seemed to shake herself and put the smile back onto her face. 'It was earlier this year. I hadn't realised it, but your grandma Alice had kept my old loom all these years. I suppose she'd always hoped I might take it up again. However, when she dug it out of the barn where it had been kept, it was in a bad way. But she persuaded Jack—dear Jack—to mend and refurbish it, and he set it up for me in the parlour.'

'And you were pleased?'

'If Ma had asked me if I wanted it, I might well have refused. But, when I saw it again, the wood all clean and shiny, my heart lifted.'

'Can I see it?'

'You can.' She got up at once from the turf bench, her eyes alight. She bent down to little Alice. 'I'm taking Dickon to see my loom, sweeting, so you keep a close eye on your sister for a while.' She wagged her finger. 'You're to stay right here. No running off.'

Alice gave a pout then smirked. 'Yes, Ma.'

To Dickon's eyes, the loom looked horribly difficult to understand. Dozens of white threads were fixed to one end of the heavy timber frame, and a number of stout wooden rods lay across them. He couldn't imagine how it might all work.

'Let me show you.' Ma sat down. Several inches of patterned cloth, in green and blue, had already been woven at the top end of the fixed white threads. Now she added more rows of colour, passing the shuttles, the green one and the blue, back and forth, back and forth, using one of the rods to press each line of colour home, and dabbing at the pedals to— well, to do what he didn't know. Ma worked so quickly, watching her made his head spin.

After she'd woven another half inch or so, she stopped and turned to him, her eyes bright. 'What do you think?'

He laughed. 'I never knew a loom was quite so complicated. I can't pretend I understood what you've just shown me. But you're clearly skilled at using it.'

'Not as skilled as I'd like to be. I need a lot more practice. But I'm enjoying it almost as much as when I was a girl. Your grandma's delighted it was worthwhile keeping the loom in her barn all those years.'

Just then, they heard a yell coming from the garden.

'That's Lizzie, complaining. I daresay Alice is being bossy again. We'd better go.'

They hurried back into the garden, and Ma rushed forward to soothe Lizzie's protest and rebuke Alice for her lack of patience. Dickon hung back a while, until his sisters were content.

He and Ma talked a little more, and he was thinking it was time to leave, when she mentioned James Paynter.

'You know James, don't you?'

'I've talked to him once or twice,' he said. 'He seems a decent fellow.'

'And a very good journeyman. But Jack thinks he's ready to move on. He will be so sorry to lose him.'

'James told me a few weeks ago he was thinking of leaving before too long.'

'Jack's already looking for a shop for him. Hopefully somewhere not too far away.'

'Has he found a girl yet?' asked Dickon, though he suspected he'd probably have heard.

'Oh, he told you he was hoping to get married? I wonder if he might have to look outside Meonbridge. There aren't many girls here of marriageable age who are level-headed enough for a man like James Paynter.' She tilted her head. 'Can you think of anyone? Though I don't suppose you know the girls in Meonbridge now?'

He nodded but then he had a sudden thought. 'I *do* know a girl who's looking to get married.' As the words left his mouth, his stomach quailed. How could he betray her, and so soon? Libby was by no means *wanting* to get married, or at any rate, not to anyone else but him.

'Who?'

'Libby Fletcher.'

'Lady Margaret's maid? I didn't know she was ready to wed. Isn't she only just your age?'

'Grandmama promised Libby's mother she'd find her a good husband as soon as she was old enough. She's beginning to look around now.'

Ma frowned. 'Fourteen is very young for a villein girl to wed. Perhaps Lady Margaret wants to get rid of her?'

He reddened. If his grandmother did somehow know about him and Libby, that might well be the truth. 'No, no. My grandmother thinks very well of her. She just wants to do the best for her.'

Ma gasped. 'You're thinking she might make a good match for James? Matilda *Tyler's* daughter?'

He started at the way she rasped out "Tyler". 'Libby's nothing like her mother,' he said. 'Don't you remember, Ma, how brave she was, when she tried to save me from the false friar, and again when that Boune rogue was carrying me off?'

'I do remember. I suppose there's no reason why a daughter should be as wayward as her mother.'

He nodded. From the little he knew of Libby's mother, Libby was nothing like her.

By the time he left his ma, Dickon thought maybe he'd persuaded her that Libby was, at the very least, a possibility for James. Yet, after what he and Libby had been to each other so recently, he wasn't sure he could bear to recommend him to his grandmother as a potential suitor. And he certainly blenched at the thought of Libby's reaction when she found out he was trying to marry her off to another man.

No matter he hadn't even told her yet they had no future together.

25

After she'd taken supper once again surrounded by the members of her household, Lady Margaret remained in lively conversation with Sir Alain Jordan as the servants cleared away, and Libby decided to slip outside a while, away from the noise and bustle.

But Dickon must have seen her move away from her ladyship, for almost at once he was at her side. 'Meet me on the bailey later,' he whispered. 'After you've taken my grandmother upstairs.'

His face was solemn, but her heart was thudding. So, he *was* still speaking to her after all.

It had been a week since their lovely afternoon at the river. She'd been so happy that evening, confident that Dickon's actions had shown his true feelings towards her. But, all next day, he seemed to be avoiding her.

She'd seen him briefly the following morning, when he came to tell Lady Margaret his plans for the day, but he hadn't spoken to her as she ushered him into the chamber. For the rest of the day, she was in an agony of unease, wondering why he'd not acknowledged her when he left. He'd not even glanced her way as he swept out through the door.

As more days passed and still he'd not exchanged so much as a simple greeting with her, let alone a smile, she began to worry something must be wrong.

But here he was, wanting to talk to her after all.

'I'll say I'm coming down for a breath of air,' she said, 'as it's so hot this evening.' She threw him her warmest smile but he didn't return it. He nodded curtly then went back to Piers, waiting at the bailey door, and they disappeared outside.

Lady Margaret was enjoying herself, and didn't seem at all ready to withdraw. Libby, on the other hand, eager to speak to Dickon, willed her ladyship to tire of her conversation. But she looked unlikely to do so soon, and Libby had no choice but to be patient. Stepping over to one of the stone benches beneath the windows, she sat down. She mused on what Dickon might be going to say to her, whilst watching out for Lady Margaret's signal.

By the time the signal came, she was so caught up in recalling once again the delicious pleasure of their river outing, she almost missed it, spotting her ladyship's beckoning hand only out of the corner of her eye. Lady Margaret's head tilted in enquiry, and Libby was relieved she was ready at last to go upstairs.

'I cannot think why I left it so long to resume taking meals with the household,' her ladyship said, when they got back to her chamber. 'It is such a pleasure.'

Libby was pleased too with her decision. Since the accident, she'd spent even more of her days alone with her. Not that Lady Margaret was disagreeable company. She could be witty and amusing, but Libby was after all still a girl and found the constant company of one old lady rather dull.

When her ladyship was settled in her chair, with the psalter she liked to study in the evenings on her lap, Libby stood before her and pressed her hand emphatically against her forehead. 'May I go downstairs again, milady? Just for a little while, to get a breath of air? It is so very hot this evening.'

'It seems cool enough up here to me.' Her ladyship raised an eyebrow. 'But, if you feel some air will help you sleep, do not be gone too long.'

Libby bobbed a curtsey and ran off, hoping Dickon was waiting for her not too far from the bailey door. The door was still wide open, perhaps to let in some air, though the hall was so vast it never became uncomfortably warm, even in the hottest weather. She stepped outside and, standing on the top step, peered across the bailey. It was getting a little gloomy now, but she could still see well enough. There was no sign of Dickon.

She waited, wondering what to do. She didn't want to leave the steps. But where was he? Had it been a trick, and he wasn't going to be here after all? He'd enjoyed playing pranks when he was younger, but she couldn't see why he'd want to do that now.

Moments later she heard a rustling at the bottom of the steps, and a whisper. 'Libby, here.' She ran down at once, and Dickon grabbed her wrist. 'Let's get away from the door, so no one can overhear us.'

Partway down the bailey, a rough wooden bench stood beneath a canopy just outside the kitchen, where Cook often sat a while when he was overheated from his labours. The kitchen was now in darkness, the kitchen workers probably amongst the crowd still in the hall, so no one would see Libby and Dickon sitting there.

She was excited to hear what Dickon had to say. He sat rather stiff-backed on the rickety bench, his hands upon his knees. She put out a hand to cover one of his but, though he didn't pull away, she was sure she felt him flinch.

'Libby...' he began.

She looked into his face and, even in the low light, could see it was serious again. Her heart at once set up a hammering. 'Is something wrong?' she whispered.

'Libby...' he said again. 'I don't know how to say this to you...'

'Say what?'

He did then withdraw his hand, but laid it gently again on top of hers. 'It was such fun the other day... I was looking forward to doing it again...' He hesitated and she heard him swallow. 'But we can't.'

'Why not?' she cried, quite loudly. If anyone was on the bailey, they surely would have heard.

'Shhh, Libby,' he said, his voice alarmed. 'We mustn't draw attention...' He pressed upon her hand. 'You must *know* why not. We both knew where it would lead. Where it *might* have led if Piers hadn't by chance arrived.'

181

How much she wished he hadn't. 'But isn't it what you want?' She was whispering again.

'What I *want* isn't important.' He exhaled. 'You must realise we can never be together. Grandmama's arranging a marriage for me, and plans to do the same for you. We have to accept our destinies—both of us. But, if we carry on the way we are, things might happen—*will* happen—that'll spoil your chances of a decent match—'

'I don't care.' Her voice rose once more.

'Shhh, shhh,' he hissed but, leaning forward, pressed his forehead against hers. 'I'm so sorry,' he said, a catch in his throat, 'truly I am. But what we were doing—what *I* was doing—was dishonouring you, Libby, and I mustn't do that— I don't want to do that.'

She jerked her head away, and wrenched her hand out from under his. 'It's Piers, isn't it?' She rasped out his name. '*He* put you up to this. Or maybe it's even her ladyship who's—'

He put his fingers to her lips. 'No, Libby, my grandmother knows nothing.'

'Piers, then,' she continued, bile rising in her throat. 'He's a prig, always trying to interfere.' Dickon didn't deny it and she jumped up, tears welling in her eyes, so she could no longer see his face. 'I can't believe you'd just go along with what he says instead of following your heart...'

If he was going to answer, she didn't give him time. Her head spinning and tears coursing down her cheeks, she fled, back to the bailey steps. But, at the bottom, she stopped. She could hardly go up to her ladyship as she was. She scrubbed at her wet eyes and cheeks with the sleeve of her kirtle then worried she might have made them red. Looking back through the gloom towards the kitchen, she could still see Dickon, sitting on the bench, his head in his hands. Was he already regretting what he'd said?

She took a few deep breaths, climbed the steps and slipped into the hall. A number of the manor servants were still there, talking and laughing noisily together. But they were at the other end of the hall, and she was able to run unnoticed to the solar staircase.

Upstairs once more, she darted along the passage to the chamber she used to share with her mother. It was used from time to time when her ladyship had guests, but no one occupied it permanently. The bed she and her mother slept in was still there, though the mattress was bare of sheets and pillows. Closing the door quietly, she lay down. She'd not stay long but had to calm herself before she returned to Lady Margaret.

Hours later, lying on her truckle bed alongside her ladyship, again she couldn't sleep. She churned over and over in her head what had happened at the river and what Dickon said this evening. It made no sense. Didn't what they'd shared at the river prove he cared for her? He'd even said, if Piers hadn't arrived, their intimacy might have been fulfilled.

How could he have changed his mind so quickly?

And *what* had changed his mind? Was it Piers? Yet she couldn't believe Dickon would let himself be swayed by Piers's prudishness. Or maybe it *was* her ladyship? Whatever Dickon said, it would be just like her to interfere, like Aunt Margery had said. Maybe she'd found out about them after all and insisted that he throw her off?

But Dickon was lord of Meonbridge. Surely, if he loved her, he could do whatever he wanted?

Wanting to cry out, she pushed her fist against her mouth and closed her teeth over her finger. She flung herself over onto her front and, burying her face in her pillow, she sobbed, her tears soaking into the feathers. It was as well that Lady Margaret was such a heavy sleeper.

As dawn's light pierced the shutter, Libby realised she must have cried herself to sleep for an hour or two at least. But her misery hadn't eased a bit.

Unable to fall asleep again, she pushed back her coverlet and rolled off the truckle. Lady Margaret was still snoring and showed no sign of hearing her leave the chamber. She tiptoed along the passage to her mother's chamber and sat down on the bed, wrapping her arms about herself and rocking back and forth.

She couldn't bear to keep this misery to herself: she had to tell someone. But who? Maud didn't approve of her friendship with Dickon, nor would she understand her grief. What about Aunt Margery? She was hardly sympathetic about Dickon either. She'd told her to forget him and accept Lady Margaret's plan to find her a husband. She'd probably say 'I told you so', but she might also be prepared to listen. Which, right now, was what she needed.

When Libby arrived at the Browghtons' farm the following afternoon, Margery was nowhere to be seen, and neither was anyone else. Knowing her aunt worked most days in the dairy, she ran across the yard, her heart thudding.

The dairy door was open. Glancing around to check there was still no one in the yard, she peeped in. Three women were working side-by-side: Aunt Margery and two much younger ones, not many years older than Libby herself. One of them was making butter in an enormous wooden churn, thumping the plunger up and down, her face red and shiny, wisps of fair hair escaping from the kerchief tied around her head. The other maid was pouring milk into a huge wide pan, presumably to sour it for cheese. Libby had seen the maids in the manor dairy do the same.

Her aunt was cleaning out some wooden tubs, scrubbing at them vigorously. Libby hesitated: should she call out? How else could she attract her attention? But she didn't want to make her cross.

Moments later, Aunt Margery wrung out her cleaning cloths and hung them up to dry. 'Right,' she said to the others, 'I am going out to milk.' She picked up a pail and the milking stool, and stepped towards the door. Libby couldn't believe her good fortune.

Though, when Margery found her hovering outside, she started in surprise then scowled. 'What on earth are you doing here, girl?' she hissed.

Libby flinched. 'I had to see you—'

'*Had* to? We'd not spoken at all till a few months ago. What can be so pressing that you must tell me of it now?'

Libby's eyes pricked. 'I've no one else to talk to. And you *are* my aunt...' She tailed off, seeing the sour expression on Margery's face.

'What of it? What advice can you imagine *I* might have for you?'

'I don't know what to *do*,' she wailed.

Margery flapped a hand at her. 'Be quiet! If you must speak, you will have to come with me. I can't idle around here.' She jiggled the handle of the pail, and strode off across the yard.

Libby hurried after her, and they soon came to a gate that opened on to some wooded pasture where four brown cows were grazing.

Margery slowed her pace as she approached the nearest cow. She set down the stool beside her, murmuring to the animal, keeping her voice low. Stroking her flank a while, she put the pail beneath her udder. She turned to Libby, her face less angry-looking now. 'You will have to come closer than that, girl, and keep your voice down. The last thing I need is a wayward hoof striking me in the head.'

Libby edged forward, and leaned against the trunk of the tree where the cow had been sheltering from the sun. 'Is this close enough?' Margery nodded but Libby chewed her lip. How could she tell her story *quietly*? She hesitated. Maybe coming here wasn't after all a good idea.

'Well?' Aunt Margery said. 'You've come all this way, putting me at risk, so just say whatever it is.'

At length Libby cleared her throat. 'It's Dickon,' she said, her mouth dry. 'We've been so close the past few weeks... But last night he told me we can't meet any more... He... He's thrown me over...' Her eyes filled with tears.

'Ha! What did I tell you?' Her aunt's tone was sour. Bending forward, she pulled at the cow's teats, slowly, steadily, crooning to the animal. 'Yet why are you surprised?'

Libby didn't know what to say.

Aunt Margery glanced over her shoulder. 'Did he lead you on?'

'Yes,' she whispered then felt her face had reddened.

But Margery didn't notice. 'I told you that would happen. He's just like his father. And why wouldn't he be?'

A lump was forming in her throat, and again she couldn't think how to answer. Her aunt too said no more for a while, concentrating on the cow. But at length she eased her back upright again.

She stood up from the low stool, and pointed to it. 'Bring that,' she said to Libby, 'and come with me. There is something you should know.' She seized the pail of milk so violently some of the milk swilled over the rim, splashing white onto the grass. Lurching towards another tree, she stopped beneath its shady branches. As Libby caught her up, her aunt snatched the stool from her and sat down.

Libby dropped onto the grass beside her. When she looked up at her aunt, the scowl upon her face was so disquieting, she was fearful of what she was about to say.

'What I am going to tell you,' said Aunt Margery, 'I doubt you already know. It concerns Philip de Bohun and your mother.' Her lip twitched into a sneer.

Libby gulped. 'My mother?'

'Indeed,' she said, her eyes narrowing. 'He violated her—'

Libby jerked upright. 'Violated?'

'I am not surprised if your mother told you nothing of it. It is scarcely an edifying story.'

Libby swallowed, as her aunt continued. 'That man—that *noble knight*,' she spat out, 'cozened my sister into sin. Mere months after he was wed, and with his wife already swelling with his child.'

Libby's head was buzzing. 'Did he love my mother?'

'Who knows?' Her eyes flared. 'Anyway, what does *that* matter? Whether he did or not, girl, he took gross advantage of her. And *she* got with child too—'

'*Me?*'

'No, of course not. You were born much later.' She scowled again. 'No, girl, when *this* child was conceived, the de Bohuns could scarcely let its embarrassing existence come to light. So, what did they do? Philip cast Matilda aside, whilst his mother insisted she expelled the child from her belly—'

'Expelled?' repeated Libby, unable to grasp what she was hearing.

'Indeed,' her aunt cried, her eyes glittering. 'Your precious *lady*ship ordered the child to be aborted, to save the honour of *her* family. She did not care what happened to Matilda.' She glowered. 'My sister suffered agonies in the ridding of it.'

Libby cried out. Her poor mama. But how could it be true that Lady Margaret was its cause? Surely she'd never do such a wicked thing? Yet her aunt seemed certain of her story.

'Neither did she care about my poor father,' Margery continued, 'a man who had served her with the greatest loyalty and devotion for years, and who held her in the highest esteem.'

Libby shook her head, confused. 'What did she do?'

Margery threw her hands up. 'She forced him... *forced* him, on pain of losing his position and his status...' she was almost shouting now, 'to arrange the murder of that child. Can you imagine what agony that must have caused him? To inflict such pain and suffering upon his own daughter? It drove him mad.'

'Mad?' whispered Libby. She'd forgotten it but now recalled her mama telling her how he'd lost his wits, so devastated had he been at Sir Philip's death. 'Because of Sir Philip?'

'Yes!' cried Margery. 'Because of what *he* had done to Matilda. Plunging her into sin to satisfy his own shameful lusts... My poor papa so lost his wits that he wanted Philip punished—'

Libby swallowed. 'You mean, *he* killed him?' She was sure that wasn't what Mama had said.

'He didn't wield the knife, but he conspired with the rogue who did.' She wrung her hands together. 'My poor papa,' she said again, 'to be so misused that he should come to that. Then to fall into such a deep despair that he took his own life, and left our family with nothing.'

Libby's head was reeling. She couldn't take in the horror of everything Margery was telling her.

'Do you see now, girl?' Aunt Margery snarled, her eyes wild. 'The de Bohuns have caused our family boundless suffering and dishonour: my sister's pregnancy, the cruel ending of it, our father's madness, the loss of everything our family had, and my own humiliation.' She lunged forward and grabbed at Libby's arm. 'And now young de Bohun is attempting to ensnare you. Like father, like son, eh? Don't you see? But it's got to stop!'

Libby flinched at her aunt's touch and pulled away. *Was* Dickon like his father? She couldn't imagine him acting like the Philip Margery had described. Yet hadn't he cast her aside too?

For a while she still couldn't speak, the lump in her throat hard to shift. But eventually she nodded. 'I suppose you must be right.'

Her aunt grunted but said no more. She stayed sitting on the stool, rocking back and forth, kneading her hands together. Libby didn't know what to do. She was so distraught by what Margery had told her, troubled too by the loathing with which she'd said it, she wanted to run away. But her aunt was in such a strange and violent humour, she somehow felt she shouldn't leave her.

They sat in silence for a good while longer. But, at length,

Margery's anger seemed to subside. Her hands stilled and she sat straight-backed again. After yet another while, she heaved herself up from the stool. 'I must get on,' she muttered. But, upright, she was unsteady, and a flailing foot kicked the pail beside her, and it tipped over and the milk gushed out, pooling onto the grass. Libby jumped up too, thinking to save what wasn't lost but most of the milk had already seeped away. She looked up, to sympathise with Margery for the loss.

But her aunt just held out her hands. 'No matter. I shall say it was the cow that kicked the pail over. It happens.' She picked the pail up. 'You had better leave.'

After supper, in her ladyship's chamber, Libby was quiet. The shock, indeed, the horror of what she'd learned earlier in the afternoon was preying upon her mind.

'Is anything the matter, Libby dear?' her ladyship said.

She lifted her face: Lady Margaret's eyes were full of concern.

Her neck grew hot. *Everything* was the matter. But she could hardly speak of any of it to Lady Margaret. 'Thank you, milady, but no.' She hesitated. 'But maybe I have a megrim coming?' In fact, she'd never had a megrim, but remembered her mother complaining of them often. Her ladyship had always been sympathetic to her requests for leave to go for a lie down.

Lady Margaret nodded now. 'Why not rest a while in your old chamber? Close the shutters. The darkness might help to ease the pain.'

Libby rose from her stool and bobbed a curtsey. 'I will, milady, thank you.'

In the other chamber, she lay down on the bare mattress and shut her eyes. Her head was thumping but it wasn't from a megrim; it was from trying to make sense of all the terrible things Margery had told her.

Had Sir Philip really seduced her mama? And got her with child? If that was true, clearly he'd behaved wickedly. But, if Mama was forced to end the pregnancy, it *couldn't* have been Lady Margaret who'd demanded it. Of course, her ladyship held great sway over all her servants and her tenants, but Libby was certain she'd never do anything so wicked as to insist upon the murder of an unborn child.

Yet what of those other dreadful ills Margery had told her of? Her father's madness, conspiring to murder Philip... Could any of that be true?

She sat up and, pressing her fingers against her forehead, she tried to recall what her mama had told her about her grandfather. She'd not thought about it for years and struggled for a while to remember what she'd said. At length, she recalled a conversation when her mother was railing against Libby's own father, Gilbert, and another man, whose name Libby couldn't remember, both henchmen, as Mama put it, of Grandfather Robert.

'It was *they* who murdered poor Philip,' Mama had said, 'and both died for their sins.' Libby couldn't remember if her mama had ever told her how they'd died. 'And your grandfather, Robert,' she'd continued, 'was so devastated by Philip's death, because he'd so loved him from when he was a boy, that he lost his wits.'

Mama hadn't said Grandfather Robert was involved in Philip's death at all. Did she not know he was? Or was Aunt Margery wrong? Or maybe her aunt wasn't telling the truth?

Libby remembered Lady Margaret talking about Robert some months ago, when she told her about her first meeting with her aunt. Her ladyship had said he'd been a fine man, for whom things had gone wrong, though she'd said no more about what they were. But she'd said how cruel it was that Margery had to become a servant because of *his* misdeeds. Her aunt had said that too, when she first met her.

She did then recollect her mama saying much the same. 'Because of his grief,' she'd said, 'he killed himself, your grandpapa. And all his property—our home, everything we owned—was forfeit to the king.'

Libby lay back against the mattress once again. What *was* the truth about it all?

Mama hadn't told her anything about her relationship with Philip, or the baby, or the abortion. Perhaps she'd wanted to protect her daughter from the horror of it all?

Perhaps too she didn't want her to know the truth about her grandfather? She'd grown up believing that Sir Philip and her grandfather were honourable men when, if what Aunt Margery said was true, in their different ways, they had both been wicked. Yet, in Margery's eyes, even if her father was involved in Sir Philip's murder, he bore much less guilt for everything that happened. She laid the entire blame upon the treachery of Sir Philip and Lady Margaret.

What's more, Margery had said that Dickon was just like his father. Was he? Libby whimpered, and tears oozed from her closed eyelids. After all, what she'd said to Margery wasn't true: she'd been so angry with Dickon for casting her aside, she wanted, at that moment, to malign him. But, although he hadn't really led her on, he had certainly made her think he wanted her as much as she wanted him, so wasn't that much the same?

She rolled over and buried her face in the coarse covering of the mattress. Her head was reeling with the confusion of it all. She let her tears ooze a while then sat up again. She had to try to organise her thoughts, else she thought she might go mad.

Next morning, Libby accompanied Lady Margaret to the gardens, so her ladyship could speak to the gardeners about their tasks for the week. The men could manage well enough without her guidance, but the gardens had always been her domain, and she was clearly glad to be fit enough to take their supervision under her control once more.

'Let us go to look at the arbour,' Lady Margaret said to her, after she'd given the gardeners their instructions. 'I should like to see how the roses are faring, now they have been pruned back into shape.'

Libby agreed but couldn't somehow put a smile upon her face. Her mind was still whirling with confusion. How could she tell whether her mother's story or her aunt's was the true one? After her talk yesterday with Margery, she was not at all sure she could trust everything, or even anything, she said.

'Perhaps you would like to gather some flowers?' her ladyship continued. 'We could make some rose water together.' Probing the pocket of her gardening apron, she pulled out her little knife. She tilted her head, but Libby shook her head. She had no enthusiasm for flowers.

Lady Margaret didn't press her and proceeded to cut some roses herself. She chose the reddest blooms, grasping the stout and prickly stems with her gauntleted left hand, whilst Libby stood at her side, holding up the basket.

'I am not sure you have spoken to Dickon of late,' her ladyship said after a while, as if it was a throwaway remark. She snipped off a deep crimson bloom and dropped it into the basket.

Libby stared up at her, unnerved. 'No, my lady, I haven't.'

'You may not know, then, that he is returning to Steyning rather sooner than he had planned?'

Her mouth dropped open and her grip on the basket faltered. 'Sooner?' Her voice was shaky. 'When?'

'Oh, a week or two, I should imagine.'

'A *week?*' She gasped and let the basket tip, spilling the gathered rose blooms out onto the ground. 'No, my lady, no,' she cried and, turning, ran headlong from the arbour.

26

'Piers, will you help me write a letter?' Dickon said, as they walked together down the bailey steps, carrying their practice weapons.

'A letter?' said Piers, a hoot in his voice. 'You've not asked me to help you with anything like that since you were a boy.'

Dickon knew his cheeks had reddened. 'It's embarrassing, but I've still not quite got the hang of it. Reading's becoming easier. But writing...'

'Who do you want to write to?'

'Lord Raoul. To ask if I can return to Steyning earlier than planned.'

Piers snorted. 'You've had enough of us already?'

'No! But Grandmama *is* a lot better. She doesn't need me here any more.'

'Have you told her?'

'She agrees. She's as concerned as me I might be missing out.'

In some ways, he'd prefer to stay in Meonbridge, but his grandmother was surely right when she said the other squires would be learning new skills. He'd already have to work hard to catch up.

'And it means I'll be away from Libby too. I'm sure you think *that's* a good idea.'

'Hmm...' Piers said, with a brief nod. 'Hopefully, her ladyship will soon find her a good fellow to wed, and Libby will discover she can be happy without you.'

'I'd like to think so. Yet I'm certain she'll be stubborn.'

'She's no choice, Dick.'

That was true, of course, but it didn't make it any more likely she'd accept it.

'There's another reason, too,' he continued. 'I enjoy our practice sessions, and our rides together, but I do miss Steyning, not just the training but, you know, the way of life, being with the other squires... or some of them...'

Piers seemed to notice his hesitation. 'Only some of them?'

Dickon flushed again. 'They're mostly fine...'

'But?' Piers led him over to a stone bench on the far side of the bailey and sat down, laying his sword and buckler carefully on the ground. 'Tell me.' He wrinkled his nose. 'I've thought for months—since last Christmas, and even more so since you've been back this time—that something isn't quite right in Steyning. I'm as sure as I can be you're keeping something secret.' He rubbed the back of his head. 'Tell me to mind my own business if you like, but maybe I can help? I was a young squire myself once, remember.'

Dickon nodded. Maybe Piers had even experienced bullying himself? Though he wasn't half a villein, but from an ancient gentry family: he'd have been prepared for knightly life from when he was a baby. Yet, if he told him about Edwin, he might have some advice to give.

Mortified by what he was about to say, he leaned forward, fixing his gaze upon his feet. Then, his voice diffident, he told Piers everything that had happened: the early petty pranking, the incident with Sir Eustace's horse, and the embarrassing episode in the dining hall and his deep humiliation. Not to mention the earl's fury...

'One day, when it seemed Edwin had given up his hounding, he challenged me to a fight.'

'Why?'

He reddened yet again. 'It was my fault. We were all practising at the quintain on horseback and, though Edwin's a good horseman, his lance kept failing to hit the mark. He must have seen me jesting with some of the other squires and thought, rightly, we were saying how useless he was.'

'That wasn't very wise—'

He snorted. 'It was *idiotic*. But I'd got so fed up always being the butt of his pranks, I couldn't help myself. I enjoyed it too because later, in the fight, he came off worse. But it was all a mistake. It wasn't an honourable act. And, of course, I got into trouble with the earl again.'

'Do you know why this Edwin has such a grudge against you?'

'I didn't then, but I think I do now. John's been telling me things I didn't know about my heritage. I've come to think maybe Edwin somehow found out the truth about my parentage, you know, that I'm only half a de Bohun.'

'Why should that matter so much to him?'

'Partly because his aunt, Isabella de Courtenay, was once married to my father, Philip. And my grandfather claimed she'd died bringing me into the world, instead of my true ma, Agnes. John said that Isabella's mother—Edwin's grandmother—was furious that her daughter was implicated in Sir Richard's lie.'

'Ah, yes, I remember that. I was still only a lad at the time of the court case, but I do recall how affronted Lady Hildegard was, and why... When the court learned that Agnes was your mother, her ladyship was made to seem a liar because she'd gone along with Sir Richard's scheme—'

'Even though she didn't truly believe it.'

'Indeed. She was humiliated in public. Reason enough, perhaps, for Edwin to believe the de Bohuns wronged his family?'

Dickon shrugged. 'I think it's more that he found out who I was,' he said, 'you know, not the son of a gentlewoman at all, but the child of a carpenter's wife. Knowing I'm only half a de Bohun—and half a villein—gave him the perfect excuse to belittle me in front of the other squires. It made *him* feel superior. He's a prig, and thinks a lot of himself.'

'Still, that doesn't warrant such crass behaviour.' Piers's eyes narrowed. 'Anyway, the earl supported your case in court, so he knows all about your heritage. Have you told him you think it's why Edwin has been bullying you?'

'How can I? That's blabbing.'

'I'm not sure this Edwin deserves your protection.'

'It's not just that. I don't want to be known as a blab. Even if the other squires want Edwin taking down a peg—and I'm sure they do—blabbing's just not done, is it?'

Piers agreed. 'But, if he starts bullying you again, Dick, you can't let it ride.'

Dickon pulled a wry grin. 'I'm hoping Edwin might have lost interest in me by now. Though I'm worried too that, since I've been here, he'll have lured my friends away again. Like he did in the beginning.'

'He might have. So, you'll have to win them back. Get them on your side. Show them you can stand up to him. They'll respect you for it.' He grinned. 'But don't retaliate again. No more fights.'

'I agree about that.'

'But, in the end, Dick, if you can't make him stop, you will have to tell the earl.'

'I thought you weren't going back till Michaelmas?' said Jack.

'I wasn't, but Grandmama doesn't need me here any more, so we've agreed I should get back to my training.'

Pa finished smoothing off a length of timber, and laid down his plane. 'You don't want to jeopardise your future.'

'That's what she said.' Dickon looked around the workshop. He felt bad he'd never confided much in Pa. But of course he had another reason for coming to the workshop today. 'Might I disturb James for a while, Pa? Do you mind?'

'Let him finish what he's doing. Then, yes, but not for long. We're too busy for him to take the afternoon off.'

Dickon asked James to go for a walk, down to the river, where they could be alone. 'There's something I want to ask you. Don't take it amiss. I'm not trying to interfere, just making a suggestion.'

'I'm intrigued.' James grinned.

They found a quiet spot on the riverbank, beneath a willow trailing its slender branches into the fast-running stream. Dickon loved the rushing sound the water made, as it tumbled over the stony riverbed. It was one of the sounds he missed most when he was away from Meonbridge.

His fingers found a dry twig in the grass beside him and, hurling it into the water, he watched it skim away downstream. He couldn't think how to start this conversation delicately, so at length he launched in. 'I wondered, James, if you'd found yourself a bride.'

James laughed. 'That's an odd question. But, no.'

'Do you know Libby Fletcher?'

James twitched an eyebrow. 'Her ladyship's companion? Isn't she the daughter of that Matilda, who brought the Bounes to Meonbridge?' Dickon bit his lip and nodded. 'Is the daughter as wayward as the mother?'

'Not at all,' said Dickon, then stared down at his feet, sure his cheeks had flushed. It wasn't entirely true: Libby certainly had a temper. 'Matilda made a big mistake, allying herself with the Bounes. I imagine she regretted it. Though my grandmother couldn't let her stay in Meonbridge.'

'She sent her away?' James found a chunky stick and lobbed it overarm into the river. It landed with a splash and bobbed away. 'But wasn't she a slut? Mebbe her daughter's much the same?'

'She's not,' said Dickon, a little too hotly. He turned away, pretending to scrabble in the grass for more sticks. Her recent behaviour might have suggested otherwise. Though at least she was still a virgin. 'I've known Libby nearly all my life. We used to play together as children, up at the manor house. She's saved my life twice, too, you know, when the Bounes tried to kidnap me.'

'Really?' James's eyes were wide. 'I didn't know that.'

Dickon briefly related the two incidents, and James seemed impressed. 'Brave maid. But maybe difficult to control?'

Dickon shrugged. 'My grandmother thinks well of her. She took her on to replace her mother, and vowed that, when Libby reached a suitable age, she'd find her a good husband.' He paused. 'That time's almost come.'

'Ha!' said James, hooting. 'So, you *are* matchmaking. I thought as much.'

He flushed again. 'I just remembered you saying you were looking for a wife. I wondered if you'd considered Libby.'

'She's certainly pretty. But very young. Would she make a good wife, d'you think?'

Dickon nodded, despite the dryness in his mouth. 'Grandmama's been teaching her housewifely skills these past few years. You know, household management, gardening, dairying, that sort of thing.'

James laughed again. 'You sound like you're her brother, trying to entice me with her many gifts.'

'I do feel that, in a way. I'd like to think of her marrying a decent man.'

'But won't her ladyship make sure of that?'

'Obviously, she'll do her best.'

James rubbed his neck. 'And she doesn't have her mother's fickle tendencies?'

Did she? The dryness in his mouth got worse. Down by the river the other week, she'd behaved most inappropriately. But twice in the past she'd put herself in danger to save him, and her forethought more recently had saved his grandmother too.

Surely her behaviour at the river had been an aberration? Her desperation to make him love her made her do it. Wasn't that it? He swallowed to moisten his throat a little.

'She's hard-working, and good company,' he said at length. But he had his fingers crossed behind his back, and felt guilty for it. If she did turn out more like Matilda than he'd claimed, James would think badly of him, and so might Pa.

As the day approached for him to leave, Dickon fretted over how to say goodbye to Libby. When he next returned to Meonbridge, she might be married and maybe even living somewhere else. He hadn't told her, but she must know he was going back to Steyning earlier than planned. Mightn't his grandmother have mentioned it? Since their "break up" they'd hardly seen each other, and hadn't spoken at all. Of course, he'd been avoiding her, which he did regret. But he couldn't put off the moment any longer.

The day before he was due to leave, he went down to the stables to ask the groom to saddle Bayard so he could take him for a last ride out across the downs. He wanted to ride alone, to drink in as much of Meonbridge as he could before leaving it behind. He'd be back again at Christmas but, in the two months he'd been here, he'd realised how much he loved it here and how much he lamented giving up its everyday familiarity.

Not that he didn't want to return to Steyning. But he'd be leaving his heart behind here when he did.

Just as he was thinking about what mattered most to him, Libby appeared at the stable entrance. His heart flipped at the sight of her. She was wearing a kirtle he'd not seen before, made from a rather gauzy fabric in a pale blue. It suited her very well. Her hair was hanging loose for once, thick dark curls that skimmed her shoulders. His groin tensed. How beautiful she looked.

Nonetheless, for a moment, he thought of hiding. Yet she must have seen him come down here, and followed. He stepped forward from the shadow of Bayard's stall. 'Libby?' he said, his throat tight.

'Did you plan to run away without even bidding me goodbye?' she said. Despite her confident-seeming appearance, her voice teetered on the edge of tears.

He felt despicable. 'Of course not. I've been busy—'

'Too busy even to *mention* you were leaving?'

The groom came forward, leading Bayard. Dickon took hold of the horse's reins. He could hardly just mount up and ride away. 'Leave him with me,' he said to the boy. 'You can go.'

The groom touched his forehead and went back inside. Dickon led Bayard from the stable. 'Let's walk across the bailey,' he said to Libby, 'to that seat over there.' He pointed.

'Can't we go down to the river?' She tilted her head a little.

His groin tensed again. 'I don't think so. I can't take Bayard there and, anyway, I'm going for a last canter on the downs.'

A scowl briefly spoiled her pretty face. 'It's not very private here,' she said, when they arrived at the stone bench. 'Can't we at least go into the garden?'

No, not there either. It was their playing at the fountain that had led to their first embrace. 'The orchard, perhaps, then Bayard can graze a while...' Even the orchard wasn't without its memories, but they were memories of childhood, of stealing apples and cherries, not teasing each other's most tender feelings.

They walked in silence across the bailey and entered the great potager, burgeoning with vegetables on every side: onion spikes, great spheres of cabbage and the frothy tops of carrots. Passing the gate that led to the herbier and flower gardens, they continued along the grassy path towards the orchard. Dickon wondered if gardeners might be working on the trees. Lovely as Libby was, he did now rather dread being alone with her. He shouldn't have agreed to it at all. They should have stayed on the bailey, where, as she'd said, it *wasn't* private.

He felt a fool for being trapped so easily again, yet he couldn't now just walk away. Perhaps he owed it to her, anyway: this one last meeting.

In the orchard, he tied Bayard's reins to a low branch of an apple tree, where the grass beneath was still lush enough for cropping, and he sat down beneath another. The tree was heavy with fruit, its branches sweeping low. He reached up to pluck an apple and bit into it. He grimaced as the inside of his mouth puckered.

'Not ripe.' He looked up at Libby, who was standing, hands on hips, in front of him. The sun hung brightly in the sky behind her, throwing her face into shadow. But he was sure she wasn't smiling.

'Were you ever going to tell me?' she said. 'Or just leave here without bothering?' There was a catch in her voice.

He swallowed. She'd come here for a fight. He should have guessed. 'Of course I was going to say goodbye—'

'And "good riddance" too?' Her voice rose.

'No, Libby—'

'You can't fool me, Dickon. You can't *wait* to get away from me.' She was shouting now.

'Sit down, Libby.' He held his hand out to her.

But she ignored it, flailing her arms. 'You're no different from your father. Leading me on—'

He gulped. 'Whatever do you mean? I haven't led you on—'

'Just like *he* did my mother—'

'*Your* mother?' John hadn't told him anything about his father and *Matilda*... 'I know nothing ab—'

'I don't believe you. You're all the same, you de Bohuns. He

199

cozened my mother into his bed, when he was already married and his wife with child. *She* got with child too.'

His mind was racing. 'Are you my sister?'

'No,' she wailed. 'Because your grandmother could hardly let her son's wicked behaviour come out, could she? She insisted the child was got rid of.' Her arms flailed again. 'My poor ma was *used*, first by your father, then by your precious grandmama to cover up what he'd done.'

Now his head was reeling. Accepting his father might have made love to Matilda was one thing, but that his grandmother demanded the murder of an unborn child? He refused to believe that.

'My grandmother wouldn't have done such a wicked thing. You must know that, Libby. It's not something—'

'But she *did*!'

He shook his head. The very idea was an outrage.

But Libby was in full flight. She lunged towards him, jabbing a finger at his chest. 'You're just the same! Leading me on, using me, then throwing me over.' Her hair was whipping from side to side. 'You're a vile, manipulating *de Bohun*, like all the others.' She spat out "de Bohun" like it was a piece of sour apple. 'I'm *glad* you're going. Good riddance to *you*, I say!'

She spun around and ran, her hair flying out behind her, stumbling over the tussocky grass, away from him and out of the orchard. As he watched her go, his heart was thudding.

He didn't get up, or consider running after her, but stayed beneath the apple tree, rubbing his back against the bark.

Trying to recall what John had told him of his father, he was certain he'd not mentioned Matilda. But perhaps John didn't know of any relationship between her and Philip? Though, even if he did, if what Libby said was true, it was so shocking, perhaps he'd not want to tell him of it.

But *was* it true? And how did Libby know of it? Had she always known, or learned of it only recently? Given her wild fury, it must be recent. What's more, if it was true, what did that mean for his father's honour? Lauded as a noble knight, had he in fact dishonoured Libby's mother as well as his own?

All these years, he'd imagined the relationship between his parents had been an amour, illicit but a thing of love. But if his father had also swived Matilda, was his relationship with Agnes truly any less ignoble?

Grief gripped his throat as he realised his father was not after all the gallant man he'd thought he was.

Yet, even more shocking was Libby's accusation that his own grandmother had ordered Matilda to abort her baby. Where could Libby have heard such an unspeakable lie? He had no plausible answer to that. Then a sudden appalling thought occurred to him: might Libby be planning to use the information in some way to shame him? He could barely believe it of her but perhaps she was so angry with him for, as she put it, *abandoning* her, she was willing to wreak some sort of retribution?

At length he stood up from the grass and heaved himself back into Bayard's saddle. They trotted down through the orchard towards a dense patch of woodland that curled around the village and at length led up onto Riverdown. The "last ride" he'd been so looking forward to was spoiled, but he'd do it, nonetheless. A gallop across the down might blow away the horror of what he'd just been told.

But, as they climbed the hill, he couldn't see ahead for tears. He slowed Bayard's pace and leaned back a little in the saddle to bring him to a halt. Leaning forward, he laid his head against the horse's damp, glistening coat, and wrapped his arms about his neck. He let his tears flow freely.

Mere hours ago, everything had seemed right: his grandmother was well again, and he was going to be betrothed to Angharad Fitzpeyne. He might have found a suitable husband for Libby, even though she didn't know it yet, and he was returning to Steyning to resume his knightly training. His only remaining worry had been whether Edwin de Courtenay might be planning to continue with his bullying, though, after his talk with Piers, he'd felt himself more confident to deal with whatever Edwin threw at him.

But now everything was turned upside down. The confidence he'd gained since being back in Meonbridge had crumbled clean away.

27

Philippa Browghton accepted Margery's claim that the cow had kicked over the full pail, causing all the milk to spill onto the ground, leaving a swathe of grass with a whitish sheen. 'It happens,' she said, repeating what Margery had herself said to her niece.

Margery had gone back and forth to milk the other cows, pondering from time to time on how the incident occurred. She knew she had kicked the pail over but why had she been in such a fury?

She had not wanted to listen to her niece's woes about being "thrown over", as she put it, by young de Bohun. Why the girl imagined she of all people might be sympathetic or be able to offer her any advice she failed to understand. Presumably the girl had no one else to talk to: the friendlessness that implied, *that* she understood only too well.

The girl was, obviously, upset by what she had to tell her but, curiously, it had upset *her* too. No, it had *enraged* her. She had already warned the girl, but either she had not been wary enough or the de Bohun boy had simply ridden roughshod over her, like his father had her sister all those years ago. Her anger that it was happening all over again, a de Bohun taking advantage of a Tyler, had seethed and boiled over, and she blurted out the misery that had been tormenting her.

Had she meant to say all that to her niece? It had not been her intention, but at least the girl now understood. If any good might come of it, she must now surely realise that she had to strike the de Bohuns from her life, to forget the young bastard lord and accept the villein husband offered her.

Nonetheless, she could not stop her rancorous thoughts rampaging in her head. Lying awake the best part of every night had become routine. It seemed impossible to cast out the bitterness long enough for more than a few moments' peace. Even when she did find sleep, it was beset by dreams that woke her with a racing heart and her sheet and pillow damp with sweat, yet they faded before she could recall a scrap of the distressing detail. Though she was sure they somehow involved her father, and possibly Lady de Bohun. Was Matilda in there too, or perhaps it was young Libby? It was hard to tell them apart.

She might have hoped the dreams would reveal to her how to gain some sort of retribution. But she was always denied an answer.

She had no idea at all of how to exact a reckoning, nor was she even sure what it was she wanted. Was it to bring harm to Lady de Bohun or her bastard grandson in some way? She surprised herself by finding her heart thudding a little at the notion. Bitter as she felt, injuring either one of them seemed extreme, as well as impossible to achieve.

Her last encounter with Pers Cokewell, on the other hand, might be something she could more easily settle. When she threatened him with a whirlwind, she had no idea what she meant, but it came to her a short while later that a charm or potion might be available to silence Pers's tongue, if only temporarily. The idea seemed appealing, yet she knew nothing of such things.

But there was someone in Meonbridge who did.

She had not seen or spoken to Ursula Kemp for years. She had met her when she first arrived in Meonbridge, ten years ago or so. Ursula's aunt, Sybil, had been a pupil of Cecily Nash, Meonbridge's mostly much-respected healer, and took over from her when she became too old to practise. But when Sybil died, a victim of the plague, Meonbridge was without a healer for five years or more, until Ursula arrived.

The return of a healer to the village was so greatly welcomed, she received a constant stream of customers for her unguents and potions. Margery had visited her just once, on an errand to acquire a remedy for megrim for Mistress Browghton. As a woman with a want of friends, Margery had warmed at once to Ursula, who was of a similar age to her, and was also apparently alone in the world.

Yet gossip had it that Simon Hogge was distrustful of Ursula's skills, and must have influenced Lady de Bohun's opinion, for Margery heard her ladyship had tried to banish Ursula from Meonbridge. But her ladyship was thwarted, for so many Meonbridge folk were eager for the healer's remedies, she merely left the village and made herself a home on the road to Upper Brooking, in the cottage once occupied by her aunt and, before her, Mistress Nash. Nonetheless, despite her loyal customers, Mistress Kemp was essentially an outcast, suspected by some of witchcraft, as was her Aunt Sibyl. Even kindly old Mistress Nash had once been thought a witch. When she was a child, Margery recalled, she and her friends had been afraid of the old woman, and were often insolent and cruel towards her, even though Lady de Bohun apparently admired her skills. Margery grunted: had it not simply always been the lot of single women to be insulted and abused?

Some days later, Margery stood before her mistress, her hands clasped before her. Philippa Browghton's eyebrows knit at her request, but Margery persisted. 'I have not seen my aunt for many years. She has no other relative but me and surely, Mistress, I should visit her in her final hours of need?'

'How have you come to learn of this aunt's impending demise?'

'I met her neighbour whilst on my recent errand for you, Mistress. It was she who told me.'

Mistress Browghton pursed her lips. 'It would be uncharitable to deny you the chance of bringing succour to a dying relative.'

Margery nodded. 'I will go tomorrow afternoon.'

Lies were coming easily to her these days. All her relatives were dead except, she presumed, her sister, Matilda, and, of course, her niece. Margery had no living aunt. Yet her mistress did not know that and, because she took little interest in the personal circumstances of any of her servants, she would not trouble herself to enquire further whether what Margery had said to her was true.

The next afternoon, Margery threw a warm cloak around her shoulders, for September was so far proving damp and cool, with a brisk easterly wind that whipped against her skirts and chilled her sparsely-covered bones. She had a long walk ahead of her.

The track out of Meonbridge towards the tiny hamlet took her past the house that used to be Matilda's, when she was married to Gilbert Fletcher. It looked unoccupied, the garden encircling it grown into an impenetrable tangle of brambles, nettles and ivy, threatening to overwhelm the roof. The property was merging into the wilderness beyond, where the track narrowed further as it plunged through tall vegetation towards the outskirts of the forest.

Before long, she came to the cottage where Ursula Kemp lived alone. It was quite an isolated place, a place where a lone woman might feel vulnerable.

Yet Ursula gave no sign of unease. 'Mistress Tyler, isn't it?' she said brightly, opening the door to Margery's knock.

Margery was astonished. 'You remember me? Yet it is years since we met and that was only once.'

Ursula shrugged. 'I've a good memory for names and faces.' She tapped her chin. 'I seem to recall you came for a remedy for a megrim?'

Margery never laughed but now could not help herself. 'How extraordinary you should remember.'

'I agree, but it's a gift I seem to have. My aunt, Sybil, had it too. Do you remember her?'

'I do. I consulted her, when I was quite young, for a—' She stopped. Friendly as Ursula appeared, she did not think she wanted to share with her the insecurities of her youthful self. 'No matter.'

The healer did not press her to continue. 'What have you come for today, Mistress Tyler?'

During her walk here, Margery had allowed her recollection of her most recent encounter with Pers Cokewell to build once more into indignation. She wanted her outrage to be evident, to encourage Ursula's support, woman to woman. She told her what Pers had said about her appearance and his "old besom" insult. 'He just does not know when to stop. It is a game to him. And I want to shut him up.'

Ursula nodded. 'When I was younger, I was often the object of men's abuse. As a singlewoman, without the crutch of a man to lean upon, I was prey to their insults. It's partly why I chose to hide myself away out here.'

Yet had she not been driven out of Meonbridge by Lady de Bohun? Though the truth of it scarcely mattered. 'Do you not find it lonely out here?' said Margery.

'I'm used to being alone. Indeed, I prefer it. My customers too prefer to seek me out in private, away from their neighbours' eagle eyes, snooping into their affairs.'

That indeed was an advantage.

They quickly developed some sort of amity. Surprising, for Margery had always found friendship difficult. But here was a woman who seemed to feel much the same as she did about the world, and about men.

'If only we could silence all the loudmouths.' The healer's dark eyes twinkled. 'So, tell me, Mistress Tyler, do you want to clam up this Pers's mouth for good?'

'I would *like* to, but...' Margery pushed out her lips.

'Maybe, then, just something to still his tongue a while?' Margery nodded. 'I'm sure you know some plants are poisonous?'

'Yes, but I have no idea what they do, or how deadly they are or otherwise. Nor do I know how to extract their venom.'

'Which is why you've come to me.' Ursula smiled. 'Come, let us sit down.'

She poured some greenish liquid from a decorated ewer into two small cups and gestured Margery to take a stool next to the table. 'This is the juice of apples I find in deserted orchards. It's a little tart but quite refreshing.'

Margery took a sip and tried not to shudder. It certainly was sour, although there was a hint of sweetness too.

'So,' said Ursula, 'let's consider the plants that might serve you well. But, do always bear in mind, Mistress Tyler, whilst small quantities may bring about, let's say, a temporary loss of speech, great care is needed to avoid a far more lasting outcome.'

'I do understand.'

'The berries of the cuckoopint, for example,' continued Ursula, 'might do the trick with Pers, for they cause the throat to swell and the breath to falter. Yet the taste of them is so bitter, it's difficult to disguise.' She swallowed a mouthful of the apple juice. 'With belladonna a person who consumes any part of it would soon find it hard to speak. Hemlock too is yet another plant that can cause the breath to stall but, with that, it's all too easy to staunch the breathing altogether.' She grimaced. 'It'd certainly stop Pers's insults but quite possibly for ever.'

'I do loathe the wretch,' said Margery. 'It would be satisfying to see him robbed of speech, but I do not think I want to watch him die.' She took a sip of juice, noticing how the tartness stung her throat. She tried to imagine the sting becoming fiery, making her gasp for air. Whilst rendering Pers speechless was appealing, choking him to death might be a step too far.

'What of the devil's helmet?' she asked. 'Might that prove suitable?'

'Devil's helmet, ha,' cried Ursula, laughing. 'Wolf's bane. Do you know it's a favourite of witches?'

'Favourite for what?'

'For murdering their foes.' Her eyebrows danced. 'Though, of course, I've never tried it—nor any of the others—as a means of trying to dispose of my gainsayers, even if I've sometimes thought I'd like to. Though I did once use wolf's bane to make a brew for dipping arrow heads, supposedly to kill marauding beasts—'

'Is that how it acquired its name? I didn't know.'

'Deadly to wolves, I understand. Again, the taste of it is unpleasant, so it would need to be disguised. Adding it to something sweet might work. Anyway, with wolf's bane it's the roots where most of the poison lies.'

'What are the effects?'

'Vomiting and tingling more than breathlessness and, at its worst, can bring numbness to the face and hands. And, as with the others, it can cause the heart to stop entirely.'

'Ah,' said Margery and pressed her lips together.

'You don't want to go that far.' She grinned. 'So maybe, say, a single cuckoo berry, ground up into this loudmouth's ale? You'd have the satisfaction of seeing him speechless for a while, but not much worse.'

After a little more conversation, Margery rose from her stool. She was loath to linger, in case another of Ursula's customers came and recognised her. She thanked Ursula for her counsel and for the apple drink, and offered her a coin for her trouble. But she waved it away. 'I'm happy to pass on my knowledge. But if you need my practical help when you're ready, do come back.'

"When you're ready" echoed in Margery's head as she hurried back to the farm. Her visit to the healer had given her food for thought. Yet what Ursula told her about the poisons had not helped as much as she had hoped it would. It seemed all too easy to get it wrong and administer too much. Though, if she was clever, no one would know it was she who had caused Pers's demise. But *she* would know, and unquestionably so would God. Insulted as she was by Pers's crass remarks, an eternity of torture in the fiery pits of Hell was far too high a price to pay for the satisfaction of silencing his tongue.

Maybe poison was not after all the answer?

28

Cook's face was grumpy, and Libby wasn't feeling up to dealing with his moods. She wanted to curl up in a dark corner and hide. For Dickon had gone back to Steyning two weeks ago, and she'd been *vile* to him before he left. What must he think of her now?

She stood at the entrance to the kitchen, loathing the wave of heat enfolding her. How did people work in here all day? No wonder Cook was so bad-tempered. It was early morning, so he was directing the kitchen boys in firing up the ovens, and his assistants were preparing the basic ingredients for dinner. Men and boys were scurrying to and fro, Cook was shouting, and Libby wanted to leave right now.

Yet, despite the deep furrows on Cook's brow, and the ill humour in his eyes, she closed the kitchen door behind her and wove her way across the busy room towards him, her ladyship's instructions for the day's meals in her hand. Lady Margaret used to come and speak to him herself but, since her accident, she'd been writing down her orders and sending Libby to deliver them. Even though her ladyship could once more speak to him herself, it had simply become one of Libby's tasks.

'It is good practice for your reading, dear,' her ladyship had said, though Cook could read as well as she could.

But, today, her heart wasn't in the effort of deciphering Lady Margaret's spidery writing, so she held out the wax tablet to him. He took it, peered at the words, then propped it on top of the saltbox.

'I'll collect it later,' Libby said, and he grunted.

She was glad to get away.

Lady Margaret had gone down to the gardens to speak to Will Greenfinger about the apple harvest. Her ladyship wasn't supposed to go anywhere on her own, but she'd told Libby she needn't accompany her, and Libby was glad to have a little time to herself.

She struck out across the bailey, thinking she'd go to the gardens too. The gardeners rarely worked in the arbour, so it was probably safe to sit there a short while without fear of being found. As she approached the arbour entrance, she could see her ladyship some distance away, talking to Will and the man who looked after the orchards. She slipped into the shade of the tunnel trellis and hurried towards the inner bower.

The fountain was still not working, but a little water remained in the pool, dark and slimy now, with a green crust around the edges, after a summer of neglect. She sat down on the turf seat beneath the roses and the honeysuckle, both still burgeoning with sweet-smelling flowers.

She recalled once more that lovely afternoon when she'd come here with Dickon, and they'd played with the water in the pool then sat together on this seat, holding hands. She'd known then that she loved him. Not with the kind of love she'd borne for him since they were children, but a grown-up love that made her heart pound and a delicious stirring deep inside her.

They'd been happy that day, hadn't they? And, later, down by the river. She'd felt he loved her as much as she did him. Yet, only days later, he'd said they could no longer be alone together.

She'd been so distraught, her misery had led her into a wicked act, telling Aunt Margery what she knew full well wasn't true. It was *she* who'd done the cozening. But what she'd said seemed to prompt her aunt to tell her things about her mother she really wished she hadn't.

At the time, she'd been so upset and angry by Dickon's rejection, she wanted to hurt him. Aunt Margery's bitterness, about her sister and her own life, had fuelled Libby's grief. Yet she hadn't really believed everything Margery had said. Not about Lady Margaret. Nor that Dickon was no different from his father.

Nonetheless, when she thought he was going to back to Steyning without speaking to her again, she convinced herself he intended to run away without even saying goodbye. She contrived the meeting in the orchard just so she could repeat all those horrible things Margery had said, knowing full well they'd cause him anguish. She wanted his heart to ache as much as hers.

Yet she'd always known he wasn't like his father, and now she was sick with anguish that she'd accused him of something he hadn't done.

In fact, she'd already come to the conclusion Aunt Margery wasn't the source of reliable information she'd once thought she was. Why *had* she told her all those dreadful things about her mother? Were they even true? When she was telling her about it all, wasn't there a wildness in her eyes?

Confused about Margery's reasons for telling her those things, and about her own reasons for maligning Dickon, at length she decided it might be best if she avoided her aunt in future. By the time she left the arbour to return to the manor house, it was settled in her mind: she'd never visit the Browghtons' farm again.

It was months since Lady Margaret first hinted it was time to find Libby a husband. She'd start looking, she'd said, as soon as she was on her feet again. Yet, as far as Libby knew, she hadn't. Or, if she had, she hadn't mentioned any likely suitors.

When Libby first heard her ladyship's plan, she'd flown into a panic. She'd claimed she was too young, though of course the real reason was her hope then that she might one day be *Dickon's* bride. But, although in her heart that *was* what she still desired, she'd accepted it would never be: Dickon would marry Angharad Fitzpeyne. Her heart ached at the thought of it, but she understood why Dickon would accept the bride chosen for him by his grandmother, even if she wasn't the one he truly loved. It was his duty and obligation to do so, and the Dickon he was now wouldn't shrink from that.

However, since he'd gone back to Steyning, her own feelings about it all had changed as well.

Dickon had said *neither* of them had a choice but to accept their destiny. He'd spurned her—yet not because he didn't love her, but because he *did*. Knowing they never could be man and wife, he'd chosen to safeguard her, by stopping her from falling into sin. She understood that now.

But it was clear too her ladyship wished the best for her, as she'd promised her mother all those years ago. Yet, Libby was still scared about what that "best" might be. Lady Margaret had said the man she chose wouldn't be too old, but supposing some rich old widower came forward, wanting a young wife? Would her ladyship refuse him? The thought of being forced to bed a thin and wrinkled, or fat and blubbery, toothless ancient—even if he was prosperous—made her stomach queasy.

Weren't there young men too in Meonbridge who might be set to marry?

She put her mind to listing all the Meonbridge men of marriageable age, say between twenty years old and thirty. She knew of three cottars: Harry Mannering, Arthur Ward and Warin Collyere. Arthur, of course, was simple, and Warin was a boor, but Harry was nice looking and sensible though, as a cottar, he had no land and few prospects. A villein was what she wanted, a man of property. John atte Wode was still unmarried and one of the most prosperous of Meonbridge's villeins. But he was the bailiff, and she could hardly imagine marrying him. She giggled at the thought of it.

But what of his younger brother? Was Matthew even ready to take a wife? He was possibly a little young yet—ten years older than her, she thought. A villein man usually didn't marry till he'd the means to support a wife and family: land of his own, or a business. So, marriageable men were often much older than their brides.

She mused upon the possibilities a while, then ran out of ideas. With a heavy heart, she supposed she'd have to wait for her ladyship to suggest someone. And for the first time it occurred to her the "someone" might not even live in Meonbridge. The thought that she might be forced to leave set her heart racing.

But more time passed, and Lady Margaret still didn't speak of prospective husbands.

Maybe she'd forgotten? Libby doubted it, but she'd not ask her. Part of her did want to marry, to have a home of her own to run, and children. But, once it had struck her that marrying might mean leaving Meonbridge, she couldn't stop worrying about what the future held.

She'd thought it before, and the thought now came to her again: making herself indispensable to her ladyship might at least delay her being married? Her best plan was to push the whole idea of husbands to the back of her mind, and work at being the best companion Lady Margaret had ever had.

The harvesting of grain and other crops in Meonbridge had been under way for weeks. The weather had been wet in August, and the start of the grain harvest delayed. Now, half way through September, everyone in Meonbridge was hastening to bring in the final crops of beans and barley.

Libby visited the demesne fields with her ladyship, to watch the tenants cutting, gathering and carrying away.

'When I was much younger,' said Lady Margaret, 'I played my part.' She swept her hand in an arc across the wide field of barley, about half of it now cut and bundled into stooks.

'You, my lady?' Libby suppressed a giggle.

'Sir Richard did not approve, so I did it only when he was away.' Her eyes twinkled.

'But it looks such back-breaking work.'

'Indeed it is. These good people labour from sun up to sun down, every day from Lammas until Michaelmas, to ensure the manor's harvest and all their own are gathered in.'

Libby's eyes widened. 'Did you work all day too, my lady?'

'Usually only for a few hours, but I did work all day just once. Albeit I was still a young woman, I suffered so dreadfully from aches and pains after that interminable day, I did not repeat it. Yet I was glad to have experienced, if only for a day, the effort that the men and women—and children—of Meonbridge make, year in year out, to keep our food stores filled.' She lifted her chin. 'The task is huge, Libby, and

I do so admire them for their labours. Which is why, on Michaelmas Day, I try to provide the most generous feast I can.'

Michaelmas was two weeks away, but the manor servants were already making preparations for the celebration that marked harvest's final day.

'Cook's very busy,' Libby said.

'Indeed. Sir Richard would often say the harvest feast I provided was too lavish. But I have learned over the years that treating my tenants—or, as I think of them, my friends and neighbours—with generosity is the right thing to do.'

Libby nodded. Aunt Margery *was* wrong about Lady Margaret.

The barley field was some distance from the centre of the village so, when the church bell of Saint Peter's rang for Sext, the sound of it drifted only faintly on the still morning air.

'Oh, look,' said Lady Margaret, as the labourers in the field stood up and eased their backs, threw down their scythes or tucked their sickles into their belts. 'Is it time for dinner?'

'Yes, milady. Did you not hear the bell?'

Her ladyship shook her head. 'I suppose it is quite far from here. But they all heard it, did they not?' Smiling, she pointed to the men and women already making their way towards the edge of the field where trestles had been laid out under a stand of trees.

As always when tenants were harvesting her ladyship's crops, she provided them with a dinner of bread and cheese and ale. The manor servants had set it up whilst she and Libby had been watching the barley being cut and gathered.

'Let us pour the ale for our thirsty workers.' Lady Margaret strode off towards the trestles. Libby had to hurry to keep up: her ladyship had certainly regained her vigour.

They stood behind the tables and, as the workers shuffled forward to take a hunk of bread and portion of cheese, they handed each one a cup of ale. Libby noticed how the men and women served by Lady Margaret tipped their hats or curtseyed.

'Very kind of ye, milady,' said one, taking the proffered cup.

'Thank ye, yer ladyship, I'm in sore need of this,' said another, downing the drink in a single gulp then holding out the beaker for a refill with a broad grin on his face.

Her ladyship laughed lightly, and chatted merrily with the man.

But, where Libby stood, further along the table, the folk coming forward were not quite so well mannered. They seized the cups of ale from her, and snatched up their share of food, lurching away to rest and eat. She felt sorry for them: the harvest had been long drawn out, hindered by poor weather. How eager they must all be for it to be finished.

'Mistress Libby?'

Deep in thought, she jumped, startled by the greeting. Lifting her eyes, she found those of James Paynter, Master Sawyer's journeyman, smiling into hers.

'Mistress Libby,' he said again. 'You playing the tapster?'

She giggled. 'Just helping her ladyship.'

Jack Sawyer came forward too, along with Dickon's brother, Geoffrey, and a younger boy she supposed was Jack's apprentice. Dickon's mother, Agnes, was with them too. All their faces were red and sweaty.

James wiped his kerchief over his brow and cheeks, then across the back of his neck. 'Hot work,' he said, and grinned again as Libby held out a cup of ale. 'Thank you kindly, Mistress Fletcher.' She giggled again at his formality.

'You're welcome, Master Paynter,' she said, feeling she wanted to curtsey.

Beneath the sweat and ruddy glow was a good-looking man. Not handsome exactly, but his nose was fine, his mouth generous, and she'd already seen good humour in his eyes. Why had *he* not been on her list? Because she'd barely spoken to him before, though Dickon had mentioned him, when he told her about his visits to see Jack—"my Pa", as he still called him—and he'd said what a skilled carpenter Master Paynter was, and what a boon to Jack.

When Mistress Sawyer stepped forward, she greeted Libby briefly then sighed. 'I don't know why I agreed to help.' She pressed her hand against her back, flinching. 'I've rarely done so before.'

Jack took two cups from Libby and handed one to his wife. 'Drink this down, love. You'll feel better, and I'm sure Libby will offer you another.' He winked at Libby. 'Anyway, you know well enough the reason: the harvest is delayed, and it's the duty of every man, woman and child to help bring it in.'

Agnes grinned at Libby. 'Yes, yes, I do know that, husband. I just find it so exhausting.'

'It seems everyone does,' said Libby, 'from what I've seen and heard. It certainly looks hard work.'

She'd not spoken to Mistress Sawyer for a long time. She'd have liked to ask her if she'd heard from Dickon, but wasn't sure she should. At length she left it. Instead she gave James Paynter a warm smile as he took his food, and his bright eyes returned her gesture as he moved away with the Sawyers to find a place to sit and eat.

When Libby returned to the hall, having delivered Lady Margaret's final instructions for the day to Cook, she found her mistress talking to the bailiff. Today was Michaelmas, the last day of the harvest, and that evening the whole village would come together here at the manor house, for the great feast her ladyship had planned.

'I am much relieved,' she was saying to John, 'that, despite the long delay in August, the harvest will all have been brought home.' She took a bite from one of the sweetmeats Libby had brought her earlier and savoured it a moment. 'All of it, you say? No field or crop still left?'

'None, my lady. By this evening, the last field will have been cleared. Everyone in Meonbridge has come together to help, even those who usually don't take part, like Jack Sawyer and his family.'

'Yes, we have seen the Sawyers working in the fields. How gratifying that folk feel they must support their neighbours, even when they have so many other obligations.'

'The food stores are for everyone, my lady, so it's fair enough withal.' He let out a bark of laughter. 'Though my sister rather wished Jack hadn't persuaded her to join in. She found it extremely wearisome.'

'I am not surprised at it. I do know how very tiring a task harvesting can be. Especially when you are not accustomed to that form of labour. As Agnes clearly is not.'

216

'Indeed, my lady,' the bailiff said. 'But at least she made her contribution.'

Her ladyship stood up as Libby approached. 'Ah, Libby, is Cook content with the arrangements?'

'I'm not sure "content" is the right word, milady.' She giggled. 'But I think everything's in hand. I saw a dozen or more geese plucked and ready.'

'Excellent,' cried her ladyship, clapping her hands. 'So, Master Bailiff, where is the last harvest taking place this year? As always, I shall go to watch the last stages and the cutting of the final sheaf.'

'I'll escort you there myself. Libby too?' He turned to her, and she nodded.

It wouldn't be the first time she'd watched the final harvesting. She'd gone years ago, when she was still a child, and her mother was her ladyship's companion. But both she and Mama had found it so dull, they didn't go again. So, when, in recent years, Lady Margaret had asked her if she'd like to accompany her, she always pretended to be too busy. But she'd enjoyed going with her ladyship the other day, and the last day of harvest was special, so why not go again?

The afternoon was still bright when John led them past acre after acre of spiky stubble towards the wide field where a dozen or more teams of reapers were competing to be the team that *wasn't* the last to finish their allotted rows.

To Libby's eyes, it looked a good-natured contest. No women seemed to be involved: the teams were made up entirely of young men, all cutting and gathering and binding as fast as they could, to ensure they didn't lose the race.

Lady Margaret's eyes were alight with the excitement of it. 'It is wonderful that they all still have the energy to work so quickly.' She pointed to the nearest team, whose reapers were shearing rapidly through one stand of barley before sprinting to the next one, not stopping to take a rest, whilst their fellows raked up the fallen sheaves and tied them upright in loose stooks to await the carters who'd come later to carry them away.

John chuckled. 'It's because it's the last day, my lady. Somehow it restores your strength, knowing this is the end of it for another year.'

'I can understand that. Indeed, they seem almost to be enjoying it.'

'Oh, they are. Vying with each other makes it a game.'

As the sun tracked down behind the distant hills, and the brightness of the afternoon waned, team after team reached the end of their rows, and sent up a cheer, brandishing their sickles in the air. At length the last team finished too, to more cheers and hooting from their neighbours. But, in a far corner of the field, a cluster of stalks remained that hadn't yet been cut.

'Don't they cut those last ones?' Libby said to John, pointing.

He chuckled. 'They do, but differently. The reapers say the last sheaf contains the spirit of the grain—the corn goddess some folk call her. With the rest of the crop all cut, her spirit's now confined to those few stalks. But, as you'll see, the reapers don't want to be *seen* to cut the sheaf, in case the goddess is angry with them for trying to destroy her sanctuary. So, they hide from her whose sickle actually makes the cut.'

'How?'

'Just watch.'

The reapers were now standing in a line some distance from the sheaf, throwing their sickles at it. The throwing continued for some time, as the afternoon faded into dusk.

'Will one of them ever cut it?' Libby asked.

'Oh, yes, it'll fall, but no one will know whose sickle did it.'

At length the stalks toppled, and a shout went up from the reapers. Then one of them ran forward and, gently gathering the cut stalks together, he wrapped them in a kerchief.

'What's he going to do with them?'

'Well, the corn spirit must be preserved,' said John, 'to ensure we get another good crop next year. The last sheaf is woven into an image of the spirit, where she lives out the winter. Then, on Plough Monday, next January, the image will be ploughed back into the soil, returning the spirit to her true home.'

Libby nodded, liking the idea. She'd not heard tell of it before.

'You will see the image later, Libby,' Lady Margaret added. 'It will be brought to the harvest feast.'

She remembered she'd seen one at feasts before, a sort of doll of woven straw and decorated with ribbons, and given a special place on the high table. But she'd never thought to ask what it was or why it was there.

Back at the manor house, they found all the servants busy, scurrying about setting up the extra trestles and benches needed to seat everybody in the village, and decorating the great hall with greenery. Her ladyship at once threw herself too into the final preparations, and bid Libby do the same.

It wasn't long before she heard the chatter and cheerful laughter of revellers approaching. 'They're coming,' she said to Lady Margaret, who clapped her hands, calling her servants to attention.

'To your places, everyone,' she cried. 'The harvest celebration is afoot.'

Libby had never enjoyed a harvest feast so much. Though she'd done nothing to contribute to the harvest, nonetheless, this year, she felt somehow a part of it all, in a way she'd never done before. Yet, although the evening was merry, with the music and the singing and a great deal of laughter, she found herself saddened too, thinking her Meonbridge life might soon be coming to an end.

But she shook her head to throw off the gloomy thoughts. Now was not the time for sorrow.

At that very moment, she realised the musicians were playing a different sort of tune and men and women were getting up from their seats, with whoops of joy, and moving to the wide empty space at the far end of the hall. At first, in harmony with the music, the couples swayed and skipped together. Then, as the fiddler struck up an even livelier melody, the dancers too became more energetic, twisting and twirling and stamping their feet.

Her shoulders drooped a little. How she'd love to join in too. But she'd never danced. And, of course, she'd nobody to dance with. She gazed around the hall, at men holding out their hands to girls and women, the women shyly accepting and being led towards the dance.

She gazed down at her lap. What fun it would be. She let out a sigh, and flicked with her fingertips at a few brimming tears.

'Mistress Libby?' She lifted her face again: James Paynter stood before her, his smile in his eyes and on his lips. 'Would you care to dance?'

She swallowed a gulp of surprise and turned to Lady Margaret. 'May I?'

'You may.' Her ladyship's eyes were bright.

Libby stood up and let James take her hand and lead her down the hall towards the circle.

'Right then,' cried the singer, as they slipped between two other couples and all clasped hands. 'Are we ready?' The dancers cried with one voice, 'Ready.'

Libby giggled. '*I'm* not ready,' she whispered to James. 'I don't know what to do.'

'It's very easy, I promise you. Just do what I do.'

With only the music of the singer's song, the dance began. Everyone in the circle stamped one foot and the other, then stepped to the left and brought the right foot across, tapping their two feet together.

'I *can* do this,' cried Libby, and James's eyes twinkled.

Then they did the same thing again, and again, circling leftwards around the singer. After a while, at the singer's signal, many of the dancers joined in the song, their voices loud and joyful too.

Unable to join in, Libby turned to James, but he wasn't singing either. Yet his eyes were alight. 'I dunno the words,' he said, 'but no matter, eh?'

Indeed, it didn't matter. She was happy simply to be taking part.

When the dance ended, James held fast to her hand as he led her back to her ladyship. As he approached the table, he bowed his head to Lady Margaret. 'May I call upon Libby tomorrow, milady?'

Lady Margaret's eyes opened wide. 'Indeed you may, Master Paynter. Come after dinner.'

He bowed again.

Libby's fingers flew to her lips as they parted in surprise. She'd enjoyed dancing with him, but hadn't expected this. She wasn't at all sure what she felt. Excited certainly a man such as James Paynter might wish to call upon her. But he was much older, surely more than twice her age? Yet he was attractive, and seemed a kind-hearted man. And hadn't Dickon said he was a skilful carpenter, so he had good prospects too.

Her heart at once turned over: Dickon! All evening long, she'd barely given him a thought.

Next day, Libby picked at her dinner, and Lady Margaret noticed. She raised her eyebrows at her. Libby put down her napkin, and her ladyship leaned forward to touch her arm.

'I think that perhaps you are a little excited?' she said, and Libby nodded.

'Be patient,' continued Lady Margaret. 'Dinner will be over soon. I suggest you await Master Paynter's arrival by the door. I shall give instructions that he is to be admitted. You may sit together on the bench close to the hearth.'

'Thank you, milady.' Libby plucked at a morsel of capon, and nibbled at it.

Yet it seemed ages before her ladyship stood up to signal the meal's end. 'You may go to the door to wait,' she said, as Libby started to clear the debris from the table as she usually did. 'For today, you can leave that to the servants.'

She curtseyed and ran over to the great door that led out onto the bailey. It seemed yet more ages before she heard a knock upon the door and a servant went forward to answer it. James stepped across the high threshold, took off his hood and gave his name, and the servant indicated Libby. She was standing straight-backed with her hands clasped before her, hoping her demeanour appeared both responsible and demure. She bowed her head a little as he approached, and he did the same.

'Mistress Libby,' he said. 'I'm glad to see you again.'

'And I you. Her ladyship says we may sit together over there.' She led the way towards the bench.

She felt strange now, being alone with him. It had never seemed strange with Dickon, perhaps because they'd known each other for so long. They never ran out of things to say. But what did she have to say to Master Paynter? Did she have to show an interest in his work? Or perhaps ask about his family? Presumably he would ask about hers? She felt suddenly a little sick: what, if anything, did he already know about all that?

What she was sure of was that she needed to be truthful. She sensed James Paynter was an honest, plain-speaking man and telling him untruths wouldn't serve her well.

As it turned out, James spoke enough for both of them, and he asked no awkward questions. She learned a little about his work with Master Sawyer, and heard too that he was planning to move away from Meonbridge, to set up his own carpentry shop.

She couldn't help but swallow at that news, and he noticed. 'You'd not want to leave here?'

She looked down at her hands, clasped tight together in her lap. 'I'd thought not.' Her voice was a whisper. 'But if I had to...'

He leaned forward a little and took her hand. 'Libby, I must move away. I'm of an age to be a master, like Jack, and I can't do that here. Jack's looking for a shop for me to take over, hopefully not too far away.'

She nodded. If James *was* the man she thought he was, and he was interested in making her his wife, she'd be reckless not to accept him, even if it did mean leaving Meonbridge. Her life would be prosperous enough—much like Agnes Sawyer's, she supposed, and that should surely not be spurned. Not that he'd asked her yet.

'I've brought you this,' she heard him say, and looked up again. In the palm of his hand lay something a little like the corn spirit doll brought to the harvest celebration, although this weaving was much smaller.

She picked it up with her fingertips. 'What is it?' Yet she knew exactly what it was, and her cheeks grew hot. It was woven from several barley straws and shaped into a heart. She'd heard about such tokens, and understood their meaning. 'Did you make it?'

'I did.' A gleam twinkled in his eye. 'Will you accept it?'

She chewed her lip. Was this all happening too quickly? Despite the pleasure she found in James's company, and her joy at being courted by such a man, she was still afraid. Though of what, she wasn't sure.

'Do you not want it?' he said.

She looked up again: his eyes were hooded. 'Oh no, it's not that...' she stumbled, not knowing quite what to say.

'If you take it, I'll not press you for an answer.' He held her gaze a moment. 'But perhaps I can call on you again in, say, two weeks?'

Two weeks? Was that long enough? Wasn't Master Paynter the right sort of man for her? He might be older, but was hardly *old*. She suspected too that Lady Margaret would heartily approve. What, really, was there to think about?

'Yes,' she said, 'that will be fine.' She folded her fingers over the token. 'Thank you for this: it's charming. I'll find a ribbon for it.' She stood up, and James stood too.

'Till next time then.' He bowed.

She dropped a slight curtsey. 'Till next time.'

Upstairs again, she found a long blue ribbon in the small box of treasures that had once been her mother's, and tied it to the token. She placed it in the box, wrapped in a soft kerchief. She had just two weeks to decide whether, when James Paynter came to call again, she'd be wearing the ribbon and his token next to her heart.

29

When Dickon first arrived back in Steyning, he couldn't shift his last conversation with Libby from his head. Shocked by the fierceness of her misery and anger, he was horrified too by what she'd told him. He was grief-stricken to think his father was somehow less than the noble knight he'd thought he was, and was even more aghast at the idea of his own grandmother being responsible for the murder of a baby. That was a dreadful calumny, even if the charge against his father had the ring of truth.

Yet, as the days passed and he settled once more back into his Steyning life, he thought of Libby less and less. There was so much to do, so much catching up, that, only a week after his return, he realised she'd slipped his mind for several days. Obviously, he'd have to deal with it again when he returned to Meonbridge for Christmas but, for now, he pushed the memory of their unhappy meeting to the back of his mind and devoted his attentions to his training.

. . .

Two weeks after his return, Dickon sensed a growing excitement amongst the squires, with a great deal of chatter between them at the dinner table, and more time spent by many of them with the hounds. He'd been very disheartened to discover that, in his absence, Edwin seemed to have won back the favour of some of the other squires, who were once more ignoring him. Though he was relieved that Nick Fenecote was not one of them.

Nick had greeted him warmly the day he arrived back at the castle. 'Good to see you again, Dick,' he'd said, then grimaced. 'I'm afraid de Courtenay's been up to his old tricks again. Wheedling the others back onto his side.' He shook his head. 'I don't understand why they are so gullible.'

'I'd thought after the fight he might not be so popular,' said Dickon.

'That was true at first. But, after you left, he somehow regained the upper hand. I don't know what it is about him. Even Alan's chums with him again.' He rolled his eyes. 'But not me, Dick, I promise. Not me.'

'Thanks, Nick. I'm glad.' He held out his hand and Nick grasped it. 'Anyway,' Dickon continued, 'is something going on that I don't know about?'

Nick's brow creased a moment. 'Oh, you mean the boar hunt? I suppose you don't know about it.'

'*Boar* hunt? Isn't that dangerous?'

Since he'd been at Steyning, all the squires had had a chance to hunt, even when they were quite young. They were learning about the process and ritual of the hunt, and practising skills that, as future knights, they might one day use in battle. The hunting master drilled them in the importance of following instructions and not stepping out of line in any way, putting everyone else at risk.

But he'd only ever been involved in hunting small deer, or sometimes foxes, and hunting them wasn't as perilous as hunting boar. Boars were powerful and fierce, and aggressive if cornered or protecting young. They could easily kill a dog and at the very least badly injure a man. What's more, harrying the boar from cover was carried out on foot, and the squires who did it needed to keep their wits about them. Which is why Lord Raoul didn't let them join a boar hunt till they were fourteen.

'Well, yes,' said Nick. 'We've been practising beating and dog handling skills for the past few weeks.'

'But I haven't, so I won't know what to do.' A knot was forming in Dickon's stomach.

Nick scoffed. 'Oh, it's not that hard, Dick. You'll soon pick it up.'

But Dickon thought he'd best ask one of the masters for some guidance, before pitching headlong into a forest full of rowdy, ferocious pigs.

By the time the day of the boar hunt dawned, Dickon was as well versed as he could be in how to track down the boar—males only—in the dense undergrowth, follow the dogs used to sniff them out, then drive the prey towards the huntsmen and their spears. He already knew how important it was for beaters to work as part of the team, to chase the animals forward in a steady line, to avoid any accidents or losses. He was excited by the prospect of the day, if also a little scared.

Though not, it seemed, quite as excited as the hounds.

At the kennels, where everyone was gathering, the handlers were struggling to control the yapping dogs, jumping and straining at their leashes, eager to be on their way. They knew what was afoot. Dickon noticed some of the dogs were different from the ones used to hunt down deer: bigger, more muscled and robust. He supposed their job was to harass the boar, maybe even to seize and hold it until the huntsmen arrived.

It wasn't long before Sir Eustace, who was leading the hunt today, rode across the bailey to the kennels, not on Morel but a smaller horse, more used, perhaps, to negotiating the dense tree cover of the forest.

The master in charge of the squires reminded them all of the rules of the hunt. 'Enjoy it,' he said finally, 'but endanger neither yourselves nor others. No risk-taking, you understand?'

A low 'Aye' rumbled around the company, then the chief huntsman blew his horn. The hunt was on.

With the dogs yelping and still straining, and the squires chatting merrily, Sir Eustace led the way towards the forest, a mile or so beyond the castle's outer walls.

At the outskirts of the wood, the master gathered the squires and dog handlers together. 'Right,' he said, 'our master huntsman has already confirmed there's a goodly number of boar here today, so it's your job now to find them. You know the drill. Look for the signs: muddy wallowing hollows in the ground, areas of uprooted soil where the beasts have grubbed for food. And, of course, footprints: you know the shape you're looking for, with the dewclaws at the back. When we're confident we've found some, we free the dogs to scent them out. You follow on, fast but never recklessly, beating the animals forward towards the huntsmen.'

A mixture of exhilaration and anxiety set Dickon's heart thumping. He knew what he had to do. But he'd not done it before and prayed he'd make no mistakes.

At first, it all went well. They found a number of fresh wallows, and trees nearby with muddy trunks, where the boars had scraped their mucky bodies clean. The ground was cratered with so many footprints, it seemed there might be several boar drifts in the forest. At length the hounds were set loose to pick up the scent. Quiet now, but with their tails still wagging, they scurried back and forth, sniffing at the tree bark and snuffling around the undergrowth. It wasn't long before they were off, their handlers and the beaters chasing after them.

Dickon was at the back of the line, trying to keep up. Not that he was unfit, just out of practice. But, as he ran forward, out of the corner of his eye he saw a smallish animal dart across his path and dive into the undergrowth. It wasn't a boar. What he saw was the right size and colour for a hound. He wasn't supposed to leave the line of beaters but, if a dog was lost, surely he should try to recover it?

Just as he turned to follow where he thought the hound had gone, he heard a strangled yelp and then a howl. The forest vegetation was dense and tangled: low shrubs, ferns, coarse grasses, the dying leaves of summer flowers, were all entwined with trailing ivy and spiky brambles, making running through it difficult. But the dog wasn't far away. When Dickon spotted it, it was clear it too had found the undergrowth a problem, for one of its hind legs was caught in the trailing stems. It must have tried to wriggle free, and the leg was now in the tight grasp of a vicious bramble.

Dickon knelt by the whimpering animal. It was one of the younger, inexperienced hounds. Its handler would get into trouble for not keeping a closer eye on it. He spoke softly to the dog, stroking its ears, then took out his knife and began cutting through the whippy, thorny stem. It was tricky, ensuring he didn't nick the leg but, before long, it was free. Yet, when the dog scrambled to its feet, it yelped again and whimpered, and wouldn't put its paw down onto the ground. It must be injured even though it wasn't bleeding. A sprain, perhaps? He groaned. He'd have to miss the hunt now and carry the dog back to the castle. But he had no choice: the other dogs and beaters would be far ahead by now, anyway, so he'd not know which way to go.

Sheathing his knife again, Dickon bent down to pick up the dog. But he hadn't yet taken hold of it when he heard a rustle and, looking up, saw a clutch of stripy, ginger-coloured piglets rushing in his direction. He stood up in alarm: their mother would surely be close by. As he thought it, the rustle became a crash and the sow burst through the undergrowth towards him. At once, he yelled at her and flailed his arms, and the dog began barking wildly. The piglets squealed and swerved aside, and the sow came to a halt. She grunted at him, lowered her head. But he shouted and flapped at her again and, after a few moments, she turned and trotted away, the piglets at her side.

His chest heaving, Dickon sunk onto his haunches, his head in his hands. Tears welled and his whole body trembled. Where had that sow come from? Hadn't they left all the sows far behind, driving only males forward?

'That was a close call, dog,' he said. 'We might've been in serious trouble.'

Yet, as soon as he'd said it, he heard rustling again and spun around in alarm. But what he saw wasn't the sow or her piglets, but Edwin. And he was strolling right across the path the sow had taken.

Dickon wondered for a moment why Edwin wasn't with the other beaters. But he'd no time to think, for he could see that Edwin hadn't spotted the sow, hidden by the vegetation as she was. If he startled her, she might attack him. He could be badly hurt.

Allowing himself no more time to think it through, Dickon ran after the sow, yelling to Edwin and flailing his arms again. Out of the corner of his eye, he saw someone else was coming into view: it was the master, calling his name. Perhaps he'd wondered where he was? Beaters were meant to stay together, yet how could he have left the dog, trapped, where a boar might find it?

Edwin also heard the master's call and, stopping, looked in his direction. Yet, unbelievably, he'd still not noticed the advancing sow, and Dickon yelled again, 'Edwin, watch out!' But it was too late. Edwin blundered through the undergrowth just as the animal reached the same point. Startled by her, he tripped, and the sow then fell upon him, the piglets squealing all around.

Edwin screamed, but Dickon ploughed on towards him. He could see the master coming too but he was still many yards away. As he closed on them, Dickon drew his knife. He swallowed: it was short bladed, not what you needed to kill a boar. Yet it was all he had.

Edwin was face down now, his arms over his head, his feet drumming the ground in terror. The sow was on his back, stabbing at him with her little tusks. His arm was already bloodied.

Dickon fell upon her, thrusting his knife into the back of her neck. But her hide was thick, and the dagger made barely any entry: he still had it in his hand. Nonetheless, the sow had felt the assault and, roaring, turned from Edwin towards Dickon. But, as she came, he lunged forward once again, this time plunging the knife into her throat. It sank up to the hilt, staying her advance, but the master was then at his side, his boar spear raised, and he drove it into the animal's flank, just behind her front leg. Instantly she collapsed at Dickon's feet. The master withdrew the spear and stabbed her once again, ensuring she was dead. The spear's crosspiece rested against her bristly hide, the shaft quivering with her dying shudders.

'A family left without a mother,' said the master, pointing to the piglets. He shook his head sadly. 'How did that happen?' Dickon pressed his lips together but didn't answer. 'Help me move her.'

He took hold of the sow's front legs, whilst the master took the rear, and they heaved her bleeding body away from Edwin. Edwin shuddered, and let out a whimper. His face dark, the master took a pot of salve and a bandage from his scrip and bound Edwin's injured arm.

'Could be a lot worse,' he said, 'but we have to get him back to the castle. You've got a lot of explaining to do, de Bohun, though I suspect Master de Courtenay might have even more.'

Dickon nodded. With little time to think about it, he suspected

Edwin was at the root of what had happened. Where he stopped to help the dog, he'd felt sure there would have been no boars around, as they had already been driven forward by the beaters. Anyway, sows shouldn't have been flushed out at all. If Edwin had *planned* to drive a boar in his direction, it must have been sheer chance he came across that sow. But, if that was his plan, more fool him for sticking around to watch instead of running off at once to join the other beaters.

'Sir Eustace will wonder where we've all got to,' the master said, 'but there's naught we can do about that now.' He heaved the snivelling Edwin up and slung him across his shoulder.

'What about the dog?' said Dickon. 'It's injured too.'

'Where is it?' Dickon pointed. 'You'd best get it, though you'll have to carry it.'

'What about the sow?' said Dickon, sorry she was dead.

'I know this spot. I'll come back for her later.'

'And the piglets?'

The master shrugged. 'Naught I can do about them. If another female finds them, she might look after them, but if it's a male, well...'

Dickon was devastated, at the sow's needless death and the likely fate of her babies. He trudged back to the castle with the master, the dog squirming in his arms, getting heavier with every step. He'd be glad to hand the wretched animal over to one of the kennel lads.

The master took Edwin to the infirmary, giving instructions he was not allowed to leave, then beckoned Dickon to follow him. 'We need to talk.'

Dickon's heart thudded. Was he in trouble yet again? Though the master didn't seem annoyed with him. 'I want you to tell me what happened.' He looked him in the eye. 'And I want the truth, Dickon. Do you understand what I am saying?'

Dickon thought he did. Nonetheless, he was torn, once more, about whether or not to say what he believed. He havered for a while before answering. 'I don't know for sure,' he said at last. 'I was at the back of the beating line and saw the dog had got separated from the others.'

'I told the kennel master some days ago that hound wasn't ready. Too skittish yet by far.'

'Anyway, it must have darted into some undergrowth, chasing a squirrel perhaps. But the vegetation was very dense, and all snarled with ivy and thick brambles. I suppose the dog charged in and got its back leg caught, struggled and became trapped. I couldn't leave it there, Master, in case a boar came and found it. So, I went to free it.'

The master nodded. 'You were breaking the rules of beating, but I commend you for your concern. Go on.' He waved his hand.

Dickon described seeing the piglets, and then their dam, and how, by yelling and waving his arms, he was able to divert them. He swallowed. 'I was terrified, Master, so sure she was going to attack me.'

'You were most fortunate.'

'Then I saw Edwin running right towards the sow. The vegetation was tall as well as thick, and he clearly hadn't seen her. I don't know why he wasn't with the other beaters. I had to warn him, so I ran towards him, yelling, but I don't think he heard me. And he tripped over at the very moment his path crossed with the sow's.'

At the time, everything had happened so quickly, he'd not had a chance to be afraid. But now, reliving it, he was trembling and felt a little sick. The master got up and brought him a cup of small ale. 'Drink this, lad.'

Dickon took a gulp, then told the master about his poor attempt to stab the sow, and her turning on him. He hadn't wanted to harm her at all, but he had no choice. Much as he loathed Edwin de Courtenay, he couldn't let the sow gore him to death. 'I was so glad you came, Master, else she might have stabbed me too.'

The master drank some ale himself and sat in front of Dickon, frowning. 'Do you think de Courtenay *drove* the sow towards you? With deliberate intent to harm you?'

He shrugged. 'Why else wasn't he with the other beaters? He hadn't stopped to help an injured dog.'

'No, he hadn't.' He stroked his beard. 'Well, if that was indeed his intention, he rather got what he deserved, don't you think?'

Dickon agreed. Yet he was glad Edwin hadn't died. Though he doubted Edwin would be grateful for his intervention.

'Anyway,' continued the master, 'I shall question him later, when he's had a chance to recover. But I daresay the earl will want to hear the tale again from both of you.'

. . .

A few days passed before his interview with the earl. Lord Raoul wanted to speak to him and Edwin together, and Edwin's injured arm—and his dented dignity—took a while to mend.

It disheartened Dickon to be in trouble yet again, when he'd only just returned to Steyning. He'd so hoped the next few months would be a time for him to catch up on what he'd missed and impress the masters and the earl with his diligence and skill. Yet here he was, once more having to justify himself, when the reason for it was almost certainly Edwin de Courtenay.

He'd thought about what had happened many times, trying to conceive a rational explanation for Edwin being where he was, instead of with the beaters. But what reason could there be, except that he was up to mischief—the sort of mischief that had Dickon as its target? Yet he couldn't have planned the incident. Wouldn't that have been impossible? But perhaps he'd noticed Dickon going to help the dog and so too hung back from the beating line? He saw his opportunity, when the sow and her young came into view. It must have been sheer chance. Though not good fortune, as it turned out.

Lord Raoul asked Edwin to explain what happened, but he prevaricated, refusing to admit to what Dickon suspected. The earl looked annoyed and turned away from Edwin to ask Dickon for his view.

Edwin interrupted and protested at every suggestion Dickon made. 'That's a lie,' he cried out, at the idea that, when he saw Dickon stop to help the dog, he too hung back, hoping for a chance to waylay him.

However, from the constant frown on Lord Raoul's face whenever Edwin spoke, it was clear he didn't believe a word he said. On the other hand, he nodded encouragingly at Dickon.

When he'd finished his side of the story, it was the master's turn. As he saw it, Edwin had no viable excuse for leaving the line of beaters. 'I can only deduce that he was up to some sort of mischief.'

Edwin tried to protest again but Lord Raoul wouldn't let him.

'Of course,' continued the master, 'neither should de Bohun have left the beating line, but he did at least have some justification for his action. He was most courageous too, my lord, in running forward to help de Courtenay, despite suspecting it was he who'd deliberately driven the sow against him.'

After listening to everyone's statements, Lord Raoul told the master to place Edwin into solitary confinement for the next few days. The master bowed and left the chamber, gripping Edwin by his arm. Dickon suppressed a smirk: so de Courtenay was about to find out what it was like being locked up on your own. He turned to leave too but the earl called out, 'Not you, de Bohun. I still have more to say to you.'

Dickon's heart sank. So, he *was* still in trouble...

But Lord Raoul asked him about the other incidents. 'Was de Courtenay responsible for those too?'

Dickon shrugged, still reluctant to blame Edwin.

The earl shook his head. 'You might not know for sure, Dickon, but I can see that you at the least suspect it.'

He nodded. 'I've never wanted to be a blab, my lord.'

'No one likes a blab. But, if you had come to me earlier with your suspicions, I could have put a stop to it all much sooner.' He sat down and invited Dickon to do the same. 'If you will not tell me, then I will question all your fellow squires. They might not be so reticent—'

Dickon was aghast. 'But a lot of them are on his side,' he cried out then hung his head in shame at his outburst.

'I am not sure that is true,' said Lord Raoul. 'Not now. As I understand it, rumour has already spread that Edwin tried to cause your death, or serious injury at least, in the forest the other day. Whereas a degree of amusement might have been caused by the earlier incidents, attempting to kill a fellow squire is not even tenuously funny. It is my belief that your fellows will agree.'

Two days later, Nick drew Dickon away from the rest of the squires. He was grinning. 'Do you know what's been going on? With Lord Raoul questioning everyone about you and Edwin.'

'I knew he was going to.' He hesitated a moment. 'What's everyone been saying?'

'I think most agree with me,' he said. 'The first couple of pranks were all very well but the incident with Sir Eustace's horse was cruel, and what happened at the duchess's birthday dinner shameful. But what Edwin tried to do to you on the hunt was way past a prank. It was malicious. Even Alan thinks so.'

'And has Alan admitted all he knows?'

'Yes. I think he can see that allying himself with Edwin isn't a good idea any more. So, he told the earl everything.' He smirked. 'I wonder what's going to happen to Edwin now?'

30

MEONBRIDGE
OCTOBER 1364

From the silence in the house, Margery supposed everyone except for her was fast asleep. She rose quietly from her pallet and opened the little wooden casket in which she stored her few possessions. She took out the remains of one of Mistress Browghton's best wax candles, which she had purloined some days earlier. Then she tiptoed from the chamber and down the stairs.

The idea had come to her some days ago, and she had already worked out what to do.

Tiptoeing along the cross passage, she opened the door into the yard and went outside. A year ago or so, the Browghtons had had a kitchen built out there, the mistress keen to rid the hall of the odour, fumes and steam from cooking. The kitchen would be empty now, as none of the kitchen servants lived in. She opened the door and stepped inside. As fortune had it, the moon was bright and shafts of light were streaming through the small, high windows, enabling her to move easily towards the hearth.

She held her hand out over the iron *couvre-feu* that was used to shield the fire at the end of each day's cooking. She hoped there would be heat enough still in the ashes for her needs. The metal lid was hot. She found a cloth and, lifting the lid off, put it on the floor. The pile of ashes in the middle of the hearth was grey and soft, but the fire was smouldering beneath it, as she had expected.

She took a small iron skillet from a hook on the wall and placed it on the ash mound, nestling it down a little. Taking the candle remnant from her pocket, she put it into the pan. For long moments, nothing happened. Perhaps the heat was not sufficient? More likely, she had to be patient. The wax did not need to melt, just soften a little, enough for her to mould it.

The light in the kitchen dimmed: a cloud must have moved across the moon. Annoyed, she reached out to feel the wax, fearing it might melt suddenly and be too soft to use. But, in the dark, her impatient fingers caught the edge of the skillet and she flinched, stifling a cry. Better to be patient, Margery.

At length, the moon's beams lit the kitchen once again, and she could see the edges of the wax were slightly liquid. Taking the pan off the fire, she put it on the floor, to wait now for the wax to cool.

Patience had never been one of her strengths. But anxiety now compounded her impatience, as she didn't know how early Cook came to start preparing for the new day's meals. Surely not yet awhile? Dawn was still a long time off.

But the wax soon cooled sufficiently for her to pick up the lump and mould it into the rough shape of a man.

How she even knew about witches' poppets, at first she couldn't quite recall. But then she remembered it was one of the things Matilda had prattled on about when they were children. Of course, they both had poppets, cloth dolls they dressed and undressed. But witches' dolls weren't playthings: they were used in charms, Matilda said, for good or evil, to make a man fall in love with you, or to curse him.

She had described the different forms the poppets took and how witches cast their spells. How Matilda knew about it all was anybody's guess. Margery never asked. It might have been Matilda's fancy, but likely too some whispered gossip she had shared with the cottar girls from Meonvale she sometimes ran around with.

When the man-poppet was shaped to her satisfaction, she added a tiny male appendage and even gave herself cause to smile. As the

236

poppet solidified, she put the skillet back onto the ash pile to melt the remaining waxy traces, wiped it with a cloth and hung it back up on the wall. No one would notice the slight stickiness when they came to use the pan again. But with no means of cleaning the cloth, she decided to take it with her, to throw into the midden later.

Back up in the sleeping chamber, she placed the poppet in her coffer and lay down again upon her pallet, hoping to snatch a few moments' sleep.

Several days later, she took the poppet with her to the barn, where she hid amongst the teetering stack of new hay bales. She brought a small cup with her too, which she dipped into the pond to collect a little of the greenish water.

In those long-ago conversations, Matilda had explained how to cast a spell. So now Margery held the poppet in one hand and, sprinkling a little of the water on its head, declared, 'I name thee Pers Cokewell', and repeated it twice more.

Then she said, three times, 'What I do to you, I do to Pers.' Taking a small brooch from her pocket, she stabbed the pin into the poppet's mouth.

'I demand, Pers Cokewell, you keep your insults to yourself. I command you to still your vile tongue.'

In truth, she felt quite foolish, addressing a lump of wax. Matilda's tales of witches' poppets *were* probably just her fancy but, in case they were not, she would come back to the barn for each of the next seven days to repeat her incantation.

Then she would look out for a change in Pers Cokewell's behaviour.

In theory, Jan and Ellen were supposed to take turns with Margery to do the milking, but they had never shown much interest. Which suited Margery well enough. Being with the cows was the best part of her day, albeit lugging the heavy pails of milk was a burden.

She was careful in her milking, massaging the udders gently before she started, and murmuring to the animals all the while.

As autumn advanced, the days grew shorter and the time for the second milking came earlier in the afternoon. The cows were kept out on the pasture for as long as the weather held, but October had brought daily rain, and she thought she might soon bring them back into the byre.

Mistress Browghton was not sure. 'It is early yet,' she said, when Margery asked her. 'Is there not still plenty of grass left in the meadow?'

'Yes. I could put them out again if this spell of rain ceases.'

Her mistress frowned. 'That is true. I suppose milking in the rain is not very pleasant?'

Margery suppressed a smirk. Philippa Browghton rarely acknowledged the discomforts of her servants. 'Indeed. What is more, I fear the milk may spoil as I carry it from field to dairy.'

At length, her mistress agreed and, early next morning, Margery led the four cows from the pasture. Two followed without hesitation, but Flora and Belle seemed slow.

'Loath to leave the grass, you two?' she said, cooing. 'But you will like your cosy byre.'

Once there, she settled them all into separate stalls, already made comfortable with a good layer of straw, and the two nearest to her set at once to browsing at their mangers of new hay. She breathed in the warm, sweet smell. How much she preferred it when the animals came indoors.

She lifted her stool and a milking pail from hooks on the byre wall, and went to the first cow. Nestling the stool firmly in the straw, she sat down. She took a cloth and, leaning forward, wiped the cow's udder clean, and kneaded it a little. The animal gave a gentle low, and her flank twitched, as Margery began to milk.

The pails of milk from the first two cows were full and frothy. Margery carried them both the short distance to the dairy and Ellen took them from her, whilst she went back to the byre.

She set her stool down by Flora. But, the moment she touched her udder, she recoiled. It was hot and swollen, much more than it should be, and felt hard instead of pliant. She saw then that Flora was not eating. In a panic, she jumped up off her stool and went into Belle's stall. As she approached, the cow turned her head and lowed. Her eyes were dull, and she too had not touched her hay. Her heart racing,

Margery bent down to feel Belle's udder: it was engorged, and red, and Belle's entire body was unnaturally hot. The cow bellowed at her touch.

'Oh, I am so sorry, lady,' whispered Margery. She had seen this affliction several times in the years she'd worked at the Browghtons'. Sometimes the milk became thin and useless, and had to be given to the pigs, or was bloody and had to be thrown away, and sometimes the milk dried up altogether. Sometimes the cows recovered, but many times they did not. No one knew the cause of it, not even Mistress Browghton, who always tried to treat it with her herbal preparations, although whether or not they had any good effect was hard to tell.

Yet one or two people—people with no knowledge of animal husbandry—thought they did know the cause. So, mixed up with her anxiety for the survival of the two sick cows was her fear of what those particular folk might say when they learned of what had happened. Nonetheless, she had to tell her mistress. Giving Belle what she hoped was a reassuring pat upon her rump, she hurried from the byre.

'Oh, not again,' cried out Mistress Browghton, wringing her hands together.

'It has been a fair while since the last time,' Margery said. More than two years, she was sure.

'You are right, of course. But that cow died.' Her hand went to her mouth, then to her forehead. 'It is always so difficult to know the remedy.'

'Shall we use the one you have made up before?'

'We must try, at least.'

Margery had never before watched her mistress blend her remedies. But, today, Mistress Browghton did not bid her leave, and she was intrigued to see the potion she was making contained a tiny dose of one of the very poisons she had learned about from Ursula Kemp.

'Belladonna, Mistress? A poison?'

Her mistress raised her eyebrows. 'What do you know about such things?'

Margery looked away. 'Oh, nothing. It is just what I have heard.'

'It is poisonous, but only in large measures. The scant amount I put in here is curative.'

239

At length, Mistress Browghton accompanied Margery to the byre to help administer the remedy. Both Belle and Flora were now lying down, their muzzles wet with froth, their tongues lolling from their mouths. Not much had touched Margery's heart for years, but the sight of such sick cows did always cause her heart to ache.

Her mistress did not blame her for what was happening. 'Dose them several times a day,' she said, 'and try to keep them cool and calm. I do not know what else can be done.'

'What of their milk? Shall I try? I fear it might pain them greatly, yet if I do not...'

'Indeed. The swelling may get worse.' She pursed her lips. 'Try, but gently.'

When Margery reported back later that afternoon, it was to say that Flora's milk was bloody, and Belle's seemed to have dried up altogether. 'I have thrown the tainted milk onto the midden, and I shall leave poor Belle alone for now.'

Mistress Browghton nodded, and Margery went back once more to the byre, intending to stay there overnight.

When Margery awoke, it was early morning and, looking out through the wide, open barn door, she saw a layer of mist hovering across the yard, and in the fields beyond. She shivered. The blanket she had brought with her was scarcely thick enough to keep out an autumn morning's chill. She paced around a while, slapping and rubbing her hands against her arms. Then she thought of the sick cows and hurried to their stalls.

Both were lying down. Had they slept at all, or lain awake all night? Surprisingly, she herself had slept for once, despite her worries about the cows.

She edged forward first to Flora. It was still quite gloomy in that part of the byre, so she knelt down by her side and felt her udder. It was the same as yesterday, but no worse. Maybe the mistress's remedy was working. Then she went to Belle. Placing her hands gently on her body, she fancied she was even hotter.

She examined the two other cows and found they still both seemed well. She would have to milk them soon. But first she would go to tell her mistress about Belle and Flora.

At the byre door, she heard voices across the yard. Her heart fell when she saw the two labourers standing outside the dairy yet again, chatting with the dairymaids. The last thing she needed right now was an encounter with Pers Cokewell. Yet she had no choice but to pass him on her way into the house.

She had seen little of him the past week or two. It was disappointing, as she had wanted to see if her poppet charm had wrought any change. The two occasions she had seen him, he was almost polite, which was not quite the result she was expecting. But, as she crossed the yard towards him and the others, all four of them turned and stared.

As soon as she was close enough, Pers jerked his chin at her. ''Ere she comes. Back in 'er usual body now, I see...' He smirked.

She came to an abrupt halt. If he had not opened his mouth, she might have hurried past. She glared at him. 'What did you say?'

He sniggered. 'We was jus' sayin'... When a cow dries up, it's usually 'cos a witch turned into a hare at night and suckled the milk away.'

Margery snorted. 'Do not be so ridiculous—' But then she understood his insinuation. 'Are you calling *me* a witch?'

Pers guffawed, and Jan and Ellen tittered.

'Or a fay,' said Pers. 'You mus' know what folk say...'

'Aw, Pers,' said Ellen. 'You shouldn't accuse our Margery of witchery. She loves them cows, so why'd she want to harm them?'

He ignored her. 'I were jus' saying,' he continued, 'I oughta pick a branch of rowan and fix it above the byre door. My gran'ma used to swear by rowan for fixing witchy cows...'

Margery's heart was thumping. Once an accusation has been made, it is difficult to gainsay it. And Pers had clearly blamed her for the cows' sickness in front of the others.

Ellen at least did seem to understand the truth: Margery was the last person at the farm to want to harm the cows. But Jan did not much like her and, for a reason Margery failed to comprehend, the girl considered Pers some sort of suitor, so she was likely eager to back up his story and repeat it whenever she got the chance.

Being called a witch was frightening—dangerous. Even coming

from the mouths of idiots like Pers Cokewell. Why had he decided to accuse her now? Was it said in jest? Or was it just another example of his foolish but malicious tongue? Or had someone seen her visiting Mistress Kemp, and concluded they might be friends? A sudden shiver chilled her. Not knowing how to respond, she said nothing more and swept past and on into the house.

When she told Mistress Browghton the latest news about the cows, her mistress sighed deeply and bid her continue to keep an eye on them.

'I must milk the other two,' said Margery.

'You must. I suggest you move them away from Belle and Flora.'

'Why?'

'I simply think they might be happier away from their sick sisters.'

'There are plenty more stalls to move them to.'

'Indeed. I shall leave it to you to manage.'

Still no suggestion, then, came from her mistress that she might be to blame for the cows' sickness. But it did appear that her wax poppet had not after all restrained Pers's vile tongue, and she would not put it past Gabriel to lend credence to the man's nonsensical outpourings.

Perhaps it was time she left the Browghtons' farm, before any more accusations were levelled at her?

31

DECEMBER 1364

Dickon's heart lifted at the sight of the Meon glinting in the winter sunshine. What a relief to be back in Meonbridge once more. As they reached the track that led up through the village, he and Piers tapped their heels against their horses' flanks, spurring them to pick up a little speed. His heart swelled as the two of them rode through the manor gates onto the bailey.

His grandmother was effusive in her greeting, as if he'd been away for a whole year instead of just three months. She still knew nothing of the misery he'd endured at Steyning. Piers was the only one in Meonbridge who knew, and he intended keeping it that way. Though he did worry that, one day, Grandmama might learn the truth by mischance, or perhaps in conversation when she next met Lord Raoul. It occurred to him too late he should have asked the earl never to tell her what had been happening, to save her any needless upset. He was sure his lordship would agree. He'd ask when he returned to Steyning.

After the mayhem of the hunting incident, and the earl's acceptance of Edwin's guilt in the affair—despite his vehement denials—Dickon had imagined Lord Raoul would dismiss Edwin from

Steyning. Yet, before he left Steyning to come home, he discovered the earl was havering.

'I have not decided finally what to do about de Courtenay, Dickon,' he said, having called him to his chamber for a private word. 'My preference is to dismiss him. I consider my band of squires elite, noble in spirit and demeanour if not necessarily in birth. They go on to join the highest ranks of England's knights. De Courtenay does not belong amidst such an honourable band.'

He paused and paced the chamber a little. 'I demand commitment and high standards from my squires, Dickon, harshly so, some of you might think.' He raised an eyebrow. 'Yet I do also have compassion, and I believe that Edwin de Courtenay is a most unhappy boy. I should have recognised it a year ago or more.'

Dickon couldn't suppress a gasp. *He's* unhappy!

The earl saw his surprise and, coming forward, rested a hand upon Dickon's shoulder. 'My deepest compassion is reserved for you, Dickon, for all that you have suffered whilst you have been here at Steyning. I am sorry for it, but trust it is now at an end. You might think that, to ensure it, I should send de Courtenay away. Perhaps I will. Yet I have concern too for him.'

'My lord?' Why might the earl feel sorry for *Edwin* of all people?

Lord Raoul smiled. 'I can see you are confused. So, let me explain. I am going to take Edwin home to Courtenay Castle and tell his grandparents about all his misdeeds. I intend to tell them also of my concerns about his unhappy state of mind. I shall ask them if they can give me an explanation for it. It will be the nature of their response that will determine whether or not I give the lad another chance.'

'You really think, my lord, that he would stop his viciousness towards me?'

His lordship pulled on his beard. 'Like you, I am doubtful. If he did return, it would be under strict instructions that he behaves himself impeccably. If he put a foot wrong again, he would be out.' He looked Dickon in the eye. 'I would rely on you and your fellow squires to be honest rather than honourable in making plain any such transgressions. The code of honour would in this case have to be set aside.'

Dickon nodded. It might work, though he was nervous of the

outcome. But perhaps even Edwin de Courtenay was capable of turning over a new leaf.

Wrapped up warm against the chilly air, in thick wool cloaks and hoods, Dickon was escorting his grandmother on a stroll around the bailey. She wanted to go further, complaining she didn't walk enough these days, but he insisted the gardens would be too wet underfoot.

'Then I shall wear my stoutest boots,' she said, but he still shook his head.

'You know the grass is likely to be slippery. You don't want to undo all the good work you've done in mending your broken leg.'

At length she agreed, and allowed him to guide her around the edge of the bailey, keeping to the drier parts, where the undulations hadn't settled into muddy puddles.

After a while, she turned to him. 'I am planning to celebrate your betrothal to Angharad Fitzpeyne in the spring. April, I think.'

'That'll be wonderful, Grandmama. Thank you.' His gratitude was sincere but nonetheless his stomach did a flip. The whole idea of marriage scared him. Not that he'd be marrying Angharad for a long while yet. But thinking of Angharad made him also think of Libby. Might she be getting married soon?

He grimaced to himself as he recalled their last conversation, in September, just before he returned to Steyning. She'd been so angry with him. She'd told him things about his father and her mother he'd not known before. It was all so shocking, he'd wondered if she'd made it up. Yet, if it was true, where might she have learned of it?

In the days before he came home, he'd become quite nervous of seeing her again. Would she still be furious with him? Or even *more* upset than she'd been before?

Yet he'd seen her twice since he'd returned and, each time, she'd curtsied to him and offered him a cheerful greeting. Even from those two brief encounters, he could see she was somehow different. *Happy.* Was she being courted by some other man? Perhaps James Paynter had responded to his prompting after all? If so, he should be pleased about it. And, of course, he was, yet still he couldn't prevent a small twinge of wistfulness pricking his approval.

When he and his grandmother returned to the house and stepped through the heavy door back into the heat and haze of the great hall, it was Libby who came forward to take her mistress's cloak and hood. She smiled at him, an easy natural gesture, not forced or insincere.

'Shall I also take your cloak, milord?' she said, and he winced at her formality.

'Thank you, Libby,' he said. Then, as his grandmother turned aside to speak to a servant, he moved a little closer. 'But please don't call me "milord", Libby,' he whispered. 'It's not necessary, not for us.'

She tilted her head. 'But I can't really call you "Dickon", can I? Not in front of others, anyway.'

She was right, yet he didn't know what else to suggest. But he had no time to think about it further, as his grandmother turned back towards him. He noticed her eyes widen: perhaps she'd seen how close together he and Libby were standing. But she didn't mention it.

'Libby, dear,' she said, 'please accompany me upstairs. There are some matters I wish to discuss with you.' She turned to Dickon. 'Shall I see you at dinner?'

'You will, Grandmama.' He bowed his head and set off to find Piers Arundale.

In the evenings, after supper, Dickon had taken to staying downstairs in the great hall, to share a flagon or two of wine with the senior members of the household: the squires and knights who'd been in service to his grandfather, Sir Richard, who now owed fealty to his grandmother, and would, in a few years, transfer their loyalty to him. He enjoyed their company. But, more than that, he relished the sense of adulthood that drinking and jesting with these men gave him.

Sometimes the banter took a bawdy turn, with tales of encounters with women, some of them local girls, but more often foreign women met whilst on campaign abroad. He never joined in these particular conversations. After all, the only "encounters" he'd have to share would be ones with Libby, and he'd hardly dishonour her by revealing what had passed between them.

Piers clearly approved of his decision. 'I've told no one what I saw,' he'd said soon after the incident at the river. 'And I never shall.'

246

Dickon had blushed. 'I'm glad of both your decision and your loyalty. Thank you, Piers.'

'It would do no one any good if I spoke of it. Not you, nor Libby, nor her ladyship.'

Yet a less wise and honourable man than Piers might have seen it differently. At that moment, Dickon had known that Piers Arundale would always be his most dependable and trusty squire.

But, even if he didn't discuss Libby during these boisterous evenings, he still thought about her from time to time. Yet, he now realised, perhaps it was more as a brother might think about his sister, rather than as a lover. Even if his grandmother might have construed there was still more to their friendship.

'You do know you could never be with Libby,' she'd said later that afternoon, when they were alone together in her chamber. It was the first time she'd ever said it.

'Of course, Grandmama. We were childhood friends, that's all.' He flushed. 'I just want to know she's going to be happy.'

'Well, I may have good news for you on that account. I think I may have found a suitable husband for her.' He looked up, both alarmed and quizzical. 'James Paynter, Jack Sawyer's journeyman, has been casting his eyes Libby's way.' She beamed, and his anxiety melted away.

So, James *had* followed up his hint. 'Oh, really?' he said airily. 'Is she responding?'

'Very much so, from what I saw at the harvest supper. They seemed enchanted with each other's company, dancing.'

Dancing! He felt a sudden pang of grief. How much he'd like to have danced with Libby. But there was no chance of that now.

'I know they have spent time together since. Alice has been my informant.' Her eyes twinkled.

'Has James asked *you* if Libby can be his wife?'

Her forehead creased. 'He has not. Which surprises me a little. He did seem so very keen.'

Was Libby also keen? She was surely happier. Maybe, then, she *had* put him behind her. He hoped so, despite his regretful pangs. 'Perhaps I'll go to talk to James,' he said. 'Find out his intentions.'

His grandmother beamed. 'I should be grateful. I should so like to get Libby settled.'

As would he. Provided she was happy too about the "settlement". He had to reassure himself of that.

Dickon pushed open the workshop door and stepped inside. The air inside the workshop was hazy with wood dust, his father, brother and James all hard at work planing or sawing great lengths of timber. A young boy was there too, someone Dickon hadn't seen before. Pa's new apprentice, he assumed.

Four faces twisted around to look at him.

Jack at once put down his plane and strode forward, his arms outstretched. 'How pleased I am to see you,' he cried. 'Have you seen your mother yet?' He enfolded Dickon in a brief embrace.

'Not yet, Pa. I'm going as soon as I've left here.'

Jack opened his arms and stepped back. 'She'll be glad to see you looking so fine and strong.'

Dickon nodded. Since he'd been back at Steyning, he'd been practising hard, to make up for the time and skills he'd lost whilst he'd been away. His efforts were paying off: he did indeed feel strong, much more so than ever, and his swordsmanship skills, especially, were improving greatly.

He said some of this to his father, but was anxious to talk to James. It was, after all, why he'd come. He let Jack ask a few more questions, then shuffled his feet. 'Pa, can I have a few words with James?'

Jack rubbed his neck. 'We're very busy.'

Dickon laughed. 'You always are. That's why your business is doing so well. But I won't keep him long.'

James was grinning as Dickon led him out of the workshop. 'Shall we go to the barn?' said Dickon.

'It's a bit chilly for hanging around in barns.'

'I know, but I want to ask you something and don't want us to be overheard.'

James grinned. 'I can guess what it's about.' Dickon felt his cheeks redden. Was he interfering where he had no business? No, it *was* his business to ensure Libby's future would be a happy one.

They sat on a solid stack of hay, the sweet smell of summer still rising from the bales. 'You want to know about Libby and me?' James said, not waiting for Dickon to ask. 'I took your advice.' He chuckled.

Dickon flushed again. 'I just want to know she's going to be content.'

'Like any good brother should.'

'Exactly.'

'Well, Libby and me have an agreement.'

Dickon nodded, his relief still tinged with regret.

'Did you know I'll be moving away from Meonbridge?' James continued. 'To set up on my own.'

'You said you might some time ago. You've found somewhere?'

'Jack's been asking around a while. And a day or so ago he heard of a shop in Wickham I might be able to take on in the spring. If it works out for me, Libby and me will get married then.'

'You need to ask my grandmother for her permission.'

'Her ladyship already knows of my intentions. But I won't ask her formally till I know I've got a proper future to offer my bride.'

Dickon held out his hand. 'I'm glad for you both.' He meant it. 'My grandmother's planning my own betrothal for the spring. April, she's said. Maybe you can marry at the same time? A joint celebration?'

James took his hand and shook it with a firm grip. 'Spring's a fine time for a celebration, and a marriage. I'll come to see her ladyship as soon as I have news.'

So, it was settled. He could be betrothed to Angharad Fitzpeyne without feeling he was letting Libby down. Nonetheless, although he trusted James's claim, he still wanted to hear from Libby's own lips that the agreement was hers as well as his. And, if it was, to tell her how pleased he was for her.

He sought her out that evening. Instead of spending the hours after supper drinking with his retainers, he asked his grandmother if she might let Libby sit with him a while. He was truthful about what he wanted to say to her.

His grandmother agreed. 'I believe she is content. But you must satisfy yourself.'

As the servants cleared away the leavings from the supper, and the knights and squires took flagons and their cups of ale to the far end of the hall, Dickon led Libby to the cushioned bench close to the hearth.

'I've something I want to say to you,' he said.

'I can guess.'

'I'll say it anyway.' He looked into her eyes. 'I spoke to James Paynter earlier, and he told me of your agreement.'

'He's a good man. You said so yourself.' She lowered her eyes. 'I was horrible to you before you went back to Steyning.' Her voice was a whisper. 'What I told you wasn't untrue, but it was vile of me to blurt it out like that.'

'I was terribly shocked. I knew nothing of what you told me.'

'I was sure you didn't. I wanted to hurt you, for you to feel the same as I had when I learned what happened to my mother. My aunt, Margery—'

Dickon frowned. 'What "Aunt Margery"?'

She flushed bright red. 'Oh, goodness, I've never told you, have I?'

'Told me what?'

'About meeting my mother's sister in Meonbridge last spring.'

'You've never mentioned her.'

She bit her lip. 'That was because she always seemed so weird...' She hesitated. 'Well, not at first. I didn't see her often but, as time went by, I realised how bitter she was about her life.'

Dickon raised a quizzical eyebrow.

'Anyway, it was her, Aunt Margery, who told me about your father and my mother. She blamed the de Bohun family, and Lady Margaret in particular, for everything that happened to her, losing her home and status and having to become a servant.'

'I did wonder where you'd learned it, but of course I didn't know about your aunt.'

'Margery was so bitter about it all. She wanted *me* to be bitter too, to hate her ladyship and your family.' She twisted her hands together. 'For a while I suppose I went along with it. I believed her. Then, when you seemed to be rejecting me, telling you about it seemed a good way of getting some sort of revenge.' Tears were moistening her lower lids. 'Yet I always knew what she said about her ladyship couldn't possibly be true. I'm so sorry.'

'I'm sorry too. I think maybe we're both to blame.'

250

She nodded. 'But I *do* understand why you had to reject me—'

'Oh, Libby, it wasn't really rejection...'

'No, I know. I understand that now. And I'm so glad of James.' She leaned forward. 'I will be happy with him, Dickon.' She smiled. 'Truly.'

'James told me Jack may have found him a shop of his own. You'll be the wife of a prosperous man.'

'I'll be sad to leave Meonbridge. But I accept it'll be to a comfortable life.' She tilted her head. 'I'd like to think we might still meet occasionally. Though I suppose when you're lord of Meonbridge, it mightn't be appropriate.'

'If you're not too far away—James said Wickham—there's no reason you can't come back to Meonbridge to visit. Not only to see me but your other friends.'

She laughed, and his heart leapt at the sight of her happiness with what her future held. How he hoped his own future would be as blessed.

32

COURTENAY CASTLE
DECEMBER 1364

The distance from Steyning to Courtenay Castle was only about thirty miles, but the weather had turned most inclement. Raoul debated with himself whether to ride or take the carriage. Being cooped up together with a surly Edwin de Courtenay would be wearisome. Moreover, with the state of the roads at this time of year, the carriage might well take longer than the horses.

Jeanne favoured wheels over hooves. 'If you go on horseback, you will soon be soaked through to your skins and freezing cold,' she said. 'Besides, is there not a chance that Edwin might attempt escape?'

'I shall be taking men with me to guard him,' said Raoul. 'Although I do agree that losing him would be an embarrassment.'

At length he allowed his wife's view to prevail. Nonetheless, the prospect of the journey was not appealing, and not only because he had to share a small compartment with a sullen youth.

What he was going to tell Hugh and Hildegard de Courtenay about their grandson he had never had to say to any family before. Naturally, there had been squires before at Steyning who misbehaved, and a few who did not come up to the mark. The former he had always managed to bring to heel before it was too late. The latter he had dismissed but their families generally accepted, if with regret, that their boys did not have what it took to be a member of his elite company.

But telling the de Courtenays that their grandson was a dishonourable *scoundrel* was quite another matter. He was not looking forward to it at all.

Sir Hugh's face was grey, his forehead wrinkled, when he welcomed the earl into the great hall of Courtenay Castle. Raoul understood why the old man was anxious: he was unlikely to be bringing Edwin home out of courtesy. Something had to be amiss, and Hugh would know it.

Raoul did not pretend this was a social visit: he clasped Hugh's proffered hand but kept his smile sober. 'Good to see you again, Hugh.'

'You also, my lord,' said the knight, his voice a little strained. 'Yet I do wonder what has persuaded you to come all the way here with Edwin instead of allowing my men to collect him as usual.'

'I regret to say it is because I am obliged to speak to you about your grandson. To apprise you of his misconduct—'

'Misconduct?' gasped out Hugh. 'Oh, my lord, I do hope nothing too grave.'

Raoul shook his head. 'Sadly, what I have to tell you is *most* grave. It appears that Edwin has been disruptive for the best part of a year, although it has only recently come to my attention.'

Hugh turned around, perhaps expecting to address his grandson, but Edwin had already slunk away. 'Oh,' he murmured and pursed his lips.

'I daresay he does not want to listen to what I have to tell you. He has already heard it.' Raoul lifted an eyebrow. 'We can no doubt fetch him later.' Hugh nodded. Raoul felt genuinely sorry for him, as his frown seemed now to have spread right down to his chin.

'Shall we go somewhere more private,' said the knight.

'Should Lady Hildegard join us?'

'I think not, my lord. I want to hear first whatever it is you have to say, then I shall decide if Hildegard should know it too.' He called for a servant and sent a message to his wife that he was in private audience with a visitor.

. . .

Sir Hugh insisted that Raoul took some refreshment prior to their conversation. 'It is exhausting travelling in winter,' he said, 'even with a comfortable carriage.'

Raoul grimaced. 'The vehicle is scarcely *comfortable*. Tolerable, perhaps, and at least sheltered from the wind and rain. But the journey was not a pleasure.'

'Good of you then to take the trouble...' Hugh poured two mazers of spiced wine and, handing one to Raoul, gulped his down in one. 'Please, take a seat.' He gestured to a cushioned bench placed before the blazing hearth.

Raoul sat and took several mouthfuls of the wine. 'Most welcome.' He raised the mazer and his eyes to Hugh, who stood before the fire, declining his invitation to join him on the bench.

'Please, my lord,' he said, 'do begin.'

He embarked upon the long litany of Edwin's misdemeanours, from the mild pranks of a year ago, to the more serious one involving Sir Eustace's horse, moving on to the mishap at the duchess's birthday dinner, then the fight Edwin falsely accused another squire of starting. Finally, the incident during the hunt surely intended to result in the other squire's grave injury or even death.

In his telling, Raoul kept the identity of Edwin's victim hidden, intending to reveal it later.

By the time the sorry saga had reached its finale, Hugh was slumped down next to Raoul. For a moment he leaned forward, cupping his face with his gnarly hands. But then he sat up again, straightening his back.

Hugh's defiant posture made Raoul wonder if he was proposing to refute what he had just told him, to deny his grandson would act so badly. Yet it seemed unlikely that Hugh de Courtenay, of all men, would accuse a superior of dissimulation. Raoul sipped more of his wine whilst the old man appeared to reflect on how best to respond.

At length, Hugh stood once more, called his servant to come and recharge the fire then, when the man had withdrawn again, he set his back towards the flames and faced the earl. His face was gloomy.

'As I am certain you would expect, my lord, I am shocked and horrified by what you have told me.'

'Are you also surprised?'

'At the degree of provocation you have described, yes, although perhaps not that Edwin might gain pleasure from teasing another boy.'

Raoul lifted an eyebrow. 'Explain.'

Hugh sat down again. 'Much as I regret to say it, the boy has had a peculiarly wretched childhood.'

'Ah,' said Raoul. 'I have suspected as much, given his, shall we say, malicious nature. Have you always known of it? Or did you first meet him only when his father brought him to England to train with me?'

'We did. We knew nothing about the boy until then, and have learned little more during his visits here.' He sighed. 'An uncommunicative lad. Yet I knew little even of my son's life in France, nor that of his family, until my youngest son, Alexander, quite recently chose to relate to me the essence of a long conversation he had had with Benedict.'

Raoul gestured to Hugh to continue.

'Alexander remains on good terms with his older brother and visits him from time to time when he is travelling in France. As I understand it, during a somewhat inebriated evening, Benedict told him things he had never mentioned before, about his joyless marriage, his regrets at throwing his entire lot in with Anne-Marie's august family, and, disturbingly, about certain aspects of Edwin's childhood. When Alexander returned to England, he felt he should acquaint me with what he had learned.' He took a deep, hitching breath. 'He was concerned at his brother's state of mind—his melancholy.'

'I am sorry to hear that,' said Raoul. 'Benedict was a successful squire, and I was truly gratified to dub him knight. When he chose to leave England, I was disappointed. Yet, in a sense, I was the author of his move, for it was soon after his dubbing that he met Lady Anne-Marie. Her mother was an acquaintance of my wife. We offered them hospitality for a few days at Steyning on their way home to France, after a protracted stay in England for some purpose that I cannot now recall. Somehow the paths of the two young people crossed.'

'I remember how excited Benedict was to meet her,' said Hugh. 'He was undoubtedly drawn to her family's great wealth, and their preeminence amongst the Burgundian gentry. I suppose he thought they would provide him with opportunities for great advancement. That may or may not have happened—I do not know—but we have never even met Anne-Marie, nor any of her family. We were not invited to the wedding, and the lady has never come to England again.'

'Disappointing.'

'Indeed. Benedict is the only one of our children whose in-law family we do not know.'

'Is Lady de Courtenay aware of Benedict's melancholy?'

'I chose to keep it from her. It is a burden I bear myself, as well as trying to determine how to help my son rise above his difficulties. But that is another issue. It is of Edwin that I must speak.'

Raoul accepted another mazer of wine. 'What did Alexander tell you?'

Hugh took a gulp from his own. 'Edwin is Benedict's fifth child and third son. For reasons not made clear, Edwin was ignored by all his siblings. Resentful, he went off on his own as soon as he was old enough, slipping his tutor's reins and making his own amusement.'

Raoul raised an eyebrow. 'What sort of amusement?'

'Nastiness of one sort or another, I understand. In particular, bullying other children, those younger or weaker, and certainly of lower status than himself, whom he encountered beyond the chateau's walls.'

'Ah,' said Raoul again.

'But it appears,' continued Hugh, 'that his family simply ignored his contemptible behaviour.'

'How extraordinary. Did Alexander know why?'

'He deduced that the boy's unpleasant nature repelled his parents and grandparents so greatly that they were inclined not to acknowledge him as one of their own.' He shook his head. 'Then, when he was twelve, they confirmed his estrangement from the family. He—and only he—was torn from his home and banished, sent away to a different country, to grandparents he had never met before.'

'To a place,' added Raoul, 'where he had to get the upper hand at once to ensure he was not cast out again. By bullying someone else who did not fit in. Which is why he picked upon Dickon de Bohun.'

Hugh gasped. 'Dickon de Bohun? Was *he* the butt of Edwin's bullying?'

'He was. Edwin isolated him by ridiculing his faintheartedness and luring his friends away.' Raoul grimaced. 'I do recall young de Bohun being somewhat reticent, overawed perhaps by what he knew of the families of the other squires. Anyway, once Edwin began playing pranks upon him, it seems the friends found it amusing too to see the boy humiliated. Although I suspect they feared retribution if they did not support Edwin in his persecution of de Bohun.' Hugh groaned. 'Then, somehow, Edwin learned what you already know, that Dickon is only partly gently born.'

Hugh looked up sharply, his eyes wide.

'With that knowledge,' continued Raoul, 'Edwin stepped up his bullying. After the hunting incident, I questioned all the other squires more closely.' He shook his head. 'I should have done so long ago. I learned from one of Edwin's former friends that Edwin considered it intolerable that a boy whose mother was a villein was sharing privileges due, in his eyes, only to those of *wholly* gentle birth.'

Hugh was leaning forward, his back bowed, his elbows on his knees, the empty mazer dangling from one hand. 'How, my lord, do you imagine Edwin learned the truth of Dickon's birth?' he said in a low voice.

Raoul's lip curled. 'I rather thought, Hugh, that you might know the answer to that yourself.'

Hugh seemed to think for several moments before letting out a deep sigh. 'Ah, yes, I probably do.'

Lord Raoul left Courtenay Castle without retelling his disturbing news to Hildegard. Hugh was so incensed when he realised she might have contributed to Edwin's misbehaviour, he asked the earl to let him acquaint her privately with the shocking information about their grandson.

Raoul was troubled about appearing discourteous, leaving without even exchanging a few words with Lady Hildegard. But Hugh was keen for him to go.

'I shall tell her you had to rush away. Another appointment perhaps?'

Raoul's eyebrows met. 'I am not sure I should condone an untruth. But it is not my place to tell you what to do in your own home, or say to your own wife.' He clasped Hugh's hand. 'You do know that my decision to allow Edwin to return to Steyning is dependent upon his future exemplary behaviour. If he puts another foot wrong, that will have to be the end of it.'

'Thank you, my lord, for giving him one last chance. If he betrays your trust again, he will have to return to Burgundy. Although I cannot imagine how he would fare there, knowing what I now do.'

'I agree. But that will be his parents' problem to resolve. Let us hope it does not come to that.'

33

Eager as Margery had been back in September to leave the Browghtons and put behind her Pers Cokewell's insults and accusations, not to mention the abuse she suffered from her master, All Saints' and Christmas came and went, and still she had not gone.

Once her anger cooled, she had considered the practicalities. How could she survive alone, with little money, no work and nowhere to live? She would be condemning herself to penury, maybe even death. Where was the sense in that? Besides, winter was the wrong time to consider giving up a roof and bed, and regular meals. She decided to sit it out at least until the spring.

She could do little to stop Gabriel doing whatever he wanted with her, although he had troubled her rarely these past few weeks and she supposed he had shifted his attentions once more to one of the others.

But at least she was rid of Pers.

It was not long after Pers levelled his witch accusation at Margery that Philippa Browghton had somehow got to hear of it. The two women were still treating the sick cows together, although the poor creatures were showing no sign of getting better.

'I hear Pers Cokewell has been throwing allegations your way, Margery,' said Mistress Browghton.

'He's an idiot.'

'An idiot with a vile tongue.' She bent down and tipped the phial of her remedy into Flora's foaming muzzle. 'I have always loathed the man.'

Margery was surprised. She had always assumed her mistress disliked her, and therefore might agree with Pers's assertion.

'I have told Gabriel to dismiss him.'

Margery gasped. "*Told*"? It was surprising too that her mistress's relationship with her husband was such that she could order him to do something. 'Is Pers leaving?'

Philippa stood up, and her lips twisted into a sneer. 'He is. Gabriel opposed me for a while, but I insisted that Pers Cokewell was not the sort of servant we want here. Moreover,' she continued, 'he has been casting his lascivious eyes in Jan's direction, turning her head, and I will *not* have my dairymaids taking up with the likes of him.'

So, it was not *she* whom her mistress wished to safeguard, but Jan. Though quite why she cared so much about the girl, when she was not even a particularly competent dairymaid, was a mystery. But she said nothing. She would be rid of Pers Cokewell after all, if not in quite the way she had planned.

For the next couple of weeks, into October, Margery and her mistress continued to spend a good deal of time together, trying to ease the cows' discomfort, hoping they might recover. She wondered if maybe Philippa did not contemn her as much as she had suspected, yet she was as cool with her as ever, and there was no sign of any softening in her attitude towards her. She seemed to have some respect for her abilities with the cows but Margery was still very much a servant in Philippa Browghton's eyes.

Neither Belle nor Flora survived despite their ministrations, and Margery was distraught. 'I was fond of Belle,' she said. 'She had such a gentle nature.'

'A good milker too. I am sorry we could not save her.'

'I shall take better care of the other two.'

But Mistress Browghton shook her head. 'This is not your fault, Margery. It is a common enough ailment. We have seen it many times here at Browghtons, and sometimes the animals have survived and sometimes not. I am sorry that this time my remedy did not triumph. But you are not to blame.'

In that moment Philippa Browghton seemed kinder than she had ever been before, although still she did not smile. Margery forced herself to smile, nonetheless. 'Thank you for saying so.'

The woman had nodded curtly, and pointed to the dead animals. 'I will ask Gabriel to deal with them. You go to help Jan and Ellen finish in the dairy.'

One of Margery's weekly tasks was to clean the parlour, a chamber reserved almost entirely for Mistress Browghton's use. It was here she had her spinning wheel, and a table for doing the household accounts. There were storage chests for costly items, and, most importantly of all, a bright-painted cupboard in which she kept her most valuable possession, her book of medicinal plants.

Of all the servants, only Margery was permitted access to the parlour, and only then to sweep its floors and dust the fine oak furniture. It was a pleasant room, with a large window that gave onto the flower garden and potager.

Usually, when Margery came to clean the parlour, Mistress Browghton would stay, spinning at her wheel, poring over her ledger of expenses, or reading from her cherished herbal. Margery always wished she would not stay, sensing she was being watched, to check she flicked the dust from every corner and wiped her cloth over every surface.

However, one day in late October, just as Margery arrived with her broom and cleaning cloth, the mistress ran upstairs to the upper chamber in a state of agitation, muttering about some problem with her youngest. Margery was astonished to see the great herbal lying open in its reading cradle on top of the painted cupboard. This was the first time she had ever seen its pages, for the mistress always made a point of locking the book away if she was to leave the chamber.

Yet here it was, surely inviting her to look.

She had almost forgotten her conversation with Ursula Kemp,

mostly because her interest in poisonous plants had waned. Whether or not her poppet charm had worked, Pers Cokewell had now left the farm, and she had no more reason to consider how to still his tongue. But the sight of the open book rekindled her curiosity.

She was drawn to its illustrated pages, and was astonished that Philippa Browghton might own such a book. How could she possibly have acquired it? But then she recalled a book her father had, not a herbal but a small missal. Each page had illustrations, much more ornate and colourful than these here, with scenes and figures amidst the passages of script, and cascades of flowers and scrolls around the edges. She never knew how her father had come by such a valuable book. In truth, she could not imagine even why he had it. He could read but, she was certain, only simple texts. Their mother could not read a word, but Father had insisted both his daughters learned, in anticipation, she supposed, of their eventual ascent up the ranks of Hampshire society. She grinned ruefully: *that* strategy certainly failed.

What had happened to that book? She had not thought of it for years. After Father's death and her own expulsion from the family home, she presumed much of the portable wealth he had amassed, in coin and in goods, was forfeit to the king alongside his house and land. The missal too, presumably.

Propping up her broom, she stepped closer to the cupboard and stared at the herbal's pages. A ribbon was tucked into the groove, marking the place where Mistress Browghton had been reading. The pages were describing feverfew, which Margery knew was a remedy for megrims. Good too, she read, for quinsy and the croup, and for reducing an ague's fierce heat. This book, she thought, probably described the properties and uses of every plant. Those plants Ursula Kemp had told her of might be here. Reading about them might refresh her memory, in case she ever decided she did need knowledge of them at some future date.

She turned the pages with care, holding the corners between her thumb and forefinger, searching for cuckoopint, belladonna, and wolf's bane. The book was huge, and it was not easy to read the words, for the script was elaborately penned, and the drawings were not much like the wild plants she had seen growing.

By the time she heard Mistress Browghton coming back

downstairs, she had found belladonna, and what she read accorded with what Ursula had told her. She flipped the pages back to where the ribbon lay and, stepping away from the cupboard, took up her broom again and began sweeping the floor on the far side of the chamber.

Philippa was still agitated and seemed not to notice Margery had made little progress with her work. But she glowered when she caught sight of the open herbal and, striding forward, folded the book shut with something of a bang. Then, opening the cupboard door, she hefted the heavy volume from its cradle, wrapped it in its linen cloth and placed it reverently upon the shelf.

Weeks passed before Margery had another chance to view the herbal, when the mistress was once more careless with her precious book. She did seem much distracted, although what might be upsetting her, Margery had no idea. Nonetheless, she had time to read about the cuckoopint before Philippa returned, again apparently unaware that her servant had been reading and not sweeping.

After that, no more opportunities arose, for she was always careful to lock the book away after she had used it. Margery was frustrated by her mistress's diligence but there was nothing she could do to make her less so. She resigned herself to never being able to read the book again.

A week or two after Christmas, the weather was not only cold but gloomy. The sun scarcely showed its face and, even at midday, the world seemed almost devoid of daylight. The house, despite its fine high windows, was dark, the solid wooden window shutters firmly closed to keep out the January chill. In the parlour, the light from the fire, and from the several candles the mistress allowed herself, did bring a little cheer but it was hard to dispel the murk of such a dismal winter's day. Nonetheless, work inside the house continued and Margery came through into the parlour from the hall, bearing her broom and cloth, ready to dust and sweep.

Mistress Browghton looked up from her reading. 'Ah, there you are,' she said. 'Are the children playing nicely?'

The Browghton children were in the hall. As far as Margery could tell, they were behaving, even though their nursemaid was not with them. 'They're huddled at the table, Mistress,' she said, 'playing a game of Nine Men's Morris. They seem content enough.'

'I am keeping an ear out for them,' said Philippa, 'whilst Nurse has an hour or two to herself.' She smiled, as she often did when referring to her children, if rarely otherwise.

Margery suppressed a snort. *She* was never given time off for herself during the working day. 'Shall I sweep up now, Mistress?'

Philippa nodded and was on the point of closing the book of plants when there came a shout, followed by another, and the sound of scuffling and a slamming door, from the cross passage beyond the hall. 'Whatever is going on?' she cried, throwing up her hands. She ran into the hall and through the door on the other side, banging the door closed behind her. Margery ran to the window, to see Gabriel hurrying away across the yard. Shortly afterwards, beyond the hall, two voices rose and fell. Who was arguing with Mistress Browghton, Margery could not be sure, but it clearly was a woman.

The argument sounded so heated, she wondered if she should give comfort to the children, who might well be frightened. But she cared little about the children, and was much more interested in taking the chance given her once more to find the page on wolf's bane.

She was so engrossed in reading that she did not notice that the arguing had stopped nor hear the footsteps coming back across the hall.

'What do you think you are doing?' cried Mistress Browghton, hastening forward, her hands flapping. She stared at the open pages. 'Wolf's bane! Why on earth are you reading about that?'

Margery stepped back at once, shuffling her feet. 'Oh, I can scarcely read the words, Mistress. But it is such a beautiful book—'

Philippa Browghton interjected, her eyes wide. 'Oh, but I am certain that you *can* read, Margery. A woman of your background would surely have been taught?' Her tone was threatening. Whatever had occurred just now had clearly shaken her.

Margery shrugged, affecting to ignore her mistress's sudden startling hostility. 'As a girl, indeed I was,' she said. 'But that was long ago, and I have had scant opportunity since to practise what I learned.' It sounded convincing enough to her ears, but her mistress did not seem reassured.

Indeed her temper rose, along with the tenor of her voice. It was then Margery noticed the wildness in her mistress's eyes, as well as the agitation in her body. 'I do not *believe* you, Margery,' she cried. 'Why *wolf's bane* of all plants? Why not strawberries or primroses?' She glowered. 'No, no, I suspect what you were actually doing, Margery, was discovering how to dispense poison— How to shut Gabriel's mouth perhaps?'

Margery gasped. 'Poison? Gabriel?'

Mistress Browghton's eyes glittered, and she let out a bitter laugh. 'You think I do not know what has been going on all these years?'

Margery opened her mouth to answer, although she had no idea what she might say in response to this surprising information. She had always presumed Philippa knew nothing of her husband's abuse of the other women in his household.

But her mistress held up her hand. 'Do not trouble to deny it. I have always known...' Her voice rattled in her throat. 'And perhaps I now know how...' Her eyebrows arched.

'How?' Margery swallowed, her mouth dry.

'Indeed, *how*. I dismissed Pers Cokewell's accusation, but perhaps he was right about you all along? They say ills come in threes...' She held up a finger. 'A good man bewitched into iniquity.' A second finger. 'Cows drained dry overnight.' A third. 'And, now, a plot?' She tossed her head. 'What does all that signify to you?'

Stunned by the sudden reversal in her mistress's view of her, and by the sheer inequity of what she was implying, Margery could not think at all how she might answer. She was still rigid with disbelief when Mistress Browghton lunged forward and grabbed her wrist, jerking it sideways in a painful twist.

'Nothing to say, you besom?' the woman cried. She twisted her wrist again and Margery flinched at the pain. 'I will tell you what it signifies. That I have been harbouring a vile *witch* within my household all these years.' The "witch" came out almost as a scream, and Margery wrenched her hand out of Mistress Browghton's grasp and darted across the room, away from her assailant. 'I do not know why I did not realise it before, with your disagreeable face, your coldness and your rancour.'

Margery stood behind an upright chair, her heart racing. Then her sense of terrible injustice—that she was being insulted *yet again*—set free her tongue.

She gripped the back of the chair as if it was a shield. 'If I was a witch,' she said, trying not to shout, 'why would I need to *read* about wolf's bane, when surely I would already know everything about it? As for the cows, you said yourself that they were *sick*, with an ailment we have seen many times before. You *denied* Pers's claim they were bewitched.' Her heart was thumping and her hands were slick against the chair, but she was determined to appear calm.

But she was having no influence on Mistress Browghton's temper.

'I want you gone from here,' she screamed. 'Tonight!'

'Tonight? Where will I go?'

'You should have thought of that before you used your sorcery and wiles on my beloved husband.'

Margery almost hooted. "Sorcery and wiles"? How utterly absurd. Yet her mistress's accusations were scarcely a matter for amusement. The case she was contriving against her might be ludicrous and unjust, but, once a woman had been accused of witchcraft, it was difficult to gainsay it.

She let go of the chair and turned towards the hall. Her mistress scowled at her but did not advance. 'Yes, I would go now if I were you, before the afternoon grows dark.'

How predictably heartless of Mistress Browghton, to turn her servant out of her home of fifteen years on a waning January afternoon. But she no longer had the energy for argument. She would just go, and take her chances. She was already done with being slandered and abused. Now she had cause too to be afraid.

Margery had almost finished stuffing her few belongings into her satchel when, glancing out of the small window in the upper chamber, she saw the children's nursemaid crossing the yard towards the road, clutching a heavy-looking travelling bag.

Grabbing her satchel and her thick cloak, Margery ran downstairs, along the passage and through the outside door, calling to the woman to wait. The nursemaid stopped. There was a faint smile on her lips.

'You are leaving?' Margery said.

She nodded. 'I told the mistress Master Browghton had assaulted me. She didn't like it.' Her smile became a smirk.

Margery gasped. '*You?*'

'Why not?'

'No reason. I always wondered if he had.'

'He's tried many times since I first came here but usually the children saved me. But now they're older, I have a little time to myself. Gabriel, of course, discovered it, and caught me when I was alone. I tried to stop him, told him the risk he was running, but he did what he wanted nonetheless.' Her lip curled. 'The last time, earlier, in the buttery, was his undoing.'

'You told the mistress then?'

She tossed her head. 'I'd had enough. I came here to bring up their children, not be set upon and ravished. I thought Mistress Browghton should know the manner of man she's married to.'

Margery could not help but grin. 'That information was not met with gratitude?'

'Hardly. She didn't believe me. Denied the possibility of it. "Gabriel has always been a most attentive husband," she declared. "A good man, who'd never assault a servant." She accused me of leading him on. Me? So, I told her I wasn't the first.'

Margery gasped again.

'I've known about you and Gabriel for some time. Always wondered why you put up with it.'

'It began when I first came here,' said Margery. 'I was young. This was my only home.'

'But that's years ago. In all that time you've just accepted it?'

Margery felt almost ashamed. 'Not "accepted", no. I had no choice. Nowhere else to go.' She frowned. 'So, you told the mistress about me?'

'Why not? It was the truth.'

'Because now she has dismissed me too. She says I *bewitched* him—'

'Bewitched?' The nursemaid's eyes were wide. 'How absurd.' She grimaced. 'And alarming.'

'Indeed,' said Margery. 'So, I must leave now too. And I still have nowhere to go.'

'I'm sorry about that, but the man's a knave, and his wife has now clearly lost her wits. You're surely better off away from here.'

'I have thought so many times, but where will I go? Who will employ me?'

The nursemaid shrugged. 'Same applies to me, but I'll not stay here to be abused. I knew Mistress Browghton would dismiss me, which is why I spoke out. We don't have to put up with it, you know.'

'I have done so a long time.'

'But not all men are like Gabriel Browghton.'

'Do you know he assaults Jan and Ellen too?'

'I suspected it. He's got no control, that man. You do know why, don't you?'

Margery shook her head and the nursemaid sniggered.

'Our haughty mistress,' she said, her voice animated, 'has been denying him his rights since Master Henry was born. She doesn't want any more children, and who can blame her. So, despite the church's ruling about marital relations, she refuses him.'

That scarcely explained Gabriel's *fifteen* years of clandestine swiving, but perhaps accounted for his ill humour of recent years. 'I am surprised she is able to refuse him,' Margery said. 'He is very forceful.'

'Ah, but she's the one with the money. He can't risk her telling her family he's a fornicator. He might lose everything.'

Well, *that* was something Margery did not know. Although she doubted Philippa Browghton would bring humiliation upon herself by revealing her husband's failings.

'Anyway,' the nursemaid continued, 'when she accused me of leading him on, I denied it. As if I would? But she refused to believe me. She doesn't want to think her husband is a sinner.'

'But now she is accusing me of practising sorcery upon him...'

'She probably thinks the same about me. About "women like us".' She raised an eyebrow. 'As if men like Gabriel Browghton need bewitching.'

She wished Margery good fortune then strode away, moments before Philippa Browghton emerged from the farmhouse.

'Margery,' she called. 'It is getting late. Perhaps you should leave in the morning?'

Margery was bemused. Only a short while ago, the woman could not wait for her to leave. Tonight, she had said. Why then had she changed her mind? Perhaps the nursemaid was right, and Philippa

Browghton had lost her wits? In truth, Margery wondered whether she even wanted to stay in the house another night. Nonetheless, she nodded, and went upstairs again with her cloak and satchel.

Yet, not long after, she decided after all not to stay till morning. It seemed dangerous to linger, with an accusation of witchcraft hanging over her. She peered through the little window in the upstairs chamber. It might be January, but the weather was dry and not unduly cold. As evening fell, she saw the moon was full. It would light her way.

When the household was asleep, she took up her belongings once again and tiptoed from the chamber, stepping past Jan and Ellen, who were both snoring and knew nothing of her going. Outside once more, the yard was almost as bright as day. The air was chilly but still. She had no idea at all where she was going but her heart was beating with excitement.

As she hurried towards the gate and the road away from Middle Brooking, she sensed a lightness flowing through her. At last, after fifteen years, she was freeing herself from servitude and abuse for good.

34

Margery had no plan.

She was grateful for the bright moon that lit her way, showing up the deep ruts in the road, and helping her avoid stumbling into the muddy ditches either side. But, at the very moment she arrived in Meonbridge, the buildings she had been able to see as she was approaching disappeared. Looking up, she saw dark clouds had formed again, the moon's feeble light almost entirely snuffed out.

The brisk pace of her flight from the farm had kept her body warm, despite the chilly breath puffing from her lips. But the sudden loss of light brought her to a halt, and the cold was soon enough seeping through her layered garments.

What precisely was she going to do? Perhaps after all she should have accepted Mistress Browghton's suggestion to stay until the morning? Leaving in the middle of the night was, in truth, absurd. But there was now no turning back. Certainly, standing still was not a good idea. She had to find somewhere to shelter for the remainder of the night.

She turned onto the main road that ran through the village, up towards the manor house. Surely there would be empty outhouses and barns, or even an abandoned cot or two where she might find refuge. Yet it was now so dark, it was difficult to discern any building that she recognised.

She came shortly to the green, in the middle of the village, and the dark shape of Saint Peter's church loomed ahead of her. Might the church door be open, so she could find shelter there a while? She edged along the green towards the lych-gate, stepping carefully upon the grass, which crunched underfoot and felt a little slippery. The gate creaked as she pushed it open. She held her breath, but everywhere was silent: nobody was abroad.

The towering yews threw the churchyard into the deepest gloom. Her heart thudded as she shuffled along the narrow path that wove between the tombs and gravestones towards the church's door, her ears alert to every small scuffle in the undergrowth, and each flap of airy wings.

The church door was locked: no sanctuary here.

She slumped onto the wooden bench inside the porch. There must be somewhere she could find shelter, if only for tonight. She sat there a while, but the chill of the stone floor was creeping into her boots, and an ache soon gripped her back and stomach. She could not just stay here.

Although, if she did, of course, come morning, her travails might all be over...

She considered that a moment. Yet she was only thirty-four; young enough still, surely, to find herself a better life?

She stayed in the porch a moment longer, then heaved herself to her feet. As she did so, a memory slipped into her head, of her and her sister solemnly following their parents up here to Saint Peter's, walking the short distance from their house. Their house, standing behind the church.

She stepped out of the porch. Would the house be empty? After her father's ignoble death, his property was given to the king. Yet, after all this time, it seemed improbable that such a fine house would still not be occupied. But it was worth a look.

Finding soon enough the connecting gate, she saw that rampant undergrowth, albeit all now mostly dead and dry, had flourished around her father's house. The tangle of brambles and ivy was, even in January, still dense enough to impede her progress towards the house's door through what had once been a glorious garden. But then the clouds parted a little and the moon once more glowed weakly, helping her to find a way through the snarl of tendrils. Her heart sank when she saw how dilapidated her childhood home had become.

Yet it was soon clear no one had usurped it. Decrepit as it was, it was still hers to occupy.

The main door was heavy and, as she shoved at it with what little strength she had left in her weary body, it refused to yield. She whimpered. If it was locked, she might not be able to gain entry. But she was tired now, and all she wanted was to lie down and sleep.

She shoved at the door again, leaning hard against it with her shoulder. A sharp pain ripped through her arm, but at length the door shifted just a little. Taking a deep breath, she leaned her whole body against the door's open edge and pushed. At last, the door moved enough for her to squeeze through the gap. She picked up her bundle of belongings and slipped inside.

At once she was choking, as a cloud of dust swirled up from the floor. Coughing, she pulled the edge of her hood across her nose and mouth. She leaned her back against the door to shut it and stared into the vastness of what had been the grand hall.

The moon was shining again, if weakly, but its beams, piercing the broken shutters, gave just enough light for her to see that the room was no longer grand. It was bare of furniture: neither the heavy trestle table, nor her father's carved oak chair, nor any of the painted cabinets were there. Everything from the hall was gone, apart from a single stool. Had it been taken for the king, or looted later? Who knew? Please God, let there be at least one bed upstairs. Letting her eyes accustom further to the gloom, she shuffled across the hall to the narrow staircase that led up to the solar.

She would deal with all the filth tomorrow. Tonight she had to sleep.

Margery slept fitfully, and awoke when morning was still some while off, although the chamber was no longer fully dark. Her sleep had not revived her, yet she was sure she would find no more. How relieved she had been last night to find a bed upstairs, though she wondered why it too had not been taken. Too big to get downstairs perhaps? In truth, it was hardly comfortable, with the mattress damp and mouldy, and the rope cording underneath it loose and sagging.

Rolling off the bed, she threw her cloak about her shoulders and stepped carefully down the stairs to the hall. She pushed open the rickety shutters to let in dawn's early light, and looked about her. The room was covered with a layer of dust and grime. Cobwebs cascaded from every beam and clustered in the corners. She groaned. How long would it take to clean the place sufficient for her to live here? And did she have the strength to do it?

A gust of air rattled one of the shutters, buffeting it back and forth against the window frame. She went over to secure it open but, as she struggled with the fixing, a chilly blast whipped in through the uncovered window, and she realised in that moment how impossible it would be to live here without adequate protection for the tall windows against the winter weather, and without some warmth.

She stared at the long-dead hearth. Surely she would have to light a fire? Yet, if she did, would it not betray that she was here in Meonbridge? She feared anyone knowing where she was, in case Philippa Browghton's accusation somehow followed her.

Perhaps staying here, in this house, so close to the centre of the village, was not after all a good idea? There must be other empty houses, more isolated than this one, where she might live out the winter. If she had any plan, it was to stay only until the spring, when better weather made travel practicable. She would then leave Meonbridge altogether. But she surely would not survive till then without at least a little warmth?

Disheartened, she sank onto the stool, pulling her cloak up close around her head. She sat there for only a few moments before she began to shiver. Hauling herself to her feet, she went to close the shutters once again. The chamber was now dark as well as cold. She could hardly live like this.

But where would she find another house? And how? She could scarcely wander about the village, looking. She thought about her visit to Ursula Kemp. Upper Brooking itself was some distance further on, even more isolated but not too long a walk to Meonbridge, when she needed to obtain supplies. Ursula had made a comfortable enough home, but her cottage had not been too dilapidated. That might not be true of the empty cots in Upper Brooking, abandoned fifteen years ago and likely in a sorry state. Yet, what choice did she have?

Despite the chilly wind and her fatigue, she wrapped up as warmly as she could and took the overgrown track out towards the deserted hamlet. As she trudged along, she wondered if she should call in to see Ursula, to tell her she was here. Yet, could she trust the woman not to give her away? She thought perhaps she could for, after all, Ursula was herself an outcast. She had also once been rumoured to be a witch, which was why she had hidden herself away out here.

Nonetheless, when she reached Ursula's cottage, she hurried past it, on towards the hamlet. There, she found four cots clustered together, hidden amidst the forest that had burgeoned since folk stopped coming here. She recalled that it had once been the home of four families of Collyeres, all charcoal burners. Every Collyere had perished in the Mortality except, she thought, two boys, who came to Meonbridge to find work.

She stepped from cot to cot, looking inside each one. The first three were in ruins, their walls mostly crumbled away, the roof thatch rotten and fallen in. But the fourth one still had standing walls, and its roof looked more or less intact. Inside, there was just one room, with a hearth in the middle of the floor. The furniture was meagre: a couple of stools, a rickety table and a mattress in one corner, even mouldier than the one in the Tyler house, its straw stuffing leaking from rips in the coarse cover. Of course, the place was grimy too but it was so small, it might not take too long to clean.

Back at the Tyler house, she searched every room for any things that might prove useful. She was glad that a few cooking utensils had been left behind in the cot at Upper Brooking, for there was little here. It was as if the house had been looted of all objects small enough to carry away. But, in the upstairs chamber, hidden behind the bed, she found a couple of small chests. Lifting the lids, she saw that one of them had been her mother's. For, inside it, amongst other items, were her sewing instruments and the pair of shears Father once gave her as a gift. There were some lengths of fabric, too, most of it bleached linen, though also a small quantity of blue wool cloth. It might all one day be of use, and was not too heavy, so she tied everything together in a bundle and took it downstairs.

She was sorry to be leaving her old home, having only just rediscovered it. But she had no choice. She had to keep herself safe until it was time to depart Meonbridge for good. Picking up her bag and bundle, she gave a wistful sigh and closed the door.

A few days later, the little cot was mostly clean, or as clean as she could make it.

It was scarcely comfortable, but at least it gave shelter from the worst of the cold and wet, and no one would discover her out here. For the time being, she would not speak to anyone outside, not even Ursula Kemp. This meant she could not purchase food, despite having a little money, saved, a halfpenny here, a halfpenny there, from fifteen years of meagre wages. For now, at least, she planned to go into Meonbridge occasionally, when the market stalls were closing, to pick up whatever scraps had been abandoned by the stallholders. There were always some: stale bread, wilting cabbage, onions with rotten cores. Her needs were small and she would make do.

Whenever she left the house, she tried to ensure she would not be recognised. Swaddling herself in layers of cloaks and shawls, and shuffling about bent-backed and leaning on a gnarled stick, concealed both her face and her true age. She thought a few folk might have noticed an unfamiliar "old crone" occasionally loitering by the market kiosks as they closed down at day's end. But late afternoons in January were so cold and gloomy, everyone, like her, was enveloped in hoods and cloaks and mufflers, and no one lingered long enough to ask her who she was.

Thus she succeeded in creeping unrecognised about the village, secreting in her satchel anything remotely edible she found discarded upon the ground. Her trips rarely yielded much, but she told herself it was enough. What she would do if there were no rejects from the market stalls, she did not know. But she determined to take each day as it came.

She found too that, if she went when it was almost dark, she could draw water from the nearest well without meeting a soul. She never took much: just enough to drink and splash her face and hands clean in the morning.

The first evening, she had lit a fire, albeit a small one. She was pleased to find a tinder box amongst the cot's former occupants' belongings, and gathered wood from between the trees that surrounded the cot.

So, she was warm enough, had water and a little food, but it was a miserable existence. Yet at least there was no one here to violate her body or denounce her as a witch. All she had to do was survive for a few short months. Then she would leave, go far away from Meonbridge, and find herself the new life she deserved.

35

It had been so good to talk to Dickon again, to find they could be friends without the complication of— Well, without any complication. Libby was so relieved that, when he asked her if she was happy, she could say truthfully she was.

James had come along at just the right time. Even though she'd already accepted she and Dickon could never marry, that hadn't stopped her worrying about what the future held. When James brought her the lover's token the day after the harvest feast, she was surprised. Yet she knew almost at once she would be wearing it when he called on her again.

He returned two weeks later, as he said he would. In the days before, she'd taken to wearing the token and, of course, Lady Margaret had noticed.

'Might a certain young carpenter have given you that token?' she'd said, a gleam in her eye.

Libby couldn't help but blush. 'Am I right to wear it, do you think, your ladyship?'

'If you believe you will be happy with Master Paynter, then naturally you must wear it when he comes to ask you for your answer.'

James's eyes lit up too when he saw his token, threaded onto the blue ribbon encircling her neck. It was resting between the small curves of her breasts. 'You've decided?' he said, and she nodded. 'Lady Margaret has agreed that I might ask you.'

He took her hand. 'So, Elizabeth Fletcher, will you do me the honour of agreeing to become my wife?'

She giggled at his formality, then flung his hand aside and threw her arms about his neck. 'Of course I will,' she cried, and kissed his cheek.

He blew out his lips. 'How glad I am to hear it.' He smiled broadly. 'I were thinking we might wed in the spring? Naught's yet agreed but the workshop I'm hoping for in Wickham might be ready then, and it'd be a fine time for us to marry.'

'The same time Dickon's getting betrothed.'

'I know. Daresay our wedding won't be such a grand affair as that.'

'But it'll be lovely all the same.'

Ever since that day, Libby had felt utterly content. Dickon would always have a small place in her heart: he was her first love, and she regretted how badly she'd behaved towards him. But his noble character had saved her. Otherwise, she wouldn't now be betrothed to a good man like James Paynter. She'd been fortunate, and she knew it.

The grand Christmas feast was the first time since the harvest celebration that Libby had been seen openly with James. Lady Margaret had agreed to her sitting with her betrothed, instead of at her ladyship's side. The atte Wodes and Sawyers were amongst the more important families in the village and always occupied a trestle close to the raised dais where the high table stood. Although Libby always enjoyed sitting next to her ladyship, elevated a little above the rest of the village, she enjoyed much more being seen at the side of such a well-respected man as James.

She looked about her, not wanting to appear immodest but hoping she might see folk acknowledging her good fortune. And, sure enough, every so often someone did catch her eye and smile, or raise their cup to her in salutation. She had felt blessed, in a way she'd never felt before. And she owed it all to Dickon.

Apart from a fleeting conversation at the Christmas feast, Libby hadn't seen Maud since late November. It had been cold and wet since then, and Libby spent most of her days upstairs in Lady Margaret's chamber, huddled with her ladyship by the fire. It was boring but at least it was warm and dry.

But January ushered in altogether drier weather and, although it was still chilly, she felt she might venture out of doors again. She was longing to tell her friend her latest news: that the workshop James had been hoping for was most definitely to be his, and they'd be marrying in April before moving the few miles down the Meon's valley to the little town of Wickham.

'I'll miss you so much, Libby.' Maud's eyes moistened.

'I'll miss you too. But James says he hopes we'll visit Meonbridge often.'

'But you'll be a married woman. Maybe even a mother?' She twisted the folds of her skirt between her fingers. 'It won't be the same.'

A married woman! Libby's stomach gave a flip. Of course, she knew it, but it sounded strange and maybe even a little frightening, the idea of *her* of all people being a man's wife. But maybe all young brides felt the same? She wished her mother was here to give her wise advice. Though perhaps her mother wouldn't be the best person in the world to give advice on marriage? Yet it would be nice to ask someone about how best to be a wife, what to expect. She could hardly ask her ladyship.

'But we'll still be friends.' She squeezed Maud on the arm. 'Maybe you'll soon be wed yourself?'

Maud pointed to her leg. 'Who'll want to marry me?'

Libby frowned. Maud always thought so badly of herself, yet she'd make any man a splendid wife, for she knew everything there was to know about managing a household, tending a garden and looking after animals and children. Yet it was true that, ever since Maud's accident, boys had looked askance at her lame leg and called her names behind her back, albeit she was still pretty. It was unkind, and unjust, but people could be cruel. She squeezed Maud's arm again. 'Someone will,' she said, with a firmness she wasn't sure she trusted.

Maud got up to add some more wood to the fire in the hearth. When she sat down again, she changed the subject. 'Anyway, I've heard something, or rather Ma has. We wondered if you knew.'

'What about?'

'Your Aunt Margery.'

Libby didn't know quite what to think about Maud's news. Had Margery left Meonbridge altogether?

Mistress Miller, Maud's stepmother, burst into the house moments later, carrying a basket with a few onions and a cabbage. She put the basket down and came to stand before the fire, slapping her hands against her arms. 'Goodness, it's cold today,' she cried. 'It's as well I had the onions in store, else I'd still be out there digging. The cabbage put up quite a fight to stay in the ground.' She laughed, and Maud and Libby joined in.

Growing vegetables might be *her* responsibility before too long, thought Libby. She was glad she'd paid close attention to Lady Margaret's efforts to teach her how.

'Maud's just told me what you heard about my aunt, Mistress Miller,' she said.

Mistress Miller took off her cloak and hung it on the drying rack. She pulled up a small stool and sat next to the girls. 'To be honest, it's all hearsay, Libby. But, as I understand it, Margery's disappeared from the Browghtons' farm. Just in the past few days. Master Browghton's been seen in Meonbridge, asking if anybody's seen her. But she seems to have entirely vanished.'

'*Nobody* has seen her?'

'So I hear,' Mistress Miller said. 'I wonder what can have happened? Do you know anything, Libby dear?'

She shrugged. 'I know she did hate it there.'

'Master Browghton was rather agitated, by all accounts,' Mistress Miller continued, 'about her leaving'.

How very odd. Why might *Master* Browghton come looking for her aunt? Was he troubled perhaps she might betray him? 'I've no idea why Aunt Margery might have left,' she said. 'After all, it was her home, as well as her job. Did Master Browghton not say why?'

Mistress Miller shook her head. 'Not that I heard. Poor woman. She's had such bad luck all her life. Ever since her father—' She stopped. 'Anyway, that's old history.' She touched Libby's arm. 'Did you even know your aunt? You've never spoken of her.'

'Hardly at all.' She turned her face away. 'Strange, really.' The truth was she was relieved by Mistress Miller's news. She'd been troubled by her aunt's behaviour the last time she saw her. If she had now truly gone away, out of her life, it was surely for the best.

Mistress Miller got up from the stool and fetched a knife and the onions she'd brought in. She sliced the vegetables with quick, firm strokes. 'Strange you didn't know her, you mean?' she said, and Libby nodded. 'Mebbe just as well,' she went on, 'for I've heard the Browghtons thought she was a witch.'

Maud and Libby gasped at the same time. 'A witch?' said Maud, her eyes wide.

Libby felt a little sick. Her aunt was certainly wild and strange, but that surely didn't mean she was a witch? How could she be? A woman can't just *become* a witch. It made no sense.

Mistress Miller noticed her unease. 'Oh, Libby dear, I'm so sorry,' she said. 'I shouldn't have said anything. I'm sure it's only foolish gossip. You know what some folk are like.' She put an arm around her shoulder and squeezed it gently.

Libby nodded and, giving her a weak smile, stood up. 'I must go,' she said, her voice tense. She needed to be on her own, to think about this upsetting news. Even if it was just gossip, the story had to have come from somewhere.

As Libby hurried back towards the manor house, her mind was reeling. What had Aunt Margery done to be called a witch? Of course, she'd probably never know, not now her aunt had disappeared.

She wondered whether to tell Lady Margaret about her. She'd not told her about her meetings with Margery, apart from when they first met last spring. But perhaps she could mention her apparent disappearance, though not that she might be a witch. That was something she'd keep to herself.

'Was it fun seeing Maud again?' said Lady Margaret as Libby hung up her cloak and came back towards the fire. 'I daresay she was pleased to hear your news?'

'Though she's sad I'm moving away from Meonbridge.'

'Wickham is not so far away.'

'That's what I said.' She bustled about the chamber, picking up the cloak and boots her ladyship must have worn this afternoon. 'You've been out for a walk, milady?' The cloak was dry enough to fold, but the boots still felt damp and she moved them closer to the blazing hearth.

Lady Margaret laughed. 'Scarcely a walk. Rather, allowing my nose and cheeks to test the chilly air for a few moments before retreating indoors again.'

Libby nodded. 'I almost ran back up the hill. It's not a day for lingering out of doors.' Which made her think of Margery, and wonder where she was. Where might she be living? Or was she homeless? Having nowhere warm to go was horrible but, if Margery *was* a witch, then she hoped she'd gone as far away from Meonbridge as possible.

'Mistress Miller had some news about my aunt,' she said.

Her ladyship lifted an eyebrow. 'Margery?'

'She's apparently left the Browghtons' farm, where she was working.'

'Left?' Lady Margaret. 'Do you mean dismissed, or run away?'

She repeated what Mistress Miller had told her. 'Master Browghton has been looking for her, as if she'd run off.'

'How very odd. I have never met the Browghtons, but John has told me they are rather withdrawn, unfriendly people.'

'Aunt Margery used to say that.'

Lady Margaret's eyebrows lifted again. 'You have spoken to her again since that first meeting?'

'Oh, only once or twice.' She turned away a little. 'I found my aunt a little strange. Albeit I felt sorry for her too, as she was so obviously unhappy. Maybe now she's gone to find herself a better life?'

'I would like to think she might find contentment somehow, although it is hard to imagine how a woman in such a difficult position as hers might achieve a more easeful life. But I daresay we will never know.'

36

Most nights Margery slept, if restlessly, but when she awoke, she never felt ready to meet the day.

She could not remember the last time her head had not spun when, swinging her legs off the noisome mattress to the floor, she tried to rise. It happened every morning now. She had to lie back again and wait for the dizziness to pass. Then, when it did, for a while she could not quite remember what she was about to do.

At length she would stand up, and wrap another shawl about her shoulders. She shuffled about the room, nibbled at a hardened hunk of bread, the remains of a stale pie or the sound part of an onion. She scooped a cup of water from the bucket and sipped it. She sat on one of the wobbly stools and gazed about her at the empty room that had probably once been full of life, if not of laughter. She went out for market gleanings only if the day was dry: despite the meagre fire, she did not want her few clothes to get wet.

If only spring would come, her misery might be relieved.

The morning she was awoken by a blackbird singing in the tree that towered feet from the cot's single tiny window, she could not help but smile. It was the first time in months she had even *thought* of smiling. But the bird's trilling song lifted her spirits, if just a little. She lay there a while longer, waiting for a few rays of sunshine to pierce the shutter. Then she eased herself upright. She splashed water onto her face and, stripping off the layers of clothes she wore at night for warmth, pulled on a different kirtle.

Her kirtles were hanging loose and long upon her now: the low neckline of her favourite slipped off her bony shoulders. To stop herself from tripping up, she had to tie a length of cord about her waist and pull the fabric of the skirt up and over it, so it did not drag along the floor.

Opening the door, she stepped outside the cot. The brambles that, long ago, had spread from the woodland floor and now flourished against the flimsy walls, were no longer just a tangle of thorny stems, mingled with rambling ivy. A host of bright green leaves was now beginning to unfurl.

She let out a sigh. Spring had arrived already, and she had not even noticed. Being so hidden amidst the trees, and overwhelmed with vegetation, the cot was dark and chilly. But the sun might be high enough in the sky for her to feel its heat.

A breath of mild air wafted against her cheek and, spurred by the prospect of feeling spring's new warmth, she hurried forward. There was a clearing at the beginning of the track back to Meonbridge. As she reached it, a patch of sunlight was casting a bright glow upon the path ahead. She stepped towards it and stood in its glow, blinking at the brightness. Then she took off her hood and bared her neck, welcoming the sun's warmth upon her skin. To enjoy it better, she closed her eyes a moment, but her head at once pitched and reeled, and she had to open them again.

She rocked a moment back and forth, then a chilly tremor twitched at her shoulders. Whimpering, she put her fingers to her naked neck: the skin *was* warm. Yet the heat was not even beginning to permeate her body. Shivering once more, she replaced her hood, her short-lived pleasure spent.

Stepping out of the bright pool, she stumbled back towards the cot and sank onto a stool.

· · ·

Subsisting on the paltry and mostly inedible supplies she still had left, it was several more days before she thought of venturing out in search of more. Even then she hesitated. It was true that, however many layers of clothes she wore, day and night, her body still never seemed to warm up. But that would not be the case for other folk in Meonbridge. If she went out as she had before, shrouded in shawls and cloaks, she would arouse suspicion. Even if she left her outings until late afternoon, as she usually did, it would be no longer gloomy or especially chilly: even on a dull day, it was still light at the time the stalls were closing.

Nonetheless, she had nothing left to eat. She had to make an effort somehow—or else accept that her flight from the Browghtons had been the journey to her death. Though, now spring was clearly on its way, she might not have much longer to endure life in this miserable place. A week or two might be enough.

But, to go out and about in Meonbridge now, she must surely assume a different guise. The old woman, swaddled into invisibility, would no longer do. Yet she could neither expose her face to recognition nor invite enquiry as to her business.

Perhaps, too, she should change her tactics? Instead of waiting for a time of day when the village was mostly quiet, when now she might attract attention, might it work better if she went at busy times and tried to blend in with the crowd? She might even try spending a little money, buying enough food at once to last for several days. Of course, that would involve talking to the stallholders, which was a risk. Supposing someone had come looking for her? Might Mistress Browghton have sent a servant to ask if anyone had seen her? But so many weeks had passed since she left the Browghtons, surely they would not be bothering about her now? Yet her reputation as a witch might be common knowledge here in Meonbridge, and folks with a taste for hunting might be eager for the chase if they espied their prey.

Though it also was quite possible that nobody would recognise her now. Seeing how scrawny the rest of her body was, her face most probably looked quite different from the way it had. Prodding at it with her fingertips told her that her cheeks were bony and hollow. She tried to see herself in the surface of a bucket full of water, holding a scrap of lighted candle up above her head. The image was shadowy and unstable, but what she saw confirmed her view.

What she needed was an enveloping sort of headdress, similar to those worn by goodwives in the village. She recalled her mother, not liking to show her face outside the house, would wrap a large linen kerchief about her head, plucking the sides forward to obscure her cheeks. She wore a wimple too, pulling it up above her chin to hide her mouth. Not much of her face was visible. Such a headdress might also work well for her.

She remembered then the things she had discovered in her mother's sewing chest: the linen was exactly what she needed.

As she now cut the bleached linen into suitable sized pieces for a kerchief and a wimple, she could not at first recall how her mother kept them secure upon her head. But, when she discovered a few pins inside the small box that held her mother's needles, different coloured threads, and a thimble, she remembered. Mother tied a fillet band around her head then pinned the kerchief and the wimple to it.

That was the answer to her needs too, yet Margery groaned. Making a fillet would require stitching: she had to add some form of tapes to fasten it. Her fingers were so stiff, just threading a needle was a trial. Pushing the needle in and out of the linen fabric made her fingertips burn and her knuckles ache.

She was much out of practice. Sewing had not been amongst her duties at the Browghtons' farm. Yet as a girl she had been a proficient needlewoman. Her mother had made both her and Matilda do plain sewing as soon as they were old enough to use a needle without stabbing themselves with it. It was not long before she was sharing with her mother the task of making shirts and shifts, and sheets and pillow covers. Matilda, however, hated sewing and proved herself incompetent—or pretended that she was—so her mother at length gave up with her. But Margery could sew a straight seam, her stitches were fine and neat, and the garments and the bed linens that she made were always of the best quality.

That could not be said of her present efforts: the fillet was a botch. Yet it scarcely mattered, for it would be hidden. All it had to do was stay tied about her head. Which, when she tried it on, it did. It took a few attempts to get the kerchief and wimple to sit quite the way she wanted but at length she was satisfied and turned her attention to her dress.

To blend in with other women in the village, she had to dress like them. She could not simply wear her outsize kirtles, hanging on her like a sack and bunched over at the waist. But a surcoat might cover up the disarray. She sighed: *more* stitching, but she would make it simple. Pray God the blue cloth would be sufficient. As she held it up against her, she could see that if she made the surcoat sleeveless and shorter than was customary, it would be just enough. She let out a deeper sigh. Cutting it would be both difficult and nerve-wracking: she could not afford to make mistakes.

All at once her resolution left her. It was the sounds and sights of spring that had encouraged her; and the warmth of the sun. Yet, what did it matter if she never left this house again? Nobody knew she was here. Nobody would know if she lay down upon the bed and let matters take their course. She would certainly not be missed.

Letting the blue cloth fall onto the floor, she stumbled against the stool as her legs gave way beneath her. She slumped down onto it, her heart thudding. Her throat tightened as she turned over what she had been thinking. It churned time and time again, till her head was reeling. But at length it stopped: her mind emptied. Pressing down against the table edge, she pushed herself to her feet. She swayed a moment then regained her balance. She must get a drink of water to ease her throat.

The coolness of the water soothed the soreness. It revived her spirit a little too. She found the last remnant of the bread she came home with more than a week ago. It had been stale for all that time. Now it was so hard, she would surely break her teeth if she tried to chew it. She poured a little water into the single bowl available and put the bread in it to soak. It was the very last morsel of food she had in the house. Tomorrow she *must* go out.

The afternoon had advanced, and it was rather gloomy indoors now for stitching. Yet if she was to mingle with the Meonbridge goodwives in the morning, she had to have that surcoat. She took up the blue wool cloth and her mother's sewing instruments once more. It was scarcely bright enough in the room to sew, but she persisted. She cut the fabric roughly into the shapes she needed then stitched the pieces together as neatly as she could. The light was fading fast as she continued, hemming the neckline and open armholes, determined to finish it. It was not a fine example of her sewing skills, but it would serve.

Whether or not she would wear the surcoat and her headdress and go out into the market was a decision for tomorrow.

The market was already busy with activity by the time Margery arrived. Keeping her head down, she tottered forward to join the press of goodwives, gossiping and examining what there was to buy.

Yet she saw at once that food supplies seemed scant: there was bread, certainly, and baskets of onions, and heaps of porray vegetables, turnips, kale, cabbage and colewort. But no eggs, no butter, no salted meat. Moreover, the man who used to wander around the market selling meat pies was nowhere to be seen. How disappointing. She had come out with a little money, hoping to buy something nourishing to eat, but there was nothing much to be had. For a while she was confused, but soon enough it came to her: it must be Lent.

Nonetheless, she made one or two purchases, keeping her face covered by her wimple and averted from the vendors. Then she walked on, unsteadily, weaving between groups of chattering women, trying not to stumble into anyone as she listened out for any crumbs of gossip that might be of use.

She soon learned from conversations that Easter was three weeks away. Not that that was of any interest to her, as she would scarcely be attending Mass on Easter Sunday. Of much greater interest was an event she heard would happen at the end of April, a week or two after Easter.

She hovered by a stall selling a few homemade pots, picking them up and turning them over idly in her trembling hands, whilst eavesdropping on an excited conversation between two women, one of whom she recognised but could not put a name to. She had pulled her kerchief well forward to obscure her face and kept her back towards the women.

'Her ladyship's putting on a grand do for it,' one said.

'Do you know who the young lord's marrying?' asked the other.

'The little daughter of Sir Giles Fitzpeyne,' crowed the first. 'You'll not know him. It were years ago he came to Meonbridge, expecting to wed her ladyship's daughter, Johanna. But he went home without his bride…' She then regaled her friend with the unhappy reason: for Philip's murder had occurred the very next day and his sister was so distraught she refused to accept Sir Giles's troth.

The woman carried on, plainly relishing the unsavoury details of what had happened. When she had heard enough, Margery put down the small bowl in her hand and stumbled away. Her heart was thumping as she reached the cot. She shoved open the flimsy door and, pushing it closed again, leaned her back against it.

If Dickon de Bohun was to marry the Fitzpeyne girl, what had happened to her niece? She had clearly been thrown over, as she had said. But had she also been sent away, like Matilda, or was she already married off to some old man, as she had feared? One or the other, Margery was certain. How typical that the de Bohun boy's glittering future was all mapped out, but that once again *her* family was being ill-used. The de Bohuns had it all; Tylers ended up with nothing.

Her bile rose. She could not just let this be.

She had imagined herself leaving Meonbridge soon after the spring weather came, although she scarcely had the energy to walk much further than the Meon. She supposed that, if she could eat a little more, she might feel stronger. Yet, what if she did not—*could* not—regain her strength?

Her legs were suddenly too weak to keep her upright; her head was reeling. She stumbled over to the rickety stool and sank onto it, dragging the wimple, kerchief and fillet from her head and throwing them to the floor. Tiredness enveloped her. Walking to Meonbridge and back was almost as much as she could manage. How could she consider travelling any distance? Indeed, she scarcely had the strength even to keep herself alive.

And, in truth, what did it matter? Who would care if her meagre efforts failed?

Sitting upright again, she turned towards the tiny window: sunlight was filtering through the slats of the flimsy shutter. Blinking at the brightness of it, an idea began to take shape in her mind.

If her remaining days were short, perhaps she should at least try to avenge the wrongs done to her family whilst she could? Did not this betrothal ceremony offer her an opportunity? Villagers would surely bring gifts to the de Bohuns. And she could do the same... Sweetmeats, perhaps? She had seen some for sale in the market.

She recalled what Ursula Kemp had told her, and what she read in Mistress Browghton's book. Wolf's bane might well do the trick. But where to find the plants? And how to extract their poison? Perhaps she could ask Ursula to help her after all?

With much now to consider, her mind began to cloud. She needed to think it all through again. How could she present the gift without anybody recognising her? Adopting her old woman guise once more might work.

She imagined herself lurking on the edge of the crowd, waiting for her turn. Then, hobbling forward, the gift in one hand, her gnarled stick in the other, she would approach and offer her good wishes, and the gift, to Lady de Bohun. To Dickon too perhaps? She would then steal away back into the crowd as others took her place.

Of course, she would not know till later if her gift had done the trick. Indeed, she might *never* know... By the time they had concluded the sweetmeats were to blame, and the constable and his men were sent to search for the anonymous old woman, she would, somehow or other, have disappeared.

It would be disappointing not to see the de Bohuns suffering for what they had inflicted upon her sister and her dear papa; a pity not to witness her *precious* ladyship's humiliation in full sight of her family and friends, with the vomiting and the flux, the loss of breath and burning fingers.

But she could not stay to watch. She simply had to trust that the poison would do its work.

37

'You're not getting wed tomorrow, Dick, only betrothed,' said Piers. 'Surely nothing to be afraid of?'

Dickon snorted. '*You've* not done it.'

It was a grand day for an exhilarating gallop across the downs. Spring seemed to arrive with Easter, and the breeze that skimmed their faces as they'd raced headlong side-by-side was almost warm. When they ran out of open ground, they had slowed to a canter, then a trot and, finally, brought their horses to a halt at the edge of a patch of woodland. They dismounted and sat down in the dappled shade of a newly greening oak.

How Dickon loved it up here, with its fine view across the Meon's valley and over the broad lands that, one day, would be his entire responsibility. He was content now with his life at Steyning, but his heart was still settled here. The prospect of being married to Angharad, living in Meonbridge and raising a family together was a good one. He was truly looking forward to that time. Yet he was nervous about tomorrow.

'I've never been offered the opportunity.' Piers's shoulders slumped.

'Why not?'

He shrugged. 'I'm a third son. Both my brothers have plenty of heirs to carry on the Arundale line. And I suppose my father thinks I'm happy enough here in your service.'

'And are you?'

Piers's cheeks flushed. 'I could hardly say I'm not to you, could I?'

'If it's true, you could.'

He shrugged again. 'Very well then, I am content, but I do think sometimes I should like a wife and children too.'

'Maybe you should look out for a suitable bride?'

'You would not object?'

'Me? Why should I?'

'We might have to spend less time doing this.' He gestured towards the horses, cropping the fresh spring downland grass, and the view.

'Ha, yes. But that might be true when I'm married too.' He laughed. 'Though that's years away from now.'

Piers nodded. 'Anyway, you're not really worried, are you, about tomorrow?'

When he travelled home two weeks ago for Easter, he'd been brimming over with confidence and joy. His problems in Steyning seemed to have been resolved, he was about to be betrothed to the sweetest girl, and Libby was going to be happy too with James. When he found his grandmother also overflowing with delight at the impending celebration, he was satisfied that all was well with his world.

Yet, as the day of the betrothal drew ever closer, he found himself unsettled by the prospect. Not that he was unhappy to be pledging himself to Angharad. It was what preparing for marriage signified.

'No,' he said, 'just a bit nervous. It seems to mark a big change in my life.'

'Becoming a man?' Piers grinned. 'Which I suppose makes me still a boy.'

Dickon hooted. 'Hardly. But, yes, that's it. Becoming a man. Of course, marrying and being knighted will be even bigger steps, but I feel that betrothal, especially *this* betrothal, to the daughter of Sir Giles, my grandfather's comrade-in-arms...' What was it he was trying to say? 'Well, I know it will be a joyous occasion, but it somehow seems a very solemn one as well.'

'Why do you think that?'

'It's part of my grandmother's plan to ensure the perpetuation of the de Bohuns. Your two brothers have done that for your family. But, with ours, it's all down to me, Piers: the survival of the de Bohun family, and of all our domains. I know it's not going to happen soon—but it's frightening to think that, one day, it's all going to be my sole responsibility.'

Dickon was pacing the floor of a solar chamber that had a good view onto the bailey, darting to the window whenever he heard the clip of horses' hooves or the rumble of carriage wheels.

Grandmama had decreed that she alone would greet the guests as they arrived. 'I think it best if you keep yourself apart,' she said, 'until nearer the time for the betrothal ceremony to begin.'

He was eagerly awaiting the arrival of the Fitzpeynes, and seeing Angharad again. She'd been a small child—four years old, perhaps?—when he left Fitzpeyne Castle to return to Steyning. She'd surely look much different now, and he was curious.

Lord Raoul and Countess Jeanne had been amongst the first to come. They had travelled from Steyning a few days ago and were staying somewhere close by. Dickon had wondered if any of his fellow squires might come, but Grandmama didn't know any of their families.

Though one family she did know was Edwin's: the de Courtenays. Dickon barely remembered Edwin's grandfather, Sir Hugh, though he'd seen him the day the Bounes brought to court their claim to the de Bohun name and lands. Yet the old man's face bore such a similarity to Edwin's that it had to be him. He stared down at the aged version of his foe, taking great care as he dismounted stiffly from his chestnut mare. Dickon grimaced: he wasn't sure he wanted any de Courtenays at his betrothal. Yet the families had once been connected through marriage, so naturally Grandmama had invited them. He suspected Sir Hugh knew nothing of Edwin's misconduct in Steyning, though, if he did, he'd surely be much aggrieved by it. For his grandmother maintained he was the most honourable of knights, who believed he still owed loyalty to the de Bohuns, despite the troubles there'd been between them.

Dickon hurried to the window often, only to be disappointed, as many guests arrived, few of whom he knew. The Fitzpeynes were travelling by far the furthest distance, though they weren't doing it all today. They'd have stayed somewhere close by before coming here this morning. So why weren't they already here? He swung around to resume his pacing, then came to an abrupt halt. How ridiculous he was being to get so overwrought. It was a long while yet before the ceremony was due to start, and he needed to relax. He sat down on the narrow bench seat by the chamber's other window, leaning his back against the wall. The view of the manor gate wasn't quite so good from there, but at least he could unwind a little whilst he waited.

At last he was rewarded by the sound of galloping horses, and a brief fanfare on a horn. He leapt to his feet once more to see half a dozen horses hurtling through the gate, their hooves sending up a cloud of dust. Behind them came two carriages, one large and splendid, the other one much smaller. It must surely be Sir Giles and his family.

He watched Sir Giles dismount then heard the excitement in their voices as his grandmother hurried forward and the two old friends exchanged their greetings. Sir Giles looked no different from when he'd last seen him: just as full of energy and high spirits as he was three years ago.

Moments later, Lady Gwynedd came forward to greet Grandmama, and there was then a lot of talk between them before Sir Giles called the children forward. At last!

The little boys came out first, then their sisters. And how elegant Angharad was as she stepped down from the carriage and glided over to curtsey to his grandmother. It was hard to believe she was still only eight. She was already lovely, prettier even than her mother, though her colouring was different, fair instead of dark. She would surely grow up into a woman of great beauty: how fortunate he was, and how much he was looking forward to the day when they would marry.

38

Margaret knew that she was beaming again. Perhaps she looked a little foolish, but she could not help herself, for her delight was overflowing.

From the top of the flight of steps that led up to the great hall, she had a broad view of the bailey and the manor gates, for once left wide open in welcome. She could see her guests arriving, on foot, on horseback or by carriage. As each party came through the gates, she had descended the steps with grace and dignity to greet them warmly, then offered them a refreshing cup of cordial before introducing them to other visitors. Although those who had travelled a long distance she invited to retire to a solar chamber for a short while in order to revive their energies before joining the celebrations.

As the guests she had waited for most eagerly had just done.

The Fitzpeyne family's arrival had been magnificent. Several days ago, she had let her memory drift back to the day, so many years ago, when Giles had come to Meonbridge, not alone, for then too he had been accompanied by a great entourage of men, although he had no family in tow. For that was the day he had come expecting to be affianced to Johanna.

Margaret had been watching from a window that overlooked the bailey, although Johanna was hanging back, nervous about the whole occasion. As Giles rode in, Margaret had cried out in admiration, and bid her daughter look. Even she, despite her affected unconcern, could not suppress a gasp.

Any normal young gentlewoman would have been vastly impressed at the sight of Sir Giles Fitzpeyne, clad as he was that day in embroidered scarlet velvet, and astride a huge black destrier. He had brought with him an enormous covered wagon filled, they later learned, with the extensive accoutrements of a knight away for a few days from home, as well as gifts for his intended bride.

Of course, that day had not turned out well. What a ridiculous understatement of the terrible suffering that followed!

Johanna had been less than enthusiastic anyway to be betrothed to Giles. Margaret knew he was a good man, but he was as old as Richard and much damaged from his years of fighting for the king. Yet it was Philip's murder that had prevented the betrothal. Johanna simply would not countenance proceeding when her brother was lying dead.

The memory of those dreadful days swooped briefly into her head again as she watched Sir Giles arrive today. But she banished it at once. This was a day for joy and merriment, not recalling the unhappy past.

Giles was once more magnificently clad, not in scarlet this time but deep crimson, more fitting for a man of his years. The members of his entourage were in crimson too. More than one carriage made up the train: one, she supposed, was again for accoutrements and gifts, but the other undoubtedly held Lady Fitzpeyne and her children.

As the carriages came to a halt close to the steps, Margaret almost ran down, her heart full of excitement and anticipation. Giles at once dismounted and hurried forward to take her hand in greeting.

'Margaret,' he cried. 'What a wonderful day this is.'

She laughed and permitted him to lift her hand to his lips and kiss it. 'Indeed it is.'

Giles let go of her hand and stepped over to the more splendid of the carriages. 'Allow me to introduce my family,' he said, his eyes alight. One of his retainers had already opened the carriage door and put a footstool on the ground beneath it, and now Giles stood by it and held out his hand. A smaller hand emerged from the carriage and grasped Giles's, then its owner, a young woman, teetered as she stepped down onto the footstool. She gave him a tender smile and smoothed her gown and adjusted her headdress. Then Giles took her arm to bring her forward.

Margaret was astonished at Lady Gwynedd's youth. Of course, she knew the lady was a great deal younger than Giles. Indeed, the difference in their ages was much more than it had been between him and Johanna.

Yet the gleam in Giles's eyes as he glanced at her face and spoke her name, 'Gwynedd, my beloved wife', was assuredly the light of love? Gwynedd's expression too was clear. These two people adored each other, and Margaret's heart flipped as she observed it. Did it not bode very well for her grandson and his future wife?

'Your ladyship,' Gwynedd said, dropping a curtsey. 'I am so pleased to meet you at long last.' Her voice had a delightful musical lilt, and Margaret at once recollected that Gwynedd came from Wales and, according to Giles, had often spoken her native language when they were first married.

Margaret leaned forward to take the young woman's hand and help her rise. 'It has indeed been far too long.' She turned to Giles with a mocking frown. 'But you have had such a lengthy journey, my dear. You must be quite exhausted.'

'We have travelled only from Winchester this morning, but it has indeed been a long and wearisome journey. But for the best of reasons.'

Giles stepped forward. 'The very best,' he said, beaming. He took his wife's elbow. 'Nonetheless, I think we all would welcome the opportunity for a brief rest and the chance to clean the expedition's dust from our eyes and ears.'

'Indeed you must,' cried Margaret. 'Your chamber is all prepared.'

Gwynedd smiled her thanks then whispered to Giles to summon the children.

Margaret had to laugh as two small boys almost tumbled from the carriage and trotted forward to bow to her. Then two young girls stepped down, much more serenely, and came over to her and curtseyed. She acknowledged each child in turn before bringing her eyes back to the eldest: Angharad. What a pretty child she was.

Of course, Lady Gwynedd was a beauty. Despite her tiredness, her skin glowed and the hair escaping from her modest headdress was the richest black. To Margaret's eyes, the lady looked as if she might come from some much more distant country, such as those Richard used to tell her of when his knightly exploits took him far away from England. Italy, was it? Or Spain? Hot countries, she understood.

Richard told her of the maidens he had met. She suspected it was more than simply "met", but chose not to let that thought concern her. Often he referred to them as "raven-haired" and "dark-eyed", as Gwynedd was. Her skin too was darker than was usual for an Englishwoman: "olive" she thought Richard would have described it. But perhaps Welsh people *were* dark? Of course, Dickon's hair was also dark, like his father's, but their skin was fair and their eyes a brilliant blue.

Yet, although the two little boys also had dark curls, Angharad and her sister had the colouring of their father, or, rather, Margaret corrected herself, the colouring Giles used to have when he was much younger. Both his daughters were fair haired and pale skinned. But Angharad did also have her mother's perfect oval face.

As her grandson's future wife rose from her straight-backed curtsey, Margaret was struck by the child's poise. She might be only eight years old, but she was already growing into a most elegant young woman.

All the guests who had travelled from afar were now either resting in their chambers or conversing amiably with others of their acquaintance. Margaret checked off her mental list of the few relatives and many friends she had invited.

It had been so good of her younger brother, Arthur, to make the trip all the way from Cheshire with his wife and eldest son. He had said he felt it only right for someone to represent her side of the family. She was grateful, for there were no other de Bohuns here apart from herself and Dickon. How very sad she was that Johanna could not come after all. She had sent a message only yesterday to say that she was confined to her bed with an ague. The infirmarian, she said, had insisted that she should not travel.

Richard's only relatives had been the Bounes, and now the sole survivor of the attack they launched against Meonbridge was the reclusive Gunnar. Not that Margaret would have even contemplated inviting him. Of course, Gwynedd was also a Boune by birth, but had long since repudiated her connection with the family, as had her mother.

'Mama is with child yet again,' said Gwynedd, after offering Alwyn's apologies for not attending her darling granddaughter's betrothal. She raised an eyebrow. 'In truth, Lady Margaret, I do wonder where she finds the energy.'

Margaret agreed. It was possible that, with this latest, Alwyn might have borne a dozen children. Not that all of them survived. 'Perhaps Lady Alwyn will be able to attend the wedding?' she said, tilting her head.

Gwynedd laughed. 'I do hope that, by then, Mama will have persuaded her noble husband that, between them, they have children aplenty and need no more.'

When Sir Hugh de Courtenay arrived this morning, Margaret was not surprised that he was alone. Naturally, she had invited Hildegard too, but Margaret did speculate about whether she would come. After all, the last time Hildegard was in Meonbridge—eight years ago—she had been deeply humiliated at the court. Hugh was more forgiving: it had been an awkward and distressing situation, but he was not one to bear grudges.

'My lady wife,' he said, after greeting Margaret most warmly, 'sends her best wishes for the day, and her sincere regrets that her present range of ailments prevents her from travelling.'

As he said it, his eyes surely twinkled, and Margaret had known Hugh long enough to construe that he was almost certainly relieved to be here on his own. She hoped the Petersfield inn where he decided to stay the night was adequate. Even spending a night or two in a less than comfortable hostelry might be a welcome respite from his wife's often acerbic tongue.

Nonetheless, she graciously accepted Hildegard's good wishes, and asked him about his family. But, before he could say much, the earl and countess had arrived, and Hugh gestured to her to attend to them.

Margaret's mental inventory of her travelling guests complete, she was now just waiting for the atte Wodes and the Sawyers to arrive. Alice had told her they would walk up to the house close to the time for the ceremony to begin, so as not to intrude upon those guests who might need her attention. Dear Alice, thoughtful as ever. But she hoped they would come soon, as everything was now in place, and she was eager to make a start.

She walked back up the steps and took her place at the top again, watching for Dickon's family. She saw then that the throng of people on the bailey included not only her invited guests but Meonbridge villagers too. Two or three groups were standing at a discreet distance from the guests, talking quietly together. She had asked John atte Wode to spread the word around the village that all could come to the great hall once the ceremony was over, if they wanted to offer their good wishes to Dickon and Angharad, and maybe even gifts. Clearly some had come early, perhaps hoping to be the first to congratulate their future lord and his bride-to-be. How very pleasing.

Looking towards the gate again, she saw that Alice and Agnes were coming, with John and Matthew, and Jack and the children all following on behind. She clapped her hands. The ceremony could now begin.

At last, everyone was being ushered into the great hall. How very splendid it all looked. The manor servants had worked hard on the decorations. The tables were all set for the banquet at one end of the hall, and the ceremony was to take place at the other. Flowers and greenery were everywhere in swags and garlands, and, despite the brightness of the day, Margaret had ordered candles to be lit in sufficient numbers to ensure that the hall gleamed.

Two great chairs had been set up for her and Dickon to one side of the hall, beneath the high windows. Her grandson was already sitting in his chair when she came to take her place alongside him. He was leaning forward, his shoulders hunched, his hands clasping and unclasping between his knees. But he looked up at her as she sat down, and gave her a wry grin.

She observed him for a few moments, awaiting the arrival of his bride-to-be. How nervous the poor boy looked, but how handsome. Indeed, how much like his father, but only in stature and appearance. From what she had seen of Dickon this past year, it was evident he had a very different demeanour from her son.

How different, too, from the arrogant little boy he once had been. She had thought then that Dickon would grow up to be as haughty as his father. But, for whatever reason, he did not. Perhaps it was the leavening of his atte Wode inheritance, or the upbringing of the Sawyers?

She speculated, not for the first time, that Philip being knighted at eighteen and acclaimed a gallant hero had perhaps gone to his head. When he returned to Meonbridge with Richard, basking in the glory he had won at Crécy, he was supercilious and rude, much more so than when he had been a boy. He treated *her*, his mother, with disdain, even contempt. It was a grievous time. She had heard too, to her distress, that he was swiving any girl in Meonbridge who was willing, and wondered idly if she had grandchildren she knew nothing of.

Margaret had loved Richard dearly. She never doubted he was a fine knight, a noble warrior for his king; but he too was pompous, quick to judge, influencing his son perhaps. Only after Philip died did Richard learn both humility and good judgement, although wisdom did eventually elude him, when he perpetrated his ridiculous untruth about Dickon's birth.

She looked across the room towards Sir Giles and Lord Raoul, talking together in a cheerful yet restrained manner. Raoul was a noble man, powerful but not overweening, wise rather than judgemental. Giles had once been handsome, but war had robbed his face of its youthful beauty, and he had also lost his sword arm. Yet, despite his prowess on the battlefield, Giles was kind and gentle, a family man now much more than a heroic knight.

She gazed back upon her grandson, sitting now straight-backed, his hands still and resting upon his knees. She threw him a smile of encouragement and, returning it with a nervous grin, he nodded.

What had changed that obstreperous boy into the thoughtful young man he now was?

Not one thing, of course, but many. Both events and people were bound to have played their part.

She was sure that *something* had happened in Steyning, something serious, even perilous. Dickon had not told her of it, but she had seen anxiety in his eyes and his demeanour. Yet that anxiety had faded, so perhaps whatever it was had been resolved. Something troubling too had occurred between him and Libby. At one time she had thought she might have to intervene, but it seemed that problem too had been settled.

She suspected that, if Dickon shared the burden of his worries with anyone, it would be Piers, standing now at Dickon's shoulder, and she was sure the squire would give him sage guidance. As she hoped she would have done herself, if she had been asked. The care Lord Raoul had shown him too was undoubtedly a factor, and perhaps even more so that of Giles? Both men had surely, in their different ways, influenced her grandson for the better.

As she then mused happily upon how fortunate Dickon would be to have a father-in-law like Giles, she sensed a change in the ambience of the hall. Out of the corner of her eye, she saw Dickon jump up from his chair, and the bustle of movement and buzz of conversation abruptly ceased. She looked up. Angharad was standing just behind the arras that screened the foot of the solar staircase from the great manor hall, with Lady Gwynedd at her elbow.

Margaret turned to glance at Libby, standing quite close by, with James Paynter at her side, his hand resting upon her shoulder. How did Libby feel about today? She was looking up at her betrothed, her face relaxed and happy, so perhaps all was well. She had genuine affection for the girl and had never wanted her to be hurt by her enforced separation from Dickon. Although she understood that Libby might have loved him—indeed that he might have felt the same for her— marriage between them was impossible. How glad she was that James had come into Libby's life at the very moment she needed him.

As Angharad entered the hall, her gaze lowered to the floor, murmurs and gasps fluttered around the company. Margaret too was captivated. Angharad's gown was a rich blue, modestly cut, as befitted a child, but embroidered at the hem and across the bodice with tiny violets and snowdrops. A circlet of fresh spring flowers was set upon her head, and her light brown curls fell below her shoulders. She did look lovely, and Lady Gwynedd, walking at her side, glowed with pleasure. The whole company applauded as she led her daughter towards Dickon and stopped before him. Dickon's eyes widened as they approached, then he glanced sideways to Margaret and grinned.

Giles stepped forward and stood beside his wife. 'May I present to you, my lord Dickon, and to this illustrious company,' he said, 'my daughter, Lady Angharad Fitzpeyne.'

Angharad dropped a low curtsey, still not lifting up her eyes.

Dickon at once reached down to take her hand and raise her gently to her feet. He gave her the broadest of smiles. 'Hello,' he whispered, and Angharad giggled.

Margaret might have giggled too, but instead caught Gwynedd's eye and they grinned broadly at each other.

'My lord,' Angharad said, lifting her eyes at last to look him in the face.

Such an expression of affection passed between them that Margaret could not help but clap for joy.

39

Libby swallowed down the small lump rising in her throat. How happy they both looked, as if it was *they* who were meant to be together. Angharad was so pretty and so graceful, even though she was still a child. Yet perhaps the affection Dickon felt for her—and she for him—was still that of playmates. What she herself and Dickon had felt for each other until only a year ago...

Her eyes misted but she shook her head, and put her hand up to where James's hand was gently laid. She must have—did have—no regrets. She rested her hand upon his and, squeezing her shoulder, he bent his head to whisper in her ear. 'They look most content.' She agreed. 'As are we,' he added, and she turned her face up to smile at him.

'We are,' she said, and meant it.

She had plighted her troth to James, and he to her, last November, in the presence of her best friend Maud and Master and Mistress Miller, and the Sawyers and Mistress atte Wode. A much simpler affair than today, it had withal been joyful, and Mistress atte Wode laid on a splendid dinner for them all.

Yet, today's grand company and lavish banquet aside, this was still a modest enough occasion.

And Dickon seemed to know exactly what to do and say. 'Let us join our hands,' he said, reaching forward with his right hand.

Angharad held out her hand too, and they gently laced their fingers.

Then Dickon spoke again, his voice strong and clear. 'In the name of our Lord, and before this company, I, Dickon, promise that I shall henceforth take you, Angharad, for my wedded wife, according to the ordinances of holy Church. Till that day I shall keep faith with you, and I shall be loyal to you all the days of my life.'

The company murmured their approval, and Dickon leaned in to Angharad and whispered in her ear. She nodded, and spoke her vows too, though her voice was so quiet it was hard to catch the words.

But the earl, who was standing close by the couple, looked up, his eyes shining, and declared out loud, 'She has responded well in kind.' Sir Giles and Lady Gwynedd laughed lightly, and poor Angharad blushed.

Libby looked across at Lady Margaret, whose face was wreathed in joy. But it was not over yet, for Piers stepped forward and placed a ring in Dickon's palm, and Dickon took Angharad's left hand and slipped the ring upon it. Then Angharad's little sister held up a tiny velvet cushion, which also bore a ring. Angharad picked it up and, lifting Dickon's hand, pushed the ring onto his finger.

The earl looked up again. 'We all here bear witness to these two young people's solemn declarations. They are betrothed.' At that, everyone applauded.

The ceremony over, Lady Margaret hurried over to Dickon and Angharad and clasped them both to her breast, then kissed Sir Giles and Lady Gwynedd on their cheeks.

Libby leaned in to James and whispered. 'I don't think I've ever seen her ladyship quite so effusive.'

'I suppose she is just very happy. Wasn't Sir Giles a close comrade of Sir Richard? Her ladyship will have known him for many years, and she may be very glad to be allying her family with his.'

Her ladyship clasped both the Fitzpeynes' hands and, turning back to Dickon and Angharad, ushered them over to the chairs beneath the window. A third chair had now been brought, and a table set up in front with a flagon of what Libby presumed was wine and three of her ladyship's finest goblets.

The three of them stood behind the table, and a servant came forward to pour them wine. Then her ladyship gave a signal to another servant who was standing guard at the great hall door, and he went outside to the bailey. Libby heard him making an announcement, and Lady Margaret stood up and clapped her hands.

'My dear friends, I have invited anyone who would like to wish our happy couple health and happiness to come forward now. Many people have been waiting patiently outside to do so, and I ask that we permit them to approach first.'

Servants moved amongst the guests with cups of wine and trays of sweetmeats whilst, from the direction of the bailey door, Libby heard the bustle of a crowd of people. Moments later, the well-wishers were spilling into the hall and the servants were urging them to form an orderly queue.

Libby took James's hand and drew him over to stand to one side of Lady Margaret, to see better who was coming forward to wish their new lord well. How many people were waiting in the queue! She glanced at her ladyship, still beaming with happiness.

As folk approached the table, most just wanted to say a few words of congratulations, but others brought small gifts, candlesticks they had carved in wood, or ribbons they had woven, some small item they had made for the occasion. Angharad appeared a little overwhelmed, but Dickon accepted everyone's gifts and felicitations with gratitude and grace, ensuring he spoke to all of them. Her ladyship did the same before a servant ushered them on their way.

Libby knew most of those coming forward, though there were one or two she didn't. According to her ladyship, many new folk had come to Meonbridge over the past year or so, and there was no reason she would know them all.

Shortly, an old woman tottered forward, her back bent, leaning upon a gnarled stick. In her other hand she carried a small box.

Despite the warmth of the spring weather, she was swathed in a dark cloak and had a hood over what seemed to be a close-fitting wimple.

'Who is this?' Lady Margaret whispered to Dickon, but he shook his head.

Libby frowned: the old woman seemed familiar. Was it the same one she'd seen a month or two ago, hobbling around the market, wrapped up warm against the cold? She'd wondered idly at the time how such an old person might have come to Meonbridge without family or friends to mind her. She'd been mildly confused too when the woman's hood had briefly slipped, and she'd thought the eyes somehow familiar. Yet how could they be? She didn't know any such old women. And she soon forgot about her.

Now, the woman stopped before the table, closer to Lady Margaret than to Dickon. She placed the box before her ladyship. 'For you, my lady,' she said, 'as grandmother of our little lord.'

Lady Margaret beamed. 'How delightful. But who is offering me this gift?'

Libby looked on in bafflement. Why might such a stranger offer good wishes to her ladyship, let alone a gift? Yet, if she had come recently to Meonbridge, perhaps she hoped to make a good impression?

'A well-wisher,' said the woman simply, and turned to go.

'How kind,' said her ladyship, picking up the box and looking inside. Her face fell. 'Oh dear. I am afraid I do not eat anything not prepared for me by my cook.' She smiled. 'So, I shall distribute these delicious-looking sweetmeats to—'

The old woman spun around, glaring at her ladyship. 'You refuse my gift?' she cried. 'You scorn my good wishes?' She let out a harsh cackle. 'Of course you do, your *precious* ladyship! As you have always scorned me, and my family...'

Gasps of surprise and horror hissed around the chamber, at the words spitting from the woman's lips.

But she had not finished. 'A curse upon you!' she snarled. 'Upon you, Margaret de Bohun, and all of your vile kin! May you burn in Hell, for your son's wicked violation of my sister, and for your murder of her unborn child!'

And, in that instant, Libby knew. She'd heard those words before.

Panic rose in her throat, as she recalled the rest of her aunt's last words to her. 'The de Bohuns have already caused our family boundless suffering and dishonour... And it's got to stop!'

What had to stop? Then, she didn't know, but now she understood. Her head was throbbing now with the horror of what was happening. Was this Margery's revenge for what her family had suffered? Were the sweetmeats poisoned? Thanks be to God her ladyship had refused them.

But, when she turned in some relief to look at Lady Margaret, she saw her ladyship's eyes were wide and staring, and her face was deathly pale. She was swaying too, her hands scrabbling at the table's edge. At the sight of her evident distress, cries of alarm echoed around the hall. Dickon moved swiftly to his grandmother's side, and Sir Giles called for calm and for the surgeon to be fetched.

And, in the growing tumult, the old woman turned once again, as if to slip away. But her foot must have caught in the hem of her long cloak, for she stumbled, giving Libby the chance she needed.

'No,' she shrieked and, wrenching her hand out of James's, she lunged forward. 'She must not get away.'

Then she threw herself at her aunt, and Margery crumpled beneath the onslaught, and fell face down into the rushes, her hood flying off. Libby knelt upon her back and, seizing the fabric of the wimple, ripped it off.

'See who it is?' she cried, grabbing her aunt's hair to pull up her head and expose her face. She glared at those people who were standing closest, alarmed and confused by what was happening. 'This is no old woman, and certainly no well-wisher. This is Margery Tyler, and she's intent on doing harm to her ladyship and our lord!'

Several of the onlookers cried out. 'But I thought she'd gone from Meonbridge,' said one.

Then Libby heard a gasping cry and, turning, saw Lady Margaret falling back onto her chair. She was clutching at her breast.

'You witch!' Libby screamed at Margery. 'What have you done?'

'Revenge!' rasped Margery, writhing and struggling to throw Libby off. Yet she had little strength. As Libby pressed hard upon her shoulders to keep her down, she could feel how thin and bony her aunt had become. Briefly she was sorry she'd come to this but, if Lady

Margaret died, had her aunt committed murder? How did she imagine she'd get away with it? Or perhaps she didn't care...

Yet, if the sweetmeats were the intended means, it surely was not them that had caused her ladyship to swoon? So, was it Margery's curse? *She'd* just called her aunt a witch, and Mistress Miller had told her she was thought to be one. Was that then truly what she was?

Libby swallowed. Nearly everyone in Meonbridge knew this woman was her aunt. Everyone except for James. If he discovered the truth about her family, and that Margery was a witch, surely he'd break off their betrothal? Tears welled. Had this vengeful woman ruined *her* chance of a happy future as well as her own? For a moment her own craving for vengeance swelled in her breast, and, pressing harder against Margery's back, she ground her face into the floor.

But then Jack and James were at her side. James took her shoulders and gently lifted her away. 'Oh, my darling girl,' he cried, clasping her to his chest, 'how brave you were.'

She crumpled into his arms, letting him hold her whilst he still wanted to. He'd soon enough understand the truth. Glancing sideways, she saw Jack grasp one of Margery's frail arms and haul her roughly to her feet. She struggled, but he held her fast. The bailiff was there too and took her other arm. 'We must hold her, Jack,' he said, 'till the constable arrives.'

Libby pushed away a little from James's chest, so she could look at Lady Margaret. She was slumped sideways in her chair, the skin of her face grey.

She caught her breath at the sight of Dickon: how very much a man he looked. A boy no longer. He wasn't weeping, but was holding his grandmother's hand and murmuring to her. But his eyes flicked often about the room, anxious perhaps for Simon Hogge to come.

Yet, the way her ladyship looked, it surely was too late?

40

How he'd like to shout and wail, and even tear his hair. But, how could he do that? He surely must keep calm, to show his courage. If he was now lord of Meonbridge, he had to act the part. Though, with all his heart, he prayed that might not yet be true.

Dickon stared across at poor little Angharad, such a short while ago so happy and excited, but now crumpled into frantic weeping on the floor. Lady Gwynedd crouched at her side, enfolding her in her arms, trying to soothe her shock and grief.

How much he wanted that: to be comforted. But, right now, his job was to *give* comfort not receive it.

In the moments after Libby's brave assault on Margery Tyler and his grandmother's collapse, the great hall had become a place of uproar and confusion, as people cried out and keened, or muttered urgently to each other about what had happened.

But it was not fitting for his grandmother to be surrounded by such turmoil. He ordered the servants to usher everybody from the hall, or at least to the far end, save for the few who were dearest to him and to her: Grandmama's brother, Sir Giles and his family, Lord Raoul and Countess Jeanne, and Libby.

Simon too, who'd been found at length and now wouldn't leave his lady's side.

'What can we do?' said Dickon, struggling to keep the panic from his voice.

The surgeon shook his head. 'I've no remedy for witchcraft, milord.'

Dickon's stomach lurched. *Was* Margery Tyler then a witch? Moments after her vile curse, Grandmama had cried out and swayed, her hand pressed to her breast. Her eyes were glassy. 'Was the Tyler woman's curse the cause?'

Simon's dark eyes misted. 'The curse itself,' he said, 'or the shock of it.'

Dickon clenched his fists, urging himself to stay strong in the face of what seemed like imminent disaster. 'You think my grandmother might die?' he whispered.

'I fear so, milord.'

Someone took his elbow. It was Sir Giles: his face was pale, the scar that slashed from eyebrow to chin somehow more livid. 'Dickon,' he said gently, 'we must urge everyone to pray for Lady Margaret's deliverance from that woman's curse. God surely will look kindly upon her ladyship?'

Dickon nodded eagerly. 'Yes, yes, Giles, thank you. Is Sire Raphael on his way?'

'He will be here shortly. But there is no reason why everybody here should not immediately fall to their knees and offer up an earnest prayer.' He laid a hand on Dickon's arm. 'I shall arrange it.'

Relieved that something was being done to help his grandmother, Dickon drew up a stool next to her chair, so he could speak words of comfort to her, though he wasn't certain she could hear him. But, shortly, she turned her face towards him and her eyes flickered open. Despite their dullness, he could tell she knew it was him there at her side.

'Poor Margery,' she whispered.

'*Poor* Margery?' he said, his voice a rasp. 'She *cursed* you, Grandmama.'

311

Her chin dipped in the slightest of nods. 'Such bitterness,' she said, and closed her eyes again.

His mouth fell open. Why was his grandmother not full of hatred for what Margery had done? Instead, she seemed to be sorry for her. He wasn't. He'd like to march over to her now, to strike her down, to have her whipped, to hear her beg for mercy. But now was not the time for that.

Grandmama's breath hitched a moment and then resumed, and her head lolled gently against his shoulder. He swallowed hard, once, twice, three times, trying to shift the lump lodged in his throat. It wouldn't move. What he wanted more than anything was to cry out, to weep. But now he had to use his voice for prayer.

He heard the whispering of a few dozen voices coming from the far end of the hall, and, looking around, he saw Lord Raoul and Countess Jeanne, the Fitzpeynes, the atte Wodes and the Sawyers were all kneeling too, their heads bowed, their lips moving in prayer. Still holding on to his grandmother's hand, he slipped to his knees as well, and begged God to vanquish Margery's curse and let his grandmother live.

Only a short while later, Sire Raphael arrived and led the prayers more urgently. Sir Giles then eased himself up from his knees and, coming over, leaned close to Dickon's ear. He spoke softly. 'Dickon, we should move Lady Margaret from this place, to somewhere more comfortable.'

'But where? We cannot take her up to her chamber: the staircase is too narrow.'

'Your grandfather was laid in the small parlour.' Giles pointed to a door at the far end of the hall.

Dickon had hardly ever set foot in the room, used as it was mainly by women servants as a place to sew and mend. 'It's very small.'

'But private. She can be cared for there until—' Giles choked back a sob.

Dickon too couldn't bear to think of it. 'Grandmama *might* recover.'

Giles nodded. 'Let us hope our prayers are finding their way to heaven.'

Dickon turned back to his grandmother. She seemed to be asleep.

Her breast rose and fell, if unevenly, and her face looked calm enough, despite its ghastly pallor. He gently let go of her hand. 'Please find some servants to assist us, Giles,' he said.

As Giles strode away, Geoffrey Dyer, the constable, stepped forward. 'Milord,' he said, 'shall we take her away?'

Dickon was confused. 'My grandmother?'

The constable shook his head sadly. 'No, no, milord, that task is for others. 'Tis her ladyship's assailant that I meant.'

'Oh yes, of course.' He swallowed. 'What must I do about her, Master Dyer?'

'We'll lock her up, and in due course you can send word to the sheriff. But not yet. In a day or so... Today, milord, give all your attention to her ladyship...' He bowed his head and, turning to his men, gestured at them to march Margery away.

He didn't much care what happened to her, but Dickon doubted Margery Tyler, in her feeble state, would survive the constable's jail, still less the sheriff's. But that was, as Master Dyer said, a matter for another day.

Grandmama stayed asleep whilst she was lifted from her chair and laid gently onto a litter. Four serving men then hefted the litter and carried it the short distance to the tiny parlour, where it was set down upon a broad table. A pillow was brought, and blankets, to give her a little comfort, and Dickon insisted that someone sit with her constantly and call him if there was the slightest change. He didn't want to leave his grandmother's side at all, but he could not ignore little Angharad, whose desperate weeping had become a swoon. She'd been taken to an upstairs chamber, and it was surely right that he, as her betrothed, should visit her to show his concern.

Simon Hogge and Libby agreed to watch his grandmother. After only an hour or so, Libby came breathlessly to Dickon to report that his grandmother had slept on a while but was now stirring. 'I think you should come,' she said.

Dickon's heart was racing as he hurried to the little parlour. Had God heeded their urgent prayers? Had Grandmama thrown off the Tyler woman's vicious curse?

He found her lying quietly, her face still waxy pale, but her eyes were open.

'Grandmama,' he cried, stepping forward to take her hand once more. 'How do you feel?'

'Not well at all,' she murmured, and his heart gave a lurch.

But he squeezed her hand gently and gave her what he hoped was an encouraging smile. 'The entire household, indeed the whole of Meonbridge, is praying for your recovery, Grandmama,' he said. 'Praying for Margery Tyler's curse to be lifted.'

She returned the smallest of smiles. 'Poor Margery,' she said again.

Anger swelled in Dickon's breast. 'Why do you feel so sorry for her, Grandmama? I don't understand at all.'

She sighed. 'What were Margery's words? Can you remember?'

Since the uttering of the curse, he'd not thought much about the words. He looked up now at Libby, who was standing at a respectful distance. He raised an eyebrow at her, and she bit her lip. In truth, he *could* remember, and he supposed Libby could as well. Margery's curse referred to what Libby had told him in that terrible argument they'd had before he returned to Steyning last September.

He'd been willing then to accept that his father had made love to Matilda, and got her with child, but not that his grandmother demanded the murder of the unborn child. He refused to believe such a dreadful lie. At the time, he'd not known that Libby got her information from her Aunt Margery. She'd not mentioned her existence until Christmas, when she told him how Margery blamed the de Bohuns for everything that had befallen the Tyler family, and how bitter she'd become.

To his relief, he and Libby had become friends again that day. They'd agreed that her aunt's accusation against his grandmother was unsupportable.

Yet, it was clear that *Margery* still believed it to be true.

His grandmother knew that she was "bitter", for she'd said so earlier. But did she have any notion about *why*? If she didn't, he scarcely wanted to tell her of it now.

She dozed a little more but then her eyes fluttered open once again. 'Well?' she said.

'Her words were too shocking to repeat, Grandmama.' Dickon's stomach was churning with unease.

To his surprise, she gave a brief shake of her head. 'Yet I think you must repeat them, darling boy. For the nature of Margery's belief must be laid to rest.'

His throat tight, he whispered the curse's dreadful words. His grandmother nodded. 'It is of course not true,' she said. 'I did not demand that of poor Matilda. But I do know what happened, as does one other in Meonbridge. Eleanor Nash.'

Dickon and Libby let out a joint cry of surprise. 'Mistress Nash?'

'Indeed.' Her voice was weak, her breathing ragged. 'Send for her, Dickon,' she whispered, 'and let the truth be told at last.'

Mistress Nash was amongst those in the hall still praying for his grandmother's deliverance, and she came quickly to the parlour. Her eyes were damp as she stepped forward to take Grandmama's shaky outstretched hand. 'What am I to tell, your ladyship?' she said.

'The truth about Matilda. So I do not go to my grave with Margery's accusation against me unanswered.'

Dickon's throat filled yet again. Was she truly going to die? It seemed she thought so. He could scarce believe it possible, but he had to ensure the truth was heard. He went to ask Sir Giles and Lord Raoul to come and also listen to what Mistress Nash had to say.

Dickon was stunned by what she said. For it appeared that it was Matilda herself who betrayed her father's crimes.

'Matilda told me that she had overheard her father plotting with his henchmen, including her own husband, Gilbert Fletcher, to murder Sir Philip,' she said. 'She told me also that Master Tyler forced her to abort the child she'd got with Philip, and made her marry Gilbert, to punish her for her sin. Poor Matty!'

Her voice was strong and steady, despite the grief that clearly lingered still, even after so many years.

'So my grandmother had no part in it, the abortion?' Dickon asked.

Mistress Nash looked shocked. 'No! She knew nothing of it, until I told her what Matilda had told me.'

'Presumably her sister, Margery, knew?'

She frowned. 'Matilda said that Margery had told their father of the pregnancy. But what Margery knew of the abortion, who ordered it and who performed it, I have truly no idea. Matilda never said whether her sister was present.'

Dickon nodded. So, presumably, Margery invented the idea of his

315

grandmother's involvement? 'Anyway, Mistress Nash, do please continue.'

'It was such a difficult thing for poor Matty to do, but she bid me share what she had told me, to ensure her father was brought to justice for his crimes, as well as her husband.' She twisted the kerchief she was holding through her fingers. 'I had to tell Lady Margaret what I had learned, for I knew that she was already suspicious of Master Tyler's recently erratic and unreasonable behaviour. I hoped that she would be able to convince Sir Richard too of Master Tyler's guilt.'

She went on to explain how events unfolded, with Robert Tyler's flight from Meonbridge, then his return and death, falling from the church tower.

By the time Mistress Nash had finished her story, it was clear that Robert's part in Philip's murder, and that played by Gilbert Fletcher and his other henchman, had quickly become well known in Meonbridge. But it seemed that no one other than Mistress Nash and his grandmother, and of course Matilda herself, knew of his other crime, forcing Matilda to abort her baby.

Dickon wondered why they chose to keep the wicked deed a secret. But now was not the time to burden his grandmother any further. She'd nodded every now and then during Mistress Nash's explanation and, when she'd finished, she sighed and closed her eyes. If she was content that the truth had now been told, why should he raise more questions? It made little difference now why the secret had been kept: they'd surely done it for the best of reasons. If he wanted to know more, he could ask Mistress Nash later.

After she had left the chamber, to return to her prayers, Dickon sat down by his grandmother's side once more. 'Grandmama, are you satisfied now the truth is known?'

She inclined her head. 'I am. And I must rest now...'

He leaned forward to kiss her lightly upon her cheek. The skin was cool and dry. He sighed. He was reluctant to leave her side again till he was certain she was recovered, but he had matters to attend to. Leaving Libby and Simon once more to watch her, he'd make his absences brief. Get others to deal with what he couldn't.

He visited the parlour every half hour or so, to find his

grandmother still sleeping. But dusk was falling and candles had been lit when he looked in for the fourth time.

Sire Raphael was now standing to one side of the table, alongside Simon Hogge. He bowed his head to Dickon. 'My lord,' he said, keeping his voice very low. 'Master Hogge asked me to attend her ladyship, as he believes she is likely near to death.'

Dickon suppressed a cry. 'But I thought she was recovering?'

'I'm sorry, milord,' said Simon, 'but I'm afraid her ladyship has worsened.' He looked away. 'It's possible she might rally, but I'm not hopeful.'

Dickon's tears brimmed, and he swiped them away with the back of his hand. 'I can't believe that she might die.'

'Indeed,' said Sire Raphael. 'Lady Margaret has ever been a force of nature.'

If the priest meant Grandmama's energy had seemed unquenchable, despite the setbacks she had suffered, how could he not agree?

Sire Raphael turned to Simon. 'Master Hogge?' he whispered. Then, as Simon looked up at him, he mouthed 'How long?'

Dickon saw it too and understood. The priest was waiting for the signal to offer the *viaticum*, not wanting to begin too soon, yet not delay until it was too late.

Simon sighed. 'Begin?'

Nodding, Sire Raphael leaned over Grandmama and recited some words of prayer. He took a phial of holy oil from his satchel and, tipping a drop onto her forehead, signed a cross upon it. Grandmama's eyes once more fluttered open as the oil touched her, and she lifted a flailing hand to clutch at the sleeve of Sire Raphael's cassock. She bowed her head briefly and he bowed in return. Then she let her eyelids close again.

Dickon stifled a whimper, then realised Libby was at his shoulder. Her eyes were red. 'May I hold her ladyship's hand, just for a moment?' she said. He nodded, and, sitting on the stool next to the table, she clasped Grandmama's hand.

'I'm so sorry, my lady,' Libby whispered, 'for the harm my family has inflicted upon yours.' Tears were dripping from her cheeks onto his grandmother's face. 'Thank you for all you have given me, and I promise to merit the faith you had in me.'

His grandmother's eyelids fluttered open once again, and she murmured 'Go well, Libby dear.' Libby stood up and, through her tears, nodded an unhappy smile at Dickon. But, moments later, Grandmama cried out and, struggling to sit up, she clutched at her chest.

Simon hurried to her, pulling a damp sponge from his scrip. 'Now, I think,' he murmured, dabbing the sponge against her cheeks and forehead. She wheezed a little, gasping for air but, at length, with the help of Simon's strong hands, lay her head back against the pillow.

Sire Raphael took the host from his little silver pyx and held it to her lips. They moved slightly, with words Dickon couldn't hear, and the priest responded. A moment later her breast stilled, and her arms dropped to the sides.

Dickon sprang forward, as if to try to stop her leaving, but she had gone. He stared down at his beloved grandmother, not believing he'd never speak to her again. Despite the warmth of the little chamber, he shivered, and he too was finding it hard to breathe. But his breath would return. As it would for all those waiting in the hall for news: Grandmama's servants and retainers, and many other Meonbridge folk who'd come, gathering in small groups and murmuring quietly together.

He left the chamber and stepped out into the hall. Someone saw him and gave a signal. The murmuring ceased and he could almost feel the air of anguished expectation.

He coughed to clear the lump that had risen in his throat again, then stood tall.

'It is my most painful duty to tell you that, despite our prayers and earnest hopes for her recovery, my grandmother, Lady Margaret de Bohun, has left this earthly life and begun her journey to the next.'

Cries of grief resounded around the hall, and every man and woman dropped to their knees.

Dickon felt unable to take in what had just happened. Fleeting images of today skimmed his mind: his grandmother's excitement at the arrival of the guests, her joy at the betrothal, the moment Margery Tyler approached the table...

His beloved Grandmama was dead. How was it even possible?

It was only yesterday he'd told Piers how scared he was that, one day, the survival of the de Bohun family and all its domains would be his burden alone to bear. He couldn't have imagined the burden would fall to him so soon.

How he wished he hadn't said it.

As he stared at his grandmother's still, silent body, he felt a tension in his jaw. He was clenching his teeth together in a growing rage, a desire for revenge. Earlier, he'd imagined making Margery Tyler suffer for what she'd done. He spun around and ran through the hall to the bailey door. Taking the steps two at a time, he raced across the bailey to the cell built into the outer wall, where Master Dyer locked up felons awaiting the arrival of the sheriff.

One of the constable's henchmen stood at the entrance.

'Let me in,' said Dickon, and the man took out a great iron key to unlock the door.

It was so dark inside the cell, Dickon told the man to keep the door open to let in a little light. When his eyes accustomed to the gloom, he saw that Margery was shackled to the wall. He was shocked by the frailty of her body, but also at the defiance with which she was glaring back at him. Her frailty made the shackling seem unnecessary, but the venom in her eyes showed she had no remorse for what she'd done.

His grandmother had been sorry for her, but he felt no compassion. Margery Tyler deserved whatever punishment the sheriff deemed appropriate.

Throughout the night, Dickon sat with Giles in the parlour, keeping watch over his grandmother's body. Somehow her face no longer bore the signs of her earlier distress, but appeared to be at peace and even joyful. It eased his aching heart a little to see it. 'I'm so glad Sire Raphael was with her at the end,' he said.

'Indeed. A good death, I think, despite it all.'

Dickon closed his eyes. He had to believe that that was true.

During the evening, a stream of folk had come to pay their respects, but the last of them had left a while ago.

He and Giles spoke little. The silence gave Dickon's imagination a chance to conjure a distressing thought. On both occasions when a betrothal had been arranged between the Fitzpeynes and the de Bohuns, a tragedy had occurred: the death of his own father, and now that of his grandmother. Was it some sort of sign? Should the two families *not* be joined? Should his own betrothal be annulled?

For a while, he couldn't decide whether or not to mention his unsettling thought. Especially to Sir Giles. Yet, at length, he felt he had to.

But Giles shook his head. He raked his fingers through his greying hair, but his voice was firm. 'I have been thinking that myself. But, each time, the tragedy was perpetrated by someone with evil and particular intent. Both times, that person was a Tyler.'

Dickon looked up. 'But why, Sir Giles?'

'Robert Tyler was once a fine, upstanding man, albeit he was a villein. Both your grandfather and grandmother held him in high regard. What led him to go against them, and to plot the murder of your father, I have never been able to fathom. And what are we to make of his second crime, the one Mistress Nash has told us of? I think we must presume some sort of madness.' He slowly shook his head. 'But what misfortune did then befall his family. His crime and his self-inflicted death threw the Tylers down from a position of advantage to the status of paupers. Although Margaret took in Matilda, Margery was forced to become a servant. That must have been very far from what she had expected from her life.'

'And that was what turned her against my grandmother. She too lost her wits?'

'So it seems.' Giles gave him a small smile. 'Anyway, there are no more Tylers left to harm you now.'

Dickon's stomach roiled. 'But *Libby* is a Tyler.'

Giles shook his head again. 'She has proved herself to be very different. She is brave, and honest. How many times is it now that she has intervened to save you, Dickon?'

'Several.' His eyes filled. 'Perhaps my grandmother had something to do with it?'

'Quite possibly. I know Margaret thought very well of her, despite her grandfather's crimes, and her mother's misdemeanours.'

'She'll make James Paynter a good wife,' said Dickon.

Giles stood up and came to lay a hand upon his shoulder. 'But you must talk to her, Dickon. She will be devastated and confounded by what her aunt has done. She might even somehow blame herself for it, even though she has no cause.'

His stomach churned again: Sir Giles was right. He had to reassure her that he didn't hold her responsible for her aunt's iniquity. She might even be afraid that James would now reject her. If he had it in his power, he had to safeguard her future happiness.

41

Early the following morning, Dickon sought Libby out. He couldn't find her in the house. Without a mistress to run errands for, he supposed she might feel purposeless. The sooner she married James, the better. If, of course, he did still want her.

He found her at last in the garden, sitting on the turf bench in the arbour. He should have guessed she would be there. At the entrance to the arbour, he stopped and softly called out her name.

'Dickon?' she responded. He could see even from a distance that her eyes were red again.

'Can I come and sit with you?' he said, and she tapped the bench beside her.

They were silent for a while then both spoke at once.

'I can't believe she's gone,' Libby said.

'I shall miss her so much,' said Dickon.

They shared a brief laugh then were quiet again for several moments until Dickon said, 'I'm so sorry about your aunt.'

She turned to him, her eyes wide. 'How can you be *sorry* for her, Dickon, after what she's done?'

'Sorry for *you*, Libby, not her.' He wondered if that sounded right. She didn't answer.

'That came out wrong—' he started, but she laid a hand on his.

'I know what you meant. I'm sorry too. Sorry to be part of that family. My grandfather, my aunt. Both so wicked. Even my mother was less than perfect...' She looked away. 'But at least she didn't murder anyone.' A sob escaped from her throat. 'I can hardly bear the shame and horror of knowing two members of my family have killed two of yours. And for what?'

'Revenge.'

She nodded. 'I don't really understand why my grandfather wanted your father dead. Aunt Margery said he lost his wits and, in his madness, decided he had to punish Philip for what he'd done to my mother.'

'What my father did was very wrong, but murdering him for it...?' He ran his fingers through his hair. 'I suppose we'll never know the truth of it. But why did your aunt want to *kill* my grandmother?'

Libby looked into her lap. 'That claim of hers that Lady Margaret forced my mother to abort her baby—'

'That isn't true!'

She laid her hand upon his. 'Yes, yes, of course. Mistress Nash confirmed what we already knew. Yet Margery seemed truly to believe it.'

'It's hard to accept Grandmama died for something she didn't do.'

'I think Aunt Margery also lost her wits. I suppose she imagined killing Lady Margaret would avenge all her family's woes.' She blenched. 'I think she might have wanted to kill you too.'

Dickon gasped. 'Me?'

She bit her lip. 'I'm so sorry but, before she made me hear all those horrible things, I'd told her a dreadful untruth...'

'What?'

She reached up for a rose branch, scattered with small yellow blooms, and pulled it across her face. 'I said you'd led me on,' she whispered, 'and then abandoned me. I let her think that you seduced me...' She sniffed. 'Whereas it was *me* who did the cozening, and I know you forsook me for the very best of reasons.' Letting go of the rose, she flicked a few tears from her cheeks. She looked at him. 'She said you were just like your father—'

'I'm not!'

'I *know* that too, Dickon. I maligned you and I'm so sorry for it.'

He slid out his hand and rested it over hers. He squeezed it lightly. 'I forgive you.'

They sat in silence for a while. At length, Libby seemed calm again, her unhappiness abated, but he was still afraid to say to her what he thought he must. He hesitated some moments longer, but he had to ask.

'Does James know about your aunt?' he said softly, willing her not to be upset.

She turned to him and nodded. 'I was so frightened he might decide he didn't want to marry me after all. Why'd he want a wife from such a wicked family? But, scared as I was, I had to be honest with him. So, I told him everything.'

'And?'

'He said I'm neither my aunt, nor my mother, nor my father, nor my grandfather, but my own self.' She looked down at her lap. 'He said it was obvious from my actions.'

He breathed out a long sigh of relief. 'I couldn't agree more. I knew James Paynter was a good man.'

She gave him a fleeting smile, but then her mouth turned down. 'What will become of her, my aunt?'

He shrugged. 'I have to send word to the sheriff, and he'll take her away. It'll be up to him to decide what happens next.'

'Will she hang, do you think, or burn?' she whispered.

'I don't know, Libby. Though, she is so frail, I'd be surprised if she didn't die in prison.'

The next three weeks were the worst of Dickon's life. Much worse than what he'd suffered at the hands of Edwin de Courtenay. The days of mourning; the funeral; meeting again those people who had come so recently to share his joy and had now come to share his grief. His courage was tested in a way he had not expected it to be for many years to come.

His aunt, Sister Rosa, insisted on travelling to Meonbridge before she was fully recovered, unwilling to deny him her support at a time of such distress. He barely knew her, but was grateful for her affection and the encouragement she gave him to be strong and brave.

She helped him too to enable everyone in Meonbridge to share their sorrow at their lady's passing. He was certain their bereavement was as genuine as his own, and he spoke to as many as he could, to listen to their memories as well as receive their condolences.

But the pain of it all was exhausting. When it was all over, and the other mourners had returned to their homes, he spent a week almost entirely on his own, or rather just in Bayard's company. He knew Piers was keeping watch on him but he didn't interfere.

At length, he let his mother and Grandma Alice attend him, to comfort him and assure him that the pain would pass. He doubted that was true, but life—his, and that of Meonbridge—had to continue. And it was his entire responsibility to ensure it did.

'Should I give up my training, Piers?' said Dickon, as they sat together on the bailey.

It was four weeks after the funeral, and Dickon had agreed it was time to resume their practice sessions. But he was proving useless against Piers, weak and incompetent. Uttering an oath, he'd thrown his sword onto the ground in frustration.

'Why are you surprised?' said Piers. 'You've not practised for weeks. And those weeks have been enough to sap the energy of the strongest man.'

Piers was right. Maybe he should be less hard upon himself. But he did need to practise more. Yet where?

'Come, let's sit a while,' he'd said, retrieving his sword. They strolled over to one of the stone benches set into the bailey wall.

'Do you want to give it up?' said Piers.

'Not really. But this is all my responsibility now.' He waved his hand in a wide arc, taking in the manor house and grounds, Meonbridge and the fields, the meadows and woodlands beyond. 'Not only this, but all the other de Bohun estates.'

'That's true, but surely you don't want to give up your opportunity to become a knight?'

That was true too. He didn't. 'But how can I do both?'

'It's quite normal for lords to be away from their estates. After all, you've not visited the estates in Dorset and Sussex, and her ladyship never went there. Neither, as far as I can remember, did Sir Richard or, if he did go, it was seldom. He, and she, relied on their steward and their bailiffs to ensure all those manors were being run efficiently. Why can't you do the same? Adam Wragge has always seemed the most reliable of men.'

'Sir Giles said all that.'

'Well, if Sir Giles has already said it, why do you need my opinion?'

'Pa said it too.'

'Jack Sawyer? If both Sir Giles *and* Jack have given you the same advice, whyever are you havering?'

'I don't want to let my grandmother down, by running away from my obligations.'

'You won't be. And you know very well that Lady Margaret, of all people, would want you to complete your training, so you have a chance to become a knight. John atte Wode's a fine bailiff, and we've already agreed that Master Wragge can be trusted.'

'But what of the security of Meonbridge?'

'Give Sir Alain authority to act if necessary in your absence. He too can be trusted. You have many good men around you, Dickon. More so than many other lords, as I understand. I think you have to put your faith in them to do their jobs, whilst you get on with yours.'

Piers was right about that too, of course. Yet it still troubled him that he'd be away from Meonbridge for another five whole years, albeit with occasional visits home.

But perhaps it simply had to be.

Two weeks before he was due to return to Steyning, Dickon sought Libby out once again.

He'd not seen much of her in recent days. She no longer had a role in the manor household, though he'd told her she could stay in the house, sleeping in the chamber she used to share with her mother, until it was time for her to marry James.

'How shall I spend my time?' she'd asked.

'I've no idea. Something in the garden? You know what Grandmama used to do at this time of year.'

'I suppose it would be good practice for when I have a garden of my own.' She tilted her head. 'I'll go to see what needs doing. Talk to the gardeners perhaps?'

'That would be helpful, Libby, thank you. I need to ensure that, once you've gone, and I have too, they all understand what's to be done, in the flower gardens as well as the potagers. I couldn't bear to find when I next return that all my grandmother's efforts have been allowed to go to ruin.'

He'd sighed: his list of tasks to be done before he left for Steyning seemed to be getting ever longer.

He found Libby now at the entrance to the arbour, the very place where his grandmother had fallen over this time last year. He hailed her from a distance. 'What are you doing?'

'Tying in the shoots of honeysuckle.'

'Wasn't that what Grandmama was doing when she had her accident?'

She nodded. 'I'm being very mindful of where I put my feet.'

'Anyway, can I speak to you about something?'

Putting down her tools, she stepped away from the pergola. 'What is it you want to say?'

'Just that I'm hoping you'll let me give you away. And host your bride ale in the great hall.'

'But Jack's already offered for the bride ale, like he did for our betrothal. It'll be held in his big barn. Mistress atte Wode's said she'll provide the food again.'

He wrinkled his nose. 'I see. That's disappointing. I should have said it earlier. But can I still come with you to the church? To stand for the brother you never had?'

Her smile seemed heartfelt. 'I'd like that very much, Dickon.'

'Good. And I'll talk to Grandma Alice about providing help with the bride ale. Perhaps I can make some contribution. In recognition of all that's been between us.'

'That's generous of you, Dickon.'

He shook his head.

'It will be a very small gesture, given all you've done for me.'

'Despite our differences?' She tilted her head.

'Entirely forgotten.'

'How happy Libby looked,' said Grandma Alice, 'that it was you presenting her at the church. As if you were her brother.' She touched Dickon lightly on the arm.

Dickon grinned. He'd been contented too: his final "brotherly" act towards her. No pangs of wistfulness intruded: Libby was marrying a good man, who'd surely give her a prosperous and happy life.

Yet, later, as Alice's splendid feast was coming to an end and the musicians were striking up the lively tune that he knew heralded the start of dancing, he stood up. There was one last thing he and Libby might do together before she left Meonbridge for her new life.

He stepped over to her and held out his hand. She turned to James, who nodded.

'You don't mind?' Dickon said to him, and James grinned.

'Of course not, my lord.'

Dickon took Libby's hand and led her beyond the tables to the end of the barn set aside for dancing. How glad he was that he'd paid some small attention to the dancing classes at Steyning. They'd never been his favourite lessons but at least he did know what to do. Not that he would occupy her for long: she was James's wife now, and it was him she should be dancing with.

But he wanted to whisper a few last words to her, to make clear to her that all was well, or as well as it could be.

She looked so lovely in her blue gown, and her face was alight with joy.

But a moment of seriousness flickered across it. 'I'll never forget you, Dickon...' She giggled. 'My lord... Nor what her ladyship did for me.'

'We are moving forward into new lives, you and I,' he said. 'But we will always share our memories, both sad and happy.'

328

Many folk had now left their tables and were gathering around, clapping their hands and cheering.

He tipped his head in their direction. 'They are eager to take their turn to dance. As, I'm sure, is James.' He led her back to where James was standing, a broad smile on his face.

Holding out her hand, he placed it upon James's. 'Your lady, Master Paynter.' He bowed his head. 'Go well, both of you.'

EPILOGUE

Alone in her solar chamber, Hildegard could still not settle to any activity without being distracted by her resentment, a resentment that had transferred long ago from the de Bohuns to her husband.

To Benedict, too. Surely he *must* have known Edwin was a malevolent and disruptive boy? Yet he imposed him upon them, simply to relieve his family from his disagreeable presence.

Months had passed since the earl brought Edwin home from Steyning, so he could relate to Hugh the shocking details of their grandson's misdemeanours. With the passage of so much time since then, she might have expected her fury to abate, and to some extent it had. She did forget about it for days together. She concentrated on her duties as mistress of her great household; invited worthy personages to dine; arranged afternoon gatherings for ladies of her acquaintance. She even paid an occasional visit to one or other of her children, those who lived no more than a short carriage ride away.

Yet, despite the many diversions of her life, sooner or later, the memory of those few days in December would worm its way back inside her head and cause her anger to ignite once more.

It was egregious enough that Hugh had kept from her for two whole days the details Lord Raoul had come here to divulge. But when he told her of the closing stages of his conversation with the earl, she was so aghast she thought her husband must have lost his wits.

She could not quite rid her head of her ill-tempered exchange with Hugh. 'You *begged* the earl?' she had cried. 'You *demeaned* yourself before Lord Raoul.'

Hugh had rounded on her. 'I did *not* beg, Hildegard. After his lordship had disclosed the sorry litany of Edwin's myriad transgressions, I decided to tell him what I have not so far told you, about what I know of the boy's life in Burgundy. Having done so, I simply asked for the earl's compassion towards him.'

She was tottering up and down the chamber, her stick tap-tapping the floor with every step. She stopped and spun around. '*What* exactly have you not told me?' she rasped out, her voice tight. 'Why was *compassion* needed?'

'If you will sit, Hildegard, instead of flouncing up and down the chamber, I will tell you.'

'I do not *flounce*,' she retorted but, noticing her husband's narrowed eyes, took the seat he indicated.

He came to stand before her. He related everything that Alexander had told him about Benedict, his family and Edwin. She listened with agitation, trying often to interrupt and make a point. But he rebuffed her interruptions. 'You may comment when I have finished, Hildegard, and not before.'

She tossed her head, frustrated. Shocked too by what Hugh was telling her: was he suggesting that her darling Benedict had somehow become feeble-minded? Preposterous! Although it would not surprise her if he was regretting his marriage. His wife's family might well sit in the upper ranks of Burgundian society but they were clearly prideful people. Not to mention discourteous. In all these years, no invitation had ever come for her and Hugh to stay with them at their chateau. Nonetheless, Benedict had made his choice, with the light of advancement in his eyes, as Hugh had said. If he regretted it now, well, she was sorry, but there was nothing to be done.

As for what Hugh told her about Edwin, neither was she surprised at that. She felt almost sorry for the boy, ignored by his parents and grandparents, and even shunned by his siblings. Yet, despite her initial dislike of him, she had spent some pleasant afternoons with Edwin, talking to him about the de Courtenay family. She had enjoyed too their exchange of letters, even if part of that particular pleasure had been the tales he had told her of the young bastard de Bohun's mishaps.

Hugh went on to describe what Lord Raoul had said about Edwin's misdemeanours. She could feel her eyes widening. In truth, she did realise that the "mishaps" that Edwin spoke of in his letters had been deliberately contrived by him. But, whilst the earlier teasing and pranking might be put down to boyish fun—even what happened at the duchess's birthday celebration—the incident in the forest was clearly no laughing matter. De Bohun might have died. Indeed, so might Edwin himself. But, if he had initiated the incident, he had only himself to blame for its disastrous outcome. It was outrageously foolhardy. She had even warned him of the dangers of boar hunting. Yet perhaps that very warning had spurred him on?

She continued to listen quietly as Hugh explained Lord Raoul's interpretation of Edwin's actions. His need to get the upper hand at Steyning, picking upon Dickon de Bohun because he thought him somehow "different", ramping up his bullying once he learned the truth of Dickon's birth.

She could feel Hugh's steely gaze upon her, and she shivered. She knew what he was about to say before he said it. And when it came, it was with a fury she heard rarely in her husband's voice.

'Most of it is your doing, Hildegard,' he cried. '*Your* prattling tongue. Your absurd unremitting resentment of what happened years and years ago. You passed on your rancour to the boy, and look at the result.'

She raised her eyes. He was standing stock still in front of her, arms akimbo, and glaring down at her. She knew, of course, that he was right... And yet?

Hugh was blaming her for deliberately fuelling Edwin's desire to persecute the de Bohun boy, in order to gain some sort of retribution for herself. But was that fair? Was she not merely giving him information about his family?

She considered for a few moments the truth of what had passed between her and her grandson. Her memory began to dim, her motivation for saying what she did to Edwin becoming clouded.

Yet she was damned if she would admit to any of it.

Instead she accused Hugh in turn of demeaning the de Courtenay name by pleading for compassion. Pah! How could he bring such ignominy upon the family? She resented hugely both his humbling himself before the earl and his holding her responsible for their grandson's wrongdoings.

However, Hugh dismissed her protestations. With a last cry of fury and despair, he turned and strode from their chamber, slamming the door behind him. The subject was closed.

They never spoke of it again, nor indeed of very much else.

Even now, five months later, they scarcely talked. Their lives always had been largely separate, Hugh spending his days managing the estates, whilst her role was within the household. But they used to meet and talk once or twice a day, at mealtimes at the very least.

Yet, now, at dinner, they sat at the long trestle well apart, eating their meals in silence. She knew the servants were whispering about them and would have liked to slap their faces for their impudence. Yet she hardly wished to draw attention to what remained an impasse.

In truth, she should be grateful that Lord Raoul had allowed Edwin to return to Steyning. She pondered occasionally on the alternative. If he had been dismissed, the boy might have—should have—returned to his family in France. But she suspected that Benedict—or his wife— might refuse to have him back, forcing *them* to give him a permanent home here at Courtenay Castle. The very idea of that was most disquieting.

Surely what she should do now was try to ensure that Edwin remained at Steyning, his reputation suffering no further blemish, until he was ready to achieve his knighthood? At that point, the boy would be a man and no longer her concern nor Hugh's.

Edwin could not decide if he was pleased or not that Lord Raoul had let him return to Steyning. He was not even certain why he had.

When the earl took him home the week before Christmas, he had assumed it was to inform his grandparents that he was to be dismissed. But, whatever was said between the earl and his grandfather, it seemed Lord Raoul had relented. A week before the squires were due to go back to Steyning, the earl sent a message to Courtenay Castle saying that Edwin could return after all.

After a brief audience with his grandfather, he had escaped the confines of the castle and run down to the stables. It was freezing cold outside but he did not care: he needed to be alone.

Given the brightness in his grandfather's eyes when he passed on the earl's message, it was obvious the old man was relieved. His grandparents did not want him to live here with them in Courtenay Castle. Neither, indeed, did he.

But neither did he want to go home to France.

He had found an empty stall, not recently used, where the bedding was still dry enough to sit on. He slumped down upon a pile of straw, and clasped his head between his hands. So, what *did* he want?

He did not know. He had not needed to give any thought to how or where he would spend the next few years, mapped out as they were in training with Lord Raoul. If the earl had *not* agreed to his return to Steyning, what alternatives would he have had?

Neither staying here nor going home appealed. Not that his family wanted him. He supposed his grandfather Hugh might have found him a place with a different lord.

Starting out afresh might work, but a part of him was loath to leave the place where he still had a chance to get revenge against the one who had put him in this position: Dickon de Bohun.

No sooner had Edwin arrived back in Steyning in January when Lord Raoul summoned him to his private chamber. A frisson of unease had chilled his stomach: had the earl already changed his mind?

The earl bid him stand with his hands clasped behind his back. He came before him and narrowed his eyes. 'When I took you home for Christmas, de Courtenay,' he said, 'it was because I was obliged to explain to Sir Hugh why you were being dismissed from Steyning.'

Edwin knew that. Why was he bothering to repeat it? But he lowered his eyes and did not speak. Submissiveness was probably the best stance to take right now.

'However, I decided at length to give you one last chance,' Lord Raoul continued, 'in deference to your grandfather, who is concerned greatly for your future. But there are conditions, de Courtenay, to you remaining here.'

Edwin had groaned inwardly: of course there were. The earl reeled off a long list of things he must and must not do. They all came down to the same thing: there would be little opportunity for finding fun in Steyning any more. Nonetheless, he maintained his outer air of deference, despite the resentment seething away inside him.

'Do you have anything to say?' said the earl.

He looked up. 'Thank you, my lord,' he whispered. 'I'll do my best.'

The earl had lifted both eyebrows at his response. Edwin wanted to grin: he rarely acted with such deference, and Lord Raoul knew it.

'Good,' the earl said, nonetheless. 'You may go. But, be very sure, de Courtenay, I shall hold you to your "best". One step out of line and that will be the end.'

Edwin let his gaze fall to the floor again and gave a nod. Then he turned and crept from the room, closing the door very quietly behind him.

Outside, he had wanted to cry '*Hourra!*', but even he would not risk the earl or any of his retainers hearing him appear to crow.

'Would you ever consider, my lord, handing young de Bohun back to me?' said Sir Eustace, as he and Lord Raoul surveyed the company of squires practising their sword skills on the bailey. He raised a quizzical eyebrow.

The earl chuckled. 'Deprive me of my best squire, Eustace? Certainly not.'

'Pity,' Eustace said. 'Now that the wretched de Courtenay has stopped his mischief—'

'Hardly mere mischief.'

'No, indeed. Knavery, more like. Or even treachery. What on earth was the matter with him?'

Lord Raoul pulled on his beard. 'If I tell you, Eustace, what I believe, it is to remain between us.'

The knight's eyes widened. 'A secret, my lord? How intriguing. Concerning de Courtenay?'

'More so de Bohun. I have never made known in Steyning the facts of Dickon's heritage.'

'I understood he was the son of Sir Philip, the young warrior you knighted yourself at Crécy.'

'So he is. But his mother was not Philip's wife but a villein girl.'

'Ah,' said Sir Eustace. 'But he is heir to Sir Richard's domains, nonetheless?'

'Indeed. And, in my view, a worthy heir, despite the irregularity of his birth.'

'I could not agree with you more, my lord. Dickon is shaping up to be, as you say, the best of squires. Already a skilful fighter, and an accomplished horseman—'

'Which is remarkable given that he did not even sit upon a horse until he was seven.'

'Brave too,' continued Sir Eustace, 'remembering his actions at the hunt.' But then he frowned. 'But whilst I can understand that maybe concealing the nature of his birth might be, shall we say, prudent, what has all this to do with de Courtenay and his evident grievance against de Bohun?'

Lord Raoul explained the familial connection between the de Courtenays and the de Bohuns, and the rift that arose between the families over the very issue of young Dickon's birth.

'Which might have been a reason for Edwin's loathing,' he continued. 'But, in truth, I am now certain that de Courtenay's grievance, as you put it, was much simpler than that. It had its roots almost entirely in the fact that Dickon is not of wholly noble stock. In his arrogance and conceit, Edwin considered that Dickon did not *deserve* to have a place at Steyning alongside boys like him, de Clyffe and Fenecote, and other sons of the most elite families in England.'

'He knew de Bohun's secret?'

'Indeed. It appears that his grandmother, Lady Hildegard, provided the information.'

'Maliciously?' Sir Eustace's mouth fell open.

'I do not believe so.' His eyes lit up. 'But her ladyship also values birth and heredity most highly and, given what I have just told you about the rift, she—perhaps inadvertently—let slip the information to her grandson. I cannot be sure, of course. But the consequences have certainly been distressing.'

'So, my lord, do you trust de Courtenay to stay out of trouble now?'

Lord Raoul smiled thinly. 'I do not. He may do so for a while, but I suspect that, sooner or later, his craving for revenge will get the better of him.' He grimaced. 'But what I can say is, when that happens, de Courtenay will be out.'

Edwin wondered if he could be bothered to stay at Steyning for much longer. Not only were there no opportunities for playing tricks on de Bohun, even the training itself was no longer any fun.

He sat at the edge of the training ground, watching the other squires take their turn to tilt at the quintain. He was better at it now: he had learned how to control the lance whilst charging forward on his mount, and he hit the target more often than he did not.

But de Bohun, damn him, was even better.

Damn him, damn him, damn him!

Edwin thumped his fist onto the stone bench he was sitting on and at once regretted it, as a shock of pain seared up through his arm.

He looked down at his hand: the skin on the outer edge was torn now and bloodied. Idiot! It was his right hand too. He must go to get it dressed. He would plead an accident. He doubted any of the masters would have observed he had had no opportunity to hurt himself. None of them took much, if any, notice of him now. Despite the great improvements he had made recently in his weapons skills, no one offered him any encouragement or praise.

It was de Bohun, de Bohun, de Bohun all the time.

Ever since the boar hunt, most of the other squires shunned him. They regarded de Bohun as some sort of hero. They said he had saved Edwin's life and he should be grateful. But he was not grateful. Why had the boar gored him and not de Bohun? Why had de Bohun not just *died*?

He stood up and, taking the long route around the edge of the training ground, skirting the tilting field, he headed for the castle. He would find a servant there to bind his hand.

As he slipped between the tall hedges that screened the area, he looked back at the other squires, racing up and down the field, lances clutched under their arms. No one had questioned his departure. He grunted. He presumed nobody would care if he departed Steyning altogether.

Nonetheless, once his hand was bandaged, he went back to the tilting field. Being missed altogether might constitute an offence in Lord Raoul's eyes and, despite his desire to leave, Edwin was not ready to risk ignominious discharge.

The other squires were resting when he returned, hunkered down in small groups upon the grassy bank that surrounded the training ground, chatting together and laughing. Heads turned as he approached but no one invited him to join them.

He no longer had any friends. Nick transferred his allegiances back to Dickon long ago, after the incident at the duchess's celebration. Then, in October, after the hunting catastrophe, Alan did the same. By Christmas, none of the other squires were speaking to him.

He had hoped that, perhaps, when they all returned after the holiday, he might be able to win at least some of them back over to his side. But, five months later, he had not yet succeeded.

In truth, there seemed little point in being here. Perhaps he should ask Grandfather Hugh to find him a new placement after all?

And yet...

The possibilities churned around his head for days. Sometimes he favoured leaving; other times he thought not.

At length, though, he refused to let himself be cowed. He would knuckle down here in Steyning. He would serve his time. He needed to succeed, to be knighted by Lord Raoul.

Then he would be a man, a knight. He could command a force, pay for the allegiance of retainers. He would be able to wreak whatever mayhem he desired.

And *then* he would have his revenge upon Dickon de Bohun.

A MESSAGE FROM THE AUTHOR

If you've enjoyed reading *Squire's Hazard*, please do consider leaving a brief review on your favourite site. Reviews are of enormous help to authors, both in terms of providing feedback and in building readership. Thank you!

And, if you enjoy my writing, perhaps you'd like to join "Team Meonbridge"?

In return for your support, I will send you updates on my books, and periodically ask for your help or feedback.
As a small "thank you" for joining the team, I will send you a FREE novella featuring some of the Meonbridge characters.

If you are interested, please visit my website at www.carolynhughesauthor.com and select **JOIN THE TEAM!** to open the sign up form.

I look forward to your company!

You can find a **Glossary** of medieval terms for the Meonbridge Chronicles on my website: www.carolynhughesauthor.com

ACKNOWLEDGEMENTS

I am indebted once more to those people who continue to help me along my writing and publishing journey. The journey for *Squire's Hazard* has taken rather longer than I would have liked but my team have been with me all the way.

For *Squire's Hazard*, I must again thank my "beta readers", who read an early version of the manuscript, to help ensure the plot hung together and the story flowed, the characters behaved consistently and appropriately (whether well or badly), and the book was, as a whole, a "good read". David, Rhonwen, and Joanna, thank you so much once more for your time and your insight. I am, as ever, hugely grateful.

I am also indebted yet again to my editor, Hilary, for helping me to wrestle this story into shape, and reassure me that this latest story about these long-ago Meonbridge folk is worth the telling.

And, of course, thank you to Cathy Helms at www.avalongraphics.org for producing another beautiful cover for this fifth volume in the Meonbridge Chronicles series.

ABOUT THE AUTHOR

CAROLYN HUGHES has lived much of her life in Hampshire. With a first degree in Classics and English, she started working life as a computer programmer, then a very new profession. But it was technical authoring that later proved her vocation, as she wrote and edited material, some fascinating, some dull, for an array of different clients, including banks, an international hotel group and medical instruments manufacturers.

Having written creatively for most of her adult life, it was not until her children flew the nest several years ago that writing historical fiction took centre stage, alongside gaining a Master's degree in Creative Writing from Portsmouth University and a PhD from the University of Southampton.

Squire's Hazard is the fifth MEONBRIDGE CHRONICLE, and more stories about the folk of Meonbridge will follow.

You can connect with Carolyn through her website www.carolynhughesauthor.com and social media:

facebook.com/CarolynHughesAuthor

twitter.com/writingcalliope

ALSO BY CAROLYN HUGHES

FORTUNE'S WHEEL: The First Meonbridge Chronicle

How do you recover from the havoc wrought by history's cruellest plague?

It's June 1349. In Meonbridge, a Hampshire manor, many have lost their lives to the Black Death, among them Alice atte Wode's beloved husband and Eleanor Titherige's widowed father. Even the family of the manor's lord and his wife, Margaret de Bohun, has not entirely escaped...

But, now the plague has passed, the people of Meonbridge must work together to rebuild their lives. However, tensions mount between the de Bohuns and their tenants, as the workers realise their new scarceness means they can demand higher wages and dictate their own lives.

When the tensions deepen into violence and disorder, and the men – lord and villagers alike – seem unable to find any resolution, the women – Alice, Eleanor and Margaret – must step forward to find a way out of the conflict that is tearing Meonbridge apart.

"A thoroughly researched book, with care given to ensuring that the characters have 14th century attitudes and knowledge...gives a strong sense of the reality of the past." Catherine Meyrick, author of *Forsaking All Other*

"A Historical Fiction masterpiece", *"it had everything I want from a book, and then some"*, *"impossible to put down"* The Coffee Pot Book Club @maryanneyarde

"A rich tapestry of mystery, intrigue, struggle, hopes and joys" Amazon reviewer

"An accomplished, fascinating historical fiction novel – and an impressive debut." What Cathy Read Next, @Cathy_A_J

"Completely intriguing, fascinating and surprisingly emotional...more please!" The Book Magnet @thebookmagnet

---

ALSO BY CAROLYN HUGHES

A WOMAN'S LOT: The Second Meonbridge Chronicle

How can mere women resist the misogyny of men?

1352. In Meonbridge, a resentful peasant rages against Eleanor Titherige's efforts to build up her flock of sheep. Susanna Miller's husband, grown melancholy and ill-tempered, succumbs to idle gossip that his wife's a scold. Agnes Sawyer's yearning to be a craftsman is met with scorn.

And the village priest, fearful of what he considers women's "unnatural" ambitions, is determined to keep them firmly in their place.

Many men hold fast to the teachings of the Church and fear the havoc the "daughters of Eve" might wreak if they're allowed to usurp men's roles and gain control over their own lives.

Not all men in Meonbridge resist the women's desire for change – indeed, they want it for themselves. Yet it takes only one or two misogynists to unleash the hounds of hostility and hatred...

"I didn't so much feel as if I were reading about mediaeval England as actually experiencing it first hand." Linda's Book Bag @Lindahill50Hill

"This book exceeded all my expectations. I did not read this story. I lived it!" @maryanneyarde at The Coffee Pot Book Club

"I adored this book! A highly recommended read for lovers of historical fiction." Brook Cottage Books @BrookCottageBks

"A treat for all the senses...totally true to its time and setting..." Being Anne @Williams13Anne

"Another fantastic piece of completely immersive historical fiction from Carolyn Hughes..." The Book Magnet @thebookmagnet

"...an absorbing account of the times" Historical Novel Society @histnovsoc

---

ALSO BY CAROLYN HUGHES

DE BOHUN'S DESTINY: The Third Meonbridge Chronicle

How can you uphold a lie when you know it might destroy your family?

It is 1356, seven years since the Black Death ravaged Meonbridge, turning society upside down. Margaret, Lady de Bohun, is horrified when her husband lies about their grandson Dickon's entitlement to inherit Meonbridge. She knows that Richard lied for the very best of reasons – to safeguard his family and its future – but lying is a sin. Yet she has no option but to maintain her husband's falsehood...

Margaret's companion, Matilda Fletcher, decides that the truth about young Dickon really must be told, if only to Thorkell Boune, the man she's set her heart on winning. But Matilda's "honesty" serves only her own interests, and she's oblivious to the potential for disaster.

For Thorkell won't scruple to pursue exactly what he wants, by whatever means are necessary, no matter who or what gets in his way...

"A lie told for the best of reasons; the truth told for the worst..."

———

"This isn't a book you simply read, but an extraordinary immersive experience"
Being Anne @Williams13Anne

"Compelling and intriguing historical fiction...it felt so real, I forgot it was fiction"
Jessica Belmont @jessicaxbelmont

"Stunning evocative writing ... a time-portal into the 14th Century" The Book Magnet @thebookmagnet

"Rich language, a great historical vibe, strong characters, treachery and villainy, community and courage – it had everything and more." Just4mybooks @lfwrites

"Once you dip your toe into the Meonbridge Chronicles, you'll never want to leave..."
Brook Cottage Books @BrookCottagebks

———

ALSO BY CAROLYN HUGHES

CHILDREN'S FATE: The Fourth Meonbridge Chronicle

How can a mother just stand by when her daughter is being cozened into sin?

1360. Eleven years since plague devastated all of England; six since Emma Ward fled Meonbridge with her children, for a better life in Winchester. But she's now terrified it was the wrong decision, convinced her daughter Bea is being exploited by her immoral mistress.

Bea herself is fearful and ashamed of her sudden descent into sin, yet thrilled too by her wealthy and attentive client.

When Emma resolves to rescue Bea from ruin, she tricks her into returning to Meonbridge, but Bea absconds back to the city.

Yet, soon, plague's stalking Winchester again and Bea flees again to Meonbridge. But, now, she finds herself unwelcome, and fear, hostility and hatred threaten...

"You don't so much read about the folk of Meonbridge as dwell amongst them for a few precious hours" WhatCathyReadNext @Cathy_A_J

"Exceptional historical authenticity, and a thoroughly enthralling story" Being Anne @Williams13Anne

"Historical fiction at its best, immerses the reader in another time" Just4mybooks @lfwrites

"Stunningly vibrant historical fiction" The Book Magnet @thebookmagnet

---

Printed in Great Britain
by Amazon

41027765R00209